TALES OF
THE DJINN:
THE
GUARDIAN

EMMA HOLLY

Tales of the Djinn: The Guardian

Emma Holly

Discover other exciting Emma Holly titles at: http://www.emmaholly.com

This story is a work of fiction and should be treated as such. It includes sexually explicit content that is only appropriate for adults—and not every adult at that. Those who are offended by more adventurous depictions of sexuality or frank language possibly shouldn't read it. Literary license has been taken in this book. It is not intended to be a sexual manual. Any resemblance to actual places, events, or persons living or dead is either fictitious or coincidental. That said, the author hopes you enjoy this tale!

Tales of the Djinn: The Guardian is an approximately 100,000-word novel.

ISBN-10: 098889436X

ISBN-13: 978-0-9888943-6-5

cover photos: istockphoto.com—Alija, Yuri

CONTENTS

CHAPTER ONE

THE djinni halted on the sidewalk in front of the tall townhome. Constructed of worn red brick and the material humans called brownstone, the residence rose six stories above the street. To Arcadius's eyes, it scrimped on embellishments. Corinthian columns framed the windows, which were topped by plain pediments. The black iron railings leading up the steps were bereft of curlicues to beckon travelers in. Compounding the general grimness, the wet snow of this unpleasant Manhattan winter clung to the building's brick, plastered there by the freezing wind. Despite his long wool coat—whose velvet collar he rather liked—Arcadius's new body shivered. He hadn't yet regained his power to change form, and the sinister sky was spitting fresh snow at them. Perhaps he'd been wrong to choose this metropolis as their spot to regroup. New York certainly wasn't what he was used to.

On the other hand, this uninspired building bore signs of what he was searching for. Within the prison of his stiff human shoes, the soles of his feet tingled. There were vibes here—definite, promising vibes.

Somewhere nearby the heart of a magical nexus pulsed.

"This is it," he announced to his companion.

"This?" His faithful servant squinted dubiously up the building's front. Like him, Joseph wore the garb of a prosperous Big Apple citizen. Unlike him, he'd flung a bright red scarf around his neck. "Master, are you sure?"

Was he sure? Arcadius was accustomed to being confident—unshakable, in fact. The situation in which they found themselves had changed many things. He studied the house again. Their hotel was a palace compared to this, but they couldn't prolong their search forever. If nothing else, they were wearing out shoe leather.

"I'm sure," he said, hoping saying so would be good enough. "My . . . spidey senses are tingling."

He thought the term he used was correct. Djinn absorbed languages from the minds of the people they moved among. Joseph and Arcadius had arrived in this teeming city a week ago, long enough to have more or less mastered the local tongue.

"There is a 'For Rent' sign," Joseph conceded.

Arcadius hadn't noticed it before, but indeed there was: a sad-looking placard taped to the window that—could one say *graced?*—a small barred door to a below-street entrance. Was this what Arcadius had come to: living in a cold damp cellar like a mushroom?

He resettled his coat for courage. "We must knock," he said, stamping up the snowy steps with the decisive stride he'd learned would lessen the chance of slipping on icy spots. "Hopefully, the manager is available."

"May it please God," Joseph murmured virtuously behind him.

Arcadius found and pressed the most-used bell.

"They likely don't have servants," he reminded himself and his companion. "We must be patient in case we have to wait."

"Hello?" said a crackly voice through the intercom.

Arcadius was too cold to be annoyed by the waste of his sage advice. He leaned closer to the ugly speaking box. "Good day. We're interested in the room for rent. Are you the individual to address inquiries to?"

"One moment," said their invisible answerer.

Beside him, Joseph shifted uneasily. The leather briefcase he carried with them everywhere *thwapped* his dark trouser leg. "That was a woman's voice."

"We will be modern, as we were with the female concierge at the Carlyle. Women here don't expect to be treated like delicate treasures."

Sensing Joseph's doubt, Arcadius felt comfortable taking the lead in this exchange. Given his former and—God willing—future position, he had more face-to-face familiarity with the fairer sex than Joseph.

Inside the brownstone, quick light footsteps descended a set of stairs, dashing Arcadius's hope that the owner would be a matron of sober years. He stepped back as the door opened, giving the female behind it room to stand on the threshold with a bit of space between them.

She was young and wide-eyed and breathless due to hurrying down from an upper floor. Her hair was black and fell to her slender shoulders without much life or style. He *believed* her eyes were green. It was hard to tell on this murky day. She was average height and not curvy. Despite a pleasant face, she wasn't the sort of beauty Arcadius had known by the literal barge load in his previous life. Her mouth was nice, he decided judiciously. And her cheeks. Very pink and soft looking.

She wasn't dressed for visitors or even for the cold. She wore a black turtleneck, faded black jeans, and a pair of slip-on shoes that sparkled—somewhat incongruously—with fake jewels. The shoes were the only part of her ensemble that resembled what women he knew wore.

Her eyes went round as she took in their affluent appearance. "*You're* interested in the apartment?"

"We are," Arcadius confirmed. Hoping to appear respectful, he removed his furry Cossack hat. He restrained an urge to bow. People didn't do that here. "Would it be possible for us to view it now?"

For reasons he couldn't fathom, her jaw dropped at the sound of his voice. Both he and Joseph were handsome men, but she didn't seem to notice that. "Uh," she said. She looked at Joseph and back at him. "It's just a garden apartment. And only a one-bedroom."

"It may meet our needs all the same."

The landlady's pale fingers clenched her large key ring. A wedding ring with a miniscule diamond by djinn standards loosely circled one finger. That was odd. He knew things were different here, but she didn't have the appearance of a woman a man cared for.

"Okay," she said. "I can show you around, I guess."

He wasn't prepared for her to step out into the snow and wind with them. He gasped in surprise as her arm brushed his thick coat sleeve.

"The street door is the only way to get in," she said at his startled reaction. "This unit doesn't connect with the lobby."

"You don't wish to get a coat?"

"This'll just take a second."

With an agility he couldn't have matched in these conditions, she trotted down the front steps and around the railing into the well that led to the second door. This walk hadn't been shoveled. Arcadius winced as her flimsy slippers sank ankle-deep in snow.

If they'd been in his native land, he'd have picked her up and carried her over it.

"Sorry about the mess," she said. "The caretaker forgets to clear this, since no one's living here right now."

Arcadius and Joseph exchanged looks as she unlocked the security gate. The bars were iron and would necessitate wearing gloves year round. Their kind didn't tolerate that metal well. Once the gate was open, she pushed two more keys into the door with the *For Rent* sign. At last, the barriers against the city's wrongdoers were undone. She hit a switch, and a line of what he knew to be pot lights sprang to life overhead.

"Hold on while I input the code," she said, doing something involving buttons beside the door. "Okay, you're good to come in."

With matching grimaces of trepidation, he and Joseph followed her inside.

The apartment wasn't quite as dire as he'd feared. It was clean, for one thing, and warm compared to the street. The windows were on the small side and set high into smooth white walls. The floor was covered in dark wide planks that seemed meant to resemble wood. A square of beige Berber carpet served in place of a decent rug. On that outrage to the weaver's art a black modern couch was placed, plus two streamlined white leather and chrome chairs. A low Lucite coffee table completed the sparse effect. The furnishings were new and useable. They weren't, however, the least bit visually appealing.

Back home, Arcadius's servants had nicer things than this.

"So, um, this is the living room," their escort said. "You could take it furnished or not, depending on whether you have stuff."

They had stuff but not the kind she meant. Being careful not to bump anything, Arcadius stepped further into the sterile room. He wasn't a puny man. If he stretched his arms, he'd touch the ceiling. Actually, if he put his hat back on, the doorframes might dislodge it.

"These items would work for us," he said, willfully ignoring how unworkable they were. Best not to waste time having them moved out. The clock was ticking for his city.

"You're sure?" she asked. "You seem like this maybe isn't your style."

The glint of skepticism in her eyes lent interest to her otherwise merely pretty face.

"I'm sure," he said, willing to lie through his teeth if it got him what he wanted. "Everything's very nice."

She shook her head, seemingly to herself. "Okay, then. Kitchen's here." She waved toward it; it wasn't a separate room, simply an area in the corner. He recognized a stove, a shiny granite counter, cabinets and a fridge. In theory at least, he understood their functions. "The appliances aren't stainless but they're new. The engineered wood floors will stand up to spills. Closet's there with a stack laundry on one side. Large three-piece bathroom. An office nook and bedroom are down the hall."

The bedroom was square, very boringly furnished, and carpeted in more beige Berber. Arcadius wouldn't have paid it much attention except the vibes he'd sensed outside the building had just increased. The hair on his nape prickled—a reaction Joseph shared, to go by the way he rubbed his neck. They left the bedroom without comment, the three of them crowding back into the small corridor. Arcadius and Joseph both dwarfed their slim escort.

Arcadius sensed Joseph forcing himself not to withdraw farther. Fitting in among the locals was important.

"What's behind that door?" Arcadius asked politely.

He thought this a natural question. The thing was right next to them . . . and padlocked. Probably original to the building, it was older than the unit's other entrances, with layers of dark chipping paint. More importantly, waves of magical energy beat through it, sure sign that here of all places the veil between the planes was thin.

Being human, the landlady should have been oblivious to this.

She looked at him. The ceiling light above them shone in her young pale face. She was too thin for his taste, but her eyes *were* green—as he'd supposed.

"That's off limits," she said flatly.

Arcadius fought a smile. To be told he couldn't do something had always been a spur.

"It's just a mechanical room," she added, seeming aware she'd been too emphatic. "The heating system and junk storage. Only the repair guy needs access." She changed the subject, gesturing in a new direction. "This hall here goes to the courtyard. Whoever rents this unit has their own outdoor space."

She led them down a short draughty passage to the outside. Weather notwithstanding, the small walled garden they emerged into was enchanting. Crooked bricks paved the sheltered area, which had room enough for a table and beds for growing things. The neighboring buildings loomed around it but didn't block the sky. The snow fell softly, like feathers and not ice shards.

Compared to the closed-in apartment, here he could breathe easily.

"This is lovely," he said honestly.

The woman sighed. "Yes," she said. "It's like another world."

She sounded sad, as though she had no hope of experiencing any circumstances except the ones she lived in. Arcadius didn't see how that could be true. She had different freedoms from those he knew, but she certainly had them.

He didn't share his thoughts. Her mental state wasn't his concern. After a moment, she sighed once more and retraced her steps inside. They stopped in the oppressive living room. The landlady was facing them.

"That's it, I'm afraid," she said. "The whole enchilada."

She put her hands on her waist, the out-of-place wedding ring tilting on her too-thin finger. Arcadius shook himself and looked into her eyes instead. He could tell she wasn't expecting a positive response.

"May we take possession of the unit now?" he asked.

Her soft pink mouth fell open. "Now?"

"If that's acceptable to you. You mentioned it isn't occupied."

"I—" She blinked, her lashes unexpectedly thick and dark. "We haven't discussed rent. Plus, I should run a background check."

A background check would be problematic, considering they didn't officially exist—an inconvenience they'd have avoided if possessing humans weren't against their own edicts.

"Will cash do?" he asked, having used it to smooth out a similar wrinkle at the hotel. "Perhaps a year upfront?"

Her mouth formed another O. Arcadius nodded to Joseph to open the briefcase. With the grace that was his nature, he set it on the clear coffee table and flipped up the gold latches. Stacks of neatly banded hundred dollar bills appeared. Arcadius thought the green color dull, but the amount ought to cover whatever she cared to charge.

"Jesus," she breathed, gaping at it. "Are you guys criminals? If you are, I'd rather you didn't set up shop in my building."

"We're not criminals," he assured her. "We simply like privacy."

This was true as far as it went. The laws of her city weren't designed to regulate magical beings. He wondered how to allay her fears, which might not be the same females he knew were prone to.

He relied on instinct to guide his speech. "I'm sure you understand the desire to be left alone."

Her gaze rose to his and stayed. He'd guessed correctly. She understood perfectly. Beneath the black turtleneck, her lungs expanded with a breath. Her breasts were small, mere oranges under the stretchy cloth. He sensed her teetering on a decision.

"We'd be most grateful," he said softly.

His old self would have swayed her with no trouble. It was confident, powerful, and catnip to most women. Fortunately, he hadn't lost all his charm. She frowned at his gentle plea for sympathy. "All right. But I'm not signing a lease agreement. You two cause problems, I'll toss you out."

"Agreed," he said, his lips curving in a smile.

She crossed her arms beneath her modest breasts, her green eyes slitting suspiciously.

"What sum would be sufficient?" Joseph asked to distract her.

She named one and he handed the cash over. She didn't count it. She must have concluded he'd be honest.

"If you wouldn't mind," Joseph said, "we'd like to settle in. Do you suppose we could have the keys?"

She stared at the hand the manservant was holding out. "I don't even know your names."

"I am Arcadius," Arcadius said, "and this is Joseph."

His answer seemed to amuse her. Shaking her head, she worked the necessary keys off her crowded ring. "I'm Elyse. Solomon. I live in 6A if you need anything." She scribbled a set of numbers on a small notebook page. "Here's the code for the alarm. Instructions for how to set it are on the control panel."

Probably due to his relief at accomplishing their first important goal, Joseph forgot himself. He bowed deeply from the waist. "Thank you, Elyse Solomon. You are a shining diamond of graciousness."

These were traditional words of courtesy, used to smooth social interactions rather than coming from the heart. The landlady scratched her smooth cheekbone. "Uh-huh," she said. "You two enjoy yourselves."

As soon as she was gone, Joseph turned to him as if he were about to burst. "Master, I know you're glad we've obtained this place but it is terrible! Look at the furniture! And the travesty she calls a kitchen! You are the Guardian of the Glorious City. I will die of shame if we stay here long."

"I *was* the Guardian of the City," Arcadius corrected. "And if you die of shame, how will I survive? I don't know what stack laundry is."

"They are machines for cleaning and drying garments. They sit on top of one another and—" He broke off as he noted the laughter in his master's eyes. "You are pulling my legs."

"A little." He squeezed his companion's shoulder. "Think what is at stake. We can both stand a bit of humbling if it saves our people."

"The church on Fifth Avenue—"

"—was far too public. We cannot do what we must in front of witnesses. You know this place is more practical."

Unable to counter his argument however much he might wish, Joseph hung his head.

"There is another consideration," Arcadius continued, wanting his servant fully in agreement. "The longer we're absent from the Qaf, the greater the consequences to ourselves. Perhaps it's not the most important issue, but I, for one, would like to wrap this up as soon as possible."

"Forgive me," Joseph said. "You are correct, of course." He lifted his head again. "Might I make your sleeping quarters more comfortable?"

"Certainly," Arcadius said. "If you feel up to it."

Pride pulled Joseph's shoulders straight. "Tramping around in the snow for days cannot make me forget my trade."

Though Joseph was his all around aide-de-camp, his original training was in magic. Grabbing their precious briefcase, he strode to the drab bedroom. This time when he opened the case, the stacks of cash were gone. In their place was a colorful array of small cloth bags. Joseph pursed his lips and selected one sewn of blue brocade. Once he'd loosened the drawstring cord, he dumped the contents onto the bed's quilted tan coverlet.

Furnishings for a Lilliputian dollhouse tumbled out. The items were almost too tiny for Arcadius's slightly better than human vision to identify.

"Perhaps you should stand back," Joseph suggested.

Arcadius retreated to the door.

Joseph checked to ensure he was far enough. Satisfied, he removed and folded his winter coat, then braced his feet wide and closed his eyes. The bright red scarf still looped his neck rakishly. Paying it no mind, he spread both hands above the miniatures on the bed. He didn't touch them, just let his energy radiate downward like heat fumes. He murmured a quick, nearly silent prayer that he immediately repeated. *Almighty God, the abundant, the merciful, creator of all beauty: allow your servant to manifest your riches into this present space. Allow your servant to bring the old world into the new.*

His focus was impressive. No muscle moved in his body unless you counted his chanting lips and furrowed brow. The items on the bed began to tremble. A tiny scroll-like roll was the first to jump. It bounced onto the floor, expanding into a Persian rug that ran like water under the servant's feet. Two more bits flung themselves to opposite walls, turning into exquisite tapestries. A table blinked into being along with a tea samovar and service to sit on top. Blue and white Iznik tiles laid themselves on the ceiling, and silk pillows swelled up heaps. So many objects were appearing Arcadius couldn't track them all. A moment later, he smelled incense and heard potted palm leaves rattle.

"Good Lord," he gasped as a large cedar wardrobe suddenly filled a cramped corner. "Perhaps you'd better stop."

Joseph opened his eyes. He was breathing harder than before. "As you wish, master. This is nearly all I fit in the bag anyway."

Arcadius couldn't resist stepping into the transformed space. Even he was amazed by his servant's skill. Allowing for the limits of the apartment's architecture, Joseph had come close to reconstituting his master's bedroom in the palace.

"My books!" Arcadius exclaimed, running his fingers over the fat old tomes. "And my favorite chair! I had no idea you brought all these things."

"I thought it would help," Joseph said. "I'm sure we're both homesick."

His former possessions made him ache for the people he used to see among them. He couldn't say that. Joseph's act had been too thoughtful.

"Thank you," he said with stinging eyes.

Joseph blushed a tiny bit, causing Arcadius to wonder if he didn't say those words enough. Joseph held one last item: a shining silver hoop five feet in diameter. "Where should I put the door to the mirror space?"

Arcadius considered. The formerly stark room was now crowded with luxuries. "Behind that tapestry perhaps, where it's hidden but easy to get to."

The tapestry depicted Sindbad's adventures upon the sea. Joseph lifted the hanging from the bottom, exposing the wall beneath. As he pressed the silver ring upon it, it sank an inch into the plaster, embedding itself in the smooth surface. The part of the wall the circle encompassed began to shine, as if the white paint within it had liquefied.

Joseph watched the fluid waver, then dropped the tapestry. "We must leave this portal alone for now. Nothing will manifest accurately for a while."

Given time, the mirror space would echo everything in the room—though the copy would be more beautiful. As Joseph fed more power into the ring, the duplication would expand to include the brownstone and maybe the entire street. The enhanced version would be an isolated piece of their world, a bolt hole no human would suspect was there. Many such mirror spaces existed, sometimes to give traveling djinn a safe place to stay but just as often for amusement. Ever since their controversy-riddled creation, the children of Adam and Eve had fascinated their djinn cousins.

Djinn spied on humans like humans watched TV.

This city wasn't as familiar to their kind as some. No counterpart to Manhattan existed in the Qaf—though one had the potential to. New York shared the same latitude as Rome and Istanbul. Both those metropolises had Qaf sisters.

Before he gave himself a headache trying to calculate the proximity of places that were more vibrations than actual locales, Arcadius turned his attention to his servant. Joseph had worked a good bit of magic. To Arcadius's surprise he seemed tired but not exhausted.

"That didn't take as much out of you as I thought," he observed.

"There was extra energy to draw on," Joseph said. "Someone died here recently."

Arcadius's brows shot up. "Here in this apartment?"

"Somewhere in the building's cellar. The death was violent. A reservoir of psychic runoff was left behind."

"Was the death related to the nexus?"

Joseph shrugged in his business suit. "I cannot say. It may be there was a fight for control of it."

Arcadius didn't like the sound of that. He'd chosen this city to avoid competition for resources. This was a modern place: Western, for the most part. Humans here might believe in ghosts or angels. Djinn, however, were figures from cartoons for them.

"Shall I investigate?" Joseph asked, seeing his perturbed expression.

"Let's leave that until our position is more secure. You need rest and I ought to procure a meal."

"Master," Joseph scolded.

"I will buy one. I am capable, you know. We have plenty of money and restaurants are everywhere."

Joseph was a young djinni, not some graybeard who'd lost every joy in life. All the same, he let out a long-suffering sigh.

"You think I cannot obtain provisions," Arcadius accused. "I, who know intimately that armies march on their stomachs."

"I think you *shouldn't* acquire our meal," Joseph corrected. "A person who takes mundane tasks on himself isn't who you are. Under the circumstances, it might be best to act in accordance with your usual character."

He was right. Then again, a person who'd admit he was wrong wasn't who Arcadius was either. "I'll consult Elyse," he said. "She can supply the name of a restaurant that delivers."

"*I* will consult Elyse," Joseph said, her name not spilling as easily from his lips. "I assure you, I'm not too depleted to handle that."

Arcadius scowled. Joseph had just turned this into an issue of honor. "If you insist," he conceded with ill grace.

Joseph smiled even as he bowed. "I do not insist, master. I humbly beg your indulgence."

Why was his servant so much better at this game? "Fine," he said, waving him away. "Go consult our landlady."

Joseph picked up his rich man's coat. "She may prove useful for other reasons. At some point, we'll need a sacrifice."

"She's married," Arcadius blurted. "Or did you not see her ring?"

"What can the vows of one woman matter weighed against every life in our city?"

Arcadius couldn't argue. He shouldn't have wanted to. They'd only been on this plane a week. Was he already empathizing with the humans he was temporarily more like? The idea unsettled him.

"As you say," he responded gruffly. "If the opportunity arises, we must consider if she'll suit."

CHAPTER TWO

ELYSE had an inexplicable urge to cook. For the last two months, ever since David's murder, she'd subsisted on canned soup and packaged sandwiches. Tonight she needed to think, and the kitchen in their apartment was her safe place. She and David tore down the wall between it and the living room, but other than that it was pretty much the same as when she was growing up. The dark cabinets that towered to the ceiling hailed from the late twenties. The dented restaurant-style stove had warmed her baby formula. Once upon a time, the countertops were too tall for her to reach. Her father—rest his soul—had purchased the colorful hand-fired tiles on a long-ago trip to Morocco.

She'd never switch them out them willingly, not for any amount of trendiness. Leo Solomon had raised her by himself, her mother having died in her infancy. Leo had been head buyer for Solomon Brothers Imports, a job that left its mark on their top-floor apartment. Souvenirs from her father's journeys were everywhere. Whatever could be shipped that took his fancy—art, furniture, tribal crafts—he'd sent home to her. She hadn't traveled with him often, because of school and because many of the areas he went were too dangerous for a young girl. The things he sent back had kept her company, assuring her she was treasured. She'd been grateful when David professed to love the place as much as she did. It would have broken her heart to move, even for the pleasure of making a fresh start with him.

"I wouldn't change one thing," the love of her life had declared. "You and this place are perfect."

She wondered what he'd say about the two strange men to whom she'd rented his pet project—*David's boondoggle,* her glamorous cousin Cara liked to call it.

Elyse shook her head, bending down to a lower cupboard to dig out the pasta pot. She hardly knew what to say about them herself . . . or about the fact that she'd given in to impulse and let them have the place. Elyse was not an impulsive person. David used to joke she thought everything through ten times, then once more for good measure.

She had a sneaking suspicion he wouldn't have liked Arcadius or Joseph. David's one flaw was that he stayed too inside the box sometimes.

"Well, too bad," she said, striving to sound independent as she ran water in the pot.

Her renters' reactions aside, David had done an amazing job carving out the basement unit from the unused cellar—as good as a professional contractor. Apart from the electrical and plumbing, he'd done everything himself, spending hours at a time on it while working his day job too. When she'd complained she never saw him, he'd said the rent would be their vacation fund, a bit of extra over what the rest of building earned. Given how nice the unit turned out, she couldn't understand why he hadn't rented it right away. The apartment had sat and sat right until he died. This was Chelsea. Those chairs and couches were classic Modern. The backsplash and all the bathrooms boasted sleek subway-style glass tile. Heck, the countertops were Brazilian granite! Add to that the top-of-the-line security system David had installed and, basement or not, the listing should have been snapped up in two minutes.

Maybe David had gotten too attached to his creation.

"So *I* rented it," she said, hefting the half full pot onto the gas burner.

She'd stowed the brick of bills her tenants paid her in her favorite mother-of-pearl keepsake box. Having so much cash on hand made her nervous. She'd gotten more than she thought she could for the place, more than comparable units in this neighborhood—which her naysaying cousin Cara could stick in her pipe and smoke. Cara always was harder on David than he deserved.

Of course, if Elyse bragged, she'd risk revealing that she'd rented the place to a pair of weirdoes . . . without getting references.

Not weirdoes, she corrected. Just eccentrics with excellent poker faces.

She honestly thought they hadn't liked the apartment. Clearly, they could afford swankier. Still, she was glad they were taking it. Maybe she'd finally stop obsessing about David's death, about her happiness dying along with him. Her new tenants would obscure that shadow. They might be odd, but they were very alive people. She'd sensed that the moment she opened the door to them.

They'd made her think of foreign dignitaries, standing on the stoop in their long wool coats and their funny hats. Okay, only the tall one had worn a hat. The shorter one had a bright red scarf flung around his neck. Their skin tone suggested they came from a sunny clime, their faces bronzed by the kind of color winter can't erase. Both their hair was dark and their eyes were astonishing. The taller man's were blue gray, the shorter one's honey gold. Their irises had seemed to glow against their contrasting skin and lashes. Both men's enunciation was remarkably precise.

When the tall man spoke, his deep voice had poured down her nerves as warmly as mulled cider.

Dad would have liked them, she thought. He'd had a fondness for quirky people—for people period, in fact. It was the biggest reason he'd loved his job.

She pulled a box of spaghetti out of the cabinet.

"You noticed them," she realized aloud.

She'd barely looked at other men once she married David. Her soul mate had been everything to her—the sweetest, handsomest, most supportive person she'd ever met. That he'd chosen her was a miracle. She knew how ordinary she was to the male species. Neither of her new tenants had looked at her the way men do when they find women attractive.

This, of course, made it that much stranger for her to have checked them out.

Cara liked to say God forgot to give Elyse the man-hunting gene. Probably He'd given hers to Cara. Elyse never could keep track of her cousin's harem of boyfriends.

The water would take a while to boil, so Elyse started on meat sauce. Garlic hit the olive oil in her skillet. She had some seasoned Italian sausage that didn't need thawing. Maybe she'd go whole hog and pour a nice glass of wine.

The sizzle in the pan didn't keep her from hearing a polite knock.

She turned down the burners and stared at the door. She wasn't expecting anyone. Did her new tenants have a complaint?

Though she was accustomed to handling renters, her pulse sped up. For half a second she considered checking her hair in the hallway mirror. Lately, she hadn't spent the time she should have on it with her flatiron. It probably looked god-awful.

Calm down, she thought, forcing herself to move toward the entrance without primping. That she'd noticed the strangers was irrelevant.

She wiped sweaty palms on her old black jeans before she turned the knob. The slightly shorter man from the new apartment was outside, the one the other had called Joseph. Once again, she was struck by his handsomeness. His face was narrow, his features sharp and striking. His dark hair was pleasantly disarrayed, his wide mouth naturally ruddy. She'd never seen skin as smooth as his on a man, though obviously he could afford regular spa treatments. A quick survey of her hormones revealed she wasn't physically pulled to him—or not so much that she'd notice. All the same, she couldn't deny he was easy on the eyes.

"Good evening," he said in his strangely formal yet not accented voice. "I hope I'm not interrupting. Could you recommend a nearby restaurant that delivers? My master likes spicy food."

His *master?* The thought that her new tenants might be a couple had crossed her mind, but not that they played with whips and chains. Was that why they wanted privacy?

Elyse struggled not to picture the man before her in a dog collar. He wore a nice dress shirt. There could be a leash under it . . . or maybe nipple clamps. She shook the thoughts from her head. The pair's personal arrangements absolutely weren't her business.

"Uh," she said. "There's a popular Indian place around the corner. And Szechuan not far from that."

"Szechuan," Joseph repeated as if she'd confused him.

"They make tasty Kung Pao chicken." Normally she'd have mentioned the restaurant was inexpensive. Chances were that didn't matter to a guy who carried stacks of hundreds in a briefcase. An image flashed into her mind of him opening the leather case at the register. This wasn't a bad neighborhood, but that was begging for trouble.

"You do have small bills, don't you?" At once, she felt stupid for asking. He couldn't be that naive. Except the term did seem to stump him.

"Small bills?"

"For paying. Like twenties. Or a credit card."

"I have the money you saw," he said.

He didn't appear to be joking—or to understand how inappropriate paying that way might be. Then again, how inappropriate was it for her to stick her nose in?

"Come inside," she said, giving in to impulse a second time in as many hours. "I've got a couple twenties in my wallet. You can borrow them and maybe break some bills at a bank tomorrow."

Joseph hesitated before entering unsurely. "The people at the hotel liked our hundreds."

Elyse laughed. "I bet they did."

Now that he'd decided to come in, he looked around. His gaze ran down the living room's wall of shelves, which overflowed with books and collectibles. His curiosity was the first unguarded emotion she recalled seeing on his face.

"You didn't decorate our apartment," he concluded.

"No," she agreed. Spotting her purse on the worn tufted leather sofa, she grabbed it and dug inside. "This place is mostly my father and me a little bit. My husband put the basement suite together."

"You husband is a paragon of . . . restraint." Joseph so obviously didn't admire this trait that Elyse had to hide a smile.

"My husband is dead," she said, the words instantly sobering her.

Joseph's face altered, though what thoughts passed through his mind she couldn't have guessed. "Forgive me," he said, offering a little bow that further concealed his reactions. "I didn't mean to cause sadness."

Elyse was struck by the thought that this was a clever man, no matter who he called *master*. Somewhat to her dismay, the realization didn't cause her to dislike him.

"You couldn't have known," she said.

He bowed again to acknowledge her forgiveness. When he straightened, his face was calm.

"I like this place," he said, actually seeming sincere. "Your belongings enchant the eyes and the fragrance is heavenly."

"That would be the garlic I'm sautéing."

"Ah," he said. "Garlic is one of God's finest creations."

He said this so seriously it was funny. Impulse washed over her again.

"Look," she said. "I'm only making spaghetti, but I'll have plenty to go around. I'd be happy to have you and Arcadius join me at my table."

"You honor us," Joseph said gravely.

Elyse felt a blush creep into her cheeks. "Well, I'm not a gourmet or anything. Come back in half an hour if your . . . if Arcadius is agreeable."

That won't do, she thought as Joseph bowed to her and left. She'd nearly called Arcadius his master too.

~

When Joseph returned to the cellar, Arcadius was studying the microwave's cryptic buttons, trying to pluck their meaning from the ethers. A gust of cold accompanied the loyal man through the door, and Joseph shut it again quickly. Arcadius saw he looked excited. His cheeks were flushed and his eyes were bright.

"I have inveigled an invitation," he announced, "for both of us."

"An invitation?"

"To Elyse's table for dinner. I played lost lamb. She is a widow. And she can cook."

These facts seemed to delight Joseph equally. Caught off balance, Arcadius rubbed his chin. "A widow?" A twinge of sympathy touched him. Though he'd never taken a wife, he imagined losing a spouse would be painful.

"Yes." Joseph rubbed his palms together. "She seemed sad about the loss. I sensed no other inhabitants in her home, no aunts or sisters. I'm sure she is lonely and vulnerable."

This *was* convenient, considering. Arcadius tried not to feel uneasy.

"Her home is nice," Joseph added. "Not like this bloodless place. I suspect her late husband wasn't compatible with her."

The logical trail he'd followed to this conclusion was unclear, but Arcadius let that pass. Joseph was probably right. The manservant was a good judge of character.

"Do you suppose the husband died violently?" he asked. "Could his death be the one whose energy you drew on?"

Joseph's triumphant grin faltered. "Perhaps it was. Forgive me, master. I should have thought of that myself."

"You can't think of everything, or what would I use my brain for?"

"Seducing her?" Joseph suggested more bawdily than he would have a week before. Arcadius's character wasn't the only one in danger of changing under their new conditions. He didn't scold the servant. They'd known each other too long and had no one else to count on their exile.

"I shall close my eyes and think of England," he promised.

"She isn't that bad," Joseph said fairly.

Elyse's soft pink mouth rose into his mind. No, she wasn't that bad. In truth, a tiny part of him was looking forward to wooing her.

~

Given that she'd told her guests to return in half an hour, Elyse had to make a choice. She could do something with her face and hair, or she could set the table. For various reasons, the table won. If her guests were gay, fussing with her appearance might make them nervous they'd have to set her straight. If they weren't, well, she wasn't ready for a new man—assuming she had the wherewithal to catch one.

No one could compare to David anyway. He'd been one in a million.

Pushing her familiar sadness down, she settled for smoothing back the crazier wisps of hair that had sprung up while she was at the stove. Her place smelled good at least. The wine was breathing and she'd tossed a nice salad. She'd gotten the impression her guests didn't cook at all. She might not possess her father's bonhomie, but she wasn't the worst hostess either. Her as-good-as-it-gets hospitality was probably good enough.

The knock that straightened her from the finished table wasn't Joseph's. This solid rap was noticeably bolder.

Arcadius, she thought, going to answer it.

To her dismay, her palm was tingling as she turned the old glass doorknob.

The taller of her two renters stood right in front of her. His sheer size caught her unprepared. This close, she could tell he topped six feet by a couple inches—and that he radiated authority. She barely noticed his friend behind him. Arcadius's presence was too intense, his chiseled face too dramatic. His fine-edged mouth could have been carved from stone. She'd forgotten how serious his expression was, as if his dark brows were thunderclouds. Beneath their shadow, the gemlike clarity of his eyes flat out transfixed her. They reminded her of chalcedony, a luminous mix of blue and gray. The way her body tightened as she stared into them alarmed her.

Joseph calling him *master* abruptly made perfect sense. The natural order of the universe demanded people obey him.

Considering the battle being fought inside her, she couldn't wonder she took too long pulling herself together.

"Elyse," came a querulous voice from across the hall in 6B. "Is everything all right? I heard loud footsteps."

Elyse smiled in spite of her embarrassing hormone storm. Her floor had two units. Only one person could be speaking.

"That's my neighbor," she informed her guests in an undertone. "Could you wait a sec? I'll let her know who you are."

"It's all right, Mrs. Goldberg," she called loudly. "We have new tenants for the basement unit. Why don't you come out and meet them?"

There was a pause. "The news is on," Mrs. Goldberg objected.

"It'll only take a moment," Elyse promised.

The old lady's protest had been empty. Mrs. Goldberg was already poised behind her door. The hinges creaked open, and she thumped out with an aluminum walker in her housecoat. Behind her thick glasses, her eyes goggled like a fish. She looked the newcomers up and down.

"Men," she said darkly, giving the tennis balls on the feet of her walker an extra *thunk*.

"Good evening," Arcadius responded in his rich dark voice. He offered Elyse's neighbor a courtly bow. "I am Arcadius and this is my friend Joseph. We're honored to make your acquaintance."

Mrs. Goldberg pursed her wrinkled lips more tightly.

"This is Mrs. Goldberg," Elyse said officially. "She's our most experienced tenant. She watches over everything."

"*Everything*," Mrs. Goldberg agreed, pointing her gnarled finger at both males.

"The building is fortunate," Arcadius said, "to have such a guardian."

He was all respect, not cracking the slightest smile. Accustomed to her longtime tenant's crotchety ways, Elyse was unprepared for her retort.

"You know it, sonny!" she cackled. "No handsome galoot like you can slip anything by me!"

Chuckling at her own wit, she turned in her bedroom slippers, shuffling relatively quickly back into her apartment.

Arcadius seemed startled by the reception he'd inspired, but Joseph grinned broadly.

"You're a galoot," he said, clearly tickled by the word.

Arcadius shook himself from his daze. "Apparently, I'm a handsome one."

"Don't mind her," Elyse said, stepping aside to make room for them to enter. "She's our resident Mrs. Kravitz."

The men looked at her blankly. "I thought you called her Mrs. Goldberg," Arcadius said. "Oh . . ." An odd expression flicked through his eyes, like he was searching an invisible data bank. "You refer to the nosy neighbor from the TV show *Bewitched*." He laughed. "That's very amusing."

Okay, Elyse thought, wondering if she should have been so quick to discard the weirdo label. "Right," she said. "She's been here forever. My dad told me she was living in that apartment back when his father bought the building. These days, her rent is so low it makes my accountant cry."

Arcadius nodded politely but not like he understood. Either the sight of her apartment distracted him, or he didn't know about rent control.

"Do you like wine?" she asked. "I opened a bottle."

She'd opened one of David's. His taste had been more sophisticated than hers.

Arcadius didn't seem to hear her. He'd stopped short in her living room, atop the antique Azerbaijan carpet with the beautiful Tree of Paradise pattern. His gaze traveled along the shelves much like his friend's before him, drinking up everything.

"This *is* nice," he said as if it surprised him.

"My personal curio shop." She knew so many colorful foreign trinkets overwhelmed some people. "A lot of the books were my granddad's. He was an antiquarian bookseller."

Arcadius wasn't overwhelmed by the collection. When he turned back to her, his handsome face beamed with approval.

"I wouldn't change one thing," he declared. "This place is perfect."

His words stirred a shiver she could have done without. All he needed to match David's bygone romantic declaration was to say she was perfect too.

One in a million shouldn't be that easy to duplicate.

~

For a moment, after Elyse opened the door to them, Arcadius thought seducing her would be smooth sailing. Finally, she was reacting like other women, who frequently threw themselves at him even before they knew his rank. As she'd stared up into his eyes, her pulse had elevated and her cheeks had flushed with arousal. Her pupils had expanded in her peridot irises. The signs of her excitement touched off similar responses inside of him. His cock had stiffened with his new body's first erection, the brush of it rising in his foreign clothes interesting. The heat and hardening felt good, as if more than one kind of potency were waking up in him.

Would sex feel different in this body? Would he like having it with her?

He'd wanted to think about those questions, not soothe her odd neighbor. Regardless, he did what politeness and strategy required. Freed then, he followed Elyse inside. As Joseph predicted, her home pleased him. It *was* a curio shop, full of interesting items. Throws and pillows softened her furniture, her genuine aged wood floors enlivened by not one but a number of beautiful area rugs. Pompeii red walls peeked between crowded bookcases and mounted fragments of Greek buildings. The lamps alone were worth investigating, coming as they did from many human countries and traditions. Arcadius spied an Indian elephant in full regalia and then an Aladdin-style oil burner. The latter had him fighting a laugh.

If Elyse rubbed the tarnished brass, would someone he knew emerge?

When he'd told her the place was perfect, the compliment was heartfelt. He had no idea why it caused her guards to snap up again.

Joseph noticed the change as well. "We brought a guest gift," he said, handing a box to her.

He used the world *we* loosely. Arcadius didn't know what the present was: some item from their magic briefcase, presumably. Elyse's face lit up as she accepted it, causing him an unexpected prick of annoyance.

He should have remembered to bring her a gift himself.

"Turkish delight!" she exclaimed, her fingers stroking the printed box. "My father used to bring me this whenever he visited Istanbul. Is that where you two are from?"

"We come from the . . . general area," Joseph conceded.

"That's wonderful," she said. "I'd love to hear all about it. Were you born there? Your English is fabulous."

It wasn't so fabulous she hadn't realized they'd been born elsewhere. Not that it mattered. The truth of their origins was beyond her power to guess.

As if the treats were precious, she carefully placed the box on her kitchen island, next to a bottle of uncorked wine from which emanated a faint but delicious aroma.

"Oh," she said, covering her rose petal mouth as she spun back toward the living room. "Should I have brought out alcohol? Do either of you drink?"

Perhaps it was childish, but Arcadius appreciated that she was asking him and not Joseph. "We aren't Muslims," he said. "The city we come from has many faiths. Whatever you serve, we'll be grateful to partake."

She laughed. "Hopefully you'll think so after you've eaten my cooking."

Humor made her more than pretty. With amusement lighting her face and eyes, she was beautiful. Arcadius breath caught halfway into his throat, his pulse skipping in a manner he wasn't accustomed to. Evidently, his new body was susceptible to simpler charms. In an instant, it throbbed with lust for her. He wanted to tear off her unfeminine clothes, to shove himself deep inside her softness and make her laugh again.

She must have seen the urge in his expression. Her manner grew more skittish than before.

"Your father travels?" he asked, hoping to calm her.

"He . . . did," she said. "He died two years ago on a trip." She lifted her hands. "Please don't apologize for asking. All my memories of him are good."

Perhaps they were, but her sense of loss was clear in her eyes. He dared not ask about a mother or siblings. He saw what Joseph meant about her being vulnerable.

"It is a blessing to have good memories," he said gruffly.

She smiled with a hint of wryness, seeming to comprehend his conflict.

Thankfully, reassuring him had caused her to relax. "Will you sit?" she asked, gesturing to a rustic round table that filled a sort of transition zone between the kitchen and living room. "Everything is ready. If you're hungry, I'll start serving."

He was hungry for more than food but pushed that from his mind. He and Joseph sat, probably equally aware they'd never navigated social territory like this before. They'd broken bread together at stranger's homes, but those strangers had been male. A female lover *might* serve a meal to Arcadius with Joseph in the room, but the servant wouldn't sit at the table as an equal. If the lover knew Joseph was a eunuch, she might not bother with a veil. Since this was a circumstance Joseph preferred not to broadcast, his experience of women was limited. His position as Arcadius's aide put him above lower class females—who'd probably have been happy to flirt with him. What Elyse's class would translate to neither of them could guess.

At least she was a widow, not an unmarried girl.

He suspected that didn't mean to her what it did to him.

She was dishing salad greens into majolica bowls from Italy. The array of crisp leaves intrigued him. He didn't recognize all of them.

"I kept the dressing on the side," she said. "I wasn't sure if you—" She broke off and turned as a knock sounded on the door.

"Elyse," a female voice called through the barrier. "I've brought sushi from Matsuri. Get off your little fanny and let me in."

Complicated emotions raced across Elyse's face. Whatever they were, they were strong enough that she took a moment to recover.

"That's my cousin Cara," she said, setting the salad tongs back in the serving bowl. "I have to answer her."

Have to, Arcadius repeated to himself. That suggested some reason for reluctance. His line of sight to the apartment door was clear. He and Joseph watched Elyse walk to it. Arcadius was surprised to discover he liked the look of her in the black jeans. Maybe little fannies *were* to his taste. Certainly, trousers for women were turning out to be.

"Sweetie!" cried the new arrival, wrapping Elyse in a tight embrace. From what Arcadius could tell, Elyse returned the hug with affection. "How are you? I was in the neighborhood. I thought I'd make sure you were eating. You've been looking so tired lately."

Elyse released her cousin. Her relative was taller by a few inches. Though their features shared a family resemblance, Cara's long straight hair was a beautiful honey blonde—not its natural color, he didn't think, but a flattering dye job. Her voluptuous figure was more his usual preference. Around its hourglass curves, her flaring red coat hung open. Multiple handle bags dangled from her hold. Her manicured nails were shiny with bold color.

"I've been eating," Elyse told her. "But thanks for your concern. I've cooked for guests tonight."

She stepped aside so her cousin could see. Minding their manners, Joseph and Arcadius pushed back their chairs and rose.

"Oh," Cara said, her face comically dismayed. "My bad! No wonder it smells so good."

"You're welcome to join us," Elyse said. "We'll have sushi and spaghetti."

"I shouldn't horn in on your evening."

"Please do," Arcadius said politely. "We're all new acquaintances."

Cara looked at Elyse. "Is it okay? I wouldn't mind taking a load off."

"You're always welcome," Elyse assured her. "You know where the closet is. Hang your coat and I'll set another place."

Before she went to do it, Cara gave Arcadius and Joseph a onceover with her eyes. The swiftness of the survey didn't keep Arcadius from feeling like he'd been stripped. This woman was a smart cookie, not to mention more confident with men than her relative.

When she returned, sans coat and packages, her stride put her considerable charms in fascinating motion. Not even to fit in could Joseph watch her knee-length knit dress cling and shift around her hips. Arcadius wasn't shy. The garment's fawn-brown color set off Cara's hair perfectly, as did three long amber-studded, antiqued gold chains that draped her lush bosom. The polished stones were good quality: honey-clear with sparkling inclusions.

"So," she said, smoothing the dress around her bottom before she sat. "How do you two know my cousin?"

"We've rented the basement unit," Arcadius said, doubting his aide would be able to speak just yet.

"Really?" Cara flipped a cloth napkin across her lap. "I'd begun to doubt anyone would take that place."

"Cara," Elyse scolded. As nimbly as a magician, she set her cousin's offering on the table, each sort of sushi arranged on a separate attractive plate. "People want different things out of apartments."

"Of course they do. Most just avoid habitations with curses attached to them."

Joseph coughed and Elyse rolled her eyes. To Arcadius's surprise, Joseph leaped up to pull out Elyse's chair. He hadn't performed the courtesy for her cousin . . . not that he'd have had the nerve to get close to her.

"May I?" Arcadius asked their hostess, indicating the open wine. She nodded and he poured for everyone. He timed his next question for when he reached Cara's glass. "Why do you say our living space is cursed?"

He looked straight into her eyes, which were green like her cousin's. Suddenly, she jumped but not on his account. From the sound of it, Elyse had just kicked her under the table. Arcadius was curious to see if Cara would obey the warning.

She flicked a wary glance at her cousin before answering. "Oh, you know, it didn't rent for a long, long time. That's as good as a curse in this neighborhood."

Finished pouring and not fooled, Arcadius sat back and smiled. Cara fiddled with one of her necklace's amber beads. He couldn't decide if she truly was prettier than her cousin or just had a different style. Her cosmetics were as skillfully applied as a concubine's.

"Arcadius and Joseph are from Turkey," Elyse said conversationally.

"Ah," Cara said, possibly not recovered from being kicked.

Elyse turned to him and Joseph. "Our family firm does business there."

"Your family firm?" Joseph asked.

"Solomon Brothers Imports," Cara answered. "Our fathers started it together. I work there too. We specialize in Mediterranean and Near Eastern goods." She lifted one of her neck chains to demonstrate. "Elyse's father was our main buyer until he fell into a volcano."

Elyse wrapped one hand across her eyes and sighed. She seemed not to like this topic any better than curses.

"He fell into a volcano?" Arcadius was startled enough to ask. This struck him as an exotic end for a human being.

Cara forked a delicate bite of salad into her mouth. "In Sicily. Mount Etna. My dad tried to warn him he was too old for daredevil tourist stunts."

"He wasn't a daredevil!" Elyse burst out. "He hired a professional guide. It was an accident."

Elyse's lovely green eyes welled up with emotion. Seeing this, Cara was instantly penitent.

"Sorry!" she exclaimed, quickly squeezing Elyse's hand. "Me and my big mouth. I shouldn't have said that, especially when I'm trying to cheer you up."

Elyse drew her hand back and shook her head. "It's okay. I know you didn't mean to upset me. Why don't we talk about something else?"

"Sure, but—" Cara turned on her chair, facing her cousin more directly. "Maybe you should accept Dad's offer to help you out. He'd be happy to take over here until you feel more yourself."

Elyse choked out a little laugh. "I know Uncle Vince means well, but I don't need that kind of help. I've managed this place myself ever since Dad died. I could do it in my sleep."

"You weren't by yourself all that time," Cara pointed out.

"For that I was. David didn't run the brownstone. He just built the new apartment."

Cara opened her mouth.

"Eat your sushi," Elyse ordered, pushing a fish roll between her cousin's lips.

Cara laughed and brought up her hand to keep the sushi from falling out. Arcadius guessed this sort of interplay was normal for the women.

"Sorry," Cara said to him and Joseph once she swallowed. "Elyse and I are kind of impossible."

"Family has its foibles," Arcadius agreed.

A cell phone rang not too far away.

"Crap," Cara said, hopping up. "That's my ringtone."

She dug the phone from a purse she'd dropped on an end table. The device was bright yellow and glossy. Though he didn't have a clear idea how to operate it, Arcadius found himself coveting one. Surely he and Joseph could afford a pair. They might come in handy for their mission.

"*Dad,*" Cara said, obviously annoyed. "I'm at Elyse's, eating dinner."

She walked to the living room's two front windows to continue her conversation in privacy. To judge by her body language, Elyse wasn't the only family member she squabbled with. She returned to them shortly.

"Ugh, my dad can be such a noodge. I'm afraid I have to leave. There's an emergency at our warehouse."

"Really?" Elyse said. Arcadius *thought* she sounded disappointed but couldn't tell for sure.

"Unfortunately, yes. You all enjoy the rest of your evening. No, don't get up. I can tell you're gentlemen, but I'm not that big of a lady." She made the words an amusing tease, her brilliant smile for both men bringing a blush to Joseph's cheeks. She addressed her cousin more seriously. "Elyse, if you find the thing . . ."

"Oh, God," their hostess groaned. "I told you, I don't have it."

"Right," Cara said. "But if you stumble across it, please let me know."

Elyse got up to hug her goodbye.

Arcadius found it all very interesting.

CHAPTER THREE

EVEN without Cara helping liven up the conversation, Elyse and her guests shared an enjoyable meal. The men had good appetites, though neither ate Cara's sushi—claiming they were allergic to raw seafood. They didn't bat an eye at her mix-and-match pasta, which she'd resorted for fear of having too little spaghetti. Their manners were excellent, their compliments for the food so flowery they were slightly embarrassing. The wine disappeared with no trouble. The Turkish delight sweets—whose brand she didn't recognize— were easily the most delicious she'd ever had. She guessed her father's favorite maxim was accurate: nobody beat locals for knowing where to shop. Nobody beat these guests for courteousness. Joseph refused to allow her to make the coffee, taking charge of her stove with easy efficiency.

Once he dropped his formality, Joseph was an amusing man. He had an endless supply of fish-out-of-water stories from his and Arcadius's time in New York. Many of the tales were accounts of dickering, for it seemed they were gem dealers. Elyse liked seeing Arcadius throw off his seriousness, laughing along with her even when the joke was on him. She concluded the part of Turkey they came from must be Old World. A lot of things she wouldn't have expected were new to them.

While Joseph bustled at the stove, Arcadius requested she show him how to use her cell phone. He pulled his chair next to hers for the lesson. Elyse tried to hide the flush inspired by his nearness, but he smelled very good— like sandalwood and frangipani and big warm man.

She reminded herself she wasn't remotely ready to move on from David. Her husband had only been gone two months, and he'd been her everything. Arcadius wasn't flirting—not that she could tell anyway. Once or twice tonight, she'd thought she saw a spark in his eyes, but each time it had disappeared. He didn't touch her as they bent together over her phone, careful not to knock her shoulder with his broad one.

Elyse wished she were as self-controlled. She couldn't help noticing the shine and luxuriance of his hair. The dark locks hung an inch below his shirt collar. His neck was nice too: tanned and muscular. The grace of his fingers as he pushed buttons per her instructions caused her thighs to go sweaty.

She didn't want to think about what he'd done to her nipples.

"Is this right?" he asked, turning the phone to show her his results.

Elyse could barely tear her eyes from his face to check. His closely shaved skin was nearly as smooth as Joseph's and, gosh, his mouth was pretty.

"Sure," she said, trying not to sound breathy. "That's how you add contacts. At least on this style of phone."

"Ah." He looked at the cell, dwarfed by the cup of his relaxed palm. "Could Joseph and I purchase these devices in not-black?"

Elyse smiled at his hopeful tone. "Probably. I use that one for business. You can also buy skins to dress them up."

"*Skins,*" Arcadius said, nodding like he'd filed the word away.

Joseph set steaming cups on the table in front of them.

Relieved by the excuse to lean back again in her chair, Elyse picked hers up and sipped. Her eyes went wide at the strong sweet taste. "How did you make this? This is authentic Turkish coffee! I don't have the equipment."

Joseph's smile was both pleased and sly. "I'm magic," he teased her.

Arcadius's chuckle set nerves tingling between her legs. No mere sound should have been able to arouse that strong a reaction. Elyse struggled not to squirm. Her dinner guest probably didn't mean to have the effect. Not that she was an expert, but she hadn't one hundred percent ruled him out as gay— nor could she swear if she wanted him to be.

Him and Joseph being lovers would make things too simple for her illogical psyche.

Despite her inappropriately eager hormones, this was the most pleasant evening she'd spent in a while. She'd *almost* forgot her troubles, and she *did* feel like her old self.

The glow lasted a whole minute after she said goodbye to her new tenants.

Without them in it, the apartment was very quiet. Maybe Joseph was magic. He'd put the dirty dishes in the dishwasher when she wasn't looking . . . and cleaned the countertops. This was nice of him, but straightening up would have settled her. Instead, she was left with her loneliness.

She let out a long slow sigh, the sound no use whatsoever for drowning out silence. It was too early to go to bed, on top of which her ability to sleep had been crap lately.

"Pull yourself together," she told herself.

With nothing particular to keep her busy, her restless feet took her the last place she should have gone. She and David had converted the second bedroom into his "man" room. His desk and computer took up one wall, furniture from his bachelor days scattered across the rest. The room smelled of him as she stepped inside. Unable to bear seeing so many reminders of her loss, she'd boxed up his things and stowed them here. She didn't know when she'd want to give them to Goodwill. As of yet, she hadn't taped the boxes closed. Probably the little book Cara had been bugging her about was in one. Elyse simply didn't have the heart to search.

David and her cousin had known each other at college, both members of a group of undergrads who'd rented a house together. They'd stayed friends, though David claimed Cara's bossiness kept them from hooking up. He liked to say the best thing Cara ever did was introduce him to Elyse.

You made my life complete, he swore.

Idly opening the desk's left drawer, Elyse found a legal pad with one of his tidy lists. *Find door*, he'd jotted and *Buy flowers for Elyse*. Her throat closed as she shoved the drawer shut again. He must have written the note while he was working on the cellar. He was always doing sweet things for her.

Sadness threatened to swallow her. She'd never be loved like that again. David had been her first and last, and now he was gone. Just like her father. And her mother, who hadn't lived long enough for Elyse to remember her. No one she needed stuck around. Probably she'd end up like Mrs. Goldberg, shuffling around alone in her bedroom slippers, calling handsome but ultimately uninterested men like Arcadius *galoots*.

Even as she choked out a little laugh, tears spilled hot down her cheeks. She'd shed far too many lately, but she let them fall anyway.

~

Lost in thought, Arcadius and Joseph dropped at almost the same moment to sit on the black modern couch in their living room.

"That was interesting," Joseph said after a short silence.

Arcadius leaned forward across his knees.

"She's attracted to you," the servant said. "I saw her pulse beat faster a couple times."

Arcadius had noticed this as well. The response was one he was familiar with. He shoved aside his irritation that her excitement hadn't been stronger. "What did you think of the cousin?"

"Beautiful," Joseph said, "but untrustworthy."

Arcadius pinched his chin. That had been his impression too. "She knows something about this basement. Why else would she suggest it was cursed if she weren't hoping to scare us off?"

"Why would her father volunteer to take over managing the building if he didn't want more access?"

Seeing they were on the same page, Arcadius turned sideways. His elbow draped the couch's back. "Do you suppose it's common for humans to turn cellars into homes?"

"I don't know," Joseph said. "If it isn't, one might infer Elyse's husband was a participant in whatever was going on."

Arcadius's mouth turned down. If that were true, Elyse might be even more alone than they'd supposed. With a start, he realized he was offended for her sake. Unsettled by that idea, he spoke firmly. "We need to examine the magical nexus. Find out what, if anything, has been done to it."

"I am ready to do that now," Joseph said. "Elyse's meal restored my strength."

His expression said he was aware of the irony. Djinn were sensitive to vibrations. Scents, emotions, even colors were alive to them. Food cooked with care was more fortifying than if it were prepared slapdash. Their landlady had unknowingly benefited their mission.

They proceeded without delay. Joseph had a key he'd stolen from his previous master, a magician to whom he'd been apprenticed—the same magician who'd cruelly castrated him. The key was enchanted to open any physical lock. The padlock Elyse had attached to the apartment's forbidden door was no match for it. Joseph slid in the instrument, released the hasp, and swung the much-painted egress wide.

Stale air rushed out through the opening. Arcadius's new body shivered. True to Elyse's claim that this was a mechanical room, the light from their narrow hall illuminated an assortment of tanks and pipes. Beyond this he couldn't see. The darkness was as thick as if it were made of fur.

"Do you wish to go first?" Joseph offered politely. His poorly hidden grin revealed he was teasing.

Amused but hiding it, Arcadius quirked one brow at him. From humans' standpoint, djinn were creatures of darkness. They wouldn't be afraid of it. "I don't suppose you packed a lantern in one of your little bags. My current body's night vision isn't what I'm used to."

"One moment." Joseph disappeared into the transformed bedroom, returning with the item his master had requested.

The lantern was already lit when Arcadius accepted it. "Watch our backs," he said, not so proud he'd pretend the territory they were exploring couldn't hold dangers. Better safe than sorry wasn't a bad tactic.

As Arcadius expected, the mechanical room provided access to the entire unfinished portion of the basement—perhaps three quarters compared to their apartment. The lantern helped them navigate. Cracked cement formed the floor, the cellar itself hewn from nearly black bedrock. Apart from an occasional stingy window, the space could have been a cave. No hallway simplified their journey. Randomly sized rooms led one to another, no seeming rhyme or reason in their arrangement. Stacks of old belongings blocked their way here and there, boxes and furniture he sincerely doubted anyone was returning for.

One small room held nothing but discarded fake Christmas trees. Another revealed a toilet and sink only the most desperate handyman would dream of peeing in.

Arcadius could almost hear spiders skittering.

"I don't sense the nexus," Joseph whispered behind him. "Something is blocking it."

"Let's be still," Arcadius advised. "If we close our eyes and breathe, its location may come to us."

He followed his own suggestion. With his sight shut off, the cellar seemed to expand in every direction, no longer a building's base but an unlimited netherworld that was neither djinn nor human. Arcadius had faced too much in his life to succumb to fear, but his skin admittedly was crawling.

"Almighty God," Joseph swore suddenly. Arcadius's eyes snapped open.

"What?" he asked. He saw nothing new in the shifting lamp shadows.

"You didn't hear that?"

"Hear what?"

"That terrible scream. Like someone . . . having parts of them torn off."

When Arcadius held up the lantern, Joseph's face shone with sweat. Arcadius didn't have to think hard to imagine what he was remembering. The servant shook himself and recovered. "It must be a psychic echo of the murder I sensed before."

"Can you tell where it happened?"

Joseph focused. "Close by. Through that next opening, I think."

They went through it. They'd reached a part of the cellar's warren with no windows. The area was maybe ten foot square, near the center of the building. Interestingly, its walls were built of new cement blocks. Perhaps Elyse's husband had erected them? The only object he saw inside was an old fashioned child's rocking horse. The toy was molded out of plastic and colored to resemble the animal.

As Arcadius and Joseph approached, the steed began rocking by itself.

"In the name of the Almighty, show yourself," Joseph said.

No mere spirit could resist the mage's authority. An ifrit appeared in the horse's saddle, roiling smoke in the shape of a small monkey with bat wings. Like Joseph and Arcadius, the ifrit was djinn. Unlike them, it viewed their Creator as an enemy. The ifrits' view was that any god who expected them to treat a younger race—i.e., humans—as superior ought to be rebelled against.

"*Mine,*" the ifrit proclaimed, its yellow eyes glaring angrily at Joseph. "My death energy to eat."

Confident in his power, Joseph crossed his arms. "I don't think so, devil."

The ifrit tried wheedling. "You don't need it and I'm hungry."

"Your kind don't frequent New York," Joseph said without softening. "How did you get here?"

The ifrit glared but Joseph's will was firm. "Through the teeny tiny hole," it answered sullenly. "None of my brothers were eating here, and many beings die badly in this city."

"Can you show us how the human died?" Arcadius asked.

Less impressed with him, since he wasn't a magician, the ifrit made its smoke nose grow longer so it could look down it. Arcadius wanted to smile but kept his face impassive.

"You will show him," Joseph ordered before the lower level demon could say something impudent.

"If I do, what do I get?" the ifrit demanded.

"How about your life?"

The demon's smoke mouth pouted. All djinn, low or high, loved baubles.

"Show us," Joseph insisted. "Or I shall use the power of the King of Kings against you."

Naturally, the ifrit disliked this threat. "Fine." It flung itself off the rocking horse, its vaporous body shredding and flickering. As Joseph had known it could, the ifrit was using its own substance to recreate past events.

The space they stood in didn't change much at first. The light was angled differently, and the rocking horse became transparent. Whatever had happened here, the toy hadn't been here then. Suddenly the figure of a man stumbled into the room, his image passing through Arcadius and Joseph on the way. He looked real but he wasn't. Neither was he a ghost. Though Arcadius doubted the ifrit knew the word, the man was a very sharp hologram—the same as he and Joseph had seen in human media.

Seeming afraid, the person who'd just appeared scrambled back on his hands and butt. Tallish and lean, he wore baggy pants with many pockets and a paint-spattered navy shirt with the sleeves pushed up. The terror twisting his features didn't hide his appealing looks. His hair was wavy and wheat colored, his jaw and cheekbones firm. Wire rimmed glasses balanced crookedly on his nose, knocked askew by his desperate flight. He shoved the spectacles straight with one finger.

"I don't have the door," he pleaded fearfully.

"You've had free rein down here for a year," rumbled another voice. The sound was so low Arcadius wondered if the ifrit were exaggerating its deepness out of some flair for the dramatic.

The frightened man was scared enough as it was. He'd retreated until the cement block wall stopped him. Now he stood, squared his shoulders, and tried to look less trembly. "I haven't found the door yet. Only the nexus, which is here."

A large man-shaped shadow fell across Spectacles. Half a moment later, the male who cast it appeared. This individual was very tall, taller than Arcadius and even thicker with muscle. His head was shaved. His scalp—and all the other skin they could see—was covered in swirling barbed black tattoos. Arcadius was relatively sure the tattooed man was human. He wasn't quite terrifying enough to be djinn.

Spectacles cowered as if he were an ogre.

"You've been seen with a magic book," Tattoos rumbled in an accusing tone.

"A f-friend loaned it to me. I didn't get it from the Qaf. The book isn't the door!"

Tattoos slapped a meaty hand around the other's neck. The move cut off Spectacles' air, trapped him against the wall, and forced him onto his toes.

"Where is the door?" Tattoos demanded.

"I don't know," Spectacles choked. "I swear I've looked everywhere. Her father hid it too well."

Tattoos released him. The other man rubbed his neck. Though his face was red from having his windpipe squeezed, being let go seemed to increase his confidence. "I just need a bit more time."

"You've had a year," Tattoos growled.

"My wife doesn't know anything. I've had to search from scratch. Listen, now that your employer knows what I'm doing, maybe we should talk."

Tattoos let out a derisive snort. "You want to talk to my employer."

"I'm sure we could come to a mutually satisfactory arrangement."

The bigger man seemed to swell. He jabbed a finger into Spectacles' breastbone. "There's only one arrangement. You give us what we want and we don't kill you."

His threat issued, Tattoos turned away in disgust. His path took him toward Joseph and Arcadius. He didn't see what they did. Behind his back, Spectacles suddenly stood straight, a look of eagerness altering his formerly frightened face. He dug in his rear pants pocket, his hand emerging with a seven-inch silver spike.

"*Heart*," he murmured as he threw it.

Tattoos' back was exposed. The spike should have hit its target. It was a magical weapon, after all. Sadly for Spectacles, the other man's tattoos sprang outward from his skin, one barbed curlicue neatly snatching the projectile out of the air, mid-flight.

"Shit," Spectacles hissed, flinching back to the wall again.

Tattoos turned. He rolled his big neck and shoulders as the swirling marks resettled on his skin. In his right hand, he held the silver spike poised to throw.

"That was a mistake," he said ominously.

"I was just defending myself. You threatened to kill me."

Tattoos lifted the spike and spoke to it. "Serve me," he said, "and I'll let you drink all of him."

The spike wriggled in his hand as if it liked that prospect.

"You need me," Spectacles said. "I'm in the perfect position."

"You've had a year in the 'perfect position.' What you are is a waste of time."

Spectacles fell to his knees on the concrete floor. "Please," he begged, his hands clutched together before him. "Don't."

Tattoos grinned, the stretch of his lips revealing big white teeth. "*Blood*," he said with relish to the spike.

The spike leaped from his hand to attack its new target. By the time it finished its grisly work, it was twice the size it had been before. Naturally, it couldn't drink all of its victim's blood. The remainder sprayed and pooled and splattered from Spectacles' uncountable slash wounds. The screams that had spooked Joseph earlier echoed around the room. In the end, Spectacles was so savagely ripped up it was hard to make out that he was human. Arcadius and Joseph had seen a lot of deaths, but they were both wincing.

"Return to me," Tattoos intoned.

The silver spike flew obediently to his hand, shining and spotless and seemingly inanimate once more.

Tattoos looked like he'd stood in a shower of blood and thicker things. If he minded, they couldn't tell. He looked down on the remains with an impassive face.

"Is that enough?" the ifrit's voice asked Arcadius and Joseph. "Shall I show you again?" The demon sounded amused. It wouldn't have minded replaying the gore fest.

"That is enough," Joseph said.

The hologram of the past dissolved. As it did, they realized the ifrit's feeding activity must have masked the nexus's location. They perceived it now, not with ordinary vision but in their minds' eyes. The magical hot spot resembled a slowly rotating sun. A micron-sized black speck, presumably the teeny tiny door the ifrit had referred to, marred the radiance. Aside from this single flaw, the nexus was beautiful. Its rays spiked upward, threw off rainbow glints, and then fell back in a surprisingly organized rhythm. Though the pattern wasn't predictable, it was visually melodic.

"Someone stabilized this power point already," Joseph said. "That dot is a tiny passage from this plane to the Qaf."

"Told you," the ifrit said.

Joseph ignored him. "I can't tell where it goes," he said with his nose wrinkled. "But not to our city."

"I come from the Great Desert," the ifrit volunteered. "Where the high ifrits travel in caravans."

The Qaf were an immense chain of mountains. Not precisely a place, no ordinary landmass connected the different territories. Sometimes you could walk from one country to the next. Other times the journey wasn't straightforward. If Arcadius understood what the ifrit meant by the Great Desert, this door didn't lead near their home.

The ifrit's mention of the caravan djinn was interesting. Though not fans of the human race, Bedouin were enthusiastic traders. If humans had contacted them, they wouldn't hesitate to do business.

"That's why the tattooed man was eager to find the door," Arcadius said. "Since this nexus is already claimed, a new door can't be created. Without the old door, they can't use this particular portal to go anywhere. With it, if they had the know-how, they could recalibrate the nexus to send them anywhere on our plane."

Arcadius knew a door could be disguised as anything. An old shoe. A hamburger wrapper. Even the proverbial needle in a haystack. He gazed around the cement-walled room. It was cleaner than he expected, given what he'd just seen. Someone, hopefully not Elyse, had scrubbed away the bloodstains.

He wasn't so busy scanning he didn't notice the ifrit trying to creep away.

"Halt, you," he ordered.

Joseph did him one better, seizing the creature by the scruff of its smoky neck. Caught, the ifrit dangled dolefully in the magician's grip. Its little batwings sagged.

"I helped you," he complained. "You said I could have my life."

"I didn't say you could have it here."

The ifrit pouted harder. "If I have to go home, I want to take my horse with me."

Arcadius and Joseph considered the sad old toy. "That isn't a door," Arcadius said, having probed it for vibes.

"No," Joseph agreed.

"The little girl who owned it *died*," the ifrit said. "*I* want to play with it."

Joseph glanced at Arcadius, who shrugged. The ifrit's interest in the plaything might be macabre, but he didn't see the harm. Ifrits could turn vengeful if you thwarted them too much. He and Joseph didn't need to deal with more nuisances.

"You may take your toy," Joseph decided. "And I shall give you a stone besides."

"A pretty stone?" the ifrit asked hopefully.

"A ruby," Joseph pledged. "Faceted by a master cutter to flash in the sun like blood."

This pleased the small demon. Sensing it would behave, Joseph set it back on the ground. Hands free then, he magically shrunk the rocking horse, pushing it through the tiny black spot in the nexus. He pulled a ruby from his pocket—as good a stone as he'd promised—and it soon made the same journey. The ifrit watched the red chip disappear avidly.

"You'd better hurry," Joseph counseled. "You wouldn't want your brothers on the other side to get their paws on your prizes."

The ifrit began to go, then looked at him. "You are honorable," he declared. "I won't forget."

Fearing it would lose its treasures, the ifrit smoked through the tiny hole.

As soon as it had gone, Joseph sketched the star from King Solomon's seal over the opening. The black spot snapped shut, no longer spoiling the nexus's glittery perfection.

With the ifrit gone, Arcadius and Joseph could speak freely.

"Well," Joseph said. "I suppose now we know how Elyse's husband died."

"The human police must have been confounded. I wonder where David obtained the blood-drinking spike. That was definitely a djinn weapon."

"Whoever installed the missing door . . ." Joseph trailed off, his gaze unfocused.

"Yes," Arcadius said. "Whoever installed it might have been visiting the Qaf for a while. The Almighty only knows what souvenirs he or she returned with."

Joseph pulled a thoughtful face. "I wonder who created those spelled tattoos for the man who killed Elyse's husband. They were of djinn origin too."

They had firsthand familiarity with magical tattoos, though the killer's seemed different from their own.

"They behaved as if they were conscious," Arcadius mused. "They knew their owner was being attacked without him turning around."

"One of our sorcerers could have infused the ink with a low level demon's spirit. The tattoos could have been compelled to protect their wearer."

"The tattooed man was human," Arcadius pointed out. "If he couldn't travel to the Qaf because this door is shut . . ."

"Then perhaps the djinni who made them was on this plane."

"Philip?" Arcadius suggested.

Joseph shook his head slowly. "I don't *think* so. He had the power for it, and I'd like to believe he's alive, but those designs didn't remind me of his style." He was silent for a moment. "Something else is bothering me. Elyse's husband said, 'My wife doesn't know anything.'"

"You think he lied?"

"I don't know. Clearly, he was practiced at deception. I can't help but wonder if he asked Elyse the right questions. This nexus is beneath her house, the house her grandfather purchased, the house her father inherited and managed before her."

"Her father who fell into a volcano."

"Yes," Joseph said wryly. "She grew up surrounded by oddities. She must know something about something—"

"—even if she doesn't know she knows." Arcadius rubbed his chin, accustomed to he and Joseph finishing each other's sentences. "I need to get closer to her."

"You do," Joseph agreed. "We need to find that door, and we need to reprogram it to lead to our city. That will require as big a sacrifice as creating one from scratch."

CHAPTER FOUR

THE return trip to their apartment felt like it should take longer. They'd learned a lot since they left.

"Tea?" Joseph offered after they were inside.

Arcadius shook his head. He wanted to think and plan—assuming his overly full brain would cooperate. He glanced at the low ceiling. Too bad he couldn't see through it to Elyse.

"I should work on the mirror space," Joseph said. "If matters here are this complicated, a hiding place might come in handy sooner rather than later. Also it wouldn't hurt to have two bedrooms."

Arcadius nodded absently as Joseph left. He lowered himself to one of the white leather and chrome chairs. The cushion wasn't uncomfortable, just firmer than he was used to. Lots of things weren't what he was used to here: the battle ahead of him, for one thing.

How did a man win a woman who didn't find him irresistible?

A rhythmic scraping drew him from his reverie. The sound came from outside their street door, so its source couldn't be Joseph. Were some of the city's wrongdoers attempting an assault? He knew from watching the news that they carried guns. Unalarmed but deciding to arm himself, he drew his favorite knife from its ankle sheath. The jewels on its hilt adjusted the blade to different sizes, suitable for anything from close-quarters jabbing to swordfighting. Most important was that the knife looked intimidating. Arcadius believed in heading off trouble when possible.

As silently as he was able, he glided to the entryway. Once the bolts were undone, he yanked the door open.

"Shit," he said, seeing who was behind it. He tucked the knife away swiftly. "What the hell are you doing?"

Elyse slapped one gloved hand to her bosom. "What does it look like I'm doing? I'm shoveling your sidewalk."

"You're shoveling our sidewalk."

"I'm sorry if I disturbed you. I know it's late, but I only just remembered it needed doing. The temperature is supposed to drop tomorrow. I don't want you two slipping if this stretch turns to ice."

She didn't want them slipping. Part of him simply couldn't accept this as an appropriate attitude for a female. His jaw worked as he stared at her, flustered and angry and at a loss as to what to say. Perhaps she was also flummoxed. Framed by the knit cap she wore, her cheeks were extremely pink. A moment later, he noticed her nose was too.

The appendage was much cuter than he was prepared for.

"Where is your coat?" he demanded.

"Shoveling is warm exercise! I'd be done by now if you weren't standing there arguing."

Arcadius couldn't take anymore. "Give me that," he said, grabbing the shoveling implement from her.

Elyse let him have it but crossed her arms. "Have you done this before?"

He hadn't but how difficult could it be? He'd mucked out stables, once upon a time.

"Sheesh," she said, watching him struggle.

"I'll get the hang of it," he muttered.

"Put your foot behind the blade. Use your weight to slide it under the load."

He did as she instructed, surprised to discover her way was easier.

"Now lift the snow over the railing and dump it into the pile I made."

He did that too and finished clearing the ramp in two more shovels full.

"Great," she said. "If you step back, I'll throw down some salt."

"Salt?"

She blinked at his tone of horror. He cursed himself for blurting out the objection. If sea salt was concentrated, it affected djinn caustically. "I use the blue stuff," she said, gesturing to a plastic bottle she'd set nearby. "It's non-toxic for pets and kids."

He gathered the container held a salt substitute. "Ah," he said, working to recover. "That's very responsible."

"Uh-huh." She seemed to find him amusing. She scattered the pellets and reached for the shovel he was gripping.

Strategy wasn't all that prevented him from releasing it. Male protectiveness was in there too.

"I need to put that away," she pointed out.

"I'll carry it for you," he said, sounding more truculent than he'd intended.

"It's just a shovel!"

"You're a woman."

"Oh. My. God," she huffed, each word a complete sentence.

"Humor me," he suggested.

Elyse began laughing. The reaction nettled him even as he appreciated how it improved her looks. "All right. Follow me to the lobby, and I'll show you where the winter supplies are stored. I'm freezing my butt out here anyway."

Oddly uncomfortable with the reminder that she had one, he grabbed the canister of blue stuff before she could. That amused her too. She hadn't quite stopped laughing by the time they got inside.

The lobby was a shoebox—barely room to swing a cat, as the saying went. He'd noted the wall of mailboxes on his earlier trip upstairs with Joseph. The hands on the clock above them pointed to twelve o' one.

"Here's the tool closet," Elyse said, opening a door paneled in the same dark aged wood as the lobby walls. "We don't lock this. If you borrow a screwdriver or whatever, just return it afterward."

Ugly metal shelves lined the closet. Arcadius set the shovel and salt where she indicated. Elyse shut the door again.

"Thanks for your help," she said, her eyes still amused. "In the future, I'll make sure the caretaker clears your walk too."

He gazed down into her face. Despite her smiling eyes, her manner wasn't flirtatious. The space she'd left between them ensured that. She'd folded her hands together at her waist, and the set of her mouth was prim. Arcadius could read body language. He knew he had to move quickly or miss his opening.

"Your cousin was right," he said. "You look tired."

Elyse snorted. "Thank you very much. At least tonight I had something to do when I couldn't sleep. Oh, I mean—" She stopped, the flush on her cheeks deepening. She was sorry she'd told him that.

"I understand," he said compassionately. "Night's hours can be difficult to endure when you've experienced a loss."

They were difficult for him, wondering how—and if—he'd save his people.

"Um," she said, seeming unable to look away from his eyes. "Sorry?"

He smiled, not out of strategy but because he found her sympathy endearing. "My countrymen know remedies to bring sleep. Stimulating special pressure points, for instance."

He let his voice deepen the way it wanted to. Seeming dazed, Elyse rubbed the hot color on her cheek. "Ah, I don't think that's really—"

"It's the least I can do. You've demonstrated concern for my safety and well-being. By our traditions, I'm honor bound to return the courtesy."

Gently, but not waiting for permission, he took her wrist to ease her forearm away from where she'd pressed it against her ribs. Exposing the special nerve center on the underside was no more complicated than sliding her sleeve upward. He rubbed the pad of his thumb in a light circle. The spot he stroked did indeed induce relaxation, though that wasn't what he was aiming for. The skin of anyone's arm right here was very sensitive. Elyse's green eyes glazed.

"Um," she said, tugging her arm back halfheartedly. "I don't think—"

"Forgive me," he said, releasing her. "I have presumed."

Her soft pink lips were parted and her breath came quicker. Her second hand rubbed the spot he'd been caressing. Arcadius noticed his own thighs were hot, the organ between his legs twitching. Elyse shook herself.

"You certainly have a way about you," she said.

He wanted to ask if it was a way she liked. Her rueful tone warned him not to be that direct. Thinking fast, he recalled her delight at Joseph's anecdotes and the many books that filled her apartment's shelves.

"I know stories," he said.

A tiny pucker appeared between her brows. "Stories?"

"Stories are only words of course, but they do fill the head when you'd rather your own thoughts did not."

He'd hit on the right temptation. Her smile was small, the tip of her tongue peeking out between her lips. "Are they Turkish stories?"

"They are the most magical Turkish stories you could imagine."

This was a lie. The only stories he knew well enough to relate were stories of the Glorious City: his stories, in point of fact. For a moment, he questioned whether he ought to tell true tales. Maybe that was risky, or just too personal.

Elyse broke into a grin. "No one's told me a bedtime story since my dad."

Her anticipation charmed him, his doubts ceasing to matter.

If it helped save his people, he'd play Scheherazade.

~

Elyse preceded him up the building's stairs with her snowy boots clumping. She had a strong suspicion she shouldn't be doing this. Never mind her dread of one more hour spent alone in the too silent apartment. She barely knew Arcadius, nor was she comfortable with his effect on her. The more time she spent with him, the stronger the attraction grew. Was the chemistry only on her side? The look in his gemlike eyes had been so hot for a few seconds . . .

Should she try to clarify the situation, or would that be embarrassing? Did he mean *pressure points* as a euphemism for something else?

She gnawed her lip all the way up the final flight.

Arcadius opened the door for her. "I'll make you a cup of tea," he said.

"You don't have to—"

"Hush," he said. "I understand grief, Elyse. It will soothe me to do this for you."

His deep voice was dreamily beautiful, his exquisite manners nonthreatening. Everything about him seemed impossible to refuse. The memory of Joseph calling him *master* returned to her. God, why did that turn her sex liquid? No one should have moved her this easily. David had been the light of her life, the only great love she'd have.

"Take off your little boots," her companion said. "Curl up in your favorite chair. I'll tell you one story and disappear."

Either her instinct was to believe him, or she didn't care if he were truthful. As obedient as a child, she removed her clunky boots—which he thought were little!—and sat on the old leather sofa in front of the flickering gas fireplace. Though the light was low, she didn't rise to turn more lamps on.

It seemed only seconds before he returned to her. He set a single teacup and saucer on the brass-topped Moroccan table and then joined her on the couch. He left space between them, as much as his height and long legs allowed. She saw he'd removed his shoes, his large male feet covered in black dress socks. The hems of his lovely trousers were damp from shoveling. He was in shirtsleeves, the perfectly fitted pale yellow garment buttoned all the way to its collar. His leather belt was narrow and sexy—as were his hips, if she were honest. Elyse reminded herself she shouldn't be studying that vicinity. Seeming unaware she'd almost measured his package, he handed her the Peruvian throw from the back of the sofa.

"Wrap this around yourself," he said. "Sip your tea and warm up."

If he'd been trying to seduce her, wouldn't *he* have wrapped her in the blanket?

Elyse pulled it around herself. "What sort of story are you going to tell me?"

He bent his arm on the sofa's back, using his elegant thumb and fingers to support his jaw and chin. The grace of the pose appeared natural, his gorgeous lips pursing slightly as he considered her. Unable to stop herself, Elyse wriggled deeper into the soft leather. "Would you like to hear the story of the sultan and the lost princess?"

"Is it exciting?"

"Do you want it to be?"

His tone was playful and she laughed. "Tell the story the way it's supposed to be, no prettying it up for the American."

His gray blue eyes crinkled with approval. "As you wish. I shall tell the tale the way it's supposed to be."

~

"I have heard it said," Arcadius began in a gentle but formal tone, "that in the golden days of the Glorious City, there lived three men who were as close in love as brothers."

"'As close in love,'" Elyse repeated, her lips curving in a smile. She'd turned toward him on the couch with her legs drawn under her and her cheek resting on her hand, as if she were half asleep already. Wrapped in the colorful blanket, she seemed childlike. Only her humorous eyes were womanly. Seeing her like this, trusting and receptive and yet unattainable, moved him in ways he couldn't quite pin down.

"The trio were great friends," he explained, ignoring the reaction. "Among the people of the Qaf, men do not hesitate to say 'I love you' to each other."

Her smile deepened at his scold. "That's nice. Friends are good."

"Yes, friends are good." He cleared his throat as emotion threatened to close it. "These three were so devoted any one of them would lay down his life for the others. They had come early to their positions, which were lofty. One of the men was a great artist and the son of the vizier. He could create any work in any medium, and it would be more beautiful than that of other djinn."

"They were genies."

"They were."

Perhaps thanks to her father, Elyse seemed to understand the term referred to more than wish-granting beings sealed up in bottles.

"Go on," she prompted. "What was the second friend's position?"

"He commanded the sultan's army. He was less interesting than the others, but he loved them and was loyal."

"I see. And the third?"

"The third friend was the sultan himself. He was known as Iksander the Golden. The sun was not more radiant than he, nor the willow tree more graceful. Thankfully, his looks hadn't spoiled his character. He was strong, cared for his people, and—in most instances—possessed a discerning mind."

"In most instances."

"Only God is perfect," Arcadius responded philosophically. "Like the others, Iksander attained his position when still youthful. His father, the previous sultan, had died recently, and Iksander was very sad. Because his friends loved him, and because they were young men, they decided to raise his spirits by taking him to a tavern.

"In order to avoid attention, all of them being recognizable, the friends decided to assume disguises. Dressed as simple workingmen and bringing only one servant, they slipped through the gates of the palace into the surrounding town. After walking about a bit, they came upon what seemed a merry establishment.

"As it happened, this particular watering hole belonged to a dangerous demon—an ifrit, who would not honor the Creator by any of His names. That is what makes a demon among the people you call genies. All djinn believe in God, but some refuse to obey."

"Why is that?" she said. "If you don't mind me asking."

"It is said that God created angels, then djinn, and finally the human race. Angels have no free will. They love and obey God, and that is that. Djinn have some free will. They may choose to love God or not, and in some cases can disregard His edicts. Humans were created with the most free will, and—

so it seems to djinn—God loves them best of all. The Creator gave dominion over the Earth to djinn, but took it back and passed it to the younger race after they were born. Djinn were ordered to bow to humans but some refused. As punishment, djinn's power to eavesdrop on angels was revoked. Djinn were also made subject to certain magical rituals. If humans know the proper formulas, as was the case with King Solomon, they can force djinn to obey them. As you might expect, this inspires resentment, especially since God seems to forgive humans no matter what they do."

"I'd be resentful," Elyse admitted.

She rubbed her cheek on her arm, making him long to brush its softness with his fingers. Her sleepy green eyes met his, giving him the odd sensation that he was falling.

"What happened at the tavern the demon owned?" she asked.

Arcadius returned his attention to his story. "The ifrit who owned the tavern was as canny as he was fiendish. Seeing his latest customers were above the common run, he gave them their own table, plying them with the best food and drink he had. Women were sent as well, to sit on the young men's laps and entertain them with sweet kisses. The commander's lap was so large three plump slave girls perched on his legs at once. With such distractions, the men forgot their troubles—their good sense as well perhaps.

"The hour grew late, but the crowd did not thin. The ifrit's friends, evildoers like himself, kept filling the empty seats. The tavern was so busy the owner's personal female servant was pressed into service. The moment the young sultan laid eyes on her, his heart fled his strong body.

"The female servant was humbly dressed but veiled, suggesting she was no pleasure slave. Though the sultan saw little of her person, what he saw inflamed him. Here was a woman, he thought, whose hand as she poured was so fair and soft it must belong to an angel.

"She filled his cup, sliding it gracefully toward him. She seemed to peer at him meaningfully through her veil, which covered not just her face but her eyes as well. The sultan truly believed that if he didn't discover what the fine silk concealed, he'd die a broken man.

"Though famed for his own beauty, the violence of the sultan's feelings embarrassed him. He dropped his chastened gaze to the cup the woman filled. As he did, he saw that on its surface a small piece of rice paper sailed.

"*Please save me* it said in miniscule writing.

"The sultan didn't know what to make of this request. He nudged his friend the commander, who sat next to him with his lap full of giggling girls.

"*Hm*, thought the commander as he also read the plea. He looked at the sultan, whose jewel blue eyes begged him to provide support.

"The commander's brain wasn't completely pickled by the strong wine they'd been drinking. He realized his friend had fallen in love. He didn't get a chance to inquire how this came to pass. At that moment, the ifrit owner, who looked like a normal djinni—simply not very beautiful—hopped onto a stool to get the crowd's attention.

"'It is time for our nightly contest,' the proprietor declared. 'Who will offer up a story to match my own? The winner receives my most priceless treasure. The loser stands me a drink of my choosing.'

"'He must mean *her*,' the sultan murmured to the commander. 'No other in this place is as priceless a paragon.'

"Unaware of this conversation or of the change in the tavern's clientele, the sultan's friend the artist jumped up from his floor cushion. 'Good Proprietor,' he addressed the ifrit. 'How are the stories judged and what are their requirements?'

"'The stories must be horrifying,' replied the tavern owner, 'and seize every soul with terror. As for the judging, I leave that to this honest crowd.'

"'Will you allow our party a moment to consider which of us should compete?'

"'Of course,' the tavern owner agreed, all unctuous courtesy. 'I'm sure it would be our honor to hear any of your tales.'

"The artist huddled back at their shared table. Sober enough to know they shouldn't discuss business in front of pleasure slaves, the commander dismissed his giggling lap companions. 'What are you doing?' he demanded angrily. 'We don't know this place's customs. This may lead us into trouble.'

"'Nonsense,' the artist scoffed. 'You heard the proprietor. Loser stands him a drink. Even if we lose, which I propose we do not, no matter what libation he chooses, it won't impoverish us.'

"'We must compete,' the sultan added. 'We must win this good woman free of her servitude.'

"The *good woman* he spoke of hadn't left with the other girls. She was silent behind her plain gray veil. Not subject to his friend's smitten state, the commander pinned her with his gaze. 'What say you?' he asked her. 'Is this contest dangerous?'

"She seemed to shrink before his challenge. The sultan touched her arm soothingly. 'You may answer my friend,' he said gently. 'As dear as you are to me, I am dear to him. He protects my interests as if they were his own.'

"The mysterious female bowed gracefully. 'Kind gentlemen,' she said in a lovely voice every bit as cultivated as their own. 'I have involved you in my troubles, and I owe you honesty. This tavern owner is a demon who kidnaped me from my home and held me captive these last two years. The drink he demands when he wins is every drop of blood in your veins. If you value your lives—and never mind my own—you must triumph in this contest.'

"The commander of the sultan's army didn't ask if the demon had ever lost. The answer to that was clear in the female's desperation and the ifrit's cockiness.

"'I am the best storyteller,' the artist said, 'and the least important of our number. I will venture my chance with him.'

"'You are *not* the least important,' the sultan protested. 'In addition to which, I have the most at stake.'

"The ruler of the Glorious City turned adoring eyes to the veiled woman, who—so far as could be told through her concealing garments—regarded him in the same fashion. The commander sighed to himself. He saw there would be no walking away from this danger. 'I shall compete,' he said resignedly. 'Though I am no great taleteller, I have been to war and have seen more horrors than all of you. Moreover, if I lose, I have the best chance of overpowering the ifrit before he drinks my blood.'

"'Sirs,' interrupted the person they'd forgotten bringing with them. It was the commander's eunuch, who had served him faithfully ever since his first employment.

"'Yes?' the commander said, only a little impatiently.

"'I wish to point out I am an excellent raconteur. Also, the account I intend to relate would curdle the blood of any male, demon or otherwise.'

"'This could mean your life,' the commander reminded him.

"'Even so,' said the eunuch, inclining his clever head.

"Thus it was decided that the commander's servant would compete. Speechless with gratitude, the sultan kissed the young man's cheeks. The artist promised him the best gift his genius could devise, if he survived the trial. The commander merely nodded, out of respect for his servant's bravery.

"The eunuch only trembled a little as he—"

A small noise caused Arcadius to lose the thread of his tale. Elyse's eyes were closed, her lashes dark and peaceful against her cheeks. Her head rested on the couch's back, her features squashed unselfconsciously on her hand. He watched a moment longer to be sure but couldn't doubt she was fast asleep.

In spite of everything, he smiled. So much for *his* storytelling skill.

Luckily, her response was just as useful for his purposes. He slid his arms beneath her knees and behind her back, lifting her carefully from the couch. She made another noise as her head fell onto his shoulder. Her weight and warmth were pleasant, the muscles of her arms and thighs intriguing.

What would it be like to bed such a slight woman? Would those muscles grip him extra well as he slid inside her? Would her body supply sufficient cushioning for the vigorous lovemaking he preferred? Slight or not, she had breasts . . . and quite a cute bottom. Perhaps her athleticism would enhance both of their delight.

It might have been smarter not to indulge this train of thought. As he carried her down the hall in search of her bedroom, his burgeoning erection made each stride increasingly difficult. He'd never made love with this body, never even taken his pleasure privately. He hadn't exercised his previous form much better—not in recent memory anyway. All in all, it had been a long dry spell.

A single lamp lit the back bedroom. Short wooden spindles marked the corners of her bedframe. The mattress didn't seem large to him, though it might have to humans. A pale blue quilt covered it neatly. Arcadius stretched one hand to tug this down while still holding Elyse. Careful not to wake her, he lowered her to the sheets.

"Hate this bed," she mumbled.

He supposed she might. Whatever her husband's flaws, he'd been company. The bed they'd shared must be a reminder that he was gone. Arcadius pulled the quilt up to cover her. She slept but her expression was fretful. Telling himself he needed her to stay unconscious, he brushed her dark hair from her forehead. Unruly curls had begun to spring up in it. She must comb them smooth usually.

"What happened t' the eunuch?" she slurred without lifting her eyelids.

"Sleep," he said. "I'll tell you the rest another time."

She rolled onto her side and hugged a pillow. Satisfied she'd stay, Arcadius turned out the light and left. As he did, he realized he'd grown even harder and his clothing was constricted. Gripping his trouser front, he gritted his teeth and adjusted the aching length of his erection. The discomfort was just too bad. He was no youth, compelled to satisfy every urge that arose. The pounding would go away. He'd ignore it until it did. He had an important search to conduct.

Now that he looked for them, signs that this wasn't a typical human dwelling jumped out at him. No wonder he'd liked Elyse's living room at first sight. Many of the items he'd admired were of djinn origin. A charming painting of a bazaar didn't depict Istanbul but a market in the Qaf. A small hide drum was meant to accompany the gyrations of magical houris. A porcelain dish held hunks of glass that weren't glass at all but uncut, gem grade aquamarines. Such stones were common in his homeland but—as he and Joseph had discovered—quite valuable here. His own people had made the Aladdin's lamp that amused him earlier. No one was trapped inside the brass, but that was beside the point.

This apartment was a treasure trove of djinn artifacts. Djinn creations sometimes found their way to the human realm, but there were too many here for the collector to have stumbled across by chance. One thing Arcadius didn't find, so far as he could tell, was the door that matched the nexus in the cellar. A glance at the watch he and Joseph had purchased with their gem money told him it was three thirty. Though he hadn't made a full inventory, he didn't dare search longer. He'd risk waking up Elyse.

She seemed unlikely to fall for a man she found rifling her belongings.

Reluctantly, he let himself out of her apartment. He was closing the door as quietly as he could when he heard someone else doing the same thing on the other side of the hall. Immediately guessing who it was, he swallowed an annoyed curse.

Apparently, Mrs. Goldberg did keep her eye on everything.

~

He reentered the cellar unit, and found Joseph asleep on the couch. Since it seemed his destiny for the night, Arcadius checked that his blankets were warm enough. When he took a peek at the mirror space, it still swirled dizzyingly within the silver ring.

Restless, he let the tapestry that covered it fall again.

He told himself they were making progress. He shouldn't be impatient. Campaigns were won one skirmish at a time.

Stripping off his clothes reminded him how chilly New York was, which reminded him of Elyse shoveling their sidewalk without her winter coat. His blasted cock bobbed straight up at that memory.

Shower, he thought, having grown accustomed to them at the hotel. The hour was late. He and Joseph had been on the go since morning. He'd have no trouble sleeping once he was clean and warm.

Thanks to being near the building's water heater, the spray emerged with great force and steam. Enjoying that despite his worries, he soaped himself. Skin tingling from the heat, he thought of Elyse. What would she look like naked in a shower? He could guess. Much shorter than he was went without saying. He knew the shape of her legs from seeing them in her jeans. Her limbs had lean muscles and pleasing curves. Her arms were slender, her breasts no bigger than handfuls.

He lathered his chest, peripherally aware that his nipples were tightened points. Elyse's skin would flush from more than one kind of heat if he lifted her by her round bottom. He'd like digging his fingers in, like pinning her to a wall of tiles with his greater weight. The tiles were plain but she'd look nice against them. He'd press her there teasingly at first, then more firmly, then damn hard as he shoved his aching cock deep into her wetness. She'd gasp as he filled her pussy. Her strong thighs would hug his hips, her little hands slide caressingly up his chest . . .

Arcadius sucked in a breath as pleasure surged strongly at his groin. The sensation alerted him to what he'd been up to. He'd done with washing his chest. His right fist was squeezing lather up his erection while his left massaged his scrotum.

His fantasy of Elyse had taken control of him.

The stimulation felt incredible: better than his first woman, better than the first time he jacked off as a randy teenager. It was like his new body was playing tricks on him. He'd always enjoyed sex. Sex was one of the Creator's best inventions. This was something else altogether, a life and death compulsion. He couldn't stop, though shock had slowed his fist's pumping. He had to have a release. More than that, he craved to have one with her.

The images that idea inspired made him moan aloud. Elyse with her head flung back. Elyse's breasts streaming water as her nipples budded up red and sharp. He squeezed his thick cock harder, the soap enabling his fingers to take a tight constriction. His veins were bulging, his nerves simultaneously begging him to draw this out and speed to completion. He spread his stance as wide as the tub walls allowed. His thighs were tense, his diaphragm jerking. His cock seemed huge as he tugged it closer to explosion. He wasn't actually sure Elyse would be able to take him.

Fuck, he thought, both aroused and alarmed.

He glanced down at his pumping hand.

He blinked and stopped jerking off.

He didn't recognize himself. His knob was fuller and redder than he was used to even when he was worked up. He tilted the shaft down to see better. He supposed the vein pattern was the same. He hadn't memorized it; he wasn't that big a narcissist. He also wasn't the owner of this big of a penis. He'd always considered himself—proportionally speaking—as slightly smaller than a man his height might hope for.

Lord, had he unwittingly corrected that imagined deficiency when he created this new body? It should have been identical to his old one—leaving aside his former powers not being online yet. Certainly, he'd meant it to be the same. The magic that replicated him relied on his memories.

Had the magic been influenced by his subconscious desires as well?

Arcadius snorted through the shower spray. If these were his subconscious desires, he was an idiot. This transformed cock wasn't simply a beast. It was a demanding one. He'd never needed an orgasm as much as he did now, which didn't strike him as convenient. How was he going to think straight and strategize with this new, not-improved part of him throwing its two cents in?

He wouldn't give in to it. With everything at stake, he couldn't afford to.

This decision coincided with noticing he'd started rubbing his cock again.

"In the name of God," he intoned aloud. "Release yourself this second."

His hand obeyed, his fingers so tense he had to flex them to get them to uncramp. More than a bit annoyed, he finished rinsing, turned off the water, and grabbed a towel. He dried himself in as businesslike a manner as he could. One truth he knew for certain.

It would take more than pressure points to get to sleep tonight.

CHAPTER FIVE

A keen sense of embarrassment dragged Elyse awake the next morning. She groaned into the pillow she was hugging. She'd fallen asleep in the middle of Arcadius's story. She'd let him tell her one in the first place.

You'd think she was five years old.

To her relief, her clothes were where they belonged. Not that Arcadius was the kind of man who'd undress a woman without permission. Oh, maybe if there was a medical emergency like her heart had stopped, or if they were stuck in sub-zero weather and she needed warming up.

"Stop," Elyse snapped to the empty room.

She had no business imagining her new tenant disrobing her.

She pushed out of the bed she'd shared with David and headed for the bathroom. On the bright side, she'd slept soundly. She glanced back at her bedside clock. Seven o'clock. Six straight hours was a miracle these days.

She felt even better by the time she'd showered. Clean and invigorated, she shoved her arms into a colorful paisley printed top she hadn't worn in a while. Her cumin orange leggings went best with it, the ones David called her booty pants.

Maybe she wasn't ready to wear those. They were kind of formfitting.

The phone rang while she was biting the side of her thumb indecisively.

"Solomon Property Management," she answered, trying to sound like she wasn't still pantsless.

"Elyse!" her Uncle Vince responded in his too-loud voice. Elyse pulled the phone farther from her ear. "What's this Cara says about you leasing the cellar apartment? I told you I'd find a renter once you were ready to face it being occupied."

He had told her that. He simply hadn't paid attention to her politely turning him down. Uncle Vince was family and she loved him. Sometimes, though, she couldn't deny he was pushy. Resigned to having this conversation, she wedged the phone between her shoulder and her ear.

"You don't need to worry," she said, pulling the vibrant orange pants from the hanger they were draped on. "These renters are okay. They paid the whole year upfront."

"The whole year! Did their check clear?"

Elyse wasn't about to tell him they'd paid cash. Uncle Vince knew a thing or two about goombahs—or thought he did. He owned every season of *The Sopranos* on Blu-ray. "It's fine," she said, knuckling her forehead. "Everything's on the up-and-up."

"Sweetie," Uncle Vince came back. "You know I think of myself as your second father since Leo . . . well, God rest my brother's soul. The thing is, sometimes your judgment isn't the best."

"My judgment will have to do. It's what I've got to rely on."

"You've got us!" her uncle exclaimed. "Me and Cara and God knows your Aunt June loves you."

"I know that." Elyse was suddenly as tired as if she hadn't slept at all. "Believe me, I'm grateful."

She zipped and buttoned the orange pants, wishing they had the power to make her bold on the inside too. Cara's family was all she had, her only relatives in the world.

"Join us for dinner tonight," her uncle invited. "I'll make reservations at the Thai place Cara likes."

"I don't think I can. I've got work to catch up on."

"I'll reserve a place for you, just in case. Show up anytime around eight. We don't see enough of you."

He hung up before she could refuse. David had been great for helping her avoid her family when she wasn't in the mood. *Date night*, he'd say, whether they had one planned or not. Then they'd eat out of cartons sitting side by side on the floor of the living room, sharing stories about their childhoods or whatever they'd done that day. David never implied she was boring or had bad judgment or looked like the cat dragged her in. *How did I get so lucky?* he'd ask instead, right before he hugged her and kissed her hair.

Elyse could almost feel his arm squeezing her shoulders.

Sighing—but thankfully not crying—she tucked the phone in her back pocket and went to make coffee. The box of Turkish delight sat open on her island, empty but for the powdered sugar still clinging to the wax paper. She'd save it, she decided, loving the painting of the Old World sweetshop on the lid. Maybe her odd new tenants would turn into friends. Maybe they'd stay a month or two and move on. Either way, the gift was a symbol that life didn't stop just because you'd lost someone. Nice surprises might be around the corner. The end of the story hadn't been written yet.

Elyse knew her dad would have approved of that attitude.

~

Arcadius spent his morning at the New York Public Library, researching Elyse's family history. Though his over-amped libido had left him sleep-deprived, his surroundings perked him up. The main branch on Fifth was lovely, the Rose Reading Room worthy of having been built by djinn, with its majestic ceiling murals and high arched windows.

No charm but simply a polite request earned him the aid of a helpful librarian. Though djinn didn't have computers, they had magical objects that served similar functions. The librarian's instructions for how to use the loaner were easy to follow.

As Elyse had mentioned, her grandfather Saul, the antiquarian bookseller, was the first Solomon to own the brownstone. He'd bought it in 1950 when he was a mere twenty-seven years of age. He moved in with his wife Mary to raise two sons. The elder, Leo, was three at the time of purchase. The younger, Vincent, had been just shy of two. Both sons grew up and married, and both sired one daughter. Of the two sons, Leo had stuck closer to the brownstone, continuing to reside there even as an adult. Perhaps because of this, the building was left to him at his father's death in 1994. Mary pre-deceased Saul, and her sons had already formed Solomon Brothers Imports —which appeared to provide them a good living.

Curious, Arcadius searched local newspapers for reports of strange happenings at the address. Elyse's husband's unsolved homicide came up, the case ceasing to appear again after a few articles. A previous structure on the site had been a Freemasons lodge. It burned to the ground in 1912, the cause for the fire listed as faulty wiring. The current building went up a few years later. No other dramatic events were reported.

Apart from an account in an Italian tabloid of Leo's death, he also found no news stories involving the Solomon brothers. If they'd come into unexplained sums of money, they weren't spending them in newsworthy ways. Leo had possessed quite a few djinn treasures before he fell into the volcano. If he'd had others he sold for profit, Arcadius unearthed no sign of it in these records.

As he shut off the machine he'd borrowed from the library, Arcadius wasn't sure what he'd accomplished. Leo or his father seemed the best candidate for having installed and then removed the door to the other plane. Perhaps one of Saul's antique books had supplied the instructions. Cara and her father's interest in the brownstone suggested they were aware of the nexus's existence, a likelihood he and Joseph had already guessed. Arcadius felt no closer to finding the door itself or to understanding the mind of whoever had hidden it.

He shoved back from the little wooden carrel the librarian had led him to. He was an active man. His back was stiff from sitting and he stretched his arms upward. Well-being rushed through him as he did, his new body enjoying the sensation of tight muscles relaxing. A different kind of stretch warmed his groin a moment later. He dropped his arms and cursed. His new cock was at it again, reminding him it wanted pleasure too.

Well, maybe it would get it. He did, after all, have a live source of information on all the Solomons.

~

Elyse ran a quick errand at the bank, picked up a few groceries, and came home. As she entered the brownstone's lobby with her bags, she noticed a man in work overalls rummaging in the supply closet. The individual wasn't her regular handyman.

"Hey," she said. "You're not Frank."

The guy stepped out where she could see him. Elyse struggled not to gasp. The stranger was very big, very tall, and very tattooed. The swirling, thorny designs covered every bit of him, even his face and shaven scalp.

He looked like a bad guy from a movie.

"Sorry for taking you by surprise," he said in a rumbly voice. He wiped his giant hand and held it out to her. It was tattooed as well, including his fingers. Elyse shook it in bemusement. His grip was firm but not bone breaking. "You must be Elyse. I'm Mario. I work with Frank on some of his other buildings. He's got the flu. He asked me to check in here. I hope that's okay with you."

Mario's eyes watched her, something about their steadiness unnerving. His irises were so dark they blended into his pupils.

"Frank gave you the keys?"

Mario held them up. "Frank told me your tenants write their repair requests on the white board in here. Do you maybe want to check the list and tell me what to do first?"

Everything he was saying was adding up, plus he had his own authentically dented old toolbox. Probably she was freaked because she didn't meet people with that much ink everyday. She told herself not to give in to narrow-mindedness.

"Sure," she said, stepping into the closet to study her tenants' pleas. "I'll call Frank later to make sure he's okay."

~

The day was sunny but bitter cold. Arcadius hailed a taxi to take him home from the library. Considering the nice warm cab protected him from the wind, he didn't long for a flying carpet to whisk him there. After paying the driver and getting out, he noticed Elyse's cousin Cara lounging outside their below-street door. Despite the arctic temperatures, her long red coat hung open.

A blind man would have seen her nipples poking behind her bra.

"Hey, there," she said, her smile as bright as the sky. "I was hoping I'd catch you. Your friend didn't open up when I knocked."

"He may be out," Arcadius responded cautiously.

"Out and about," she laughed, like it was a joke. "What exactly do you two do?"

"We're gem dealers." This was what they'd told Elyse, and it was true enough.

Cara seemed simultaneously amused and dubious. "Interesting digs for that."

He took a moment to grasp her meaning. "Living modestly draws less attention. We have security concerns."

"Well, sure. Who wouldn't?"

He couldn't tell if she meant this or why she was here. "Did you have a reason for wanting to speak to us?"

She laughed as if that were funny too, pushing off the building's brick to stand directly in front of him. *Getting up in his grill*, he believed the saying went. She tapped his chest playfully with her fingernail. Though he found her actions presumptuous, he couldn't deny she was beautiful with the icy wind blowing back her honeyed locks. Her lipstick was shiny peach today. "I have a favor to ask."

"A favor."

"Nothing big. I borrowed this antique book from my dad's library and loaned it to Elyse's husband. It's a collection of love poems. David wanted to read them to Elyse." She rolled her eyes like this was silly. "Anyway, he died before he could return it, and we can't find it anywhere in Elyse's place. I'd really like to put it back before my dad notices it's missing."

"Forgive me," Arcadius said politely. "But what does this have to do with me?"

She blinked, clearly expecting a warmer response. "Well, it might be in your apartment. David spent a lot of time fixing up the place. Possibly he mislaid it down there. If I could just take a quick look around—"

"No," Arcadius said firmly. This really set her back on her heels. "Joseph and I value our privacy. If we find your book, we'll let you know."

"O-kay," she said, hesitation breaking the word apart. "It's small. About the size of cigarette case and bound in embossed leather. The pages are kind of fragile, so if you find the thing, you probably shouldn't open it."

"We'll keep your wishes in mind," he said.

She pulled her coat around her. He sensed her deciding whether she should try to flirt harder. Maybe he should have let her, but he kept his expression cool. He had enough concerns without trying to juggle fake pursuits of her *and* Elyse.

"Okay, then." Cara tossed her hair behind her shoulders. "Thanks for agreeing to look for it. —Hi, Elyse," she added sunnily, lifting her hand toward the steps above them.

Elyse stood there in snug orange pants that made his mouth go dry. The dismay on her face said she'd drawn her own conclusions about his and Cara's proximity. His stomach dipped even as his annoyance spiked. Cara was swanning away down the walk as if nothing at all were wrong. She must not have realized his ears were sharper than a normal man's.

"All right, mofo," he heard her murmur beneath her breath. "Don't say I didn't try to do this nice."

~

Cara hadn't simply cozied up to kissing distance from Arcadius. She'd also treated him to her trademark hair flip. To a practiced flirt like Elyse's cousin, this was pulling out the big guns.

Elyse's gloves tightened on front stair railing. This wasn't her business. She had no dibs on the man. Anyway, Arcadius hadn't been smiling back at Cara.

Of course, his habitual expression was kind of stern.

Even as she tried to comfort herself, his head snapped around to watch Cara sashay away. Elyse's cheeks burned with embarrassment. Arcadius twisted back before she'd recovered. His blue gray eyes were highly observant. She had a feeling he knew what she was thinking better than she did.

"Your cousin asked if we'd seen a book of poems she lent your husband," he volunteered. "I told her we'd let her know if we did."

"She's, uh, kind of got a thing about that."

Arcadius nodded, still looking serious. Elyse cursed herself for finding that sexy.

"Did you have something to say to me?" he inquired.

"Oh, um, yes." She fought another blush. "The repair guy is here. Have you or Joseph noticed anything not working in your unit?"

"Everything seems functional," he said.

"Okay . . . I'll . . . just see you around then." She turned and began to climb the stairs, every step in the formfitting leggings feeling incredibly awkward. For just a flash, she had the weird impression he might be staring at her butt.

"Elyse," Arcadius said.

She stopped and turned back to him. Her pulse was going to get whiplash from the way he made it jump around. "Yes?"

He was a ways beneath her, down on the basement unit's entry ramp. He lifted his face to speak. "Would you like to have dinner? With me? At a nice restaurant?"

He was asking her on a date. Though she'd been out of circulation for quite a while, she couldn't mistake that. Struggling to recover from her surprise, she shut her gaping mouth.

"I enjoyed your company last night," he continued, his expression still serious but gentler. A tiny smile pulled one corner of his kissable mouth upward. "If you're interested, I'll tell you the rest of the sultan's tale."

She started to assure him she didn't need a bribe but pressed her lips together before she could. He was asking her on a *date*. Dates implied things she wasn't ready for.

Arcadius must have sensed she was on the fence. "Food," he enticed, the curve of his mouth deepening. "Wine. Some hopefully pleasant conversation. *Lots* of wine, should that not work out. It's easy to say 'yes' to . . . unless you have something more important you need to do."

He reminded her she had something she'd rather avoid. If she had dinner with him, she couldn't cave to Uncle Vince.

"Can I pick the place?"

"No." He paired the refusal with a truly brilliant smile, the first she'd seen him break into. His exotic handsomeness dazzled her—and his obvious enjoyment in teasing her. "I'm the man. I want to surprise you."

An unexpected and very hot wet quiver seized her between the legs. When it passed, desire ached deep inside of her.

"I hate Thai food," she said, because she couldn't just give in.

"I'll come for you at seven," was his undeniably smug answer.

~

Elyse managed to put off worrying what to wear until her day's duties were fulfilled. These included calling Frank her handyman a couple times and getting no response. She shrugged off a pinch of unease. If Frank had a bad case of flu, he might not be up to answering. Mario of the head-to-toe tattoos seemed to be filling in okay. She'd crossed his path earlier, while he was patching a wobbly baluster on the stairs. Also promising, the hall light on the fourth floor wasn't flickering anymore. Probably she was right to give Frank's choice the benefit of the doubt.

Her upcoming date was another matter. Low-grade anxiety turned to panic the moment she surveyed her closet. She had nice clothes, or nice enough for her. She just had no idea what would be appropriate. Was a dress too dressy? Or would pants be too casual? Not knowing where they were going made her selection more difficult. She didn't want to be rude, but she also didn't want to send the wrong message. She flipped through her rack again. Cleavage sent the wrong message. She could eliminate any choices that exposed that.

"Yoo-hoo," called her cousin's voice from the foyer.

Elyse's heart jumped into her throat. Cara had a key but she usually knocked. She also didn't usually tear herself away from work this early. Cara loved her job at Solomon Brothers.

"In the bedroom," Elyse answered reluctantly.

Cara hugged her when she came in. Her skin was cold and she smelled expensive. "Hey, sweetie. I came to see if you were joining us for dinner. Not that," she added, gently returning the navy pantsuit she was considering to the rack. "How about your red dress with the low shoulders? It puts color in your cheeks."

"Bare shoulders are as bad as cleavage," Elyse said without thinking.

Cara looked at her. Oh, this was going to be awkward.

"I have a date," she admitted.

Cara's eyebrows went up. "Aren't you the sly one? Who with?"

"Arcadius."

Elyse returned her attention to the closet. She knew she didn't want to witness the expressions crossing her cousin's face. Arcadius might not have realized Cara was flirting this morning, but Elyse knew better. The idea that Elyse could have caught his interest instead would seem ridiculous to her.

Cara took a second to find her voice. "Your new tenant, Arcadius?"

"I don't know any other men by that name."

"But . . . you barely know him. And David's only been gone two months."

"It's not a serious date," Elyse said. Probably it wasn't, she being who she was.

"What about the sidekick?"

In spite of her qualms, Elyse pulled the red dress out and looked at it. "As far as I know, Joseph's not invited."

"As far as you know."

Frowning, she hung the red dress back up and pulled out her trusty LBD. The dress's cut flattered her slim curves but showed zero cleavage. She held it up to herself, confirming it didn't expose too much leg either. Would wearing black count as reminding Arcadius she was in mourning? And if it did, was that a bad thing?

"Elyse!" Cara said.

"What?" Elyse asked, startled by her exasperated tone. She guessed she'd been zoning out.

"You need to be a little careful. Don't get all—" she pulled a comic face "—like you did with David."

"All what?" she asked, not understanding the semaphore.

"Don't throw your judgment out the window just because this man pays you more attention than you're used to."

"My judgment was fine when it came to David."

Cara pulled the face again.

"It was!" Exasperated now herself, Elyse plunked her hands on her hips. "You never gave David a fair shake. You were always running him down, rolling your eyes at the nice things he did and said. You only introduced him by accident when he came to visit with that ex of yours. From the start, he treated me like I mattered, like I wasn't a two-year-old. I would have loved him for that alone."

"Jeez," Cara said. "Sorry for ruffling your feathers."

Elyse knew she was supposed to say she was sorry too. Rather than give in to the urge, she pressed her lips together stubbornly.

Cara heaved a dramatic sigh. "Fine. Consider the subject dropped. I'll tell Dad you made other plans for tonight." Her cousin's anger was already fading. She smiled at Elyse indulgently. "Wear the red," she advised, wagging her finger playfully. "Recent widow or not, you need to show that man what Solomon women are made of."

~

Against her better judgment, Elyse wriggled into the shoulder-baring deep red dress. Her reflection in the closet mirror told her Cara was right. She looked sexy, and the dress did throw color into her cheeks. Pinning her hair up hid how much it needed a cut and style. Her flatiron *might* have helped, but if she weren't careful, the straightener just made her hair more insane. Cara was luckier on that front. She'd inherited Aunt June's hair. Elyse put on a necklace, then took it off. Ditto for a delicate diamond tennis bracelet David had given her on her birthday. She'd have gone without makeup except the shadows under her eyes needed concealing. She pulled on hose, not stockings, and slid into a pair of taller than usual black heels.

Her heart clenched a little when she surveyed the end result. Within their frame of mascaraed lashes, her eyes sparkled. She looked like a woman who was excited to see a man.

Maybe she shouldn't have put on real lipstick?

Her phone rang before she could wipe it off.

"Solomon Property Management," she answered, per usual.

"Elyse," Arcadius responded in his sexy baritone. "I'm in front with the vehicle. If you're ready, I'll come up and knock."

He was calling to see if he could come up and knock? Then the light bulb went off. "You bought yourself a cell phone."

"It is bright blue with an ocean wave pattern! I can surf the net on it." He wasn't quite crowing, but he was close.

Elyse smiled to herself. He'd wanted to use his toy. "I look forward to admiring it."

"Are you ready then?" he asked in a more moderate tone.

She glanced at her reflection, reluctantly relinquishing her chance to swap out red lipstick for colorless. "I'm ready. I'll come down and meet you. No need to run the meter."

When she stepped out onto the front stoop, she didn't find the taxi she expected. Arcadius had hired a shiny white limo. For a moment, she couldn't move. No one had picked her up for a date in a limo since her high school prom—and that ride had been shared between three couples.

Arcadius waited on the sidewalk, holding the rear door open. His gorgeousness put the vehicle in the shade. He'd left off his Cossack hat, possibly deciding it was too eccentric for a date. Elyse had liked the thing for precisely that reason. Still, she couldn't deny he looked like a million sexy bucks in his slick European overcoat and suit. He was tall and built in a pale blue dress shirt and dark trousers, his sober necktie smoothed down his front just so. She was glad her own coat was buttoned. She totally wasn't ready for him to see her outfit.

Ordering her legs to work, she continued down the steps.

"Is this all right?" he asked, his amazing eyes studying her expression. "The limousine seemed nicer than a cab."

She felt dazed as he took her hand to assist her in. She'd forgotten to grab gloves. His palm—which pretty much swallowed hers—was warm. As his long fingers curled around hers, they felt both smooth and strong.

"It's beautiful," she said, conscious she was a bit throaty. "You didn't have to fuss so much."

"Ah," he said. "My apologies."

He slid in after her and shut the door. He didn't actually seem sorry for overdoing. He was too confident a male for that. She couldn't help noticing he filled a lot more of the seat than her. He wasn't trying to crowd her, though his greater size created an undeniably pleasant sense of vulnerability. The limo rolled away from the curb. There must have been a driver, but Elyse couldn't tear her gaze from Arcadius's handsome face to check.

She guessed he noticed. His lips curved slightly. "You're beautiful tonight."

"The magic of make-up," she managed to respond.

Arcadius caught her chin with one finger, gently turning her face from side to side. Light though the contact was, it set her nerves humming.

"No," he said. "I'm pretty sure it's you."

She blushed like a schoolgirl. *Don't squirm*, she ordered herself a second before she did. The move forced her to realize her panties were dampening. "You, uh, were going to show me your phone."

"Was I?" Arcadius's smile deepened as he leaned in to her. "I think my former intentions have slipped my mind."

She wanted to head him off by saying his name but no longer had the breath. His big hand cupped her cheek as lightly as his finger had held her chin.

"Don't be afraid," he said.

Was she afraid? Her lips certainly trembled as he brushed his across them. Gosh, his mouth was soft. And warm. And he smelled amazing up close like this. His hand slid behind her neck, his fingers supporting her skull as its weight fell back helplessly. His lips pressed a little harder, their softness molding over hers.

His tongue touched the very center of their closed seam.

Elyse found herself clutching his coat's lapels as if this were her protection against drowning. That seemed a real danger. Her panties had gone from damp to wet. He moved his hand again, sliding his big palm across her shoulder and down her tweed coat's sleeve. Was Arcadius breathing harder? She couldn't tell over the sudden thundering of her heart. He squeezed her elbow through the cloth, and a zing shot straight from the nerves there to her clit. Elyse gasped against his lips in shock. Her nipples had just hardened like they'd been pinched. Arcadius smiled, kissed her one more time very softly, and backed away. Elyse blinked rapidly.

"I had to do that," he said.

"Well," was all she could think to say. She pressed one hand to her mouth, aware her lips were buzzing. David's first kiss, which had included considerably more tongue, hadn't set off fireworks this intense. To her dismay, she didn't have the presence of mind to feel disloyal.

"Should I apologize?" he asked.

His voice was deeper than before, and his blue gray eyes smoldered. *Bedroom eyes*, she thought, a fresh rivulet of heat escaping her sexual folds. She really, *really* wanted to check out his crotch, to see if he was affected too.

"Um," she said. "No?"

He chuckled at her lack of certainty and sat back against the seat. His face was still turned to her, his expression hot and sleepy. He'd sprawled his knees, but she resisted the temptation to peek between them. When he ran his tongue across his lips, she shivered.

"This is going to be an entertaining night," he observed.

The gleam in his eyes made her as nervous as his kiss. She knew she shouldn't say what she did next even before the words blurted out. "I guess this settles the question of if you're gay."

His dark eyebrows arched upward. "What?"

"I'm sorry. I didn't really think you were—and there wouldn't be anything wrong with it—just, well, Joseph *did* call you 'master.' You know, like master-slave and . . ." She trailed off. Arcadius was staring at her as if she'd spoken an alien tongue.

A moment later, he shook his head and pulled himself straighter. "Joseph must have been confused about the term. I'm his employer, not his master. We don't have that kind of relationship."

"Right." Elyse's hands clenched her knees as she fought not to mention how fluent Joseph's English was. *Way to go*, she thought. *A guy gives you one great kiss and you insult his manhood.* Her dating skills were beyond rusty. She snuck a look at him.

"Our work here is sensitive," Arcadius said—not angrily, thank goodness. "It's easier and safer if Joseph and I live together."

She supposed gem dealing was dangerous. And he and Joseph came from a different culture. Maybe in his country, two straight guys sharing a one-bedroom was no big deal.

She *would* have shut up if Cara and her uncle's digs about her judgment hadn't prodded her. "Why my building? Why live in a basement apartment when you can afford better?"

Arcadius smiled. He'd relaxed, his clothes whispering on the limo's leather as he turned on the seat toward her. His tone was teasing. "Are you trying to convince me to move out?"

"No," she said. "As your landlady, your reasons aren't my business. As your . . . date, I admit I'm curious."

"We're very superstitious. Your building had the qualities we look for."

"Like good feng shui?"

"Something like that."

Elyse wondered what their superstition said about violent murders taking place a stone's throw away.

Her mouth must have made a funny shape. Arcadius brushed her lower lip with his thumb. "Could you not worry for one evening?"

"Maybe," she said none too surely.

Arcadius seemed to find that amusing.

~

Arcadius wasn't amused. He pretended to be, but her assumption took him aback. She'd thought he was a lover of men? *Him?* Whom countless women had fought to bed? Maybe he was silly to take offense. His calculatedly gentle kiss had moved her . . . until she started babbling about him and Joseph being gay S&M lovers. He couldn't help but scowl at that. If he was going to make anyone his sexual captive, it was her. He'd very much enjoy chaining her to a bed for a night or two.

He tugged the crease of his trousers, conscious of how strongly the kiss had affected him—too strongly, considering how circumspect it had been. He was uncomfortably hard, as if the pole for a battle standard were planted between his legs. Elyse cleaned up well, as the humans said. Her tapering ankles in those high-heeled black shoes were impossible not to fixate on.

She'd be perfect wearing heels, a collar, and nothing else.

Arcadius's engorged cock throbbed more energetically. He shouldn't have let that image into his head. For that matter, he should have satisfied his lusts in the shower last night. To hell with discipline. He was supposed to be in control of tonight's seduction.

"Is this it?" Elyse leaned slightly across him toward the window. Her neck was exquisite with her hair pinned up. Belatedly noting the car had stopped, Arcadius glanced outside.

"Yes," he said gruffly.

The forgotten driver had gotten out. Crisp and polite in his uniform, he opened the door for Arcadius. Humor crinkled his eyes, so probably he'd seen them kissing in his mirror. He stepped back as Arcadius emerged. "You got my number," he said in a thick New York accent. "Call me when you want to be picked up."

Arcadius nodded at him and helped Elyse out himself.

Her hand felt nice in his: little and feminine. In spite of his resolve to remain coolheaded, the widening of her eyes as she studied the French restaurant's pretty front charmed him.

"This is fancy!" she exclaimed.

She didn't seem to be complaining. "The concierge at the Plaza recommended it."

The helpful man hadn't forgotten Joseph's hundred-dollar bill supply. His suggestion certainly delivered on atmosphere. Formerly an elegant townhome, La Vérité gleamed with gilded chairs and candles and pristine white tablecloths. The diners were as glamorous as the decor: quick-witted, well dressed humans sipping wine and forging alliances over fine china.

The maître d' led Arcadius and Elyse to the third floor.

"Wow," she breathed. "Our own private room."

Arcadius couldn't miss the war between her pleasure and her fear of giving into it. "I thought it would be nice to hear each other without raising our voices."

Elyse had handed off her coat downstairs. Arcadius gritted his teeth as he pulled out a chair for her. The red dress she wore hugged her body like a lascivious second skin, drawing his admiring gaze to every asset she possessed. Her slender shoulders were bare and creamy, her cleavage more than hinted at from his angle above her. The dress was lined. She hadn't worn a bra under it. He couldn't see her nipples but it was close. When Arcadius tore his attention from her alluring curves and hollows, the waiter who held out *his* chair suppressed a knowing grin.

Arcadius tried not to glower. If he'd been in the man's position, he probably would have done the same.

Recalling their clash of wills over shoveling the walk, Arcadius didn't order Elyse's meal. If nothing else, her dress reminded him this city had its own customs.

His attempt to put her at ease wasn't successful. As the server left, she was fidgeting.

"I should tell you something," she confessed.

"Yes?"

"It's about your apartment and the reason my cousin implied it was cursed."

"Ah." He relaxed back in his chair. Discussing this topic suited him.

Elyse bit her lip guiltily. The effect this had on her painted mouth was rather distracting. "My husband was killed down there. Not in your actual apartment but in the cellar."

"I see," he said, already aware of this.

This wasn't the reaction she expected. Her tempting lips fell open. "His murder was kind of violent. Lots of folks wouldn't want to rent a place where that happened. You know, if they were superstitious."

"Oh," he said, understanding now. A funny little warmth expanded in his chest. "It's honest of you to tell me, but it won't bother us."

"You're sure?" She leaned forward across the table. "It's not like I spent your rent money. I only put it in the bank this morning."

"I'm sure, though I'm sorry for your loss. Did the police catch your husband's killer?"

Elyse shook her head. "The police think it must have been someone hopped up on drugs, looking for stuff to steal to support their habit. I'm not sure I believe it. David always set the alarm, and the cops didn't find signs of a break in." She shrugged and looked unsure. "I guess David might have forgotten. He could have surprised the intruder."

She shuddered, her gaze focused on the past.

"Are you the one who found him?" he asked.

Tears glimmered on her lower lids. "It was bad," she said hoarsely. "Really bloody and really bad."

Unable to help himself, he drew her hand to his mouth to kiss its tense knuckles. He patted it before setting it down again. "Images like that stay with you, but eventually they fade."

"You've seen dead bodies?" Her green eyes were big.

"Many," he said solemnly. "Once upon a time, I served in the army."

He hoped he wouldn't ask which army. He didn't have a lie prepared.

Elyse drew a long breath and blew it out. "Sorry. This isn't ideal dinner conversation."

The waiter returned with their wine. Arcadius waited until her glass was filled. "Our pasts cannot be erased. Sometimes we have to share them to get to know someone. Tell me about your father. From what you said, those are happier memories."

~

Being easy to talk to wasn't a quality Elyse expected to find in a man as handsome as Arcadius. As it turned out, he was as good at listening as telling tales. Over a selection of delectable food and wine, Elyse shared stories of her father: trips they'd taken together, crazy purchases he'd shipped home while she was stuck in school. Once, he'd sent a life-size Egyptian faience hippo, thinking she'd like keeping it in her room.

"I was eight," she said. "And I adored it. Unfortunately, it was so big I had to climb over its back to get in or out my bedroom door. When my dad came home and saw how much space it took up, he agreed maybe we should let the auction house sell it."

"Your father didn't take you everywhere," Arcadius observed.

"No," Elyse agreed. "I had school, and some of the places he went were too dangerous for a child." She smiled, turning her half full wine glass in a circle. "Dad was a charmer, really amazing with people—probably because he was genuinely interested in them. I never worried about him. No matter where he went or how different the culture, he made friends."

"That is indeed a gift."

Elyse laughed. "One I sometimes wish I had."

"Perhaps you have more of it than you think."

Though she wasn't convinced, his words warmed her. This evening had been a gift. Talking about her dad brought back the feeling of being loved by him. "I've talked your ears off," she said guiltily.

Arcadius pressed his palms over them to check, his eyes gleaming with mischief. "I believe they're still there."

"You promised me a story."

The lines around his beautiful mouth deepened. They weren't dimples, but wonderful signs of humor and having lived. When he didn't smile, he was still gorgeous—in a foreboding way. When he did, boy, was he edible. He ran one finger around his wine glass's rim, and she swore she felt it touch her.

"I *would* keep my promise," he said, his voice dropping intimately, "but I fear we're keeping our waiter from his beauty rest."

He turned his wrist to display the face of his gold Rolex. For a second, she couldn't read the hands. He'd rolled up his cuffs and his forearm was sexy. Dark hair, olive skin, strong muscles and tendons . . . When her eyes agreed to focus, she was shocked by the time.

"Oh, my gosh," she exclaimed. "I really did talk your ears off. I had no idea it was that late!"

"I encouraged you," he said smoothly, "though I think I should call our driver to pick us up."

The restaurant was nearly empty when Elyse and Arcadius descended the stairs from their dining room. The staff who were cleaning up wished them goodnight. They seemed to mean it, and Elyse suspected Arcadius had tipped well. Outside, the street was quiet, the cold air refreshing on her face. She was surprised to discover she wasn't drunk. The glow she was experiencing came from the nice night she'd spent. Disconcerted by that realization, she sat without speaking for the ride home.

I'm getting over David, she thought.

Did this mean something was wrong with her? Two months was no time at all. She bit the side of her thumb, sneaking a look at Arcadius. Even sitting down, he was tall. He watched the city's skyscrapers and late-night traffic roll by outside. His sharp-as-a-statue profile was almost too perfect to be real.

Would he be a good choice to get back in the saddle with? Leaving aside his claim of enjoying her company, the chance he was interested in her in any long-term manner seemed miniscule. A man like Arcadius enjoyed conquests, not commitments. He'd bed a woman a couple times and be on to the next challenge.

Could Elyse stand that, or would it hurt her feelings?

She wasn't sure, only that he attracted her immensely.

I'll leave the next move to him, she thought, *and decide how to cross that bridge if I come to it.*

Arcadius seemed unlikely to complain. He struck her as the sort of man who'd want to hold the reins himself.

CHAPTER SIX

ELYSE'S mood had turned thoughtful since leaving the restaurant. Arcadius suspected she was deciding whether to sleep with him. Her having to think about it annoyed him. Yes, she'd been widowed not long ago. Arcadius knew her husband had been no prize, but Elyse loved the man she thought he'd been. He couldn't expect her to fall into his arms just because females usually did. The fact that he'd put actual effort into seducing her was beside the point. Feeling insulted gained him nothing. Patience was the weapon that would win his desire.

That he did desire her was obvious.

How had this happened? She was supposed to be a strategic target, a means to a crucial end. Instead, he craved her irrationally. To touch her skin. To kiss her neck. To slide his hands up her firm slim legs. Right that moment, he longed to draw her across the seat to him, to simply hug her against his side. That was no sexual fantasy, or not one he recognized.

He rubbed two fingers across his lips, wondering what was wrong with him. The limo ride was smooth, the lights turning green for them as if by magic. They were coming up on the meeting of two four-lane streets. Arcadius recognized a storefront on the right, so they must have passed this way earlier. He was glad the city was becoming decipherable. Something ought to go right for him.

The thought had barely finished when an out of place streak of motion caught his eye. All alone, with no other cars to block it, a white van sped down the intersecting street. The red light faced it. It should have been slowing down.

The limo driver noticed the same thing.

"Shit," he said, spinning his own wheel to get out of the way of the vehicle. "You two hold on back there."

The white van gunned its engine and veered toward their adjusted course.

Arcadius had seen soldiers spurred to extraordinary feats by surges of adrenaline. The phenomenon was rare but not unheard of. Until that moment, his experience had been secondhand.

Many thoughts flashed through his head at once. He knew the other driver meant to hit them, and hit them hard. Elyse was on the oncoming side. No matter how sturdy the limo was the collision would crumple it. More importantly, it would crumple her. She was a breakable human being. Chances were she would die.

The idea of allowing that to happen filled him with agony. Despite it being too soon for his former powers to activate in his new body, his magic flared within him like an exploding sun. Every cell burst its bonds as he returned to the smoke and fire from which the Creator had fashioned him.

Startled, he took an eye-blink inventory. He was bigger, perhaps eight feet tall but still manlike. Two arms extended from his developed torso, two legs, two feet made of black vapor. He was his inner nature: a nightmare creature from an exotic tale. Elyse hadn't noticed yet. She was leaning toward her window.

"What is that idiot doing?" she murmured.

She wasn't afraid of the purposefully accelerating van. She didn't scream until she turned and saw the unfamiliar being he had become.

The shriek she let out was blood curdling.

Arcadius didn't have the luxury of minding. Though he wasn't solid anymore, he had an ability to move matter similar to a strong magnetic field. Seizing Elyse in his smoky arms, he barreled so quickly out his side of the limo that the door ripped off its hinges.

He and Elyse escaped disaster by milliseconds. The van hit the limousine with a squeal of rubber tires and a resounding crunch of metal. A third car honked and slammed on its brakes, narrowly missing the others. The van and the limo spun across the road as if dancing with each other. As the spin completed, the limo tumbled onto its roof, wheels whirring like an upended beetle's legs. Big white pillows exploded in front of both drivers.

Airbags, Arcadius thought, the word popping into his mind in spite of the situation's stress.

He didn't get a chance to see more details. By this time, he'd whisked Elyse a couple hundred feet into the night sky. He remembered to stop before it was too late. Humans didn't do as well as djinn at high altitudes. He was lucky the office building next to them was dark. If anyone had been working late, they'd have had quite the water cooler tale.

"Wha-" Elyse gasped, her teeth chattering, her hands instinctively trying to clutch his non-shoulders. She gaped in terror at the street grown tiny under them.

"It's okay," he said. "I've got you."

He forgot how different his voice would be. Her head jerked around at the fiery hiss. His eyes were more fire within the smoke, blue gray like his normal ones. Though somewhat larger, his features were basically the same.

"*No,*" she said, recognizing him.

Probably they were fortunate her overloaded system chose then for her to pass out.

Sirens wailed in the distance, reminding him he'd better hightail it out of there. Being seen in his current shape wasn't a good idea. This was the city that never slept, where every other phone—as he'd learned today—had a miniature camera. Arcadius zoomed off, flying his burden homeward as swiftly as he dared. Some detached corner of his mind observed that nighttime Manhattan twinkled beautifully from above, the snow like whipped icing where it clung. Elyse was secure in his arms, if limp. The biggest danger was that she'd freeze before he got her to the brownstone.

Smoke was a terrible insulator for body heat.

By the time he touched down in her building's courtyard, her unconscious body was shuddering.

If he'd thought about it, changing back might have been difficult. Luckily, he snapped to solid form automatically. He was shuddering himself, the expenditure of energy leaving him weakened.

"Joseph," he bellowed, not caring who heard him.

Afraid to set Elyse down, he staggered toward their "garden" apartment's back entrance. Joseph met him in the draughty passage that connected outside to in.

"Master!" he cried in alarm.

Later, Arcadius decided, he'd discuss the importance of Joseph not calling him that.

"Take her," he said. "You're warmer than I am."

Joseph took her, for once not shy of having a woman in his arms. "What happened? Were you flying? I didn't think we could change form yet."

"Let's get her to her apartment. She's had enough shocks tonight."

Arcadius explained the crash as succinctly as he could, his breath and nerves steadying in the process. Joseph was ahead of him, carrying Elyse.

"Did you see the driver of the van?" the servant asked over his shoulder.

"It happened too fast. Afterward, I couldn't afford to linger. I heard sirens and didn't want to be spotted in my smoke form. I'm not sure who notified the police. I only pray our driver survived."

"Human cars have 'systems' to call for help," Joseph informed him.

They hastened into the lobby and began climbing the staircase. Joseph handled Elyse's weight as easily as Arcadius would have. Perhaps he shouldn't have found that noteworthy. Elyse was slight, and Joseph, despite his . . . lack in one area, was as able-bodied as anyone.

"I assume the airbag helped protect the chauffeur," Arcadius said, careful to speak quietly. "The other driver's went off too. What sum do you suppose a person charges to use a vehicle they're operating as a weapon?"

"I couldn't guess," Joseph said. Something else occurred to him. "What name did you use to hire the limousine?"

"Cade Smith. I paid cash, which is harder to trace than credit, but the company will have this address on record from the pickup."

"It would be best if we avoided police questions. Perhaps I can speak to them."

Joseph meant more than *speak*. He meant use magical persuasion to fuddle the limo service's recall. The spell wouldn't work unless its subjects were more or less willing, but hopefully his hundreds could smooth the way. Memories people were determined to hang onto were more difficult to erase.

Arcadius wondered how determined Elyse would be to preserve her memory of him transforming. "Are you certain you have enough power in your reserves? You've been expending a lot lately."

"I attended two funerals today," Joseph admitted. "The deceased were much beloved. The mourners threw off a lot of grief energy."

Joseph wouldn't have harmed anyone by taking this—aside from the mourners recovering sooner from their sadness. All the same, feeding at funerals or graveyards was considered uncouth by their class of djinn. Some humans didn't want their tears prematurely dried.

"Under the circumstances," Arcadius said, "I won't scold you about ethics."

Joseph paused ahead of him on the steps. "We must take care. This is Elyse's floor. We don't want to wake her neighbor."

They covered the final distance silently. Joseph used his universal key to enter Elyse's apartment. He didn't have to, as it turned out. Amazingly, Elyse's little clutch purse remained safely tucked in her coat pocket.

Joseph settled her on the couch in the living room, where Arcadius immediately bundled her in blankets. Elyse began to stir soon after. She sat up, fought one arm free of the swaddling surrounding her, and rubbed her forehead. Arcadius sat next to her on an ottoman. She wasn't fearful when she looked at him, though her brow furrowed.

"What happened? Were we in an accident?"

"I'm afraid so," he said, wondering how fuzzy her recall was. Traumatic events could cause short-term memory loss. "Another car hit the limousine. We were thrown clear when it rolled. Do you feel all right? You seemed unhurt, so I didn't take you to the hospital."

Her nose wrinkled. "I passed out?"

"From shock, I believe. If you feel dizzy or nauseous . . ."

"No. Just really cold."

"Joseph is running you a hot shower."

"Joseph is."

"When you didn't wake up, I was worried," he confessed. "I summoned him to assist."

She smiled, her expression still unsure. "Is our driver all right?"

"Banged up but okay," he said, praying this was true.

Elyse rubbed her forehead dazedly. "I was having the strangest dream. Something about the Chrysler Building and flying through the air."

"Shock is a funny thing."

Joseph returned to the living room. With one swift glance, he registered the fact that Elyse seemed comfortable with Arcadius—as she'd hardly be if she remembered him changing. "The water should be the right temperature now."

"Joseph," Elyse said, drawing the servant's gaze to her. "Thank you so much. You're a truly considerate man."

Joseph's cheeks went half a shade darker. "I'm honored to be at your service."

As far as Arcadius could tell, the bow he offered before he left was sincerely respectful.

~

A couple pieces of Elyse's brain felt like they were missing. Her dream about the Chrysler Building had been strange for more reasons than the flying. Instead of lights to warn off planes, the skyscraper's iconic crown had sported two glowing blue gray eyes—the same blue gray that made Arcadius's visage so amazing. That had to be a Freudian message. Probably she shouldn't mention it. Definitely she shouldn't pay too much attention to him sitting as close to her as he was. His knee touched the couch, his dark gray trousers shaped by the strong muscles of his thighs. She *almost* let her gaze slide higher. Maybe the sight of *his* Chrysler Building would warm her up.

Really, if you thought about it, her libido's ability to be turned on by him so soon after passing out was impressive.

"So," she said. "I'm just gonna take that shower."

She still had her coat on, plus the blankets he'd thrown around her to warm her up. Given all that wrapping, she couldn't stand without help. Worse, her hands shook too much to unbutton the coat herself.

"Sheesh," she said as Arcadius undid her like a kid.

On the bright side, the clenching of his jaw when her snug red dress reappeared was satisfying—even if her sense of payback was short-lived.

Being freed from the extra weight left her lightheaded. Arcadius caught her hand as she swayed.

"Sorry," she said automatically.

He shook his head in amusement. "I'll help you walk. I don't want you going lights out again."

She let him assist her, inescapably glad the bathroom was in good order. This was the only part of the apartment that was all her. She'd done the renovation after her father's death but pre-David, stealing a less-used closet to expand the space. The fittings were white, black, and satin nickel: all classic turn of the century reproductions except for a drop-dead luxurious steam shower.

That sleek glass cylinder could have doubled as a transporter pad on the Enterprise.

Thanks to Joseph's consideration, vaporous white clouds rolled up in it. At the sight of those, an inexplicable shiver gripped Elyse. Memory teased her. She heard the icy wind roaring all around her and felt strong arms, their muscles real but not quite solid.

The fragments eluded her. She'd forgotten something important.

"I'll handle it from here," she said to Arcadius.

He had one hand under her elbow. "You're sure?"

"Absolutely. Now give a lady some privacy."

To Elyse's relief, he couldn't refuse this request. She undressed slower than usual but without falling. Curiously, though she'd been in an accident, she didn't notice a single bruise.

The limo's roll must have thrown her onto a featherbed.

That was weird, but not something she could figure out right then. She checked the temperature Joseph had set for the shower, pursed her lips on a silent whistle, and turned it down. Arcadius's friend must like being boiled. She'd rather not faint a second time, thank you.

A tap sounded on the door, loud enough to hear but still polite. "I'm not opening this," Arcadius said. "Just call out that you're still alive."

Maybe what happened to her next could be explained as a reaction to escaping death. Maybe it was her tenant's low sexy voice. Whatever the cause, arousal crashed through her body in an unstoppable rolling wave. The effect was his kiss times ten. Her pussy clenched hard enough to ache, her nipples contracting, her palms itching to stroke him. Every inch of her skin woke up simultaneously. Physically, she lusted after Arcadius. Whether the rest of her was ready didn't seem to matter.

Then again, if her subconscious was lending his eyes to one of the city's biggest phallic symbols, her mind might be more decided than she believed.

"Elyse?" Arcadius asked through the bathroom door.

"I'm alive," she said. Because she was her, she cogitated a couple more heartbeats. "You *could* come in. You know, make sure I don't drop the soap and slip."

She'd taken him by surprise. There was a weighted pause, during which Elyse's desire to grin fought with her impulse to grab a towel and cover her nakedness. The latter urge she managed to control. The crystal knob to the bathroom turned.

"Okay," Arcadius said. "I'm coming in."

He was in shirtsleeves, his cuffs rolled up like they'd been at dinner. It was a testament to how well that shirt hugged his muscular chest and shoulders that, for a second, she forgot she was starkers.

His eyes sliding down her reminded her.

"Whew," he said, not so much comment as reaction. His gaze stopped at her feet and made a slo-oww reverse trip. He wet his lips when he reached her breasts, no amount of gentlemanliness able to prevent him from lingering there. His breath rushed out. He seemed to have trouble forcing his eyes to continue on to hers. "That's a prettier sight than I imagined."

Elyse hadn't forgotten how to trade teases with a man. "In that case, I hope you imagined something good."

To her surprise, Arcadius blushed. He *had* been thinking about her—and in some way that embarrassed him. That was flattering, and a boost to her confidence.

"There is one problem." She drew a fingertip up and down between her breasts. Her nipples grew even harder from the knowledge that he saw them.

Arcadius swallowed, his eyes following her motion. "There is?"

"Oh, yes," she said, pleased with him. Since his gaze was occupied, she finally let hers travel to the crotch of his nice trousers. Now that was a national landmark! The ridge that pushed out his zipper was large enough to steal her breath, maybe large enough to recommend caution. Elyse ignored the warning. "The problem is you're incredibly overdressed."

He dragged his attention up to her face again. Another man would have laughed, but perhaps he was too wound up. His expression was intense: dark brows lowered, chalcedony eyes hot enough to set her ablaze. "I'd be happy to address that oversight."

"Could you do it slowly?" she asked. "I've been imagining you naked too . . ."

~

She wanted him to do it *slowly?* Did she know the effect she'd had on him? Djinn loved overdoing decoration. The more the better was their aesthetic. Elyse's unclothed form was simple and perfect. Everything a woman required for beauty she possessed. Her waist was slender, her hips curving out from it just so. He'd already admired her legs in her jeans, but their naked paleness, their shape and their long muscles, even her knees somehow undid him. He wanted to lay her down and press them apart as he pushed his cock into her. Her triangle of curls invited petting. Her breasts . . .

His breath caught a bit when he gazed at them.

They looked so soft, so delicate and creamy mounded on her ribcage. Their slight size made him feel both protective and ravenous. His fingers curled with longing to cup what weight they had toward his lips. Those tight nipples needed kissing, right on their rosy tips.

Loveliness like Elyse's could crack the heart.

He shook himself. He was being ridiculous. Brand new hormones at work, no doubt.

"Your wish is my command," he said huskily.

She liked that. She bit her lip as he started undoing shirt buttons. One by one, he thumbed the disks from their holes. He opened the pale blue shirt all the way to his belt.

"Pull the tails from your pants," she said.

He obeyed, able then to free his arms and toss the garment behind him. Elyse's gaze traveled up his hairy chest and across his shoulders. He guessed she enjoyed what she saw. Her fingertips pressed her palms like his had when he looked at her.

"Belt," she said throatily.

Steam from the shower was beginning to fog the room. That couldn't explain why his pulse suddenly beat harder and his groin flashed hot. He pulled the tongue of the belt through the buckle, then freed the metal rod from the hole. Slowly, letting the leather hiss around his waist, he dragged the length of it through the loops.

When that was done, he wound the belt around one palm. The feel of that strip of hide circling his hand, of her gaze magnetized by everything he did, hardened him even more. Her eyes dipped to his cloaked erection, measuring it the way women do. He didn't mind then that he was bigger than before. Her breath came faster and his did too.

"Ready for the rest?" he asked.

She blushed like a summer rose, took one step back, and nodded.

He smiled. He frightened her a little, not because he was a monster, but because he was a man. Luckily, he didn't frighten her too much.

"Sure?" he asked teasingly.

She put both hands behind her back. "I'm trying not to jump you before the show is done."

Oh, she made him laugh—and when he least expected it.

"I'll give you a show," he promised. Setting the belt aside, he took off his shoes and socks. He possessed enough sleight of hand to remove his knife and ankle holster without her noticing. Best not to alarm her with that, he thought.

Her toes curled against the tiles as his bare feet appeared.

"Big feet," she said when he raised one eyebrow. "No wonder you thought mine were small."

"They *are* small, you silly girl."

She grinned, impish delight beaming from her face. She brought her hands from behind her back to gesture for him to resume. "Come on, then. Let's see the full Monty."

He didn't know that term. When he plucked it from the linguistic ethers, he huffed his breath out in mock offense. "I'm just your toy."

"Not yet, you're not."

He couldn't recall experiencing precisely this blend of lust and humor while undressing for a woman. It felt good, like light was filling him up inside. He undid the tabs on the waist of his trousers and drew the stretched out zipper carefully down.

That hurdle cleared, he dropped trou with a whoosh of fine tailored wool. Elyse laid one slim finger beside her mouth. "That settles that question. Boxer briefs. I would have guessed commando."

"The weather is too cold for that."

"So it is. And the red and yellow horizontal stripes?"

"Are festive!" He crossed his arms at her amused tone. "The clothing store offered ship's anchor patterns too. And ducks."

"Ducks." The corners of Elyse's mouth twitched deeper into her cheeks. Her green eyes sparkled. "Are you saving them for a special occasion?"

"Maybe," he said, pretending to be grumpy.

She stepped closer, laid her hands on his folded forearms, and went on tiptoe to kiss his chin. "They're beautiful. You're beautiful. Every . . . delicious . . . inch of you."

Her fingertips skated across his forearms, stroking the dark fine hair that grew there. To his elbows her caress went, over his hipbones and the apparently too-festive underwear. Skirting around his bulge, she smoothed a path to their hem and back. His skin tingled underneath.

He couldn't forget she was already naked. He enjoyed looking down her too much.

"May I?" she asked, her body almost touching his.

"May you what?" His voice was thick, his arms seeming to unfold by themselves. Mesmerized by her shining eyes, he laid his hands lightly on her hips. When he rubbed his thumbs there—noting she wasn't chilled anymore —her skin was velvety.

"May I remove your beautiful boxer briefs?" she asked.

"I thought you wanted me to strip for you."

"Now that I've seen you in these, I've changed my mind." Her thumbs moved too, feathering the stretched cloth to either side of his erection. His body shuddered with pent desire, his testicles drawing up.

"That is a woman's prerogative," he admitted.

She grinned, cupping one hand directly over his straining cock. Arcadius's libido went haywire, liquid excitement squeezing from the slit at his tip. Elyse stretched up his front with the clear intention to kiss his mouth. Arcadius caught her firm upper arms.

"Don't," he said, though the very tips of her breasts trembled in his chest hair.

"Don't?"

"If you kiss me, I'll forget to be a gentleman. You won't have any more say in what happens."

Elyse dropped back to her bare heels. "Good to know," she said teasingly.

He almost lost it at her joke. He wanted to maraud her, to conquer and command and drive himself deep inside her softness until they both broke into pieces. Instead, he stood respectful and unmoving as she pulled the boxer briefs down his braced legs.

She bent to complete the task, her unintentional genuflection doing bizarrely powerful things to his arousal. He couldn't doubt he liked the thought of her on her knees, servicing his raging cock with the soft pink mouth that had earned his appreciation from the start.

When she straightened, her brows went up at his expression. "Are you all right? You look thunderous."

"I desire you very much. It is hard to wait."

"Oh." She smiled beatifically. "Will you wait long enough for me to explore you?"

"Yes."

He probably sounded as thunderous as he looked, but she displayed no fear as she pushed spread fingertips up his chest and across his shoulders. Her fingernails scratched gently, not leaving marks but only warm pleasure trails. Sensing she preferred him not to interfere, his dropped his arms to his sides.

"You're big," she said, her eyes seeming to touch him too. "Not just your . . . cock but all of you."

He liked that she said the word—and that she was a little shy of it. "I am proportional."

He *thought* this was true. He hadn't really overdone his copy by that much.

Elyse circled around to his back, her softly scoring nails doing deliriously nice things to his muscles there. She laughed at his comment. "You're more than proportional. You're massive."

He wanted to turn and look at her. "I'll be careful with you."

"I'm not worried that you won't."

She kissed him between his shoulder blades, her hands sliding down to cup his gluteus maximi. She squeezed the muscles with surprising strength. "Nice butt, by the way, big guy. Very bitable."

That image lashed him, a perfect storm of lust whipping through his veins. Apparently, he liked the idea of her nipping him as much as vice versa.

"Touch my cock if you're going to," he warned.

This time she didn't laugh. She slid her slender arms around him, hugging him from behind. The unthinking tenderness of her embrace made his ribcage contract. Had she held her husband this way? He pushed the question determinedly from his mind. Her cheek pressed his upper back, her soft breasts his mid, and her satiny belly his clenched rear. Her fingernails combed the hair on his thighs. Then her thumbs and fingers enclosed his thudding shaft.

"Is this good?" she whispered, tightening the wrap as she pulled upward.

Arcadius's entire body tensed with delight. He felt as if he'd never been touched before. Hot chills chased along and inside his cock, causing the tip to pulse and leak more excitement.

He put one hand over both of hers, stopping their motion. "That's *too* good, sweetheart."

He turned to her, his shift forcing her to release his erection. Their gazes met like laser beams in the steamy room.

"If you kiss me . . ." she said.

"If I kiss you."

Her tongue curled over her upper lip. "I'm on birth control."

His mind sorted through the implications of the phrase. "My body is as clean as a virgin's," he responded honestly.

Her laugh was partially a snort. She knew he was experienced. He sucked his breath in sharply as she took him in hand again. Eyes locked on his, her thumb pushed up the side of his shaft to circle the swollen head. Round and round she went, each pass intensifying his sensations. He couldn't imagine what she saw in his expression. She switched from circling to a crosswise rub. Pre-come made her thumb pad slide. A low moan broke in his throat as pleasure blurred his vision.

"I love the way your skin feels here," she said throatily. "So smooth. So hot. I'd love to feel it inside of me."

"Then you will. And soon, if God allows."

She shivered at the deepness of his voice.

He dropped his head and kissed her.

This was no teasing brush of lip on lip. This was the slow deep burn of passion. He pushed his tongue inside her mouth, sucking, drawing, sliding his arms around her back and lifting her to him. Her naked body felt amazing plastered tight to his. Conveniently, he could cover her rounded bottom with just one hand. Since this was the case, he used his second to tilt and support her head.

"Mm," she hummed, her tongue stroking alongside his. Her hands clutched his shoulders from behind. "Arcadius."

He kissed her graceful neck and then her mouth again. She had no coyness. She was responsive and sleek and utterly delicious. He could have kissed her all night.

Of course, he needed to fuck her too.

"Elyse."

The shower door opened on a curved track. He slid it aside and stepped into the spray carrying her.

"Oh, that's good," she moaned, her head dropping back at the water's heat. It *was* good, nearly as steamy as a Turkish *hammam*. Water ran down her breasts, enticingly skirting her flushed nipples.

Arcadius smiled at her sensual reaction. "Let me help warm you."

Her head came up. She framed his face in her hands, kissing him just as intimately as he'd kissed her. Oddly, her boldness had the same power as her kneeling.

He didn't know if he could stand wanting her this much. His body felt so good, so ready to plunge into hers and pump. He pushed her into the thick glass wall, careful not to use all his strength on her. Controlling himself was an increasing challenge. Every time he thought he couldn't get more excited, another wave of arousal washed through him. Unable to resist, he ducked his head to her breasts. The beads that tipped them were as smooth as butter, as sweet to his suckling mouth as strawberries. She liked him pulling on them. She made little pleasured noises and wriggled in his arms, obliging him to grip her rear tighter.

That was no hardship. Her curves there were a delight to squeeze.

When she lifted her legs around him, crossing her ankles behind his hips, he couldn't contain a groan. The muscles of her calves were as firm as apples.

"Please," she said, her hand traveling down his front to find his erection. "Warm me from the inside now."

~

Elyse had never had her hands on a man as hard and perfect as Arcadius. His muscles were hot marble, every part of him a joy to touch. His back called to her, his arms, the taut rounds of his buttocks.

The part her fingers curled around next was especially rewarding.

She pushed aside her niggle of intimidation over how large he was. He knew what he was doing. The confident way he held her left no doubt of that. He'd know how to bring her pleasure with this too.

She placed his erection's silky pulsing head at her gate. Arousal welled from her at the contact, the ache in her increasing. How much she wanted him was ridiculous. Since he was where she wished, she let go to grip his shoulders.

The shower pounding on them felt good too.

"Elyse," he said in his seductive voice. He brushed her wet hair back with one hand. Though his body vibrated with desire, he didn't press inward. Maybe he wasn't sure he should?

"I trust you," she said.

Something flickered behind his eyes. He put his second hand underneath her bottom. The feel of his big warm palms was sexy.

"Just relax," he said, purring the instruction. "I have you. You don't have to hold your weight. *Feel* me push into you. I'll take my time. You can just enjoy it."

"I'm not supposed to do anything?"

"Later," he growled, his hypnotizing eyes glowing. "When I'm all the way in you."

His hips gave a slow firm push. The pressure of his cock on her entrance increased, the effect so pleasurable she gasped. The flare of the head squeezed in, stretching her passage without the least discomfort, no doubt because she was so wet. The muscles of Arcadius's face tightened—at how good the entry felt, she supposed, and maybe from curbing his natural male urge to go faster.

He pushed again, still slowly, and slid deeper. He tensed more, but Elyse's spine lost its last iota of stiffness. His heat and thickness felt so good. This was primal. Being taken. Being owned. She was ready to surrender. Or certainly her pussy was.

"Oh, my God," she breathed as he forged in to his last inch.

Her pussy was in love. His huge hot cock had conquered it. She knew she'd never forget the sensation of him throbbing and alive inside of her.

"Okay?" he asked breathlessly.

His heart was pounding in his big chest. Elyse had locked her arms around him without thinking. She bit her lip and grinned.

"Much better than okay," she said.

He rubbed their noses together, his smile a subtler curve than hers. "All right. I'm going to move now. Don't do anything until I get the feel of you."

She got the impression he liked that: him acting, her accepting what he did. For the moment, she didn't mind. Him pulling gently back and forging in again felt incredible.

The growl of enjoyment that rumbled from his chest wasn't bad either.

She twined her fingers in his thick below-the-collar hair. The next time he pushed, she met him with her own forward tilt.

"You want to help me," he observed.

"I do. I'm a fan of a good team effort."

He blinked before letting out a low male laugh. "All right. See if you can keep up."

The steam shower was spacious—or so she'd thought before he got into it. He braced the sole of one foot on the curved wall behind him. Evidently, one leg was all he needed for balancing. He nuzzled her neck, somehow finding just the right spot to make her melt. Only when he had her trembling did he begin moving.

She gasped as his cock withdrew and thrust in smooth back and forth motions. He did it again and again, gradually speeding up until he was definitely pushing her up the slope to climax. She didn't know if it was due to his thickness or if his technique was just that good, but every inward shove gave the nerves of her clitoris a solid jolt.

He didn't seem to mind that she dug her heels into him as she met his motions. Though she couldn't help crying out, she didn't have a chance to be self-conscious. He was groaning himself, as if everything they did was extra good for him. His cock grew harder inside her—and it had been plenty hard before. His grip on her butt was tight and exciting.

In truth, everything about this was exciting: his cock, his heavy breathing, the bunching power of his big muscles. Elyse held on tight and gave herself over to the ride. Her pussy contracted on his shaft, eager to pull the wonderful sensations more greedily into her.

Arcadius cursed in a foreign tongue. He shifted their angle of conjunction a few degrees. Suddenly wonderful sensations changed to insanely amazing. His cock hit something good inside her, and hit and hit it until her body seized with a huge climax. Her head arched back on the shower wall, her fingernails digging into his shoulders.

Arcadius grunted and pumped faster, stretching out her sharp orgasm.

Somewhere in the middle of her bliss, she noticed him start thrusting for himself.

The sounds he made then were more urgent, the length of his strokes shorter. Each thrust stayed deeper inside her in his quest for maximum friction. Though this felt great to her, she didn't want to miss what it did to him. She forced her gaze to refocus.

The effort was worth it. His eyes were screwed shut, his gorgeous face twisted into a mask of need.

"Yes," she encouraged him. "Come, Arcadius."

His erection pulsed. He slammed it up inside her even as his tight grip on her hips dragged her pussy down. Their pelvises smacked together. His head flung back, the groan that tore from him rough enough to scrape his throat. Heat flooded her deep inside.

"Ah," he sighed as the pulse came again. One more burst warmed her, and then his eyes opened.

Water beaded his dark lashes and cheekbones, his blue gray gaze sleepy. Elyse's afterglow spread through her like warm honey.

"Wow," she panted, her lungs not recovered yet.

Arcadius's lips quirked at their corners. "I concur."

His voice was hoarse, which gratified Elyse. His cock remained inside her, not as big or stiff as before but comforting. His weight pressed her more heavily to the shower's curved glass wall, both his feet on the floor again.

Giving in to temptation, Elyse rested her cheek on his broad shoulder. "You have to stay where you are," she said. "I don't think I can walk."

"Was I too rough at the end? I'm afraid I was more . . . enthusiastic than I'm accustomed to."

Elyse grinned. *Enthusiastic* was a good word for it. "You were perfect. All my kinks are worked out."

She patted his wet back and yawned. Maybe that was rude, but after the night she'd had, she couldn't restrain herself.

Arcadius let out a quiet laugh. "All right, sleepyhead. I'll carry you to bed."

To herself, Elyse admitted being toted around like a girly girl was nice. David hadn't been a wimp, but Arcadius was a regular Hercules. And maybe a sexual Einstein. That climax had knocked her socks off—and his had seemed pretty much the same. She and David had worked their way up to being good in bed together. Though Elyse had never thought she was missing out, she'd never experienced pleasure this epic. As Arcadius settled her on her bed, she was kind of sorry she wasn't up for another round.

His manner as he pulled the sheets over her was nice but not overly romantic. He didn't join her in the bed himself. In her current mood, that seemed fine. She was alive, and David wasn't coming back, but that didn't mean she had to skydive that very second into something serious.

However long Arcadius stuck around, she decided to enjoy him.

CHAPTER SEVEN

ARCADIUS hadn't forgotten Elyse's bed was the same she'd shared with her deceitful dead husband. Because he had no desire to stir up memories of the man, he didn't attempt to join her there. Instead, he pulled a broken-in leather chair closer to the bed. As he sank into its cushion in his comfortable boxer briefs, he realized his core hummed with repletion.

The climax he'd enjoyed with her had been one for the record books.

He wouldn't have minded another. His recovery time seemed to have been reset to that of his youth. His cock was heavy again, needing little encouragement to stir. Unfortunately, he'd tired out his partner.

Clearly drowsy, Elyse turned her head to him on her pillow. "You're staying?"

The question offended him. Of course he was staying. Not that she was aware of it, but someone had tried to kill her. He wasn't leaving her unguarded for one instant.

"I'm staying," he said. "Just in case you hit your head in the accident."

"My head is fine." She wriggled around onto her side without exposing her nakedness. "Neither of us has a scratch."

"We were fortunate," he said sincerely.

She smiled, one hand under the pillow beneath her head. The fingers of the other drew an idle pattern on the sheet in front of her. "I'm not quite asleep. You could finish your story."

"Ah," he said. "You'll have to remind me where I was."

"In the tavern. With the sultan and the artist and the commander. They'd just decided the commander's servant would compete for who could tell the most horrifying tale."

"That sounds right," Arcadius said, pleased she'd remembered. "So, to continue . . ."

* * *

The Servant's Tale

AS you'll recall, the tavern's demon proprietor issued the challenge for the duel. According to the rules, he told his story first. He related the account of a hideous female ghoul, notorious for lying in wait for travelers near a graveyard. Disguised as a lovely woman, she'd promise unsuspecting gentlemen a night of pleasure. Once they were enticed, she'd lure them to her crypt, where her bloodthirsty children would eat them up. The tavern owner's storytelling style was lively, involving acting out gory scenes. His ifrit friends enjoyed it immensely. Whether they were horrified was a separate matter. One or two among them might have been ghouls themselves.

As the audience clapped and whistled, the eunuch rose and came forward.

"What a marvelous story," he said, his manner all modesty. "No doubt I should concede, but for honor's sake, I will try my humble best."

The audience quieted as the servant began.

"Once upon a time," he said, "but not too long ago, a male child was born to a poor family. At the age of fifteen, because he had certain talents, the boy's parents apprenticed him to a powerful magician.

"What the parents didn't realize was that the magician's nature was black as night. He worked the boy like a slave and demanded other terrible things besides. Every month, when the dark of the moon arrived, he ordered the boy to kill one of his relatives. 'I own you,' the magician would remind him. 'And you must do as I say. If you refuse, I'll summon a demon to murder your entire clan. Then what good will your scruples do?'

"The captive boy could make no argument. Luckily, he knew a few tricks himself. Each month, when the dark of the moon arrived, instead of a relative he sacrificed a poppet—a straw doll he'd animated with his own blood. He would do this alone in his little chamber, whisking the relative by magic to a far-off town. Such was the apprentice's skill and such were the shrieks of the poppets as they were slain, that the subterfuge was successful for many years.

"In the seventh year of his apprenticeship, the last according to the agreement his parents signed, one of the magician's associates happened to travel to the village where the young man's relatives now lived. Furious over being made a fool of, the magician sent his men to arrest the apprentice's father. He would be the next sacrifice, and the death would take place in public, in the magician's green courtyard.

"The young man begged his master to relent by all the names of God, but the djinni was deaf to his pleas. He even refused the apprentice's offer to give up his own life instead. When the father heard this, he tried to intervene.

"'You must do as he asks, son,' he said. 'I sold you into servitude. Though I only wished you to have a trade, my ill-considered bargain led you to this trouble. Surely the debt is mine to pay.'

"What son could murder a father so loving? Not the apprentice certainly. Enraged, the magician ordered his personal pack of demons to torture him for the next fortnight. Every moment the fiends were at him—pinching, biting, whispering any nastiness they could think of to drive the young man to despair. If the apprentice slept, there was no escape. The demons entered his very dreams, turning the smallest scrap of sweetness into a dark nightmare.

"Finally, at the end of this period, the magician came to him. 'Kill your father, or suffer the same again.' The apprentice was exhausted but once more he refused. Another fortnight commenced, with no pleasanter activities. One difference struck the apprentice. Before, the magician only checked on him occasionally. Now he came every night to ask the young man if he'd changed his mind. To the apprentice's weary eyes, he seemed almost desperate.

"'You are wise,' the apprentice said to the old woman who each morning left a heel of bread and a cup of water outside the bars of his cell. 'Can you explain this mystery? If our master is so enraged with me, why not simply end my life and have done with it?'

"'I will answer,' said the woman, 'both for the sake of your pretty manners and for my own hatred of the man. You are the seventh apprentice our master has taken on, none of whom resisted as long as you. The murders he wishes you to commit are his means of blackening your soul. As each apprentice becomes irredeemable, he gives him to a terrible demon king in payment for a debt he owes. It is this demon who gave the magician his great powers. If our master fails to pay, the demon will visit worse sufferings on him than you have undergone. The final installment is due tomorrow. If you hold out a little longer, the demon king will kill him and you'll be free.

"The old woman's revelation filled the apprentice with fresh resolve. Through all his tortures, the young man had kept silent, refusing to let anyone hear his cries. Tonight, however, when the magician returned to ask if he would submit, the giddiness of his hope robbed him of caution. 'Have you nothing more to bring against me?' he taunted his oppressor. 'These fiends are no worse than kittens nibbling at my toes.'

"The magician's fiends—who were in fact his former apprentices, merely without their souls—had done the worst they could devise. Knowing this, and aware the clock was ticking for himself, the magician seized upon the first terrible idea that came into his mind. Storming into the cell, he kicked the weakened apprentice until he lay moaning on the ground. Then the magician bent, grabbed the apprentice's testicles, and ripped them from his body.

"'These are my hostages!' he cried, shaking the bloody things. 'Kill your father before the next rising of the sun, and with my magic I shall return them. Defy me by a single second, and I'll feed your jewels to my so-called kittens.'

"The apprentice knew the magician could do this. He'd seen his master remove and reattach people's limbs for amusement. Sadly, the awareness only made him feel worse. He curled on the floor of his cell in shock, clutching his wounds and knowing his own rash words had condemned him to suffer them forever.

"If he stood his ground, he *and* his father might survive. The apprentice simply wouldn't survive as a whole man.

"He must have appeared beaten as he was led out trembling into the courtyard the next morning. His father was there, and the fiends, and all the magician's servants. Torches burned, for the sun hadn't yet risen.

"'Now,' the magician said, so confident of his prey that he held a knife hilt toward him. 'Kill your sire and live to have children yourself someday.'

"The apprentice took the knife, hung his head in defeat, and heaved a sorry sigh.

"'I forgive you,' his father said. 'It is right that a parent's life end before his child's.'

"'Do it,' said the magician.

"Dawn began to glimmer behind the near rooftops. The apprentice knew this was the deadline for the magician to pay his debt to the demon king.

"'*Do it,*' the evil man repeated more urgently.

"Half-starved, tortured, and weak from loss of blood, the apprentice leaped toward the magician. With the last measure of his strength, he drove the knife meant to kill his father into the black heart of his oppressor.

"Given the magician's power, perhaps he could have healed the injury. He wasn't given the chance to try. Thunder cracked as a split appeared in the ground nearby, infernal light glowing in its depths. A terrible form of smoke and fire emerged. The demon king had arrived.

"'You have failed!' the great ifrit rumbled. 'Now *your* soul is forfeit.'

"With no more ado, the demon king snatched the dying magician down into his hell with him."

This seemed to be the end of the servant's story. The young man stopped speaking and bowed his head, politely awaiting the tavern crowd's judgment. His listeners gazed at each other uneasily. This indeed was a tale of horror, no less so because the evil magician—with whom their sympathies naturally lay —had been defeated.

"Hm," said one audience member. "That is a disturbing tale."

"I don't believe it," declared another. "The magician had the apprentice where it hurts. He would have given in!"

"Would he?" the modest servant asked. "What if the apprentice had been me?"

The eunuch lifted his robes, revealing his awful scars. His audience gasped, each imagining himself similarly unmanned. As the servant predicted, he'd succeeded in curdling their blood. Slowly, one by one, the ifrits began to clap. The clamor grew and grew until it was noticeably louder than the applause the proprietor had inspired.

Though he was an evil djinni, the tavern owner knew what honor required.

"I concede the win," he said. "Though I do not see how you will enjoy her, my greatest treasure belongs to you."

This treasure was the veiled woman who'd begged the sultan to save her with the note dropped in his wine cup. The eunuch accepted the trophy graciously. Then, as quickly as discretion would allow, the eunuch, the sultan, the artist, and the commander escorted their prize to the safety of the palace. The eunuch petitioned the sultan to take the veiled woman as a gift, which the ruler gratefully did.

For her part, the woman would not agree to be returned to her home, nor would she tell them where it was. Because her heart belonged to the young sultan, she swore being parted from him would be worse than servitude. Knowing such a sensitive woman must possess noble blood, the sultan asked her to marry him. She agreed and was revealed to be a beautiful princess. The couple married and were showered with presents by her royal father, who had thought his child was dead.

Thus they lived joyfully together, for as long as it was God's will.

* * *

Arcadius had been speaking for a while. To his surprise, Elyse wasn't asleep yet.

"Very good," she said with a crooked smile, "though you might have rushed the romance-y part."

"It was the eunuch's tale," Arcadius reminded her. "Those events weren't relevant to him."

Elyse hummed skeptically. "The eunuch didn't get much out of his victory. I felt bad for him. He was so clever and suffered for so long, and because of a few rash words, he couldn't live as a whole man."

"It *is* sad," Arcadius agreed. "Though there is more to life than sex."

"So says the man who just knocked boots with me in my shower."

"I wasn't wearing— Oh." He rubbed his chin. "'Knocking boots' doesn't seem . . . expressive enough for what we enjoyed."

Elyse waggled her eyebrows. "It *was* kind of awesome. Probably I should thank you."

"I'm sure that isn't necessary."

"Maybe it is." She pushed up on her elbow, her expression serious. "I wasn't sure when I'd recover enough from David's death to want to do that again. You got me over the hump, so to speak. So . . . thank you."

He couldn't put his finger on exactly what about her words nettled him. "You're extremely welcome," was the response he came up with.

Elyse's lips curved as she put her head on the pillow and closed her eyes. "Thanks for the bedtime story. I should probably walk you to the door, but now I'm too sleepy."

She thought she should walk him to the door? Arcadius snorted in his head. If she didn't wish to share her precious bed, he'd walk himself to her couch, thank you.

~

Elyse woke at the crack of dawn from a confused dream involving a smoke monster and the commander's eunuch servant. The end of Arcadius's tale truly hadn't been fair to him. With all that magic flying around, couldn't someone have magically fixed him?

"It's just a story," she mumbled to herself.

Half asleep, she shuffled to the bathroom, noting only when she finished that it was a shambles. Damp towels lay everywhere. As she picked them up and hung them to dry, she found Arcadius's soggy dress socks and now water-spotted shoes. His beautiful pale blue shirt, which had been tossed onto the floor and stepped on, might never recover. His rolled-up belt and watch perched beside the sink basin.

Wait a second, she thought. What had he worn to get home? Arcadius didn't like the cold. He'd have grabbed shoes at least before he braved the outside.

Pulling on a Japanese silk robe she'd ordered through the family firm, she walked quietly to the living room.

Her brand new lover was sleeping on the couch. That was weird, right? She hadn't invited him to stay. On the other hand, she couldn't deny her pulse skipped with pleasure at seeing him. Had he been that worried about her nonexistent bump on the head? Did he, maybe, *like* her more than she'd given him credit for?

She edged closer. By New York apartment standards, the old leather couch was big. Arcadius only fit on his side with his knees drawn up. In the gaps between colorful layers of throws, she saw he wore trousers. His feet and torso were bare. Even in sleep, he hunched into himself as if he were cold. His features were pinched with worry or possibly a bad dream. This didn't lessen his handsomeness. He was still the most gorgeous male she'd ever laid eyes on.

She sat on the same ottoman he'd used last night, pulled the top blanket higher, and touched his hair gently.

His amazing eyes opened.

"Good morning," she said, surprised to sound so calm. Those eyes of his would give any girl's heart a jumpstart.

His gaze sharpened. "What's wrong?" He sat up, covers falling from his naked chest. "Has someone tried to get in?"

"What? No." He must have woken up confused. She tore her attention from his six-pack. "It's morning. You're at my place. You fell asleep on my couch."

He scrubbed his face with one hand. "Sorry. I didn't mean to fall asleep. You're all right?"

"Perfectly fine."

His gaze dropped to the place where her robe crossed her breasts. "That's pretty. You look nice in dark blue."

Did she? She must have more color in her cheeks than usual.

"The gold chrysanthemums are an attractive touch," he added.

The flowers were printed on the silk—big, cheery, shiny bursts of petals. As luck would have it, the bloom Arcadius seemed fixed on draped her left breast. He shifted on the couch cushion as if something might be making his pants too tight. Elyse's nipples contracted.

"They're festive," she said, repressing a little smile.

His gaze came up to hers. "Please remove your robe for me."

Elyse's blush heated her cheeks like coals. Seeing this, a grin spread across his face. Slowly, gently, he slid one hand beneath the robe to mold over her trembling breast. Though his hand didn't move, her nipple went fiery.

"I can help you take it off, if you like," he offered.

"Uh," she said, stunned by the effect he had on her. Shouldn't his touch be less powerful than last night, now that it wasn't new? It seemed not. Delicious sensations coursed through her, from no more than the warm pressure of his palm.

"No answer?" Arcadius teased. "I suppose I will have to take charge of you . . ."

~

Asking permission didn't seem like the right approach. Arcadius undid the simple belt of Elyse's robe, quickly rolled it, and stashed it in his pants pocket for later. The halves of the robe fell open, baring her centerline. Elyse didn't tug it closed.

She was too fascinated by the sight of him tucking the tie away.

"You'll see that again," he promised.

"What?" Her startled gaze flew to his.

Arcadius didn't answer. He enjoyed teasing her too much. He slipped the silk from her shoulders and then her arms, allowing the rest to fall. Her body was as pretty as he remembered, as perfect and simple. While she gaped at him, he lifted her from the ottoman and laid her on the couch. Pillows propped her back, the sofa's arm supplying a resting spot for her head.

She tried to sit straighter.

"Stay," he said. "Relax. I have things I want to do to you."

"What things?"

Her suspicious tone amused him. "Things you'll enjoy."

"I—"

"Shh." He pressed her lips closed with one finger. The couch was wide enough for him to climb over her on his knees. He was much bigger than she was. He knew he must appear to be looming. Elyse's dark lashes blinked rapidly.

"I'm kissing your neck first," he warned.

He stroked the graceful column in preparation for nuzzling it. A few whispering passes of his lips identified the special hotspot that made her melt.

"Oh," she said, her hands fluttering to his back.

He didn't let that distract him. Instead, he teased the sensitive area with his tongue and at the same time slid one hand down her naked side. When he reached her hip, he anchored it to the couch. The pressure he used wasn't enough to control her, but Elyse began to squirm. She didn't do this to get away—though perhaps she thought she did. Arcadius knew better. His sensitive djinn nose told him what she was hoping for.

"Arcadius," she said breathily. "I don't think . . . the couch—"

"—will smell all the better for having your scent on it," he purred.

Her cheeks turned as pink as if she'd leaned near a fire. "Arcadius—"

He pressed his lips to hers to seal the protest in. "'Stop now' are the only words I'm listening to this morning. Feel free to scream any other ones you like."

Her cushiony mouth fell open. His mention of screaming took her aback. Grinning, he kissed a soft trail across her collarbones, down the satiny hollow between her breasts, and onto her left nipple. The feel of him sucking there calmed her—more or less. He knew how to make the nerves of woman's nipple connect to lower things. He did so, tickling her with his tongue and pulling on her sweetness. The fragrance of her arousal rose, her hips bucking slightly beneath his hold on them.

When her legs started shifting restlessly as well, he moved to the other breast.

She let out a pleasured noise, her fingers forking into his hair to keep him where he was. Arcadius's prick was about to burst through his trousers, but he didn't rush his activities. Her enjoyment was his reward, the gradual loosening of her spine. Her involuntary undulations grew increasingly erotic.

Concluding the moment was right to take his next liberty, Arcadius swung off the couch. Elyse seemed a different woman as he stood looking down at her, much more sensual and relaxed. She lolled on the couch rather than simply lying there.

She didn't resist as he sat her up and shifted her body to face forward.

The sofa cushion was deep, and she had room to lounge back. Arcadius sat on the ottoman facing her. Her green eyes were hooded, her expression simultaneously secretive and watchful. He liked that. He wanted her attention on his actions—but also on what occurred inside of her.

"What now?" she asked in a slumberous voice.

"This," he said.

He stroked her thighs up and down, his pressure gentle but persuasive, until her slightly tense knees agreed to sprawl. Wanting more of that reaction, he drew her left foot onto his thigh and then her right. This position exposed her sex to him, not simply her dark curls but the rosy folds they protected. Moisture was welling from her, causing them to glisten. Elyse noticed what he was looking at. She tried to draw her feet away.

"No," he said, gently holding her calves trapped. "Don't hide. Everything about you is beautiful to me. You bring me pleasure when you let me watch what I do to you."

She stopped tugging but bit her lower lip. With his thumbs, Arcadius drew tiny circles on the sensitive skin inside the bend of her knees. Elyse's eyes were round but not afraid. Nervous, maybe. Her pupils had swollen with arousal.

"Okay," she whispered.

Arcadius pulled the tie to her robe from his pants pocket. Her feet rested on his thighs. Pleased that she wasn't struggling, he covered their tops to warm them and rubbed their soles with his thumbs. Elyse's toes curled with enjoyment. Judging that she was ready, he wound the length of silk around her ankles until he'd secured them together.

"Wait," she said. "You're binding my *feet?*"

He guessed she'd expected something else.

"You'll like it. It will change what you feel when I go down on you. You'll be able to tug the tie all you want without breaking it. Also, this leaves your hands free to hold my head—assuming I'm doing a good job."

"That's very practical," she said faintly.

"It is. A woman like you with such nice firm legs might strangle me at my work."

"Oh, come on," she said, sensing he was teasing in spite of his straight face.

Arcadius pushed all eight fingertips up her thighs. "All right, maybe I shouldn't call it *work*. More like a labor of love."

He slid his thumbs up the groove where her legs and torso met. One of her muscles twitched as he bent forward.

"Arcadius," she said.

He laughed. He knew that tone. She was going to warn him off. "Elyse, don't you think you'll enjoy me doing this?"

"Yes, but—"

"But?"

She squirmed, and not entirely with embarrassment. "It's personal, and it's only our second time."

"Is there a rule?"

"No." She didn't say *but* this time.

"I want to," he said. "I want to take your taste inside me. I want to hear and feel and cause you to fly apart. I want that power." He searched for an appropriate phrase. "I get off on it."

She touched the side of his face, stroking a stray lock of hair behind his ear. "You're a unique man."

"Strange, you mean."

"No." Her finger traveled around his lips, her green eyes considering. Her touch left a warm humming trail behind. "I mean unique. Like an incredible artifact someone unearthed from an ancient tomb."

"You're comparing me to a mummy?"

Her smile slanted to one side. "You're better with words than me."

He leaned forward and kissed her navel. "I'm good with my mouth," he promised.

He put his hands on her pussy first, stroking, tugging, oiling her with her own arousal. Her head arched back as he found the areas she liked to have massaged.

"You could close your eyes," he suggested.

"I like watching your expression."

He curved two fingers inside of her. That drew a nice throaty sound from her. He parted her folds with his other hand. Elyse's curled into fists. Despite her claim to like watching him, her eyes were nearly closed already. He rubbed up and down to either side of her clitoris, admiring its flush and swell. One slow lick introduced him to her delicate taste. Then he sealed his mouth over her hot bud.

Her moan of pleasure was an aphrodisiac, causing his erection to surge longer.

She reached for something to hold and at last settled on his head.

That's it, he thought. *Teach me everything you like.*

Her body taught him with each roll and moan and catch in her breathing. When it came down to it, she wasn't so foreign from djinn females. Women were all their own country, each similar to the others but also different. This was territory Arcadius enjoyed conquering. He didn't tease Elyse. He took his time, letting her enjoyment build.

He wanted to teach her to trust him.

He slid off the ottoman to his knees, finding better leverage for what he did from the floor. It made sense to duck beneath her legs, to let her bound feet rest on his back.

"God," she groaned, clearly liking this new position.

She began to tug at the tie that held her ankles, to feel how the restriction intensified the sensations inside her sex. Being bound played with people's minds, but it had physical aspects too. Certain things had to stay in certain places and maintain their relation to each other. Leather creaked from Elyse's slow motion writhing. Arcadius's heart pounded harder, looking forward to her release as if it were his own. That was a new experience. He generally kept an emotional distance when pleasuring a female—if only out of strategy. He decided he enjoyed this sense of involvement. Elyse's body felt so alive. She was losing her inhibitions, her motions begging him for more. He gave her more pressure with his lips and tongue.

"*Arcadius*," she pleaded.

Her pussy contracted around his fingers, that tightening another plea. With his other hand, he pressed the bone over which her clitoris anchored. He squeezed slightly from either side, effectively holding the rod captive. Every good nerve bundle that he was able to stimulate he did. Elyse's back arched dramatically.

Arcadius drew a breath and spun the dial on his mouth to ten.

She cried out with a hard climax, not screaming but close to it. He kept at her—fast, firm, his tongue lashing her clitoris as his cheeks pulled it rhythmically. When she sagged with satiation, he gentled.

"Holy smokes," she breathed as he backed off from her.

He wiped his face on his forearm and grinned. To his surprise, she broke into a laugh. "You should see your expression. Like the fox in the chicken coop."

"Is that bad?"

"Nothing about you is bad. Not that I've seen anyway."

Not that she *remembered*, he realized.

~

Sadness ghosted across Arcadius's face. Did some secret guilt trigger the expression? Elyse supposed everyone had a history. However decent a person Arcadius seemed, he'd be no exception.

Still vibrating from her orgasm, Elyse bent forward on the couch to unbind her ankles.

"Shoot," she said after a moment's struggle. "I tugged this tie pretty tight."

"Let me help," Arcadius said.

"You should," she joked. "You made me do it."

Arcadius smiled faintly. She wouldn't have guessed his fingers were nimbler than hers, but apparently there was a trick to the knot. He had her free in seconds.

"Don't tell me. You were a sailor in a past life."

"I have been to sea," he acknowledged.

He sat on his heels, the hint of wistfulness lingering in his expression. The sight pricked her conscience.

For goodness sake, she scolded herself. *Stop being so damned uptight. This is a good man, who just gave you a very good orgasm.*

Simple fairness suggested she ought to do something nice for him.

"It's still early," she said. "I'm not sure what you planned for today, but since the sun isn't up, you probably can't do it yet. I could make you breakfast, or maybe you'd like a couple more hours sleep on something more comfortable than a couch."

He cocked his head in surprise. "You mean sleep *with* you? On your bed?"

"Well . . . yes," she said. "Or, um, maybe you're not into the snuggling thing—though we wouldn't *have* to sleep."

"We wouldn't."

Now he was teasing her. She knew that despite his deadpan tone. She pretended to smack his chest. "I've been out of the dating pool. I can't help it if I'm awkward."

"Forgive me," he said, his gemlike eyes crinkling. "I can't seem to resist twitting you. I'd be honored to join you in your bed, for cuddling or anything else you have in mind."

The suggestiveness of his voice abruptly swung her into the *anything else* column. Elyse had always assumed her sex drive was normal. If that were true, Arcadius seemed to have superpowers for arousing her. Maybe every woman he met reacted to him this way. Rather than think about that too hard, she hopped onto her feet and offered him a hand up.

"Follow me," she said as he accepted it.

He followed, seeming bemused to have *her* tugging him down the hall. That made her laugh, which made it easy to tug him through the bedroom door. She told herself this didn't have to be a big symbolic deal. She and Arcadius could simply have some fun.

"Hold on," he said as she reached the foot of the bed.

When she turned, he lifted her in his arms for a full-on lip lock. That was fun, especially when he grabbed her rear in one hand and started grinding his pelvis against her. To her delight, he was erect. His cock felt like actual wood behind his zipper.

He broke free to gasp for air and growl. "Feeling you come made me so fucking hard."

How could she want to laugh and jump him at the same time? She rolled herself seductively over him. "I can tell. Put me down and I'll help you get naked too."

He set her on her feet and she started attacking his waistband. God, she wanted him inside her, like she'd die if she couldn't come around his raging dick.

Evidently, she was too slow for both of them.

"Let me," he said, which he followed up by toppling her onto the mattress.

Elyse had no objection to him taking the lead right then. The problem was, the moment their bodies hit the bed, a giant shock zapped her in the butt.

"Ow," she said, rubbing it.

Arcadius felt it too. "What the hell was that?"

He touched her hip and the shock came again. Though less intense than before, it seemed too big to be a static charge.

"Huh," she said. "This bed is wood. It can't be electrified. Unless some wire came loose and is arcing on the mattress springs."

Since the mood was broken, she got out to check beneath the frame. Nothing was under there but dust and a long-missing sock. When she clambered back to her feet, Arcadius stood on the opposite side from her.

"There's something between the mattress and the box spring," he said.

She didn't know how he knew that, but he sounded so grim she didn't question him. "Okay," she said. "Help me lift the top."

Sure enough, pushing up the mattress revealed an object that didn't belong there. It was a book, a small one, bound in embossed leather. Elyse was no expert, but the design looked Persian, possibly thirteenth century.

"That can't have caused a spark," she exclaimed.

"You should remove it," Arcadius advised. "I don't think it will shock you again."

Realization dawned. Or sort of. "This must be the book Cara was looking for, the one she said she loaned David. What's it doing between my mattresses?"

She pulled it out, barely noticing Arcadius setting down his side of the bed. Despite knowing leather and paper couldn't shock her, she undid the ribbon that bound it gingerly. Uncle Vince probably would be angry if he knew this was gone from his library. The antique embossed leather was beautiful, the yellowed pages edged with gold.

Elyse lifted the front cover.

"Careful," Arcadius murmured.

Elyse glanced at him in confusion and looked at the book again. The words inside weren't written in English. "I think this is Arabic." Her brow furrowed. "David didn't speak Arabic. Why would he borrow a book of love poems to share with me if he didn't understand what they meant?"

Arcadius wore his grim face again. "Because they're *magical* love poems."

Elyse started to laugh but stopped. "You're serious. Just how superstitious are you and Joseph?"

She blushed as soon as she'd asked. That was a rude way of putting it.

Arcadius didn't seem insulted. Instead, he held out his hand. "May I?"

She passed the little book to him. His big hand dwarfed it as he ran one finger down the lines on the open page. Seeming satisfied, he closed it again.

"Yes," he said. "If you turn these pages and concentrate on your intended target, whoever it is will fall in love with you."

"That's silly!"

"Is it? You're the one who said you hated this bed. You must have known, subconsciously, that the spell was still functioning. It was causing you to feel things you wouldn't have otherwise."

Elyse plunked her hands on her hips, the move reminding her she was naked—not her favorite state for having an argument. "I told you, David didn't read Arabic. Anyway, we fell in love the normal way, bit by bit, from getting to know each other."

"The charm would have magnified your feelings. Kept your attachment strong no matter what he did—or even if he died."

"No." She wagged her head back and forth. "This conversation is ridiculous. None of this happened."

"The person who activates the charm doesn't have to speak the language it's written in. All they have to do is run their eyes across the words."

"No!" Elyse protested with real anger. Arcadius regarded her calmly. "Why are you saying these things?"

He let out a weary sigh. "Not to hurt you. At some point, I was going to have to explain why I wasn't leaving you alone. Why I was guarding you."

That didn't make any sense either. Cara might have a point about her judgment. Elyse had slept with a crazy man. "Give me the book," she said firmly. "I need to return it to my cousin."

Arcadius weighed it in his hand without complying. "Your cousin was rather anxious to get it back. She must want to use the spell herself."

"There's no spell! Honestly, I'm sorry to be rude about your beliefs, but you're taking those stories you tell too seriously."

"It can't be a coincidence that the book released its charge now, when you were about to . . . explore your feelings for someone new."

Of all the irrational things he'd said, *this* drew extra color into his chiseled cheeks. Was *exploring her feelings* his euphemism for having sex? Ignoring her discomfort at being naked, Elyse stalked around the foot of the bed to tug the book from him. As she yanked it—probably too hard, considering its likely value—something fell from between the pages and the back cover.

Elyse picked the something up. It was a micro memory card in a small plastic case. "ELYSE" was written on it in David's handwriting. She touched the letters and shivered.

"That's a computer storage device," Arcadius said.

"I know what it is." Her anger drained from her. This was all very strange.

"You'll want to see what's on it," Arcadius said. He hesitated. "I'll wait in your living room."

CHAPTER EIGHT

DAVID'S laptop was in his office. Happy to get some distance between herself and Arcadius, Elyse threw on clothes and took the memory card to the room next door. There had to be an explanation for all of this. Probably she'd laugh when she discovered it.

Once she'd shifted a box of David's packed-up stuff from the desk chair, Elyse sat. She booted up the laptop and stuck the memory card into its slot. The only content was a video file.

Crap, she thought, her stomach knotting. Whatever this was, she didn't think she was ready to find out.

She clenched her jaw and clicked "play."

David's pleasant features appeared on screen. From the looks of it, he'd filmed himself in the basement unit with the built-in camera on this laptop. He adjusted the screen, lowered himself to the white Barcelona chair, and smoothed his shirtfront down his lean chest. The familiar sight of him pushing his wire rims up his nose made her eyes burn with emotion.

It totally felt like he was alive again.

So there, she told Arcadius in her mind. If her love for David were a trick, that couldn't have happened.

"So, Elyse," David said in the comic-sheepish voice he used to confess he'd forgotten to pick up supplies for dinner. "If you're watching this, I'm either dead or you'll wish I was in a few minutes."

What? Elyse thought, not liking the sound of that. She almost clicked the "stop" button but restrained herself.

"Here's the thing," he said, leaning forward across his knees so that his face came closer. "Your life might depend on what I'm about to tell you, so take a deep breath and hear me out. First off, know that I really love you. Our marriage might have started out as a way to get information—" Elyse bit her thumbnail and kept watching "—but you're a seriously nice woman. You're fun and you're sweet and, believe me, I know I don't deserve you." He pulled an ironic face. "*Didn't* deserve you, I guess. Anyway—"

His voice had roughened. He dragged his palms down his cheeks, obviously working to compose himself. "There's so much to tell you. I guess it starts with your Grandpa Saul. You know how weird your Uncle Vince gets when anyone mentions him? Like he wants to say something bad but has to keep whatever it is to himself?"

Though David couldn't see her, Elyse nodded. She'd chalked up the behavior to sibling rivalry.

"Your dad and your Grandpa Saul were extra close. Kindred spirits, as people say. Even as a kid, your dad would hang out at the Solomon bookstore and help with customers. Vince was the younger brother and not much of a bookworm. I suppose he felt left out, especially when Saul wouldn't let Vince in on his 'Big Secret.'"

What secret? Elyse wondered. In the video, David put on his sincerest face.

"I know this will be hard for you to believe, but stick with me, honey. Before the brownstone was built, this address used to be a freemasons lodge. That burned down, but one of the Grand Poobahs held onto his hush-hush papers and what have you. When he finally kicked the bucket, your grandpa bought his collection for the bookstore, which is when he discovered some crazy stuff.

"There's another world, Elyse, just out of sight from ours. I guess a scientist would call it an interpenetrating dimension. The people who live there are called the djinn—genies, to you and me. They know a lot about us, but most of us humans—Westerners, anyway—think they're only characters from cartoons. Their world is sort of like ours and sort of not. For one thing, it's filled with riches. You could walk into a djinn orchard and, instead of fruit growing on the trees, you might find emeralds. The djinn have powers we'd call magic. They can change into animals or turn to smoke and actually get stuck in bottles when people know the right spells. If they get into our reality, they can do magic too—not as much as in their homeland but plenty compared to us. The thing is, they can only get through at certain energetic points, where the separation between the dimensions thins. One of those points is under this brownstone. That's why Saul bought it. The freemasons drew on its energy for their rituals, but he believed the power nexus could do more. Your grandfather and your father made a lifelong project of trying to open a portal, so they could travel to the djinn world. And here's the God's honest truth . . .

"Your dad succeeded."

David looked straight at her through the screen. He was totally serious. Elyse pressed her hand to her mouth.

"It's true, Elyse. Cara thinks he used his job at Solomon Imports to search for clues in countries where the djinn travel back and forth more frequently.

Your dad certainly had a knack for finding magical artifacts. He left quite a few hiding in plain sight in your living room. This isn't me getting carried away with one of my enthusiasms. I've actually seen them work.

"Your Uncle Vince knows about this stuff too. As a kid, he eavesdropped on Saul and Leo. As an adult, he did his own research, sometimes retracing Leo's tracks, sometimes taking his own sidetrips. He told Cara he knew the first time Leo crossed into the djinn dimension. Claimed he could see the excitement in his eyes afterward. I don't know exactly when he confronted your dad about it. I do know your dad admitted he'd cracked the secret to the door but wouldn't let Vince have access. He didn't trust Vince not to abuse it. Leo was all about the wonder. Meeting the different djinn. Being their friend. Learning about their world. I don't think he was as distrustful of Vince as your grandfather, but Leo did accuse your uncle of wanting to steal the djinn's treasures, of wanting to use their magic to get unfair advantages here."

David hitched his shoulders. "From what I've seen, that's probably true. Your Uncle Vince is kind of ambitious. I admit, the power angle was how Cara roped me into courting you after your father died, to find out what you knew. She remembered from college that I was into the paranormal. We'd stay up after everyone in the house, talking ghosts and psychics over cheap wine. That was all it was, though. We never did sleep together, but she thought I was the type you'd go for. Before I met you, I'd never had anyone just love me and not be out for their own interest. You made me want to be decent, to be the man you thought I was. It's no excuse, but I was afraid if I told you the truth, those feelings would go away. Hell, I was afraid if I didn't keep the charm going on the magic poetry book, they would. I'm sorrier than I can I say, Elyse. I wish I weren't too much of a coward to tell you this face to face."

He did look sorry, though Elyse had trouble swallowing what he said. Maybe she didn't want to swallow it. Him saying Cara "roped" him into courting her put a big enough lump in her throat. The David in the video cleared his.

"Ironically," he said, "Cara figuring out I love you is what makes me think my life might be in danger. Aside from it bugging the hell out of her, she doesn't trust me like before. When I swear you don't know your dad's secret, I can tell she thinks I'm lying. She thinks we're in cahoots together, and keeping it from her and her dad. She knows how much Leo loved you, and she assumes he must have shared what he knew with you. I think he meant to. I think he would have if he hadn't feared the truth would put you in danger."

David heaved a sigh. "Please listen to this bit, sweetie, even if you doubt everything else I said. That thing with your dad falling into the volcano is just too damned crazy. I don't have proof, but I think maybe Vince arranged to have your father killed before he got the chance to share the truth with you. He must have thought that without your dad around to block him, he'd be able to find the secret to controlling the door himself. He must not have expected Leo to lock it up so effectively. You can't trust him, Elyse, and you can't trust Cara either. I only pray you trust me because, honey, I'll love you forever."

A single tear rolled from his eye and down his cheek. He tipped his glasses up to rub it away. "Okay," he said. "I guess that's it. I don't know if you'll want to try to open the nexus yourself or get the hell out of Dodge. Either way, if there is such a thing as an afterlife, I'll do whatever I can to look out for you. Bless you, Elyse. You're the best thing that ever happened to me in my whole sorry life."

The video ended, leaving Elyse stunned and crying a bit herself. She hadn't known her husband thought of his life as sorry. She'd understood his parents were kind of horrid, the sort who hurt without hitting. The few anecdotes he'd shared hadn't been detailed. *They're the past,* he'd said. *Not worth ruining the present thinking about.* Maybe they'd damaged him more than she'd realized.

She wiped her cheeks. David's upbringing didn't explain a wholesale descent into delusion. On the other hand, if this crazy account were true, David's interest in hearing stories about *her* father made a new kind of sense. As did Cara pretending to dislike him. And her uncle's offers to "help" her manage the brownstone.

Come to think of it, Arcadius had encouraged her to talk about her dad over dinner. Was he trying to control the mythical door as well? Was that why he and Joseph rented the apartment?

God, her brain was going to explode. She snapped the laptop shut and stood. Before she could decide what to do, Arcadius appeared on the threshold.

She didn't think that was a coincidence.

~

Arcadius lied when he said he'd wait in the living room. He *had* to know what was on David's recording. The potential fallout for himself and his city was too great. Because of that, he didn't feel guilty for lurking in the hall listening. A little embarrassed, maybe, and worried for Elyse.

When he stepped into the doorway, she spun around in the office chair. He met her accusatory glare stoically.

"Are you after this door thing too? Have you convinced yourself there's a real djinn world you can steal magic from?"

He'd braced himself for anger. Elyse's misinterpretation of his position momentarily tied his tongue. "Elyse, I *am* a djinni," he said once he recovered. "I'm here because my city is in danger, and I need to get back to it."

"Oh. My. God." Elyse slapped the heels of her palms over both her eyes. "You're crazier than I thought."

"I'm not crazy. I had to escape a grave danger, one that would have rendered me useless for helping my people. To prevent that from happening,

I projected part of myself into your world."

"The part that, coincidentally, looks like a regular human being?"

"I looked human before. Many djinn do in their daily form. Unfortunately, my projection can't get home without your father's door."

"Arcadius," Elyse said, enunciating precisely. "There is no such thing as djinn. Consequently, you are not one."

Considering what had transpired last night, Arcadius hadn't expected convincing her would be hard. Were humans truly this good at denial?

"Elyse," he said. "Don't you remember what happened in the limo?"

"You told me what happened. There was an accident. We were thrown clear and I passed out."

"What about before you passed out? Don't you remember what you saw?"

Uneasiness crossed her face, but a moment later it tightened stubbornly. "I saw the white van speeding toward us down the cross street. After that, everything is blank."

Her husband's office was small. Arcadius reached Elyse in two strides. Frowning, she craned her neck at him from the swiveling chair.

"I know you're scared," he said gently. "But I also know you're not fragile. It's important that you not run away from your own knowledge. You saw me, Elyse. You saw me change into my smoke form. You screamed bloody murder, as it happens. *That's* what made you pass out. I pulled you from the limo before the crash, which is why neither of us was hurt. I flew you home far above the city."

"The Chrysler Building . . ."

"Yes, I expect we passed that."

Elyse stuck her thumbnail between her teeth. "People don't turn to smoke," she said less surely than before. "And sometimes otherwise rational people hallucinate nutty things. They catch beliefs from each other. Like UFOs or Bigfoot. That's how mass hysteria works."

He let out his breath slowly. "What if I showed you?"

"You can't."

Possibly he couldn't but he could try. "Watch my hand," he said, holding it out flat in front of her.

He closed his eyes and concentrated. Back home, this would have been as easy as a human standing up or sitting. He told himself the power was within him and ready. He simply had to find the right metaphysical muscles to direct.

The surface of his hand tingled, heat beginning to radiate outward. Matter was mostly empty space. Solids and gases were simply different energetic states. He fed more energy into his, imagining soft black smoke supplanting flesh and bone.

Elyse gasped like a rifle shot.

He looked down. He'd done it. A dark gray cloud-hand swirled at the end of his arm. Its shape was blurred but identifiable. He curled his smoky fingers then opened them one by one.

"This is my other form," he said. "What I look like out of my human shape."

He reached toward her. Elyse shrank back before he could make contact. Her eyes were huge, her lips trembling visibly.

"This won't hurt," he said. "This is what I used to carry you from danger."

He brushed her cheek lightly. He knew she felt the subtle magnetic touch because she immediately kicked the rolling chair back from him.

"I can't do this," she said, jumping up from the seat. "I have to get out of here."

"Elyse—"

She paused at the threshold. "I'm sorry. I don't mean to hurt your feelings, but I can't be this close to you. I need a chance to . . . process all of this."

Arcadius assured himself being hurt was irrelevant. He had to focus on what mattered. "You're not safe on your own, Elyse. Last night's crash wasn't an accident. I believe someone meant to harm us both."

Her already wide eyes widened. "I won't go far," she said, her voice almost too breathy to understand. "I just can't stay here right now."

~

Elyse wanted to run screaming from the building and hire the first cab she saw to drive her to Canada. She settled for the shared hallway on her floor, with the door to her apartment shut firmly behind her. She couldn't get the hell out of Dodge anyway.

She'd left her purse back in the living room.

Her panicked laugh stayed mostly in her throat.

She must be the stupidest woman in Creation, either for giving any credence to David's story or for not suspecting all along.

Could her father have discovered a secret world and not told her? Was Arcadius actually a genie? Maybe she'd hallucinated what he'd done to his hand. People's minds could play tricks on them. Look how she *almost* recalled being flown across Manhattan now that he'd planted the idea in her head.

Think, Elyse, she told herself. *What do your instincts tell you is true?*

That was her father's advice. Not "what do other people think?" Not "what's the most sensible explanation?" He wanted her to trust her own take on things.

A man who used that as his yardstick might be open to believing in genies.

Elyse let her eyes open. Her instincts told her to believe what she'd seen. Arcadius wasn't human and David hadn't been lying. She also believed he loved her, so on that score her judgment hadn't been abysmal. Maybe on other scores as well. For most of her life, she'd had mixed feelings about Cara and Uncle Vince. She'd shoved those feelings aside because they were family.

She thought back to her father's death. Uncle Vince always seemed to work to make people like him, with his loud jokes and his fancy house and his big gestures. Her father had drawn people to him without effort. One conversation at an airport, and he'd have a lifelong friend—as if being loveable was simply his nature. Uncle Vince was sad after her father died, but he'd also seemed more relaxed. Elyse had assumed this was due to being out of his big brother's shadow, to finally being free of the inevitable comparisons.

What if the reason for the change were more sinister?

David's claim that him falling for Elyse bugged the hell out of Cara was credible. Murdering him for it seemed a stretch, unless maybe Uncle Vince was responsible for that? She didn't want to believe either of them capable of killing him so horrifically—or of hiring someone else. Clearly, people she thought she knew had the power to fool her. She glanced at the door behind her. She wanted to trust Arcadius, though that could be because she'd slept with him.

Not trusting anyone struck her as unpleasant.

The door across the hall creaked open, causing Elyse's heart to jump. She sagged as she saw Mrs. Goldberg. The old lady was shuffling out in her housecoat and slippers with a little tied-up bag for the garbage chute. She nearly dropped it when she saw Elyse.

"Goodness," she said. "You startled me."

"Sorry," she said—or tried to. Her voice was scratchy from her turbulent emotions.

Mrs. Goldberg cocked her head at her. "Are you all right, dear? You look upset."

Elyse's nosy neighbor was no monster, but she was often crotchety. Her unexpected concern caused Elyse's tears to spill over.

Mrs. Goldberg immediately tut-tutted. "You should come in for tea," she said, waving her toward her door with a gnarled hand. "You can tell me all about it."

Elyse nearly laughed. She couldn't tell her anything, not without Mrs. Goldberg having too tasty a story to spread around.

"Oolong," her neighbor said temptingly.

Elyse gave in. Anything that delayed her having to deal with Arcadius seemed like a good option.

She hadn't been inside the other sixth floor unit since Mrs. Goldberg's sink backed up while the plumber was on vacation. The decor was the faded jumble she expected from a tenant who'd lived here forever. Too many chairs and tables crowded the space, topped by too many cheap knickknacks. The paintings on the wall were so bland and muddy it hardly seemed worth the trouble of hanging them.

Old motel art, Elyse thought, catching sight of some blah pink flowers in a blah brown vase.

Mrs. Goldberg ate a lot of meals in front of her TV. A rickety folding table with a tray stood by the recliner that faced it. To Elyse's surprise, the television was a large LED model. Maybe her tenant didn't need rent control as much as she'd thought.

"Come into the kitchen, dear," Mrs. Goldberg said. "I'll get the kettle going and we can be cozy."

Cozy was right. Though the layout of this unit mirrored hers, the wall between Mrs. Goldberg's kitchen and living room was intact. The enclosed cooking space was tiny, the Formica table tucked in the corner barely big enough for two. Despite the lack of space, the kitchen was cheerier than the rest of the apartment.

"This is very kind of you," Elyse said. "Can I help with anything?"

Mrs. Goldberg set the kettle on the gas burner. "I may be slow but I do everything. Tea is in that cabinet by you. You could get it down for me."

The cabinet held pretty tins with loose leaves. Elyse placed the oolong where her neighbor could get to it. As she leaned back against the edge of the countertop, she noticed a sleek little notebook computer open on the cutting board opposite.

"That's cute," she said. "Is it the kind where the keyboard snaps on and off?"

Mrs. Goldberg turned to look. "Silly me, leaving that there. I was typing out a recipe for a friend of mine. I should finish doing that before I forget. I love email, don't you?"

Amused, Elyse watched her abandon the kettle to peck a quick message. The steam began to whistle as she clicked "send."

"Perfect timing," her hostess said, shutting the tablet with obvious satisfaction. She hummed as she prepared a tea ball to steep. Elyse didn't think she'd heard her do that before. Was the old lady grumpy because she didn't have enough company?

"Delicious," Elyse said, sipping the cup Mrs. Goldberg poured her. The oolong was smooth and rich and just the right temperature.

"Years of practice," Mrs. Goldberg said.

A click from the outer room, like a door opening, jerked Elyse's head around.

"That's just the forced air blowers going on," her hostess assured her. "Such noisy things. Now that you have your tea, why don't you tell me what's troubling you?"

The thickness of her corrective lenses made her eyes look big and interested.

"It's not that important—" Elyse began to say.

Something pricked the side of her neck, as if a bee had stung her. She lifted her hand to touch the spot, but her knees went out from under her. Just as shocking was someone catching her from behind.

The arms that held her were familiar.

"Mrs. G," her cousin Cara praised. "You really should have been on the stage."

"Shouldn't I though!" The old lady seemed unsurprised by this turn of events. Elyse would have sworn the woman and her cousin only knew each other well enough to nod "hello."

"Crap," Elyse said. She sat on awkwardly folded legs on the kitchen floor. She'd have gone down completely if Cara hadn't been holding her. Elyse's arms were limp, her tongue thick feeling. "She emailed you that I was here. She's been your spy all along."

"'Spy' is such a judgey word," Cara scolded. "Mrs. G and I are friends."

"She told you when I rented the basement unit. You crashed that dinner with Arcadius and Joseph because she'd given you a heads up."

"I had to see if they were threats to my interest, didn't I?"

Her interest, not her and her father's.

Elyse shut her mouth against commenting and twisted around to see Cara's face. It wasn't easy. All her muscles were rubbery.

"What did you give me?" she slurred.

Cara smiled pleasantly. "Nothing that will kill you. I am fond of you, you know. And now I think I should return you to your apartment. Family business should stay that way, don't you think?"

"Mrs. G" probably would have preferred to be included, but "Enjoy yourself, dear," was all she said.

Before it occurred to Elyse that she could still scream, Cara whipped a dashing Emilio Pucci scarf from around her neck and used it to muzzle her. Elyse was unable to walk or stand. Cara had to grip her under the arms and drag her backwards through the living room to the building's hall. Elyse estimated it was around seven a.m. by then. One of her tenants was going out the street door to walk her dog. She couldn't see Elyse, of course. When the little terrier barked, she just shushed her.

Cara laughed softly. "This is a bit undignified, isn't it?"

Be there, Elyse thought to Arcadius as Cara opened Elyse's door. Elyse hadn't locked it when she came out. She'd been too eager to get away. If only Arcadius were a mind reader, she could warn him to do something.

"There we go," Cara said, using one beautifully shod foot to shut the door behind them.

She was huffing but not a lot. Elyse wished she'd been eating more pasta. Maybe with a few more pounds she'd have been harder to lug around. She growled through the scarf as Cara dropped her a little roughly into an armchair.

"Sorry," she said, not meaning it. Her eyes danced with enjoyment as she flipped her honey blonde hair away from her face. "Stay there while I find something more to tie you. Oh, wait, you can't move, can you?"

There was an upside to getting taken captive by her cousin: Elyse was too irritated to be fearful.

Cara strode briskly down the hall as if no one could possibly stop her. Had Mrs. Goldberg not noticed Arcadius staying over? Or did Cara have better knowledge of his whereabouts than Elyse? Had he left when she ran out on him? God, she hated being gagged. Not being able to ask questions was really annoying.

She heard drawers opening and shutting in David's office. Sadly, no one seemed to be leaping out to subdue her captor. Cara said "ah-ha!" and then fell silent. When she returned to the living room, she was beaming from ear to ear. A roll of duct tape circled one forearm like a cuff bracelet. This, however, wasn't the reason for the joy in her expression.

Between both hands, which she'd lifted to breast level, she held the little volume of magical love poems: the same volume Arcadius and David believed would ensure she loved him. Elyse had left it on David's desk, where anyone—including potentially homicidal relatives—could find it.

Fuck, was Elyse's fervent mental reaction.

"Thank you for still having this," Cara gushed. "You have no idea how useful this is to me!"

She wasn't kidding. She opened the book then and there. She filled her lungs, exhaled, and settled her shoulders. When she'd composed herself, her gaze lifted to Elyse. A glint of anticipation lit her green eyes. "Brace yourself, cuz. Only one person at a time can use this charm. You may find you don't adore your departed husband quite so much in a few minutes."

Elyse had assumed the love spell ended when the book shocked her. Maybe Cara didn't know that, or maybe something new would happen. She tensed as Cara turned the pages in sequence, running her manicured finger across the lines. Her eyes moved but not her lips, so Elyse guessed Arcadius was right about the caster of the spell not needing to know Arabic. When Cara reached the final page, she closed her eyes, shut the book, and pressed it against her breasts.

"Infinite Power," she murmured, "binder of hearts: cause the man whose image is in my mind to fall in love with me."

Elyse couldn't help but be fascinated. As Cara finished speaking, some sort of energy wisped out from the book's pages. Though the wisps took the form of smoke, they glowed golden. For a few seconds, the tendrils whirled around themselves in the air, pretty but aimless.

"*Do my bidding*," Cara insisted.

The smoke brightened, spread out, and winked out of sight.

"Good," Cara said, like she'd ticked off number two on her to-do list, right after *Drug and kidnap Elyse*. She tucked the book beneath a pile of other leather bound volumes on a shelf.

"Feel any different?" she asked Elyse.

Elyse shook her head, annoyed that even this small motion made her dizzy. She curled her hands around the arms of the chair she was sitting in, her grip sufficient to keep her from falling over but not to push her up.

"Ah, well," Cara said philosophically. "Perhaps the hero worship takes a while to wear off."

A really, truly annoying possibility occurred to Elyse. What if Cara had just caused Arcadius to fall in love in her? She huffed around the scarf Cara had stuffed in her mouth. Cara glanced at her but was occupied with pulling down the shades in the living room. Once the windows were blocked, she returned to Elyse with the duct tape at the ready. Something shiny on the couch caught her eye.

"Hm," she said, slipping whatever it was into her pocket.

Go right ahead, Elyse thought, pointlessly infuriated. *Steal anything you want.*

At the moment, Cara seemed immune to shame. As adeptly as if she took hostages all the time, she attached Elyse's wrists and ankles to the chair.

Elyse didn't bother making angry noises, but she glared really hard.

"Oh, don't be that way," Cara said. "You didn't have to choose to side with David. All right, maybe you did but that's water under the bridge. Now we'll just tackle this head on and make things turn out the way they should." Crouched down to strap her left ankle to the chair leg, she patted Elyse's knee. "I should probably warn you not to count on your new friends coming to the rescue. They're currently indisposed, though you were a clever girl to spot what they were and recruit them to your side.

"I didn't know for sure myself until you escaped that car crash. Funny how the driver saw all that smoke and nothing had caught on fire. Even funnier was both his passengers disappearing without a trace. The crash wasn't supposed to kill you, by the way, just put you out of commission. As a general thing, Dad doesn't like having family blood on his hands."

As a *general thing?* Did that mean he sometimes made exceptions?

Elyse shivered. She'd fallen down a rabbit hole where her uncle might very well have killed her father and her cousin might still kill her. She wished she'd been as clever as Cara thought. Not that pleading ignorant would help. Cara was one of those people who couldn't be convinced they were wrong.

Satisfied Elyse was secure, Cara rose and dug out her cell phone. She called someone she had on speed dial.

"We're a go up here," she said.

CHAPTER
NINE

ARCADIUS hadn't wanted to let Elyse leave. This dimension's attitudes about not overprotecting women confused him. He'd said himself she wasn't fragile. He knew she could run her own life. Being bulletproof, however, wasn't a quality she could claim. She also wasn't magic-proof, which was just as relevant.

Hearing her go into the neighbor's unit eased his mind somewhat.

Hoping to ease it more, he dug out his new cell phone. Joseph should be told what was going on.

Joseph didn't answer even after many rings.

Arcadius's chest tightened. Joseph had been quick to adopt this world's technology. He wouldn't turn off his phone any more than he'd ignore his master's ring. Something was wrong. Arcadius needed to get to him.

He grabbed his coat but didn't bother to find his shoes. If Joseph were in trouble, time was of the essence. He bounded down the building stairs, pausing at the vestibule to scan the street outside. The metropolis's morning was getting into gear. Vehicles trundled by and pedestrians strode the sidewalks in work attire. One dark sedan was begging for a ticket from the police. It had parked in front of a fireplug. Other than that, he saw nothing suspicious.

Cursing under his breath, he covered the distance from the brownstone's front steps to their below-street entrance as nonchalantly as a barefoot person could pull off in the snow. Remembering the window, he approached the door at a crouch. What he spied through the security bars made him glad he'd taken the precaution.

Two men stood in the small living room. The first was well dressed and slightly portly, with striking salt-and-pepper hair. The second was tall and muscular and wore handyman overalls. Joseph didn't appear to be enjoying their company. He sat on the modern black couch—not in a relaxed pose.

The better dressed of the intruders had a gun trained on him, which probably explained why Joseph hadn't answered his call. Arcadius instantly recognized the other man, due to his distinctive shaved head and thorny black tattoos.

He should have known he'd cross paths with the man who killed Elyse's spouse. He reached for the blade he kept in his ankle sheath . . . and remembered he'd left it tucked beneath the pillow on Elyse's couch. Cursing didn't make it reappear. He'd have to do this unarmed.

He reassessed the situation. Tattoos' broad back was angled to the door. He held something in his hands, over which he was chanting. Allowing that to continue didn't seem like a good idea. Joseph's face was tight with dread, the older man's gun preventing him from fleeing.

Arcadius prayed a distraction would allow his associate to save himself.

Testing the door revealed that the knob would turn. Arcadius eased it open and slipped silently inside. There was no cover to hide behind. He had a second to debate which target to address first.

The man with the gun decided for him.

"Hey," he said, his arm swinging around toward Arcadius. His voice was deep, his face oddly familiar. Arcadius ducked to make himself a smaller target and ran for him. Unfortunately for his spur of the moment plan, the man didn't lose his cool. As he faced Arcadius's rush, he planted his feet squarely. His second hand joined his first on the grip, and he pulled the trigger.

He didn't miss.

Arcadius grunted as a bullet hit him high in the chest, beneath his left shoulder. The room flashed hot. He assumed it was a pain reaction, but as he fell forward onto his hands, Joseph screamed. Thick billows of black smoke erupted through the room. The cloud swirled and hissed as if it were angry.

"*Do my bidding*," Tattoos intoned ritually. He lifted his hands, which held a small brass oil lamp—the same lamp, Arcadius suspected, that recently adorned Elyse's living room.

As if he were being sucked by powerful vacuum, every bit of Joseph's smoke essence disappeared into it.

"Don't get any funny ideas," the man pointing the gun ordered Arcadius.

Funny ideas seemed unlikely. Serious ones maybe. On the floor but half sitting up, Arcadius pressed one hand to his chest. His head was swimming, the hole the bullet made bleeding copiously.

"I can stick him in here too," Tattoos offered. "Killing him seems a waste."

"Fine," said the older man. "Just do it quickly. He'll bleed out if he doesn't change form soon."

Their awareness of this was interesting. Suddenly Arcadius knew why the gunman's features were familiar. "You must be Uncle Vince," he wheezed.

Uncle Vince snorted as his accomplice recommenced chanting.

Magic wasn't simply the djinn's birthright, it was their Achilles' heel: the Creator's way of evening the scales if the more powerful race tried to take advantage of humans. Tattoos had his chant down pat, or he couldn't have transformed a skilled practitioner like Joseph against his will. He wrenched Arcadius into his smoke and fire shape even more speedily. While Arcadius didn't regret losing the pumping bullet wound, the sensation of being squeezed into the lamp was highly uncomfortable.

As soon as he was all in, he popped back into his normal form. From his captors' standpoint, he'd shrunk down to toy size. From his perspective, the lamp had grown very big. The reservoir was empty, though the musty smell of old olive oil overwhelmed. Joseph was there already, dry heaving on his hands and knees by the curving wall. He wasn't far from the nozzle hole, through which the wick would feed if it were lit. The floor of the lamp bobbed like an anchored ship in a rough harbor. Grateful the motion wasn't worse, Arcadius lurched carefully to Joseph. The oil residue was sticky beneath his feet. Because Joseph wasn't getting up, he knelt down and rubbed his back.

"Sorry, master," the servant said miserably. "I wasn't clever enough to stop them."

At moments like this, when Joseph took so much weight upon himself, Arcadius felt like his father.

"Neither was I," Arcadius said. "But in every battle some events go awry. The important thing is not giving up. Take a minute to recover. We'll figure a way out of this."

Joseph groaned. "My body wasn't ready to be changed. I feel terrible."

Arcadius supposed he had his rescue of Elyse to thank for the fact that he felt all right. He'd already cleared that hurdle. "Lift your head closer to the spout where the air is fresh."

Without air, they'd have had to stay in smoke form. Arcadius helped Joseph move, keeping his arm around his shoulders even after his shakes lessened.

"All right," he said then. "Tell me everything you've learned."

Joseph had been paying attention. He'd discovered the tattooed man's name was Mario. Elyse's Uncle Vince acted like he was the boss of the partnership, but Mario had betrayed signs of having his own ambitions. "Mario doesn't respect him," Joseph said. "I saw him sneering behind Elyse's uncle's back. From what I pieced together, Mario plans to enslave a gang of djinn to commit crimes for him. After he's honed the art of control on us, he'll journey through the nexus to capture more. Vince doesn't seem to care about that. He's interested in treasure. He views Mario as hired muscle. I don't think he suspects his associate wants to take over."

"You learned a lot," Arcadius observed.

"They weren't careful how they spoke. I don't think they saw me as a threat."

"What about the spell? Did Mario leave any holes your magic can sneak through?"

"Not that I could tell." Joseph's shoulders sagged. "I fear our gooses are truly cooked. Elyse's too. They believe the three of us are working together, and that she knows more than she's admitted."

The message David left for Elyse made this unsurprising news. Arcadius very much disliked being unable to go to her, but hopefully she'd stay safe with her neighbor until he could. "What about this lamp?"

"It is a proper djinn artifact. The lid is stamped with the full Seal of Solomon, the same as the wise king wore on his signet ring. No spell I know can break through that."

Arcadius recalled picking up the lamp at Elyse's place. He'd been convinced it was empty, though he hadn't tried opening it. Something about the memory nagged at him.

"The spout," he breathed quietly. "It had no stopper. And this Mario fellow hasn't yet put one in. He probably doesn't know he should."

Joseph's eyes went round. "We *can* get out. Master, you are the wisest djinni who ever lived."

Arcadius knew that wasn't true. Neither of them would be in this fix if it were.

"We'll watch for our moment," he said. "They'll probably take the lamp with them wherever they go next, but at some point their attention will shift to something else."

"And out we'll smoke," Joseph said. "May God the Merciful smile on us."

Arcadius murmured a quick prayer of agreement.

~

Cara paced the length of the living room, waiting for whomever she'd phoned to arrive. Elyse had plenty of time to admire her figure-flattering white blouse and black trousers. Her crisply clacking heels looked like Jimmy Choos.

Cara dressed stylishly for every occasion, she supposed.

Under the circumstances, feeling frumpy in her jeans and T-shirt was pointless. She focused on her relief that whatever Cara had drugged her with was wearing off. She was duct taped to a chair and couldn't escape, but at least her head was clear enough to consider how she might.

It was also clear enough to realize she'd kill for a cup of Joseph's spine-stiffening Turkish brew.

Oh, my God, she thought, a tingle sweeping across her scalp. When Joseph said he used magic to make the coffee, he hadn't been kidding. He was a genie too.

All right, Elyse's thought processes really had been sluggish.

Normally, she tuned out the building's various noises. With nothing to do but listen, she heard multiple sets of feet coming up the stairs. Cara heard them too. She immediately fluffed her hair, undid two more buttons on her white blouse, and turned to face the door. She rubbed her lips together to ensure her bronzy lipstick covered them evenly. Finally, she took a deep breath and smiled. A quiet knock sounded.

"It's open," Cara called.

After witnessing that little preparation, Elyse was interested to see who came in. The chair she'd been taped to faced the front windows. If she turned, she could see the fireplace on one side and the door on the other. The first person to enter was Uncle Vince—surely not who her cousin had primped for. Unable to speak, Elyse met his gaze unflinchingly, telling him as clearly as she could what she thought of his behavior. He looked away, irritation and a hint of shame fighting for the upper hand in his expression. Defensiveness defeated both.

The reaction was classic Uncle Vince. Nothing could ever be his fault.

Then Elyse noticed the man behind him.

Damn it, she *was* the biggest idiot in Creation. Uncle Vince's companion was Mario, her tattooed substitute handyman. Screw being PC. She should have trusted her original suspicions.

He seemed to enjoy her reaction. He grinned, tipping two fingers from his temple to her in acknowledgment. Then he caught sight of Cara.

His stride faltered, his jaw dropping. He acted like he'd never seen her before, though Elyse was under the impression the trio had been conspiring for a while. That didn't seem to matter. Mario's breath sucked in, one fist pressing his breastbone. His eyes were actually glazing as Elyse watched color bloom in his cheeks.

Oh, she thought. *He's the man Cara wanted to fall in love with her.* She couldn't deny she was relieved. A second later, she felt unnerved. Had she looked like that the first time she met David?

"Dad," Cara said with a little smile. "Mario." She put an extra purr in his name. "As you can see, I've been busy."

Mario shook himself, immediately looking more normal or trying to. He was carrying something like a football in the bend of his arm.

"Cara," he said gruffly. "Good job as usual."

"Can we get on with this?" Uncle Vince prodded impatiently.

"Are the djinn secured?" Cara asked Mario, temporarily ignoring her father.

With one tattooed hand, Mario tapped the object he held. Elyse sat straighter. That was *her* Aladdin's lamp, one of her favorite presents from her father. Cara must have stolen it to give to him.

"Locked up tight," he said.

His gaze connected with Cara's. He'd lost his glaze. He reminded Elyse of a badass biker guy in a bar who'd settled on his night's target. *Yes,* his dark eyes were saying. *You're coming home with me.* Pleased with the attention, Cara simpered and stroked her neck. Mario didn't seem to mind.

"For God's sake," Vince snapped. "My daughter flirts with every male on two legs. Set up the shield so we can interrogate my niece."

Mario appeared startled to have been so transparent. He set the Aladdin's lamp on a table—not the table it belonged on, Elyse thought in annoyance. Hands free, he pulled a ball of twine from one of his work uniform's side pockets. He unrolled it quickly, forming a wiggly circle around her living room, perhaps ten feet in diameter. When he ran out of string, he tied the ends together and muttered a single word. Elyse's ears popped. She guessed the shield was in place.

"The twine blocks sound from leaving the circle," Cara explained helpfully. "You can scream all you want and no one will hear."

Uncle Vince didn't seem to want to remove her gag. He waved for Cara to handle it. She leaned closer than she needed to untie the scarf, which Elyse childishly hoped her spit had ruined.

"Just cooperate," Cara said in Elyse's ear. "I can keep you safe if you don't resist."

Elyse wasn't sure what her cousin meant by *cooperation* or *safety*. For the moment, she didn't care. She worked her jaw, swallowed, and turned her head to her uncle. She had no idea in her mind of accomplishing anything. She simply had to ask.

"Uncle Vince," she said. "Did you arrange for my father to fall into that volcano?"

He was leaning back against the fireplace, thick and solid in his expensive suit. His shoes were inside Mario's sound-cancelling twine circle, so presumably he'd heard. He didn't speak. He crossed his arms and glared.

This was answer enough for her.

"You did," she said. "God." Her voice broke and she swallowed again. "Uncle Vince, he was your *brother*. How could you do that to him?"

Suddenly he was so angry his eyes practically spit fire. "Leo kept me from what was mine. He and my father. Their precious djinn were more important to them than me. They acted like a goldmine shouldn't make a profit! My whole life, they treated me like dirt they were too good to step on."

Elyse knew that wasn't true, not in her father's case. Leo sometimes treated Vince cautiously but never with meanness. She shut her open mouth. There was no point in saying this.

"Dad." Cara went to his side to pet his arm soothingly. "We don't need to get into this. Elyse understands you had your reasons." She shot Elyse a pointed glance, one whose meaning she didn't comprehend. "She's going to help us make things the way they ought to be."

Elyse didn't see how she'd manage that. She didn't have the secret to opening her dad's door. She wasn't much of a liar either, which Cara really should have known.

Arcadius and Joseph shelved their plan to escape the lamp as soon it became clear their captors had Elyse. Judging by the briefness of the trip and the steps Mario had climbed, they'd been taken to her apartment. They could hear but not see what was going on outside.

Listening to Elyse ask her uncle if he'd killed her father caused Arcadius's heart to clench.

"Her speech is slurred," Joseph said, his head cocked toward the nozzle hole. The lamp being set down on a flat surface made it easier to stay crouched by it. "I wonder if she was drugged."

Arcadius's fingers curled into fists. "I need to assess the situation. See who's where and what weapons are in play."

"Could you smoke out invisibly?"

At home, he could have. The more refined version of his non-solid form was no more noticeable than vapor above a cup of tea. "You don't think *you* can?" he asked Joseph. Normally the servant was better at these things.

"I doubt I can change at all. Being forced to shift seems to have interfered with my abilities. But if you want me to try . . ."

"No." Arcadius saw he'd grown too accustomed to Joseph taking the lead in magical matters. "We may need your powers later. I don't want you straining them again now."

They fell silent, focused on what was happening in the room outside.

"You do it then," Vince Solomon was saying. "Make her tell us what we want to know."

"I don't know anything," Elyse said. "I didn't know there was a nexus in my basement until today."

"Elyse." Her cousin's tone was gentle and disappointed. "Don't lie to us. None of us wants to be forced to hurt you."

"I could live with it," Mario said.

"Shush," Cara scolded. "She'll tell us. I know she will. Think, Elyse. What did your father use to open the portal? It could be anything. Maybe an item he carried with him all the time. Or a gift he sent home that he told you to take extra good care of."

"He never said things like that," Elyse responded. "I was the only one upset if I broke something."

"Tell us!" her uncle burst out in a roar.

"*Dad.*"

"She has to answer," Joseph said in an undertone as Cara calmed her father. "They won't believe she doesn't know."

Arcadius jerked. Someone had just been slapped. Though no one cried out, the obvious victim was Elyse.

"Tell us, bitch," Mario said. "We've wasted enough time tiptoeing around you."

"Mario!" Cara cried.

"Stop shielding her," Mario said. "She's in your way. You're a queen. You deserve to have everything you want."

"He's been spelled," Joseph said, his practiced ears instantly picking up on it.

Cara must have found the book. Clearly, she didn't realize charming a man to love her didn't necessarily mean she could control him. The situation seemed destined to spiral into disaster soon. Fueled by a sense of urgency, Arcadius began to slip his form.

"Give Elyse something to give them," Joseph advised hastily. "A genuine artifact preferably. Tattoos will know the difference between an object that's magical and one that's not."

Arcadius nodded before letting go of his solidness. He needed to find a likely fake quickly.

~

Elyse's cheek still stung from Mario's slap. Her eyes had teared up, but she'd clamped her mouth against crying out. What was the point if no one helpful heard?

"I'm taking you seriously," she assured him, staring straight into Mario's hard black eyes. "I simply don't have the answer you're looking for."

His brows lowered with suspicion, the movement causing the markings on his face to shift more than they should have. Maybe fear was making her see things. For a second, his tattoo seemed alive.

He lifted a finger to point at her. "You'd better find the answer."

"My father gave me lots of presents. Why don't you try them all?"

"Because every trial costs time and energy, and we still might not find what we need. Think, little girl. Your life depends on it."

Elyse was surprised he'd explained. She looked away, partly because his tattooed face unnerved her but also so she'd seem like she was doing what he'd said. Her attention settled on the Aladdin's lamp. It sat on a low drum table, maybe six feet away. Though Cara had pulled the shades, the day was brightening behind them. Light glinted on the pattern engraved in the tarnished brass.

Her mind flashed to Mario patting it.

Oh, hell. When he said the djinn were "locked up tight," he meant Arcadius and Joseph were in there. He'd forced them in magically.

Her heart thudded harder, the reality of all this craziness sinking in. Then she noticed something else. An ephemeral ribbon of vapor was issuing from the antique spout. Were the djinn escaping? Was it possible they could help? Not wanting anyone else to see, she blurted the first idea that came to her.

"Maybe the door thing is in my dad's safe deposit box. I have the key to that."

Mario looked intrigued, but Uncle Vince shot down the suggestion. "Leo wouldn't have locked the door away. Whatever the object is, he'd have kept it where he could get at it easily."

"What about the storage rooms in the basement? There's tons of stuff down there."

"We've gone through those," Mario said. The faintest smile touched his mouth, as if he'd recalled something that amused him.

Elyse's skin went cold. Had he gone through them before or after David's death?

The possibility stalled her brain. "I . . . don't know . . . what else to suggest," she stammered.

The hippo, the softest possible voice murmured in her ear.

It was Arcadius's voice, sort of.

"The hippo," she repeated, because she assumed she was supposed to. All her kidnappers stared at her. "It's a blue faience statuette. Egyptian. My dad gave it to me to replace one he sent home that was too big. You remember, Cara. It took up half my bedroom."

"I remember," her cousin said slowly.

Tell them your father said it was magic, Arcadius directed.

"Dad told me it was magic. At the time, I thought he wanted to make me feel better for having to give up the other one. It was exactly like the original, only small."

This brought a gleam into Mario's eye. "Where is it?"

"Um," Elyse said, momentarily stumped.

Top shelf, Arcadius said. *Over the fireplace.*

Elyse looked where he'd said. To her relief, she spotted a bit of blue. "There. At the very top."

The built-in shelves ran up to the high ceiling. Though he was tall, Mario needed to climb onto a chair to reach the statuette. He turned the hippo between his hands after he stepped down.

"Well?" Uncle Vince demanded.

"I can't tell if it's the door," Mario said, "but it's definitely been charmed."

Cara's father thrust his hand out imperiously. "Give it here."

Mario stared at him. "I'm the one who knows the spell."

"You're not the only one who knows it. Or have you forgotten who gave you the books you've been studying?"

"I haven't forgotten anything, including the 'favors' you had me do because you're too proud to get your hands dirty. You think it doesn't matter how many people a man like me kills."

"*Mario*," Cara exclaimed.

"Every man has his talents," Vince sneered unrepentantly.

Mario pulled a pistol from another of his pockets. Elyse had no idea what kind, just that it was big and black.

"Thanks for reminding me," he said. He clucked his tongue when Vince's hand started to move to his jacket. "I wouldn't if I were you. You're not quick enough to quick-draw me."

"Stop it!" Cara protested, putting the sound-cancelling twine to the test.

Mario barely glanced at her. "Come on, Cara. How many times have you called this old man a pain in the ass? We don't need him. You've got twice the brains he does." He laughed and cocked the hammer. "Actually, so do I."

"He's my *dad*." Cara's face was a study in panic, Vince's one of arrogant disbelief.

Fuck, Elyse thought, sensing what was coming before it did.

"He's not *my* dad," Mario said and calmly pulled the trigger.

The bang was loud, though she supposed no one outside the circle heard. A neat red hole appeared in the center of Vince's brow. His body jerked and fell over. The bullet's exit was messier. The shelves he'd stood in front of were sprayed with gore.

"Holy crap," Cara breathed, chalk white with shock. She crouched down to check for a pulse. "Holy crap, Mario, he's dead."

For a couple seconds, Mario looked abashed by her reaction. Then he rolled his big shoulders and recovered. "We're better off without him. All he did was piss people off, and that's not good business. Pull yourself together. Let's see if this little hippo is the real deal."

Cara's fear-round eyes glistened with unshed tears. She stood shakily, swiping her hands down her nice trousers.

"Thatta girl," Mario praised. "I'll call my boys to come clean this up. Grab that lamp while you're at it. You never know when we'll need three wishes."

Elyse couldn't tell if he was joking. Her breath caught unpleasantly in her throat when he looked at her. The glitter in his eyes was considerably different from Cara's. Elyse didn't think it was a trick of the light that his tattoos seemed to have taken on their own mocking expression.

It was like they were sentient.

"You'd better not be wrong," he said. "You don't want to find out what happens if I have to question you again."

Elyse was too terrified to utter a single sound.

Like her father before her, Cara avoided Elyse's gaze as she trailed her new lover out.

~

Arcadius rematerialized as soon as Cara and Mario trooped out. He looked around for something to release Elyse. When he lifted the pillow on the couch, the harness was there but not the knife he kept in it.

Well, fuck, he thought, mystified.

"Letter opener in that drawer," Elyse said, nodding toward where she meant. "It should be sharp enough."

He found the item and started sawing through the tape that bound her. "We have to get out of here. What happened to your neighbor?"

"She was Cara's informant," Elyse huffed. "So of course she's perfectly fine." Her gaze fell on her uncle's corpse, which was crumpled on the floor and not fine at all. "Jesus, what was wrong with that Mario guy? Cara's book of love poems didn't affect me that weirdly."

Arcadius finished freeing her second wrist and started on an ankle. "I think the spell must have interacted badly with his possessed tattoos."

"His *what?*"

"They're animated by a djinni's spirit, probably an ifrit. The spirit protects him from attacks, but it seems to have bonded with his own consciousness. Djinn are more susceptible to magic than humans. The love spell influenced Mario more intensely because of that."

"Jeesh." Elyse rubbed her unbound wrists.

Arcadius cut through the last stretch of tape. Since he was kneeling, he gripped her calves to focus her. "I have to go after them. Joseph is still in that lamp. He wasn't able to change and get out like me. Is there somewhere safe I can leave you?"

"Leave me?" The extent to which she was startled surprised him. "No way. I'm helping you rescue him."

"Elyse."

"You're not talking me out of it. I don't know who did what exactly, but because of Cara and Mario's scheming, my dad is dead. And David. And you and I could have been. I'm too involved to be left somewhere."

Arcadius searched her determined face. "You're not afraid?"

"I'm terrified. I'm just so mad I don't give a shit. Anyway, maybe I *do* know something. Those three certainly thought I did. —Just to be clear, that hippo wasn't the real door."

Arcadius smiled. "It wasn't, though hopefully we've gained time while they work that out."

"Shit," Elyse swore suddenly. "I hear people coming up the stairs."

"Mario's 'boys,'" Arcadius guessed. "They must be coming for the body."

Elyse jumped up and grabbed his arm. He noticed her hand was cold but steady. "We'll go out the back, down the fire escape. We can get into the basement from the courtyard. We'll steal the lamp back from them."

Arcadius saw a few gaping holes in this strategy but had no better plan to suggest.

"Okay," he said. "Try to stay behind me."

~

Elyse amazed herself. Despite the chaos in her brain, she had the presence of mind to grab Arcadius's shoes out of the bathroom. No one should have to climb down a fire escape in winter in bare feet. She descended first, forcing her knees not to wobble by sheer will. She was strangely glad to be obliged to *do* and not think.

After what seemed like much too slow a journey, she dropped into the cold still courtyard. Though his elegant wool coat flapped around his legs, Arcadius landed noticeably more nimbly.

She had her keys, so she let them into the back hall. At this point, Arcadius went ahead of her. "Stay close," he said very quietly.

They had to go through his unit to reach the unfinished section of the cellar. Elyse hadn't been here since padlocking the door to the mechanical room. This was the part of the basement where David had been slain, an event she now suspected involved the supernatural. Arcadius paused long enough to squeeze her shoulder. She appreciated the attempt at comfort but wasn't sure how she felt about him right then. He wasn't who he'd pretended to be any more than Cara or her uncle or Mario. Whatever his real agenda, he seemed to be on her side. She guessed she was on his, since she was doing this with him.

Her instincts told her he wasn't feigning his protectiveness of her.

He used the light from his cellphone screen to lead them through the maze of rooms. It didn't escape her notice that he knew where he was going. He must have searched the brownstone's cellar already.

When they reached the creepy janitor's john, he gestured for her to stop.

"Wait here. I want to see what they're doing and where they've put the lamp." She opened her mouth but he shook his head. "Don't worry. I'll be back."

She was nervous enough that she let him go.

He returned from reconnoitering in barely a minute. "They're in the center room with the nexus. The room where your husband died."

"The one with cement block walls?" She asked this without flinching.

"Yes. Mario is still chanting. He's trying to make the fake door you gave him open a portal to the djinn dimension. Your cousin has the lamp he trapped Joseph in. I know she's bigger than you but she isn't armed. If I provide a distraction, can you dash in and grab him?"

Elyse's throat felt tight. "Does this distraction involve you getting killed?"

Arcadius's mouth slanted to one side. "Hopefully not. I'm going to try something that should take them by surprise. I'm not sure I can pull it off, but my former powers do seem to be coming back online."

That piqued Elyse's curiosity. She trailed him nearer to the room where the magical nexus was. They stopped when they heard Mario's voice. Elyse couldn't tell if he was chanting in English. His words were running together.

They'd come close enough to see a blue luminescence within the room, too close to talk without alerting their enemies. Arcadius handed her his cell and began taking off his coat. She supposed the heavy garment would hamper him. Since she held the glowing phone, she got an unobstructed view of his emerging back.

She sucked in a breath of shock. Arcadius had a tattoo. He was shirtless, and the thing wasn't small. A raven with wings outspread stretched the full width of his broad shoulders. Was this part of what he meant by his powers coming back online? She *couldn't* have missed seeing the design earlier. She'd circled him in the altogether that first night in her shower. And she'd certainly had a sightline to the relevant area when he'd gone down on her on the couch.

That memory drew heat into her cheeks. Arcadius glanced at her, probably in response to her quiet gasp.

She pointed to his back and made flapping motions with her fingers.

Maybe he guessed what else she'd been thinking, because his grin smoldered.

He turned away to compose himself. His breath went in and out, and the musculature of his back relaxed. A thin seam of light appeared around the outline of the tattoo, like a distant galaxy peeping through his skin. Before the rays were bright enough to attract attention, the seam disappeared.

So did Arcadius.

A large black bird, every bit as real as she was, stared up at her from the cement floor. From beak to tail, it was bigger than most house cats. Its feathered head tilted to the side as if it were studying her.

Holy crap, she thought, her lips moving with the words.

The raven lifted its wings, its head swiveling toward the room from which the chanting came. With a little hop to get it started, it flew like a shot through the opening.

Elyse gaped after it like a dunderhead.

Cara and Mario began to shriek. The raven must be attacking them. Its wings were flapping, and it cawed a battle cry. In the middle of the mayhem, Mario's gun went off.

"Shit," she hissed, springing into action. This was the part where she was supposed to take advantage of Arcadius's distraction.

She ran into the cement block enclosure, remembering to crouch low at the last moment. She didn't have time to dwell on the last time she'd seen this room, with David's torn up body. Arcadius's raven swooped from Cara to Mario, flying at and pecking them. He didn't seem to be hurting them, but they certainly were freaked out. She caught sight of the source of the blue luminescence: a beach-ball-sized floating orb she assumed was the energy point.

Not important, she told herself. She looked around for the Aladdin's lamp. Cara didn't have it anymore. She must have dropped it when Arcadius dive-bombed her. Elyse spotted it lying on its side near the wall. She darted in and seized it.

"Stop her!" Mario shouted.

Cara was in no state to accomplish that. Mario tried to shoot Elyse, but the bullet just struck sparks off the wall and floor. Elyse ran out with her prize, hoping Joseph wasn't being bounced around inside the container. She heard Cara scream a second before the radiance from the nexus went out.

The cellar wasn't pitch black but it was close. Elyse had Arcadius's phone and could see where she was going. Of course, this meant the others knew where she was as well. Desperate to slow them down, she shoved whatever obstacles she could find in her wake. They wouldn't bother Arcadius. He could fly over them.

She pelted through the room with the fake Christmas trees. Strong wings beat the air behind her. Figuring Arcadius was faster than she was, she didn't wait for him. She spied the hot water heater up ahead, plus a crack of light where they'd left the door to the basement unit ajar. Arcadius sailed past her, knocking it farther open with his bird shoulder.

She ran inside after him, cursing as she tried to re-secure the padlock. This would have been easier if she'd set down the lamp, but she didn't want to let go of it. She shot the hasp home just as a burst of light flashed in the hall behind her.

Fortunately, the light was Arcadius changing form.

"Good," he panted.

Something heavy, presumably Mario, slammed into the now locked door.

Arcadius grabbed her elbow, pulling her toward the living room. They skidded to a halt at the sound of glass shattering.

Mario's boys were breaking the street door window. Mario must have called them away from body disposal. The alarm didn't go off. It wasn't set—not that alerting the police would help them in the short term.

"This way," Arcadius said, yanking her after him into the bedroom.

For a second, all she could do was goggle at the luxurious furnishings. This absolutely wasn't how David had decorated it.

Rather than try to block the door with the mammoth wardrobe—which would have been her choice of barricade—Arcadius tore a beautiful Middle Eastern tapestry of a boat off the wall.

"In here," he said.

He beckoned her toward a silver hula-hoop mysteriously inset into the paint. The area within it was strange and shadowy. Elyse's nerves chose then to balk.

"Hurry," he urged. He swung one leg into what should have been solid wall.

The street door burst open, raised male voices quickly closing in on them. Arcadius stretched his arm to her. There was nothing else to do. Elyse swallowed her fear, gripped his hand, and followed him.

CHAPTER TEN

ELYSE seriously considered changing her name to Alice. She seemed to have stepped through that character's looking glass and not just a wall. As soon as she was inside . . . wherever they were, Arcadius grabbed the silver hoop in both hands, using brute strength to rip it from the plaster. Her view of the room they'd exited disappeared, leaving their current location dim.

"There," Arcadius said, resting the hoop against a shadowy chair. "I've only removed the ring from this side, but its absence will make it harder for the others to follow us."

"Follow us where?" Elyse's breathing came shallowly. She clutched the lamp, relieved that she still had it. "What is this place?"

"Hold on. I'll get the light."

He found a switch and flipped it. Though the fixture above them held normal looking bulbs, no bulb she knew provided the sort of illumination that flooded through the room. The light was as fresh and clear as sunshine, revealing—without a doubt—that the ceiling wasn't flat anymore. It also wasn't low. Blue-and-white porcelain tiles lined a lovely four-section vault.

"Holy cow," was all she could say. If the space they'd left was luxurious, this put it in the shade. Their surroundings were an *Arabian Nights* illustration come to life: silks and rugs and pillows, all in the most delectable shades and patterns. The tapestry Arcadius had torn from the other wall still hung here. Its colors were even richer, the boat and waves more lifelike.

"Sindbad," Arcadius said, pointing to the tall young man who stood proudly at its prow.

"I don't understand," she said. "This isn't part of my basement."

"It's a mirror space—a magical 3D copy machine that automatically enhances what it replicates. See, there's the bed your husband supplied for the apartment. Joseph added some belongings from our home to dress it up. He shrank them, like your dad had someone do—or possibly did himself—to your blue hippo. That's why the statuette gave off an enchanted vibe."

Too many questions whirled in her brain to ask them all. "Who made this place?"

"Joseph. He's a skilled magician. We should get him out, by the way. I doubt he's happy stuck in that lamp."

Elyse held the vessel out to him. Arcadius shook his head and smiled. "I'm afraid you have to do it. A human trapped him. Therefore, a human must set him free. It's inconvenient but that's the way these matters work."

"Don't tell me I have to rub it!"

Arcadius grinned. "In a circle. Three times around the seal that marks the lid."

Elyse's jaw had dropped. "Will he owe me three wishes?"

"You'd be within your rights to claim them, but between friends it's considered rude. Also, wishes can be tricky. Sometimes it's best to leave them be."

He wasn't kidding. Or he didn't look like he was.

"Rub clockwise," he specified, "and say, 'If you are one who honors the Holy Name, I free you from captivity.'"

She did as he instructed. The brass hummed each time she ran her hand around, like a pager set to vibrate. After the third rub, Joseph smoked out so quickly she dropped the thing. Returning to his solid man shape seemed more challenging. Feeling like maybe she shouldn't watch, in case he had performance anxiety, Elyse turned her back on the churning cloud.

A real gold table, set beautifully for serving Moroccan tea, occupied her stunned attention.

"Thank you," Joseph's normal voice said after an interval. "I was getting a headache from the smell of that olive oil."

Elyse faced him. Arcadius's friend looked tired but otherwise okay. He'd smoothed his dark hair already. His beautifully tailored suit, the same type he always wore, was only a bit crumpled.

"You're dressed," she burst out.

Joseph smiled. "Everything near our skin transforms when our bodies do."

She rubbed her jaw, oddly self-conscious now that she knew what he was. It was like meeting someone from a new culture for the first time. She didn't want to put her foot in it. "You made this place," she said.

"I performed the ritual. Mirror spaces take on a spirit of their own once they're seeded. I'm glad enough of it was complete to shelter us."

"How big is it?"

"Just the basement for now. Given sufficient time and power, there's no limit to the size a mirror space can grow."

"You mean you could copy the whole brownstone? And the street? What about the people? Would the mirror space clone them?"

Joseph laughed as her questions tumbled out. "No people. No animals. Plants, though. I once knew a mage who could recreate a whole forest in just one day."

Elyse's mind boggled. "That is so weird. And cool."

She dropped onto the end of the copied bed. The coverlet was velvet soft, the mattress so inviting she nearly curled up to take a nap. Her thoughts were too busy to let her sleep. Though she was aware of Arcadius and Joseph watching her, she took a minute to sit like a lump and think.

No wonder her father always seemed so interested and full of life. He'd been in on some truly marvelous secrets. Maybe she should be angry he'd kept them to himself, but she was too caught up in amazement.

At last, she looked up again.

Arcadius was smiling at her faintly.

"What are we going to do?" she asked. "I gather we're safe for now, but we can't hide out here forever. It's a closed system, yes? Nowhere to go but here. We'll run out of tea in no time. On the other hand, if we leave, Mario and his boys will pounce." She turned her gaze to Joseph. "I don't mean to offend you, but his magic trumps yours, doesn't it? Because he's a human being."

"To a certain extent," Joseph said. "Fortunately, he's not experienced. He hasn't mastered the nuances of the craft as I've had a chance to do."

"Can you nuance us out of this? Not that this ought to fall on you. My family is responsible for causing a lot of this trouble."

Joseph sat beside her. Remember the shyness he'd exhibited around women—certainly around Cara—she took this as a compliment.

"This isn't your fault. You didn't know about the nexus, and you weren't involved in the struggle to control it."

"Arcadius said—" She glanced at the other man briefly. "He mentioned your people were in trouble, and you need the nexus to return to them."

Joseph nodded soberly. "If we can't save them, every soul in the Glorious City is doomed to die."

His golden eyes filled with tears. This was no tale to him, no beguiling cabinet of curiosities. Real people he cared about would be lost.

"Can I help?" she asked shyly.

Joseph patted her knee. He probably didn't know how condescending the gesture seemed.

"I mean it," she said. "I'm not afraid—or not too. Having a human on your side might be handy."

"If you could help us find your father's door," Arcadius put in, "that would be invaluable."

~

Perhaps it was shameful to admit, but Arcadius couldn't recall feeling such unadulterated respect toward a female before. Elyse wanted to help. And she'd asked to do so as if them allowing it would be a favor to her. She could have been the most hideous being on her plane, and he'd still have admired her.

Joseph was moved by her offer too. He sat next to her as easily as if she were a man.

"I've been trying to think what the door could be," she said. "Uncle Vince wasn't wrong to say Dad would have stashed it where he could get at it easily. Plus, if my father really wanted to keep me in the dark, he wouldn't have hid it in the apartment. I think the door must be here, in the basement somewhere."

"Mario likely searched it from top to bottom. And your husband too."

Arcadius didn't relish bringing him up, but Elyse absorbed his words calmly. She rubbed her hands along her blue jeans, unaware that the motion drew his gaze to her strong little thighs.

"One thing about my dad," she said. "He had a goofy sense of humor. He loved puns and wordplay and riddles so obvious you couldn't believe you didn't guess the answer right away. I'm pretty sure the opener for his precious nexus is an actual door."

"An actual door," Joseph repeated, turning his head to her.

"Well, maybe part of one," Elyse amended. "I suppose dragging a whole door around would be awkward."

Joseph and Arcadius looked at each other.

"The door to the mechanical room," they said in unison.

"Sure," Elyse said. "It's original to the brownstone, so it would have been around when he was alive. Maybe Dad spelled a hinge. Or the doorknob. Or something along those lines."

"*Someone* would have thought to examine it," Joseph said.

"Could Dad have found a spell to avert their attention?"

"Maybe." Joseph rubbed his chin thoughtfully.

"Unfortunately—" Elyse heaved the word as a sigh "—if I'm right, it doesn't do us much good. The real door is on the other side. Mario will notice if we sneak out to check."

Depending on what he knew about mirror spaces, Mario might figure out where they'd disappeared. Arcadius was willing to go up against him, but the human's magical advantages meant this was better avoided. He'd long ago learned strategy was more useful than raw courage.

"Joseph," he said, drawing his associate's eyes to him. "Will the mirror space include a facsimile of the nexus? And if it does, might the relevant portion of the copy door open it?"

Joseph's gaze sharpened. "Yes, and yes, though I can't swear either will function."

"If we had enough energy to pump into them . . ."

Joseph knew that by "energy" he meant a large enough sacrifice. He glanced at Elyse and back to him. His expression probed Arcadius's a bit more deeply than was comfortable. "We could probably open the nexus. Whether we could get it to transport us where we want in the djinn dimension, I couldn't say."

Ironically, Elyse was more excited by this prospect than they were. She bounced a little on the mattress. "It's worth a try, right? We could slip away without getting shot by Mario."

"Yes," Joseph said. "I expect we could do that."

Arcadius wasn't looking forward to what came next. He'd avoided thinking about it too hard as he got to know and like Elyse. Regrettably, he couldn't postpone it much longer.

As they left the bedroom, Elyse put her hand on his arm—not to stop him but because touching him seemed to make her feel safer. Her approach to venturing farther into the mirror space was a mix of caution and curiosity.

Once in the hall, she peered toward the living room. "There's no *out* outside the front door. All I see is swirling mist."

"That's right," Joseph said. "Beyond the mirror space is simply unformed potential."

She gnawed her lower lip. "What would happen if I tried to step into it?"

"You'd feel a very strong aversion before you did. If you persisted, your soul would separate from your body. You'd need a good necromancer to call it back."

"In other words, don't do it."

"That would be best," Joseph conceded. Elyse's question had amused him. "Why don't we concentrate on the door here for now?"

The replicated entrance to the mechanical room was in the hall. Its multiple layers of paint were as ancient looking as on the original. Joseph and Arcadius scanned the panel for enchanted hotspots while Elyse removed the padlock.

"My key still works!" she exclaimed, sounding pleased by that.

"The hinges aren't spelled," Joseph said.

"Or the knob," Arcadius added. His statement wasn't as sure as Joseph's. *Was* there a tickle of something there?

"Maybe there's something inside the mechanism," Elyse suggested.

"We'd need tools to take it apart," Joseph said.

Elyse responded with an eye roll. "Guys, I *am* this building's in-a-pinch handyman."

She had a miniature toolset attached to her key ring. The clever folding collection included a screwdriver, a penknife, plus a number of utensils he couldn't identify. With their love of unusual gadgets, Arcadius knew he and Joseph immediately coveted the thing.

Elyse opened the door cautiously, seeming relieved to find a dust-free and very shiny mechanical room behind it. Reassured it was safe to do so, she knelt and began disassembling the knob. The apparatus was the same dull old brass as before—a circumstance he found noteworthy. Mirror spaces usually prettied up their contents.

"Here we go," she said. "The threads on this screw are more worn down than the others. It's been removed and put back in more often."

The screw was the length of her index finger. She handed it up for Joseph to examine.

His eyebrows rose as he ran one thumb up the spiraled shank. "This is it. I can't believe you found it so easily."

Elyse grinned. "See? Already I'm convenient."

Joseph's answering grin was forced. He knew how they were going to repay her.

Elyse used the side of the door to pull herself to her feet. "Should we try the screw on the duplicate nexus now?"

Joseph rubbed one eyebrow. "No point putting it off. Why don't I lead the way? In case any parts of the mirror space are wonky."

They weren't wonky in the way he meant, but the improvements the mirror space had produced did distract Elyse's attention. The room with the abandoned Christmas trees brought her to a halt. It was as picturesque as an old-fashioned holiday card.

"The trees are *lit*," she said wonderingly. "And decorated. Gosh, is that real snow on the floor?"

Arcadius stooped to touch it. "White sand," he answered her.

Elyse let out a soft laugh. "This is too crazy. How does the mirror space decide?"

"Religious scholars say each time a mirror space is seeded, God gives it its own angel. The angel's intelligence guides it."

Elyse looked at him. "You absolutely mean that—as if there's no question God and angels are real."

Arcadius shrugged. "Djinn don't understand how humans doubt."

She laughed again, sounding like she enjoyed the differences between them.

He hoped she still enjoyed them when this was over.

They reached the cement block room without more delays. In this version of the basement, the blocks were sugar white and twinkled. Wariness marked all their footsteps as they went in. To Arcadius's relief, he sensed the presence of the nexus. The vibration was slightly different but it was strong.

"I don't see anything," Elyse said. "I saw the other glowing beach ball thing. Is the one on this side working?"

"You saw that nexus because Mario activated it. Joseph will do that here."

Before Joseph could try, the energy center flickered brightly and then pulsed off.

"Uh," Elyse said. "Is it supposed to do *that?*"

"No, it isn't." Joseph stretched his palms toward the power as if warming them. He snatched them back abruptly. "Shit. Mario is trying to force a portal open without the door."

"He can't do that," Arcadius protested. "Can he?"

"He might be able to if he isn't trying to go far. This copy connects more closely to *his* nexus's vibration than any spot in the universe."

"He knows we're hiding in a mirror space."

"That is the logical conclusion." Joseph looked worried. "We need to hurry this up."

Arcadius's stomach plummeted, as it hadn't for Joseph's previous bad news.

"What's wrong?" Elyse asked, noticing his dread.

Arcadius ordered himself not to lose his nerve. This wasn't the first time he'd broken this sort of news. In the past, his partners' reactions had ranged from anger to tears to throwing an entire collection of perfume jars at his head.

"Elyse," he said, taking her hands in his.

"Closer," Joseph instructed from the side of his mouth.

Joseph held the enchanted screw at the ready, poised to shove it in the nexus the moment the signs seemed right. Arcadius shifted himself and Elyse nearer to the power center, near enough that its energy wisped along their skin like smoke. The next time the illumination flickered it stayed on. Arcadius wasn't certain, but he thought he heard Mario chanting. Elyse didn't seem to. She lifted her face to him, her green eyes wide and perplexed. She was a good woman: bright and warm and endowed with rare spirit. He told himself he had to do this, no matter how little she deserved it.

"Elyse," he repeated, aware that his palms were damp. "I'm not in love with you."

Her eyes grew wider, and her mouth formed a little *O*. Even though Arcadius felt awful, he forced his expression to remain unyielding.

Then Elyse burst out laughing.

Okay. This was the first time a woman had done *that.*

"Arcadius!" she exclaimed, snorting a bit with her inexplicable amusement. "Why would I think you were? Is it because we slept together? It's nice of you to worry about my feelings, but women don't take that as seriously here. Sometimes, sure, but not necessarily. Anyway, it doesn't matter. I'm not helping you because I think you love me. I'm helping you because I think it's right."

Arcadius felt very strange, as if a large sack of rocks were sitting on his chest. He and Joseph had been hoping to draw on a very specific power. From a magical standpoint, it exceeded the potency of a hundred mourners' sorrows. Only a true heart could produce it . . . and only when it broke.

Arcadius couldn't doubt the goodness of Elyse's heart, though evidently she wasn't in love with him. He'd ended her husband's spell. He'd exerted himself to court her. She'd trusted him enough to share her bed. Nonetheless, he hadn't broken anything.

Was it normal for people in his position to want to dig a hole and crawl into it?

Her hand lifted to pet his cheek, her brows beginning to pucker above her nose. "Are you okay? You look funny."

"Got it!" Joseph announced before he could answer.

Arcadius jerked himself alert. For a second, he'd forgotten the very important goal they were trying to accomplish.

Joseph was dragging the tip of the screw down the center of the nexus, magically cutting a swath through it. The nexus itself was blue, the slit within bright white gold. Arcadius couldn't tell where the opening led—not that they had a choice about stepping into it. Mario's chanting was louder now, his will attempting to battle through to them in pulses.

"Hurry," Joseph urged. "His magic is pushing against mine."

He held his arm out to Arcadius.

"Ready?" Arcadius asked Elyse. He gripped her right hand snugly. He noticed her eyes were huge.

"Yes," she gasped like she'd lost all her breath.

Arcadius didn't wait. He slapped his other palm around Joseph's.

Joseph pulled them all into the sunny glare.

Arcadius had traveled this way before, but the experience never failed to disorient. For long moments all he saw was light, and all he heard was ringing. Numbness overtook his body, his thoughts seeming to speed up and slow down at the same time. Not wanting to accidentally lose his grip on Elyse, he willed his fingers to stay secure.

"Ow," she said as their new reality buffeted them.

She fell forward onto her hands and knees, less accustomed to the jolt of transition than either of the men. They staggered but didn't lose their footing. Elyse sat back on her sneakered feet, absently rubbing the hand he'd squeezed too firmly.

"Sand," she said, stating the obvious.

They'd landed amidst an ocean of empty dunes. Arcadius turned in a circle to scan their surroundings. Wave after rippling wave of golden sand stretched to every horizon. At those horizons, craggy vertical mountains rose. These were the Qaf, the mountains of the djinn dimension. Every djinn territory possessed a stretch. Here they wore their most forbidding aspect: no grass, no trees, and no sparkling white snowcaps. Though beautiful, the massifs were stark brown stone without adornment.

The time of day appeared different from what they'd left—the shadows suggesting late afternoon rather than morning. If that was true, he knew which way was west. At the moment, the knowledge was of useless.

"This is the Great Desert," Joseph said, echoing his conclusion.

"Is that bad?" Elyse accepted Arcadius's help to regain her feet. His awareness of her feelings, or lack thereof, gave the contact an odd poignancy. As she swiped her knees free of sand, he was very conscious that she'd left her other hand in his.

"It isn't great," Joseph said in answer to her question. "Our dimension isn't as linear as yours. The Great Desert is the equivalent of a distant island from the Glorious City."

"The Glorious City is where you live."

She'd turned to Arcadius. He tried to force the grimness from his expression. "We'll get there," he said. "Just not as conveniently."

"At least it's not deathly hot." Compared to Manhattan, the desert's warmth was wonderful, with a sage-scented breeze whispering softly across the dunes. The gentle tousling was curling Elyse's hair. She raked it back from her pretty face. "We're not going to die of thirst, are we?"

"We're not," he assured, unable to refrain from rubbing her hand soothingly. "People live here. And there's more magic to draw on in this plane. Even I could cast a spell to find them."

Elyse smiled at him. "Even you, eh?"

Had his spirit swooped like this when she smiled at him before? Had he simply not noticed? The light of the djinn dimension caused her green eyes to gleam like gems. God, she was beautiful. He knew then why the nexus had opened for Joseph. Someone's heart *had* broken. Unfortunately, it was his.

Joseph pulled Elyse's attention from Arcadius by politely clearing his throat. "Forgive me, but I don't think a spell will be necessary. Someone seems to be approaching us."

~

Elyse wasn't sure what she was looking at. The shape in the distance was dark and fuzzy, and it didn't get clearer when she squinted. A bobbing motion marked its progress across the golden sands, like whatever it was might be riding an animal.

Though the rider wasn't familiar, the animal somehow was.

"Stay behind me," Arcadius said in a low tone.

She stepped a little behind him but she wanted to see. Soon the image was more defined, though not really more sensible. A person made of smoke, no larger than a four-year-old, galloped toward them on a plastic rocking horse. The toy's rockers hung a hand span above the sand, each forward lean of the rider propelling it toward them. Little misty batwings stuck up from the rider's back. Elyse couldn't decide if they were cute or just devilish.

Well, then, she thought, working to get her brain to accept this reality. Clearly, they weren't in Kansas anymore.

"Friends!" cried the small being on the peculiar steed. It rose in the plastic stirrups to wave at them. "It is I, your ifrit friend, Samir! See how beautiful I have made the horse which you graciously gifted me!"

"Oh, boy," Joseph muttered beneath his breath. "What are we in for now?"

The ifrit, Samir—who Arcadius and Joseph appeared to know—swung off the horse in a dashing manner. He wasn't a child. Children weren't that graceful. He dropped to one knee with his smoke fist pressed to his presumably smoky heart. "Honorable sirs, have you come to request a return favor?"

As Samir returned to his feet, Elyse saw glowing yellow flames where a human would have had eyes. She didn't know what to make of his manner, but those eyes seemed very intelligent. Her hand rested on Arcadius's back, which was bare and warm and still marked by his bird tattoo. Though she didn't remember touching him, she was glad for the contact. The ifrit had just sniffed the air and peered straight at her. She forced herself not to flinch before his alien gaze.

"You brought a human with you," he exclaimed, sounding surprised and perhaps a bit repulsed. "Are you hoping to trade for her?"

Excuse me? Elyse thought.

"That is not your business," Joseph said sternly.

Arcadius crossed his arms, projecting disapproval without a word. Samir looked from one tall man to the other. Although he was made of smoke, Elyse swore she could see the ifrit's mental wheels turning.

"What would you like Samir's business to be?" he asked.

Joseph glanced at Arcadius, who nodded for him to handle this.

"Samir," Joseph said more respectfully. "Have you knowledge of the caravans hereabouts?"

"Of course," said the ifrit. "Samir knows and is known everywhere."

"We would appreciate an introduction to a tribe from which we could expect hospitality, one that wouldn't harm our human companion."

Samir cocked his smoky head to the side. "All the tribes near here are ifrit."

"Some ifrit are more tolerant than others," Joseph observed.

"You have presents?" Samir asked.

"You have witnessed my gifts yourself," Joseph said calmly.

Elyse interpreted this to mean he didn't have the sort of "presents" Samir referred to. Samir seemed to reach the same conclusion. His smoke face formed a clear frown. "All guests need presents."

"Not all presents are things."

Samir's yellow gaze slid to Elyse again. "*She* would make a good present."

Arcadius's broad back tensed beneath her palm. Sensing this wasn't the time for a lecture on women's lib, Elyse held her tongue.

"Samir," Joseph said, drawing the ifrit's attention his way again. "You let us worry about our guest gifts. Can you discharge your debt to us or not?"

Samir looked longingly toward his waiting plastic horse. It sat on the sand now, a perfectly ordinary slightly old-fashioned toy.

"Oh, my God," Elyse blurted. "That's Melanie Turner's old rocking horse! I stored it in the basement after she died, in case her mother returned for it."

"*My* horse," Samir said fiercely.

His voice hissed like a fiery wind. Elyse blinked and shut up.

"Yes, it's your horse," Joseph soothed. "Our companion has no wish to reclaim it."

Elyse supposed she didn't. Melanie's mother had moved away years ago. "You *have* made it beautiful," she said.

Samir regarded her slightly less hostilely. "I also made it fast."

"Impressively so," she agreed.

This compliment warmed him even more. "The little girl's pain from her illness is still inside it. I haven't drunk it all up yet."

Elyse didn't know what to say to that. She hoped her face wasn't horrified.

"So we're all agreed," Joseph said smoothly. "The horse is yours, and your debt to us will be discharged once you provide us an introduction to an honorable tribe of nomads."

Samir thought this over. "Agreed." He mounted his plastic steed. "Follow me," he threw over his shoulder.

They followed at a necessarily slower place, their feet shushing through the seemingly endless sand. Though their guide soon grew distant, neither Arcadius nor Joseph appeared concerned that he would ditch them.

Arcadius rubbed her arm before taking her hand in his. Elyse wasn't sure he knew he'd done it. His manner was preoccupied. She felt preoccupied herself. She was in the desert of the djinn. She'd been magically transported. If the sand hadn't been such a chore to trudge through, she'd have concluded she was dreaming.

Arcadius's steps slowed unexpectedly. "You understood Samir," he said to her.

Elyse's eyebrows rose. "Wasn't I supposed to?"

"He spoke our language. I've heard being around djinn helps humans comprehend our tongue. I guess Joseph and I have rubbed off on you."

"Handy. I don't suppose you could teach me French that way."

He smiled absently, his attention moving to other things. "What shall we do about a guest gift?" he asked Joseph.

"Hope his sorcerers aren't as powerful as me. I expect I can provide some service he'll appreciate."

"Assuming you're willing to provide it."

"Assuming," Joseph agreed.

"Guys," Elyse said. "Are we in trouble here?"

"No," Arcadius denied at the same time Joseph said, "Not exactly."

Elyse coughed out a little laugh. She looked at Arcadius. "You said before that ifrits are demons among your kind."

"I also said they aren't necessarily evil."

"They aren't necessarily good," Joseph felt compelled to put in.

"Ifrits don't love God," Arcadius explained. "They believe in Him, because that's hardwired into all djinn, but they don't obey His laws. They're also . . . sensitive about humans."

"You mentioned your people believe God raised humans above the djinn, and that He ordered you to bow down to them."

"That is correct."

"So basically," Elyse said, "it's like Uncle Vince's resentment of Grandpa Saul on steroids. Grandpa Saul played favorites, and Vince couldn't get along with my dad because of it. I'm human, and a woman, and these tribesmen aren't going to want to play nice with me."

Arcadius's sigh was a reluctant admission.

"There is one thing we can count on," Joseph said, clearly trying to inject a little optimism into the discussion. "Only the most degenerate djinn wouldn't observe the rules of hospitality. These will be higher-level ifrits than Samir. If we can get an invitation to break bread with them, we'll be safe until the next sunset."

"Except we probably need a present to get the invitation."

Neither of the men denied this.

"I should have grabbed our briefcase," Joseph said, shaking his head in irritation. "Even if I was being sucked into a lamp, emeralds are always suitable."

They didn't have emeralds. They had the clothes on their backs and the shoes on their feet . . . and the things in their pockets.

"What about my Swiss army knife?" she suggested, remembering the gleam that had lit the men's eyes when she brought it out. "It's the SwissChamp model. It has thirty-three implements. If I were a nomad, I'd want one."

"Hm," Arcadius said. "That might do. I doubt a nomad will have seen one before. Novelty is a great temptation."

"I recall it's a little plain," Joseph said, "but if we blinged it up . . ." He stopped walking to look at her. "Would you be willing to give me your wedding ring as well?"

"Uh," she said, taken aback. Despite everything that had happened, she felt wrenched by the idea. "I . . . guess so. Under the circumstances, I don't actually need it."

"I'll give you a new one." Arcadius blushed as soon as he said the words, obviously still embarrassed about his kind but unnecessary warning that he wasn't in love with her. "I mean I'll supply another to replace it."

"I know what you meant," she assured him.

Amusement cured her niggling reluctance. She slipped the ring off her finger and handed it to Joseph. The Swiss army knife took longer to twist free of her key ring.

When he had both, he cupped them between his hands. He closed his eyes, furrowed his brow, and whispered a quick prayer. Light flared behind his fingers, turning their edges red. He opened his palms. Elyse leaned forward to see the outcome.

"Ooh," she said. Her old army knife was better than new. It was—as Joseph had said—"blinged up." He'd used the gold from her ring to plate all the steel gadgets, which no longer had a scratch on them. The diamond sparkled brighter than she remembered, replacing the Victorinox cross-in-a-shield logo. "Now *that* would be any handygirl's best friend."

"I only polished it up a bit," Joseph said modestly.

"It's very good," Arcadius praised. "No djinni could resist it."

Joseph's blush was as adorable as his.

"There's just one more thing," Arcadius said. He shoved his hand in his trouser pocket, bringing out the tie from her Japanese robe, the same one he'd used to bind her ankles so erotically on the couch.

Elyse's cheeks flashed hot—and other parts of her as well. No doubt she deserved that for being smug about their blushes.

"Master," Joseph said. "I don't think a sheikh will be impressed by a strip of silk."

"It's for Elyse. It isn't safe to take her among the tribe as our companion. I think we'd better take her as my pet."

"Your pet!" she burst out before she could control her mouth.

Arcadius stared gravely down at her. His eyes were even more striking seen in his own dimension. The look in them slid through her like molten steel, causing her sex to quiver strongly with arousal. If they'd been alone, she'd have done things to him she'd never done to a man before. She couldn't have said what those things were precisely, only that she'd do them with great fervor. And nakedly. She'd do them very, very nakedly to his big hard body.

"If you were my pet," Arcadius said in a low thick voice, "any insult to you would be an insult to me. We wouldn't have to negotiate for your safe passage separately."

Elyse had to clear her throat. "Two for the price of one."

"Exactly. Joseph can transform this tie into a slave rope. I promise it will be comfortable."

The rope might not hurt her, but Elyse rather doubted it would be *comfortable*. "As your pet, I'd have to do things to keep up the pretense."

"You might." He stared at her harder, so hard in fact that she had to press her trembling thighs together. "Would you find that too difficult?"

"I'm not an idiot. I understand we're in danger."

His expression softened. His hand rose, his fingers caressing the side of her heated face. "While I live," he said softly, "I swear I shall keep you safe."

Her jaw dropped in astonishment. He meant every word of the extraordinary oath. She felt off balance, as if the Earth had bobbled on its axis. Hell, maybe *she* was bobbling. David had been a good partner in his way, but she'd never expected a man to say something like that to her.

Seeing her shock, Arcadius dropped his hand. "You need not fear this bondage," he said stiffly. "I won't take undue advantage."

The thought hadn't crossed her mind, and that was startling too. She *really* trusted him, more than she had reason to. Her trust had led her astray before.

"All right," she said, too confused by her feelings to attempt to answer more lucidly. "Tell Joseph it's okay with me."

Joseph had stepped away while they spoke. His back was to them, possibly to give them privacy. He looked surreal standing in the empty desert, tall and solitary in his beautiful three-piece suit. She knew even less about him than Arcadius. He'd called Arcadius *master* again. Arcadius must actually fill that role. He wore no slave rope, but perhaps he was one. Or maybe Joseph was just a servant. Either way, he was devoted to his employer. Did he mind her intrusion in their lives? He didn't seem to.

He's sad, she decided. *But I don't think he's sad because of me.*

He turned back as she had the thought. His face was calm and watchful: the perfect servant, prepared to do whatever was asked of him.

"Are you ready?" he asked.

"I'm ready," she answered.

Joseph did his whispered spell thing to transform the tie into a length of rope. As promised, it was soft against her skin. With the matter of fact motions of a tailor, Joseph tied it around her waist. He muttered a word at the knot, which caused it to grow snugger. Then he handed the trailing end to Arcadius, who wound it twice around his strong wrist. The remaining rope stretched about five feet between the two of them.

Elyse tried to squelch the rising erotic buzz inside her, a goal made more difficult by Arcadius studying her up and down. As far as she could tell, he was only gauging the result. The effect his attention had on her, however, was unquestionably sensual.

Her nipples hadn't been this hard since he almost ravished her on her bed. At the moment, she deeply regretted he hadn't been successful.

"I don't think that's enough," Arcadius said.

"It's enough for tradition," Joseph countered, considering her from his place at his master's side.

"She needs to look more . . . claimed. Give me your belt."

Joseph's brows rose along with hers, but of course he obeyed. Arcadius didn't have a belt on him, just his trousers and shoes. He exchanged his end of the rope for Joseph's accessory, causing Elyse to feel as if she were being passed from man to man. With no more fuss than Joseph used to perform his tricks, Arcadius turned the black leather belt into two wrist cuffs and a neck collar. The restraints were thick but pliant. A spaced row of silver studs circled each—the former buckle, she presumed. To be honest, they looked cool, though maybe a little Goth for a landlady.

He put them on her gently.

"That's the first time I've seen you do magic," she said. "Apart from you changing form."

His eyes came up to hers. He was fastening the neckpiece and they were close. His pupils were dilated, his body heat noticeably higher.

"I wanted to do part of this myself," he said.

He spoke softly, the answer intended for her alone. Their gazes held a few seconds longer. Elyse felt arousal run hot and silky from her body.

Arcadius finished with the collar and took a step back from her.

Had he meant to excite her? His face was closed, and she couldn't tell. She did know aspects of their chosen pretense wouldn't require acting. Her enjoyment of being tied by him hadn't been a one-time fluke.

So, she thought, struggling not to be unnerved. *Learn something new about yourself everyday.*

In her distraction over her new self-knowledge, she nearly missed Samir's return. His reappearance was worth watching. He slalomed down the nearest dune like his toy horse was on snowboards.

"Slowpokes," he chided as he stopped in a spray of sand. "Samir has found what you seek. A good honorable tribe has made camp beyond that crest. You can walk there in five minutes. Ten if you keep dawdling."

The ifrit did a double take when he saw the changes in her outfit. Elyse discovered she didn't like *him* examining her.

"Well, that makes more sense," was all he said.

Dismissing the issue with a shrug, he turned his steed around by its reins to lead them toward their unknown fates. Though his pace was slow enough for them to keep up, Elyse had the impression he didn't care if this turned out badly.

CHAPTER ELEVEN

THE descending sun stained the desert copper as they crested the next big dune. All of them, Samir included, halted at the sight below.

Elyse experienced a moment of pure wonder. She was one of very few humans ever to see its like.

A level plain, scattered here and there with silvery scrub, extended from the base of the dune they stood on to the stark brown heights that edged this area of the Great Desert. The plain was beautiful in the way any wild place can be, but it also served as a startling contrast for a not at all humble encampment.

Dozens of dazzling white round tents had been set up on the sand. Their peaks flew pennants: some red, some gold, all fluttering in the balmy breeze. Small robed figures scurried in an organized fashion between them. These were solid beings, not smoke demons like Samir. They appeared to be lowering rolled-up tent walls, possibly to shield against the cool of the coming night. A large cooking fire glowed in a central clearing. Next to that was a hive-shaped mound Elyse recognized as a mud oven. Heat waves shimmered from its sides, the rich scent of roasting lamb confirming her assumption. Most marvelous, beside the largest of the tents a single palm tree grew—as in, its fronds were literally stretching taller before her eyes.

"Wow," she said, at a loss for a better word.

Arcadius and Joseph appeared impressed as well, though maybe not for the same reasons.

"That is a *large* tribe," Joseph commented carefully.

"A wealthy one," Arcadius added, his leeriness echoing the other man's.

"This is Sheik Zayd's caravan," Samir announced smugly. "He is the greatest sheikh in the Great Desert."

The ifrit was enjoying their reaction, as if a private prank were playing out as he'd hoped. Joseph sent him a cool look, but didn't speak to him directly.

"I don't see women," he observed.

"Or camels," Arcadius said.

"A sheikh that rich could afford a lot of wives. If Zayd has housed them elsewhere, he won't leave them alone for long."

"No, he won't," Arcadius agreed. "He must be traveling back and forth."

He and Joseph seemed to understand what this exchange was about. Elyse didn't have a clue, only that they believed they'd discovered something significant. Whatever it was slid over Samir's smoky head as well.

"Samir can take you to the sheikh," he announced.

"In a moment," Arcadius said. "Wait for us at the bottom."

The ifrit pouted but went ahead. Once he was out of earshot, Arcadius turned to her. His expression told her he was braced for objections. "I need to give you instructions."

Elyse nodded, so he went on.

"I'm aware that holding your tongue doesn't come naturally to females of your plane, but please, for all our sakes, leave the talking to me. Whatever you do, don't argue with the sheikh or any of his high-ranking men. They won't abide rebellion from a woman they're not sleeping with—certainly not a human one. Joseph and I respect you. You can trust us not to let them go too far."

She didn't mind his warning as much as she minded him thinking her incapable of self-control. "I understand. My lips are zipped unless you give me the go ahead."

"Or Joseph."

"Or Joseph," she agreed, striving not to sound huffy.

He sighed but seemed to believe her. "I need to take back the rope."

She'd been holding the end while they climbed—like a dog walking itself, she thought wryly. She handed the leash to him. He wound it around his wrist as he had before. The carnal shiver she couldn't seem to suppress shook her. Maybe Arcadius felt it too. He caught her gaze, wet his lips, then abruptly turned away.

So we're both hot to trot, she thought. *Great timing.*

Thanks to this and a temperature near eighty, she was more than a little glowy by the time she clambered awkwardly down the sandy slope. Walking at the end of a rope someone else was holding was harder then she'd thought. Hitting flat ground came as a relief.

The snow-white tent village remained a ways off. No one challenged them as they approached, though they certainly drew glances. She noticed there was a graduated dress code in effect. Servants wore the hooded white tunics Moroccans called djellabas, plus long indigo scarfs they tossed once around their necks. Fancier outfits involved white shirts tucked into loose trousers with indigo over-robes. Grander still were individuals displaying gem-studded waist sashes.

When a tall djinni dressed completely in indigo strode toward them, she was relatively certain they were going to meet the sheikh. His waist sash was stiff with pearls, his Turkish-style slippers shining with twenty-four karat embroidery. Despite his ornate dress, he didn't seem effeminate. He walked like a winning fighter—like the greatest sheikh in the land, she supposed.

"Greetings," he said, stopping a body length away from them. His skin was golden brown like Arcadius's, perhaps a shade darker. His eyes were ash gray and, though curious, very cool.

Elyse blinked when she saw his long waving hair was actually waving smoke.

"Greetings," Samir replied, immediately falling prostrate to the dry cracked earth. "Great sheikh, your humble friend Samir begs you to make the acquaintance of these pitiful God-fearing travelers."

Elyse couldn't view this as a nice introduction, but Arcadius didn't seem insulted. He bowed politely, straightened, and waited calmly for a response.

"I am Sheikh Zayd," the tall man who'd met them said.

"I am Arcadius," Arcadius responded. He gestured to Joseph, who bowed lower than his master, though with a similar composure.

"I am Joseph, his servant."

"And your friend?" Zayd asked in a silky, suggestive tone.

"She is my pet." Arcadius lifted the slave rope as evidence. "You may have her name if you wish, but she isn't important."

"She is human."

"She is," Arcadius agreed. "However, she is docile."

As the sheikh shifted his gaze to her, Elyse realized she ought to cast down her eyes.

"Can she dance?" he asked as she stared at her scuffed sneakers.

"No," Arcadius said.

"Sing?"

"Alas, only if you are tone deaf."

"She is good in bed then."

"Moderately," Arcadius conceded. "I confess I like my women soft."

Sheikh Zayd snorted. It seemed this wasn't a taste he shared or approved of. Elyse tried to look meek—which damn well better be what Arcadius meant by "soft." She was no triathlete, but she wasn't a wimp either. She settled for pretending she couldn't hear what they said. They were acting like she was deaf, after all.

The sheikh made her jump by leaning close enough to sniff her neck. He chuckled at her reaction, a low mocking sound that set her nerves on edge. As if it had a separate existence, his vaporous hair retreated more slowly than the rest of him.

"This one would be fun to whip," he said. "My hospitality is yours if you loan her to me tonight. I won't even fuck her, since you claim she's not very good at it."

Okay, biting her tongue was harder than Elyse thought. She managed not to curl her hands into fists. Avoiding clenching her jaw was impossible.

This time Sheikh Zayd laughed like smoke flowing over stone. "City man," he said to Arcadius. "Never try to fool an ifrit. Your God-loving faces aren't made for it."

Elyse felt rather than saw Arcadius bow slightly. "You are too wise. The human has made me heartsick. I cannot be parted from her for even one minute."

"Now *that* I believe." Sheikh Zayd slapped Arcadius on the shoulder. "What else have you to bargain with?"

"It is too paltry," her protector said modestly. "A mere human trinket of no value. I hesitate . . . no, I cannot waste your time."

"Show him, master," Joseph urged, falling in with his playacting. "Perhaps he'll find it useful. No other sheikh in the Qaf has one."

"Show me," the sheikh ordered, thrusting out an imperious hand.

As if he hardly dared, Arcadius laid her army knife in his palm.

"Hm." The sheikh held it up to the dying light, fortuitously causing her former wedding diamond to flash. "What is it?"

"It is a Swiss army knife. It has thirty-three implements, including a fish scaler and a corkscrew!" Suddenly radiating enthusiasm, Arcadius showed the sheikh how to fold them out one by one. The Philips screwdriver was a stumper, but the other tools were hits. Sheikh Zayd especially admired the ballpoint pen.

"It writes *blue*," he praised. "Signing everything in blood gets monotonous." With an air of satisfaction, he closed all the bits and bobs, slipping the knife away somewhere in his robes. "I accept your gift. Please come break bread with me. You too, Samir," he threw over his shoulder.

Elyse guessed the smoke demon hadn't lied about everyone knowing him.

~

Arcadius allowed himself to feel a cautious measure of victory. He'd maneuvered the sheikh into catching him in a lie, thus reinforcing Zayd's sense of superiority. Most great men enjoyed thinking of themselves as impossible to trick. Even Iksander had now and then.

Iksander **did,** Arcadius thought, correcting the past tense.

A servant showed their scraggly trio to a communal ablutions tent.

"You may wash," the man said, his snooty tone implying they needed to. "Please avail yourselves of the extra robes in those baskets."

"They have water," Elyse exclaimed, once they were alone again.

They had more than water. They had a lovely blue-and-white tiled fountain splashing within the tent.

"Water crystals," Joseph mused, lifting one from a notably generous pile.

"That looks like a piece of quartz," Elyse said.

"Break it," Joseph suggested, handing the small point to her.

Elyse took the crystal to the fountain, where she snapped it carefully in two. The moment she did, at least five gallons of icy H2O sprayed out and soaked her. She gasped in shock before bursting out laughing.

"Bad genie," she scolded Joseph.

He grinned delightedly at his successful trick.

"You're almost clean," he pointed out.

She flicked her wet hands at him.

Arcadius smiled fondly. Seeing them happy gave him an unanticipated sense of well-being.

Playtime over, they washed as quickly as they could while giving each other privacy. The clothes that had been left for them were beautiful: soft and clean without a single mend or tear. Their fineness reassured him Zayd took offering hospitality seriously. One set of garments was actually small enough for Elyse.

"This suits you," he said, tying the slave rope back around her waist. Though he didn't need to, he smoothed the vivid blue outer-robe down her hips.

"My hair's a mess," she said, touching it.

"Your curls are pretty," he assured her.

She looked up at him, her eyes enchantingly wide. Their brief trek across the desert had added color to her face. He wanted to kiss the roses in her cheeks and lips, followed by unpeeling every layer she'd just drawn on to caress the soft delights of her nakedness. His cock began to harden, its rise within his loose trousers too swift for his peace of mind. He shouldn't have let himself linger over helping her. The slave rope was too good at giving him ideas.

God, he wished that damned book of love poems hadn't prevented him from taking her on her bed.

"People are heading to the fire," Joseph said from the slit he'd cracked in the tent's entrance. "We should probably join them."

His words pulled Arcadius back to the task at hand. "Could you accidentally forget your manners while we're eating?"

"Of course," Joseph said. "Are you intending to send me away as punishment?"

"I am. I'd like to know the scuttlebutt among the sheikh's servants before we proceed further."

~

Joseph seized his opportunity as soon as the roasted lamb and other dishes were divvied onto brass platters. Though Samir had been invited to join them, he'd slipped away with his plate. Perhaps the smoke demon disliked others seeing how he ate. Who knew how he managed it without a solid form?

"Good appetite," the sheikh wished the remaining company.

"God be praised," Arcadius's obedient servant responded.

Every ifrit seated around the fire glared at him.

"Idiot," Arcadius rebuked, clouting Joseph behind the head. "Have you forgotten where we are? Get away from me before I do worse than rattle your pea-sized brain."

Joseph begged forgiveness, bowed, and slunk hastily into the shadows.

"My sincere apologies," Arcadius addressed the sheikh. "My man is a skilled magician, but his intelligence sometimes fails him in other areas."

"Sorcerers can be hard to manage," Zayd acknowledged. "Tell me, what do you think of this couscous?"

Arcadius complimented him fulsomely on the food—not difficult to do since he was hungry and it was good. Unused to eating hot meat with her fingers, Elyse was having a harder time. Other than that, she was behaving better than he'd hoped. She'd known to crouch at his feet rather than joining him on his rock. She did nothing to draw attention. She even made herself smaller. He wondered where she'd learned the skill. Not from her father. Leo Solomon wouldn't have wanted his daughter to be invisible. But maybe the knack had helped her get along with Cara when they were young. He could imagine Elyse's cousin wanting the spotlight to herself.

As he ate, Arcadius watched the sheikh interact with his men. Zayd definitely ruled from above but didn't seem resented—not even for his hard temper. Twice, he struck associates across the face for small infractions, an act that inspired not even half the disapproval Joseph had for his prayer. Iksander was a different type of ruler, but his people were different too. These djinn respected violence. Being top dogs of the desert was more important to them than being loved. The only weakness Arcadius saw was that they were a smidgen bored.

Maybe the other dog packs were too cowed to start up a good war.

He asked Zayd's leave to retire before the other man was ready to let him go. His polite insistence earned him a barrage of jests, most along the lines of his "pet" needing seeing to.

"You city men," Sheikh Zayd mocked. "You'll never stiffen up your swords if your dick is the hardest thing about you."

Arcadius smiled and bowed as if the words weren't a grave insult. He laid his hand behind Elyse's neck. Though he didn't think the ifrit saw her trembling, he registered the vibration through his fingers. She'd bottled up enough tension for one evening.

"Oh, as you wish," the sheikh relented, seeing his guest's will was fixed. "My good wine would be wasted on your city mouth anyway." He snapped for a waiting servant. "Take them to the tent I told you to prepare."

Despite mocking him for his softness, the tent Zayd provided was large and luxurious. The floor was a plush red and yellow carpet, the walls double layered to keep out the blowing sand. In one corner was a bath carved from emerald green desert glass. Someone had filled it. The water was steaming.

Their escort had departed, so Arcadius turned Elyse to face him. Her eyes were too bright, her lower lip shaking. Arcadius touched it and she stilled the trembling with her teeth. His urge to soothe her was very strong. Uncertain how to go about it, he caressed the sides of her face gently. His little fingers brushed the leather collar around her neck.

"You did well," he said. "Even better than I asked."

She nodded—not ready to speak, he guessed.

"I'm sorry they frightened you," he tried. "They are rough men."

Elyse swallowed. "When Sheikh Zayd said I'd be fun to whip, he meant *really* whip, didn't he?"

"You didn't realize that?"

"Not at first. Not until I saw him draw blood when he struck those men."

He stroked her unruly hair, liking—inappropriately, perhaps—how the waves clung to his fingers. "To a certain extent, most djinn can draw power from human emotions. Ifrits especially relish drinking pain."

"Like Samir and the sick girl's rocking horse."

Arcadius nodded. He didn't evade her eyes. "Djinn are different beings from humans."

Thoughts ran behind her expression. She looked away, keeping them to herself.

"There's a bath," she said, spotting it.

"And a commode. Zayd is either showing off or trying to put us off our guard."

"Or both." Her rueful smile said her spirit was coming back.

He slid his hands to her shoulders, feeling their slender strength beneath the borrowed clothes. He wanted to undress her but wasn't sure he should suggest it.

"Arcadius." The throatiness of her voice drew his gaze to her face again. The look in her eyes was unmistakable. She wanted him. Her hands slid up the shirt and robe that draped his chest. Heat flashed across his skin as her wrist cuffs brushed him. They were alone. She could have removed them. So could he, if he'd wanted to.

"Elyse," he whispered, lifting her off the ground for a ravenous kiss.

He'd dropped the slave rope when the servant left, and she hadn't picked it up. The leash dangled over his embracing arm, yet another reminder of their pretend roles. When he drove his tongue into her mouth, she sucked it, locking her legs enthusiastically around his waist. He had to touch more of her, had to remind her she was safe because she belonged to him. He palmed her bottom and squeezed the firm lush flesh. Like him, she was wearing loose male trousers. The cloth was thin, the halves of her ass nearly naked for his fondling. He pushed his stroking further, groaning when his fingers found a stretch of dampness on the inseam. Her labia were hot and wet and clearly ready to be played with.

She made a noise, wriggling in his hold until her folds molded around his rigid length. This was what they both needed, or part of it. She thrust up and down his cock, her body growing wilder, wetter, rubbing his erection from base to tip.

That felt so good his scalp prickled.

"Elyse," he gasped, wishing there were a wall to slam her against.

He settled for holding her tight to him, for pushing his hips in movements that made the most of hers. His nerves grew hot, his balls beginning to tingle. She couldn't seem to slow. She nipped the cord at the side of his neck and worked herself on him faster.

"I'm going to come in my clothes," he warned, gripping her harder still.

Behind him, from nowhere near great enough a distance, Joseph politely cleared his throat.

"Shit," Elyse gasped, scrambling down from him.

Arcadius fought his desire to curse. He'd been a breath away from exploding, which would have been a shame if he hadn't known himself capable of taking her quite a few times tonight. His erection thrust like a pole in his loose djinn pants, thick and hard and not going down for any reason soon.

He didn't turn around right away. It seemed insensitive to let Joseph see him in this state, like rubbing the servant's nose in what he couldn't experience himself.

"Forgive me, master," the servant said, sounding uncomfortable but not unsure. "I wouldn't interrupt if I didn't think you'd want to hear this immediately."

Arcadius heaved a sigh. "Let me hang a tapestry for you," he said to Elyse. "So you can bathe privately."

She nodded and leaned around his side. "Sorry, Joseph," she said.

Arcadius hung the tapestry on the appropriate hooks in the tent's structure. He heard Elyse test the water, gritting his teeth at the thought of her undressing without his help. He sighed again. There was no more putting this off. He turned to Joseph, drawing breath in preparation to ask what he'd discovered.

To his surprise, Joseph held up a finger for silence.

He used the heel of his slipper to draw a faintly luminous five-foot circle in the pile of the carpet floor. He beckoned Arcadius to step into it. The thickening of the air in his ears told him the circle was a magical sound shield.

"We're being spied on?" he asked.

"You didn't notice?" Joseph paused and shook his head. "Of course you didn't. You were . . . worried about Elyse. There's a small seeing crystal buried in the main tent pole. No, don't look. We're angled away from it. Elyse should be all right. You hung the tapestry between her and it."

"Damn," Arcadius said. "I should have expected that."

Joseph smiled. "If I remind you only God is perfect, will you clout me again?"

Arcadius laughed sheepishly. Joseph was a rock, and a good man to have at his back. "I wouldn't have thought I'd say it, but I grudgingly thank you for interrupting. What did you find out?"

Joseph turned serious. "Not as much as I'd like. Zayd runs a tight caravan. I was able to discover he visits his women once a fortnight. They live in a carved stone palace hidden in the mountains." The other man wagged his eyebrows, saving the best for last. "He travels there with his most trusted guards on a flotilla of flying carpets."

"A flotilla," Arcadius marveled. "One would get us home. Do you know where they're kept?"

"I have a suspicion, but I couldn't get close enough to check. It's early, and his patrol is alert."

An idea sprang into his mind, so complete and compelling he couldn't dismiss it. He wanted to. It was sort of horrible. "What if—" He rubbed the groove of his chin. He thought some more but couldn't come up with a better option to put forward. "What if Zayd's patrol were tempted from their duties?"

"I don't see how," Joseph said. "Even if we had a sultan's ransom, Zayd would kill them for taking bribes."

"Not a bribe. A distraction. They've been top dogs too long. They're bored here and so is Zayd. Most of them probably haven't seen a woman in a while. What do you think will happen if someone starts a whisper that Zayd is watching a 'special' entertainment in his tent?"

"I expect they'll wander by to check. I expect his tight patrol will develop a lot of holes." Joseph looked at him. "Are you sure? Elyse would be very uncomfortable if she knew."

"I won't tell her," Arcadius said grimly. "Her safety depends on us getting out of here. On top of which, Zayd would know something was up if we simply slept. We may as well make hay of this."

Joseph blew out a breath. He didn't like the plan, but he knew what was at stake.

~

Elyse sank down in the steaming bath, trying to throw off the last of her shakes. She'd grown up female in New York City, accustomed to the need for caution in regard to her safety. She'd thought that would prepare her but she'd been wrong.

Sitting through that meal with Zayd and his men had chilled her to the bone.

She'd had to stay smack dab in the middle of circumstances smart women avoided, aware that her only shield was Arcadius. If Zayd's men had been human, it would have been bad enough, but they were something else, something alien and unpredictable. The thoughts behind their strange eyes were different. Their voices had a foreign timbre, their movements more fluidity. A few—those in Zayd's inner circle—sported smoke hair like him. She suspected it was a form of boast. Look at me: I can hold two forms at once. One thing she was sure of: These djinn weren't bound by rules unless they chose to be.

Her gratitude to Arcadius for getting her away was almost too strong for words.

She thought it likely the powerful feeling was why she'd leaped on him. She wasn't falling in love. She knew love made her stupid. Lust was safer. Anyway, gratitude wasn't love. So Arcadius respected her. So he told her she was pretty. David had done as much. Both men had lied about things that mattered. She wouldn't go down that road again.

Arcadius didn't lie selfishly, she thought. Plus, she was getting a chance to know him without deceptions. David hadn't given her that option.

Stop, she mouthed. Talking herself into being more susceptible wasn't constructive.

She soaped the sea sponge some nameless ifrit servant had left for her. She could do this: wash her skin, rinse her hair, pretend being here was just another challenge she'd rise to. Lose her father—sure. Run the brownstone by herself—why not? Watch her cousin's magically infatuated boyfriend shoot her uncle in the forehead . . .

She covered her face, overwhelmed by the litany. A moment later, she blew out her breath and dropped her hands again. She had to keep it together, not just for her sake but also for Arcadius and Joseph's. They were two men against a literal enemy camp. The least she could do was not add to the weight they carried.

Remember the cool things, she told herself. This was a one in a million, unbelievable adventure, the same sort of adventure her dad adored.

She got part of her character from him. She'd been tested, and she hadn't crumpled yet. Maybe, ultimately, she was as spirited as him.

She'd finished washing up and was simply lolling when Arcadius stepped around the tapestry.

"Stay," he said, moving a little stool so he could sit by her. She had her head on the rim of the clear green tub, her body almost relaxed in the warm water. Having him sit with her felt easy, like they'd known each other longer than they had.

"Do you feel better?" he asked.

She nodded. "How is Joseph?"

"Wandering the camp. He won't be back for a while."

"What did he want to—"

Arcadius laid two fingers across her lips. "Let's not speak of serious matters. Let's enjoy a moment of peace for us."

The light touch coupled with the heaviness in his eyes heated her. His attention fell to the water, which was scented with lavender oil. A Moroccan lantern hung from a strut above her, its gentle radiance revealing her submerged curves. Arcadius dropped his hand to her breast, cupping its side with his fingers while his thumb drew circles around the rosy peak. Elyse's pussy contracted with desire, echoing the tightening of her nipple.

"You're so lovely," he said, his eyes on the wet flesh he stroked. "You make me wonder that I ever found other women attractive."

For some reason this amused her. "The world does contain a few more than me."

"You're the only one who's beautiful to me now."

She touched his face and smiled. He was the beautiful one, too beautiful to convince her he meant the words. "You're silly if you think I need overblown compliments."

His hand slid beneath the water and over her belly. "I'm being honest."

She started to laugh, but just then he enclosed her pubis within his hand. The laugh became a gasp of pleasure. He squeezed the softness of her mound, one long finger burrowing between her labia.

She bit her lip as its tip penetrated her vagina.

"Do you want me?" he whispered. He worked half the finger in and out, slowly, gently, making her squirm around it. The stimulation felt very good and not nearly good enough. Elyse clutched the sides of the tub harder.

"You're . . . in a position . . . to know I do," she managed to choke out.

He eased his finger out of her, changing strategy to rubbing two along the smooth channels to either side of her clit. Teased by the glancing friction, the little peak of flesh swelled and grew more sensitive. Her pulse quickened inside it, the ache of want deepening inside her.

When she tried to rise, he held her more firmly.

She couldn't deny that excited her.

"I want you," he said. His eyes were the same burning steel blue she'd seen in his smoke form. Right then, the glow was too sexy to frighten her. "I'm so hard I feel like I could fuck you all night, like I'd just keep going and never want to stop."

His words were enough to get to her, but he also squeezed her entire mound, his capable hand massaging her eager flesh. Too aroused to be still, she bucked helplessly in his hold.

Arcadius's chiseled cheekbones flushed darker. When he spoke, it was huskily. "Would you let me take you wearing the cuffs and collar?"

"I'd let you take me any way you want," she said.

He saw she meant this. He released her sex, drawing his palm along her inner thigh. Down from one knee he glided, across her mound, and up to the other. The admiring stroke made muscles all over her body clench.

He looked at her, his eyes searching hers. His breathing was deeper than before, his expression tight with want. He had to know she was ready. She didn't understand what he was waiting for.

"Let me up," she said, too impatient to remain where she was. "I left the cuffs over there so they'd stay dry."

He drew his arm back from her.

She rose, water sheeting down her naked body into the bath. She didn't hide herself. If he enjoyed ogling her, he was welcome to.

Her nipples sharpened even more as the air hit them.

The sight inspired him to stand—too quickly, apparently. The stool nearly toppled over, but he caught it with his foot. Unable to resist a survey of her own, she was gratified to discover a tent pole behind his pants. That was worth a stare or seven. The cotton trousers he wore were thin. Nothing stood between them and his stiff sword. She saw it clearly through the cloth, including the spot where pre-come glued the fine weave to the rounded tip. Blood flushed that part of him, making her mouth water. The blackness of his pubic hair was X-rated. Ditto for the heavy hang of his balls. The way his shaft jerked and throbbed seemed an engraved invitation to jump his bones and ride.

A shudder of anticipatory pleasure rolled down her spine. When she dragged her eyes up from his erection, his lips had curved into a smirk.

"Fine," she said. "I like looking at you too."

Grinning, he offered her his hands to step out.

"Wait," she said when he seemed about to swing her up in his arms. "The cuffs and collar are on that painted chest with the vessel sink."

He spotted them . . . and handed them to her.

Okay. He wanted to watch her put them on. She'd already discovered how easy they were to unfasten. Their overlapping edges stuck to each other with invisible magical magnets. Even the neck collar was surprisingly comfortable.

It looked like bondage but didn't constrict her throat at all.

As she checked the straightness of its silver studs, he inhaled sharply. His reaction sent an answering pulse through her, as if two of his strong fingers had just pinched her clit between them.

"Sheesh," she breathed. "What a pair we are."

"You like it too," he said.

"I like it like crazy," she confirmed.

He swung her up in his arms, and suddenly everything was good. No more fear for tomorrow or even the next minute. She was lost in the heady pleasure of being with him.

The bedroll lay on the floor in the main area of the tent. It was a generous square of striped linen stuffed with something comfortable. Arcadius showed off his strength by lowering her easily onto it, then staying there to kiss her. Being under his weight, feeling his chest and abs and gloriously hot erection was wonderful. Rubbing their fronts together, she kissed him deliriously.

As much she enjoyed this, she wanted him free of his clothes even more.

"Take these off," she panted, beginning to tug at them. "I want you inside me."

He looked at her—dark-faced, panting. Decision shifted behind his features. Whatever the decision was, once he'd made it, he got himself naked fast.

She purred when his big bare body came back to her.

"You're so hot," she praised, her hands roaming his smooth warm back. "Your cock feels incredible."

It felt huge: thick and hard and thoroughly tempting.

"God," he gasped as her wandering hand wrapped it and stroked upward. "I don't need that, sweetheart."

"I want to." Her thumb rubbed silky wetness around his tip. "I love touching you."

She pushed down and found his balls, stroking their weight gently. Arcadius groaned and ducked lower, his head covering her breast as his mouth sealed hungrily over one nipple. The pull of his lips and tongue caused her spine to arch. Needing more, she took his hand and moved it between her legs.

He twitched when he felt the wetness of her arousal, quickly proving he loved exploring her as much as she did him. His warm blunt fingertips rubbed her, parting her folds, circling her clit and then tugging it. As he slid two fingers inside her, he backed his torso up to watch them penetrate. That was good. Elyse's eyes closed without her willing them to shut. How natural this felt amazed her. Gone was any hint of self-consciousness. Her bent legs dropped to the side, all the tension washed out of them. She wanted him to see what he did to her, wanted him to have any pleasure that excited him.

"Wait," he said as her body rolled with desire for him.

He stretched to the side to get something. Elyse's eyes opened in surprise. He was pulling a sheet over them.

"I'm hardly cold," she said, amused by this unnecessary consideration.

"You might *get* cold," he said, his answer choppy with arousal. "Desert temperatures drop at night."

She laughed, gliding her hands up his chest to pinch his tight nipples. She gave them a gentle twist. "Maybe you need warming up," she teased.

His pelvis jerked against her, his seemingly mile-long cock strafing her inner thigh. "Never around you. You heat me up whenever we're together."

"Prove it. Put that tent pole where it belongs."

His eyes flashed silver blue fire at her. The sheet covered them to their waists. He didn't bother tugging it higher. He pulled her thighs apart instead, his hands strong and hot on her knees. She didn't wrap her legs around him. She wanted him to move as he pleased without restriction. Seeming to share the preference, he took his hard cock in hand and placed it at her entrance. The contact with his fingers was intimate.

His face flickered with deep pleasure as he shoved halfway in.

"Mm," she hummed, her spine stretching and undulating, her feet digging in to the firm mattress.

She was wet, but his thumb rubbed her wetter by manipulating her little rod. She squirmed around the flesh inside her, wondering at her unexpected sense of power—as if she were the one on top. His pulse throbbed inside her, his wide chest heaving over hers. Enjoyment weighted her eyes. She couldn't resist pricking his ribs where her nails held them.

"Give me the rest of you," she said. "You know I've been waiting."

Thankfully, he didn't need more encouragement. He screwed his eyes shut and shoved. Two thrusts surged lubriciously in and out, easing and pleasing her. On the third, he grunted and found her end. One hand closed possessively around her bottom, the fingers of the other fanning her shoulder. His lashes rose, his pleasure-blurred expression sharpening when he found her gazing back at him.

Neither of them looked away. His eyes were saying something she thought she ought to be able to decode. Whatever the message was, he felt it intensely. Instinctively, she gentled her grip on his ribcage. She expected him to speak. Instead, he lightly kissed her right cheek and then her left.

Then he smiled and began pistoning into her.

She had a hard time remembering they were in a tent, and she shouldn't cry out too loudly. His long hard strokes felt so good, so totally, one hundred percent what she was craving. She guessed he agreed with her.

"Yes," he praised as she shoved back at him.

This was going to end fast. Pre-orgasmic sensations were already gathering in her sex. "I hope . . . you're not . . . trying . . . to draw this out," she gasped.

"No," he panted. "I'm going to lose my mind if I don't come soon."

He shifted angles and went deeper. She couldn't help it; the inner friction was heaven. She hooked her heels behind his hard butt and pulled.

"Don't," he said, immediately dragging them off again. With an efficiency that startled her, he rearranged their legs. Now his calves pinned her ankles, pinning them under him as he thrust.

She gasped, remembering when he bound them with the tie to her robe. The feeling was the same—that somehow being kept in this position improved every sensation. He was forcing her to take his cock in precisely the right spots, making it impossible for her to do anything but go out of her mind with bliss.

Her pussy tightened hungrily around him.

He let out a low noise, seeming to like that a lot. "Is this okay?" he asked anyway. "Tell me if my weight presses you down too much."

"Just don't stop," she said, grinding her teeth as he went faster.

Her ragged plea snapped some restraint in him.

His hips thumped hers more determinedly, each thrust scooching them slightly higher on the bedroll. Loving how his strength stimulated her, how it made her feel wonderfully overwhelmed, she clung to his bunched shoulders.

"Oh, yeah," he said, sounding so male his voice alone was a thrill. His pumping cock seemed to swell, stretching her inside even more. "God . . . Elyse . . . you feel . . . so *good.*"

He sucked air between the words, slamming into her with each utterance. The deep jolts knocked her nerves to the brink of orgasm. When he said "good," she went over. The delicious narrowing down of her ecstasy clamped her sheath snug on him.

He felt that, no mistake. He flung his head back with strain and bliss, his Adam's apple standing out. "In the name of God, turn my seed to smoke."

The prayer meant little to her. His big body had her attention as he drove in and burst, groaning rough and low with relief. Something about his ejaculation was unexpected. She registered heat and throbbing but no wetness —or not apart from her own and the sweat running down his abs.

She took a minute—a pleasant one—to realize what was off. Her climax had dwindled to warm honey, and he pulled his cock free of her. He sank face down beside her, one arm slung over her at the waist. Her body hummed with satisfaction, not simply in her pussy but all over. She didn't notice the wisps of smoke rising through the sheet in one particular area until she curled her toes and stretched.

Shocked, she slapped her hand over her pudendum. It didn't hurt. In truth, it felt really good. Even so, she had to ask.

"Arcadius," she gasped. "Did you just set my pussy on *fire?*"

He chuckled against her shoulder. "Genie prophylactic. I wasn't certain the birth control you mentioned earlier was in place. Smoke doesn't make babies."

She goggled for more than one reason. What sort of incredibly responsible, self-controlled male remembered to consider this?

"It won't hurt you," he mumbled. "Perfectly hygienic, I promise."

He kissed the breast that was nearest him, covering the other with his palm. Elyse twisted on her side to face him. His head was lower than hers but she saw the edge of his smile. Her fingertips followed a slightly sweaty path to his breastbone, where his heart was thudding slower but steadily. Their knees bumped before he edged one hairy leg between her smooth ones.

She liked having those big muscles to tighten her thighs around.

"Arcadius," she said, trailing her touch low enough to circle his navel. "What would you say if I told you I wasn't done with you?"

His smile deepened. "I'd say I'd be honored to pleasure you again."

"Actually," she said, "I have a hankering to ride you."

That brought his head up. The look in his eyes was uneasy. "Uh, I don't think—"

She cut him off by clasping his fading erection. She used all her hand—fingers, palm, muscles—to caress it as persuasively as she was able. He squirmed, his flesh immediately stiffening. He put one hand over hers. Maybe he meant to stop her. Stroking him again seemed to change his mind. He let his hold ride along with hers instead.

"Um," he said, pleasure blurring his eyes as her grasp pulled slowly, luxuriantly up him.

"'Um?'" she repeated, teasing him.

"I don't think . . . that is . . ."

Sensing she had the upper hand, she nudged him onto his back and straddled him.

"I *do* think," she contradicted. "I have no doubt you'll rise to the occasion of having me in your saddle."

He blinked. Possibly the metaphor confused him. Her fondling was easier to follow. She had his cock against her belly and was pulling hand over hand up the anterior of his shaft. He hardly needed the help. He was very firm, very ready to gallop toward the finish line. His tip stretched an admirable distance up her belly.

He squirmed, the same small wriggle he'd failed to restrain before. He looked at himself in her hands before gaping at her face. He seemed at a loss to give her a clear thumbs up.

"Should I use the leash on you?" she asked. "Would that make it easier for me to be on top? I, um, gather the men of your plane prefer to be in charge."

"I don't . . . have a problem with you being on top."

She smiled at his breathless answer. One large part of him had no problem with it at all. Her teeth caught her lower lip. His body made such a picture under her: so male, so strong, so completely unable to remain motionless.

"Maybe I'd just *like* to use the leash on you," she confessed.

He flushed, his hands settling on her hips. The restless kneading of his fingers caused arousal to well from her. "This position is . . . I can see everything."

"I thought you enjoyed that."

"I do. Believe me." As if he couldn't help it, his gaze fell to and locked on her breasts. The modest swells shook with her renewed heartbeats, her nipples reddened and drawn tight. He wagged his head then slid his hands up to cover them. "Anything you want, I promise I'm game to try."

That was quite the offer.

"I tossed the leash out here," she informed him. "It's lying in a coil above the bedroll."

"The slave rope, you mean."

"Yes."

His powerful chest went up and down. "Where would you put it?"

She thought. "I'd bind your left arm to the tent pole. I like the way the rope looks circling your wrist."

Her cheeks went hot as she realized what she'd said. This was how he held the tether when she was tied. Arcadius's grin turned devilish.

"Do you now?" he asked. "That's where you'd better put it then."

~

Maybe Arcadius should have found a way to dissuade her. When he settled on this plan, he hadn't intended to make a show of her—of their lovemaking, yes, but not her. Then again, what did he truly risk if she discovered he'd done this without her okay? She'd be furious, and probably mortified, but she couldn't fall out of love; she wasn't in it in the first place. He couldn't deny she made an excellent distraction. Certainly, he couldn't tear her eyes from her.

Actually, he wasn't sure how clearly he was thinking.

He didn't resist as she wound the soft rope around his left wrist. Her breasts jiggled temptingly as she moved, her budded nipples mesmerizing him.

"That's not too tight, is it?" she asked.

Had she tied his wrist already? He glanced over and saw she had. His brain went a little weird. He was the sultan's commander. Up until the end, he'd never lost an important battle. Most definitely he'd never been trussed like a captive.

"That's fine," he said in an odd strangled tone. His penis thought it was fabulous. It was as rigid as it had been in the seconds before he came.

Seeming unaware anything was wrong, Elyse patted his thudding chest. She hopped off him, nimble and naked, to attach the rope's other end to the tent's center pole. "You won't tug too hard, will you?" she asked as she crouched. "I wouldn't want the roof to come down on us."

Arcadius hoped Zayd's seeing crystal was too high to get a clear eyeful. Elyse was such a pretty woman, her body so neat and well formed. Zayd's men didn't deserve to see her, much less to pass judgment on how she "stacked up" to females they knew.

"Arcadius?"

"No," he said. "I won't bring down the roof."

She hesitated, finally noting something off in his expression. "Maybe these aren't the right circumstances for trying this."

He rolled onto his side to see her. He was glad he'd told the sheikh she made him heartsick. He didn't have to hold back his words. "All the moments I share with you are gifts. Everything we do excites me, even acts I haven't tried before."

Elyse looked shyly pleased but also amused. "You say the nicest things," she laughed.

"Come back here," he growled. "I wish to demonstrate how earnestly I mean what I say."

He clenched the muscles of his ass, causing his erection to bounce higher. He intended the display to be slightly comical. Elyse pressed one palm over her snicker. Suspecting he almost had her, he did the trick again.

"All right," she surrendered. "I can't resist that offer."

She crawled back to him on her hands and knees, the litheness of her body making her look like an animal prowling. That caused his prick to bob without assistance.

She laughed as she noticed the telltale throb. "You really do like me on my knees."

"I'd really like you on my cock. Please 'save a horse,' as the human saying goes."

She swung one leg over him. She was on her knees in a different way, his pocket Amazon, poised for conquering. Her pussy was above but not on his dick. She drew all her fingers playfully up his shaft. He'd noticed his sexual nerves were sharper than in his old body. Her light touch teased him so effectively he truly felt desperate.

"I want you," he reminded her.

"You just had me."

"I guess I wasn't done with you yet."

She smiled and bent to kiss him. His right cheek received the press of her lips, then his left, and finally the tip of his nose. The sweet little gesture, which echoed what he'd done to her, touched him to a ridiculous degree. He fought not to let the emotion burning behind his eyes rise high enough to show. Luckily, she was ready to move their game along. Her fingers stroked his erection more purposefully.

"You ready for me, cowboy?"

He cracked a grin, the idea of being one humorous. "I am," he promised her.

Despite his amusement, nothing readied him for the bliss of her sinking down on him. She was hot and soft and as slick as if she'd been oiled. Waves of pleasure had his body writhing in slow motion, had him pushing his pelvis eagerly to her. He gripped her hip with his untied hand, urging her down on him. Wanting to use both hands, he forced himself not to tug too hard with the other. The pole that braced the tent peak was sturdy, but djinn were strong. He really might pull the roof down on them.

His Amazon sighed and gave a delicious wiggle as she finished engulfing him. Arcadius's eyes had closed. He opened them dazedly. Elyse pressed one hand to her pubis as if trying to feel him from there.

"You're pounding inside of me," she whispered.

He felt her heartbeat too. "I think you'd better ride me hard, sweetheart, before I go crazy."

She lifted, snug flesh dragging delectably upward. She sucked in a breath and paused. "God, you feel good. Will you remember to do that smoke thing again?"

"I don't have to. The one spell will last all night."

She bit a sudden grin. "I don't have to be careful?"

"Only of yourself," he said.

She bent to kiss him—once, deeply, her tongue driving in and retreating before he could hold it there. The kiss stole his breath, but when she began to ride him, that stole his mind. She was fast and strong and every nerve in his cock instantly blazed with sensations.

Her fingers kneaded his chest, her breasts bouncing gorgeously. Each time she lifted, his cock gleamed bright from her secretions. The primal appeal of that visual couldn't be resisted, no more than being her steed could. He was used to being in charge, and this was a fresh pleasure. His wrist twisted on the slave rope, longing to snap it even as he felt an unexpected exhilaration at it restraining him. Elyse seemed to know. Her hips rolled faster, harder, as smoothly as if her joints were on wheels. She was making him forget everything: how to be careful of the force he used, how to hold back his climax until she had hers. The need to explode expanded, the pressure both delicious and unbearable.

Elyse growled and thumped her pussy more energetically down him.

Watching her go wild sent his excitement into the stratosphere. In the end, though, he couldn't bear the thought of anyone but him seeing her come.

"Kiss me," he demanded, his free hand sliding behind her nape.

She cried out as he tugged her down, her sheath starting to ripple with contractions. Maybe his aggression triggered her. He cursed, planted his feet for leverage, and drove into her from below.

His orgasm burst from him like fire, white gold, blinding, so powerfully sweet new words had to be invented for the pleasure. Elyse clung to him, not kissing him but holding tight. Her nipples were sharp as pebbles, her heart pounding crazily. His thumb found her clit and ground it, partly to increase her bliss and partly for the lovely tightening that inspired. A second astronomical climax subsumed his first.

"*Cade*," she gasped, the nickname instantly charming him.

He had no strength left. The world could have ended, and he wouldn't have been able to lift a finger to prevent it.

"Mmm," he moaned as she panted against his neck. She was a hot sweaty limpet on top of him. He stroked her spine and patted her trembling butt, his hand unwilling to stir once it was there. Elyse wriggled until her head found a comfortable hollow on his shoulder.

Her satiated sigh was music to his ego. "I'll get up in a minute," she mumbled.

"No need," he said, tightening his one-armed hold on her. "I want to sleep with you just like this."

~

Elyse didn't know how long she was unconscious before her eyes snapped open. She was curled against Arcadius's side, hugging him in her sleep. The colorful Moroccan lanterns had gone out, leaving a bright quarter moon to light the tent from outside.

Shoot, she thought. *I forgot to untie him.*

She checked his arm, but of course he'd removed the slave rope himself. She *had* only bound one wrist. Her touch on his forearm caused him to stir sleepily.

"Everything's fine," she said, rubbing his bare shoulder. "Go back to sleep."

He wasn't going to take her word for it. He opened his eyes, stared at her for a moment, only closing his lids after he was satisfied.

Since she was awake, she pulled her knees up and hugged them. The ifrit camp was quiet except for the apparently constant whisper of the wind.

I'm in the world of the djinn, she thought, still not quite believing it. In spite of the dangers involved in this, she grinned.

Then she noticed a shadowy hump in the opposite corner of the tent. She pressed her hand to her throat a second before recognizing the shape as Joseph. He was curled on the carpet floor, seemingly fast asleep. He had no bedroll and no blanket. He'd removed his outer robe and was sleeping under that.

That didn't seem right. Elyse found her own robe and tied it. Because Arcadius had plenty of body heat to share, she eased one of their blankets from the pile and carried it to the servant.

Joseph turned out to be as light a sleeper as his master. He turned onto his back while she was laying the cover over him.

"What's wrong?" he murmured.

Elyse crouched beside him to speak. "I was going to ask you the same thing."

He rubbed his face. "Nothing's wrong. Or not any more wrong than before."

His wry response amused her. "Now *there's* an answer I can believe."

"You brought me a blanket," Joseph said, sounding surprised as he touched it.

"You looked cold."

He gazed at her. "Thank you."

"Thank *you* for reconnoitering."

She assumed this was what he'd been doing. Her words seemed to make him uncomfortable. It occurred to her he might have returned while she and Arcadius were still at it. That would be awkward. Elyse wasn't the sort of person who wanted the whole world to know when she was getting some.

"I should sleep," Joseph said in a calm soft tone. "So should you. Tomorrow may be challenging."

"Oh. Of course. I'll just . . . go back to Arcadius."

Mildly embarrassed, she did just that. Joseph's prediction wasn't exactly soothing. All the same, when Arcadius wrapped himself around her and kissed her hair, she only took a moment to drop off again.

CHAPTER TWELVE

ARCADIUS woke before the others early the next morning. He made use of the extravagant magically powered bathroom, dressed, and slipped out into the camp to scrounge breakfast for his tent mates.

The rules of hospitality—assuming they'd be honored—guaranteed their safety until sunset, at which point they'd need another invitation to continue as Zayd's guests. Arcadius was on guard for threats but was directed politely to the cook tent. Given the number of speculative looks he attracted, he concluded his and Elyse's performance had drawn its intended audience.

The only appropriate response was to pretend he didn't see. Though his cheeks were a degree hotter than usual, he maintained a bland expression.

His color didn't truly darken until he ducked into the tent and Joseph spotted him with the laden tray. Arcadius had forgotten how out of character his behavior was.

"Master!" Joseph exclaimed. "I would have gotten us breakfast."

"I know you would," he said gruffly. "I was up."

Both Joseph and Elyse were awake and dressed. They sat on the floor in Joseph's sound-cancelling circle, probably because the younger man had steered Elyse there. Arcadius set down the tray, allowing Joseph to take over the process of serving.

Elyse, he noticed, looked to be in good spirits and beautifully well pleasured—certainly none the worse for wear for having been dragged into danger.

"Coffee!" she burst out delightedly. "My God, I adore you!"

That caused his cheeks to darken a little too.

"So," Joseph said after they'd taken the edge off their hunger. "My suspicions were correct. There's an outcrop of rocks not too far from camp that Zayd's guards include in their patrol. I expect there's a cave underneath where the flying carpets are stored. It would make no sense to protect it otherwise."

"How close were you able to get?"

"I spent two minutes right on top of the thing while the guard was . . . distracted. The entrance is password protected. I couldn't break through it magically. Probably only Zayd knows the open sesame."

Elyse's jaw had dropped at the mention of flying carpets. She did a double take at his choice of words. "'Open sesame' isn't really a thing."

Joseph smiled. "It isn't anymore. These days, it's the first code anybody tries."

"Do you think you could crack the spell if you had more time?" Arcadius asked.

"I wouldn't bet our lives on it," Joseph said. "Zayd's sorcerers are topnotch."

"Is there a reason we have to have a flying carpet?" Elyse inquired. "Trying to steal one seems like asking for trouble."

"Unfortunately," Arcadius said, "we can't walk from this stretch of the Qaf to ours, not if we had unlimited supplies and all the time in the universe. The two areas aren't physically connected. We need magical transport."

"Maybe this is a stupid question, but could we ask Zayd to loan us one?"

"Out of the goodness of his heart?" Joseph shook his head doubtfully. "I wouldn't bet our lives on that either."

The flatbread Elyse's fingers were tearing into pieces suddenly fascinated her. "What about another bribe?"

"No," Arcadius said firmly.

"You don't know what I was going to say."

"No," he repeated. "You will not offer yourself to him. I forbid it."

"You can't forbid it. I belong to me."

"Zayd would *kill* you, Elyse. He's a different type of djinni from Joseph and myself. He'd whip you as fiercely as if you were an ifrit—and then he'd lose control. He wouldn't be able to help himself. And you'd never survive it."

Her mouth formed a crooked shape. "Okay, I'm not saying I *want* to do it, or that I doubt your words. Just . . . what if there isn't another choice?"

"There's always another choice."

"There is," Joseph seconded, inspiring more gratitude in Arcadius than he probably realized. "We'll watch for an opening. The solution will come to us."

~

Joseph had already gone out. Elyse couldn't be left alone in the tent safely, so Arcadius retied the slave rope around her waist.

"Keep you eyes down," he reminded her. "Don't speak to anyone even if they address you." He pulled up her djellaba's hood, using this as an excuse to caress her head. "Joseph spelled the circle we're standing in to muffle sound. Try not to talk about our business outside of it."

Her brows went up, but she didn't make the leap to the full extent of spying that might go on. "Do you know what's happening today?"

"Most likely Zayd will demonstrate the strength of his position and try to assess ours. I predict we'll see training fights between his men and be invited to participate."

"Will you accept?" Her fingertips rested on his chest. He doubted she knew how much he enjoyed standing with her like this.

"My answer will depend on what we stand to gain."

She tilted her head to consider him. "You aren't a rash person."

"Not if I can help it."

"Neither is Joseph."

Joseph was more impetuous by nature, but he'd learned to suppress the trait. "When it comes to protecting you, neither of us will lose our heads."

She smiled. "I'm concerned for your safety too."

Of course she was. She was a caring woman. He hadn't missed that business with Joseph and the blanket this morning. He rubbed her shoulders, reluctant to let go of her. He dreaded the day when she regarded him with anger. A question rose inside him. Though he suspected he shouldn't voice it, he couldn't seem to stop himself. "Do you wish I were more dashing?"

Her soft pink mouth fell open. "I find you extremely dashing, exactly as you are. Good Lord, how could I not?"

He couldn't answer that. Her feelings about him were murkier than he wished. Had her husband been dashing? Or better at romance? Con men sometimes were. He shook his head to clear the irrelevant concerns. Their current situation demanded his complete attention.

~

Arcadius's question knocked Elyse off balance. Why did he care if she thought him dashing? He was of course—along with being gorgeous, sexy, intelligent, and considerate. Being reckless wouldn't have improved him in her eyes. Being more honest, perhaps, but not that.

She trailed after him through the camp, her mind occupied with trying to sort this out. He'd sounded unsure of himself. Was his pride at stake? He'd warned her he didn't love her, a claim that was beginning to sting more than it should have. *Was* he falling for her? Or was this some crazy trick within a trick? She couldn't rule that out. Her instincts, such as they were, told her he wasn't being frank about everything.

But she had to push that aside. She needed her wits about her, in the present. Even with her eyes cast down, she noticed they were getting a lot of looks. How noisy had she been last night? Was she the reason Joseph had drawn his circle for silence?

She pulled her head covering closer, hoping it hid her burning cheeks. They came to a sudden halt on the path between the tents.

"There you are," Sheikh Zayd said too pleasantly to be believed. "I trust the night left you well rested."

"Your accommodations were everything the most particular guest could wish." Arcadius bowed, which djinn seemed to do a lot.

"I am gratified to hear it. My men are training today. I thought you might enjoy watching them. And your slave as well, if it won't distress her too much."

Arcadius had certainly called this right. Elyse was tempted to look up. Staring at the sand that clung to her slippers didn't tell her if the sheikh truly wanted her in the audience.

"Your offer is magnanimous," Arcadius said. "Hopefully her spirit will not quail at your men's fierceness."

"Her spirit may be stronger than you have said."

Well. Elyse recognized *that* tone as sulky.

"Only a fool would give his slave a swelled head."

Arcadius's response was mild—too mild, maybe. Zayd's words had put her protector on his guard. Elyse touched the rope that bound her to him, one thumb nervously rubbing its smooth surface. Realizing Zayd might see the gesture, she forced herself to stop.

"As you say," the sheikh returned smoothly. "Shall we proceed to the fighting ground?"

They proceeded.

The fighting ground was a cracked sand flat. Using the tip of a gold plated stick, one of the tribesmen drew an oval the size of a hockey rink around it. Elyse assumed any fighter who crossed the border lost. Or who died. Probably that qualified as a loss as well.

The sun was bright and the day warming. Zayd and his closest tribesmen took seats beneath the shade of a small canopy. Arcadius and his "pet" were also welcomed there. The sheikh's throne-like chair put him higher than their cushions. Elyse didn't care. She was grateful she didn't have to stand.

At first the matches were interesting. Some ifrits fought each other in whirlwind form, dashing at each other like tornadoes and taking crazy shapes until one or the other was shoved over the penalty line. The battles with exotic weapons kept her attention too. The ifrits were fast and strong and as balletic as movie stunt people flipping around on wires. Thus far, no one had died. The injured either healed themselves by changing form or by requesting the aid of Zayd's sorcerers. The magicians were easy to identify. They wore black robes that covered everything but their eyes, perhaps to make them seem mysterious. Elyse counted seven—enough to outmatch Joseph, she concluded reluctantly.

The problem, at least for her, was that there were simply too many fights. The winner of each battle got to choose the terms of the next, along with whom he fought. None of Zayd's men wanted to be left out. As the day wore on, the matches grew bloodier. Elyse didn't enjoy watching people get stabbed and hacked, no matter what sort of beings they were. As she flinched, the sly sideways glances the sheikh sent toward her frayed her nerves even more. Arcadius had warned her drinking in too much pain could cause an ifrit to lose control.

Was her distress at the violence enough to send Zayd around the bend?

Arcadius continued to watch with calm interest, but that was SOP for him. He kept weaknesses—when he had any—to himself. Elyse decided she should stop paying attention, since she couldn't control her reactions. As she wrenched her gaze away from the current fight, she spotted Samir the smoke demon in the crowd. Without his horse, he seemed different. He perched atop a barrel, stretched to see over the taller djinn around him. His vaporous batwings quivered with excitement, their edges wispy beneath the sun. As one fighter skewered his opponent with a disgusting squelching noise, the demon pulsed down to a pinpoint. The crack of bone followed a moment later, causing the crowd to roar. Samir's smoke flashed back to its previous size, darker and thicker than before.

She couldn't doubt he liked the blood and gore.

She didn't want to know what had happened, though all seven sorcerers rushing onto the ground at once was a hint.

Sheikh Zayd rose, addressing the victor even as a limp, red-soaked body was carried off. Elyse didn't hear the congratulations. Her blood roared too loudly in her ears. She was pretty sure someone had just been killed. Though she tried not to look, she saw an arm trailing in the dirt between the sorcerers. That one limb gave off an indefinable no-one's-home impression she'd forever recognize. She'd noticed it the moment she found David in the cellar that awful day. Arcadius's heavy hand settled on her shoulder, but she didn't lift her head.

Arcadius was already being challenged before the words people spoke started making sense to her again.

Shit, she thought—and a few other curses besides. The djinni who'd slain his opponent wanted to fight Arcadius next. Arcadius couldn't risk himself like that! What if he were killed? Stopping her mouth from opening to protest took all Elyse's strength. She had to trust he knew what he was doing.

Arcadius came gracefully to his feet, exuding the modesty he and Joseph excelled at. "The chance to test my mettle against such a champion honors me. If I am to say 'yes,' I have two requests: that our fight end with first blood drawn, and that this be my only match. I am a visitor among this tribe. To even hope for more glory would be inappropriate."

She probably should have known the sheikh would agree to this. He wanted Arcadius to fight, no matter what.

Arcadius lifted his arm. Joseph must have been nearby. He appeared as swiftly as if he'd been magicked. Arcadius handed him the slave rope's end.

"Watch my pet," he said, not asking for Zayd's permission.

Joseph bowed and stepped beside the cushion on which she sat. Arcadius strode toward the fighting ground without a backward glance. One small sound broke in Elyse's throat. Joseph squeezed her shoulder but then let go. Her heart pounded so hard she thought she might be sick.

She absolutely refused to check if Zayd was drinking in her terror. Out on the fighting ground, Arcadius stripped down to his trousers. Though Joseph seemed unruffled, she couldn't help gnawing on her lip. Arcadius's opponent was as tall as he was and bulged with muscle. He was one of the ifrits who kept his hair in smoke form. As he warmed up for his next battle, he made an impressive show of whipping his scimitar and dagger around. Arcadius was given the same weapons. He rolled his head on his neck, stretched his arms until they cracked, and crouched in readiness.

The bout was over in less than five minutes.

Arcadius was breathtakingly quick and powerful. He made no show of anything, getting in and getting out with the minimum necessary motions to defend or attack. The nick he dealt his opponent to end the match was so tiny the audience saw the streak of red before Zayd's man registered the sting and gaped at it.

"Wonderful!" cried the sheikh. He leaped from his throne clapping. "You must fight another match, if only to allow my men to study your technique."

Arcadius inclined his head. "Far be it from me to deny my host anything he wishes. I would suggest, however, that the day grows late. Even men as formidable as yours require breaks for sustenance. Might I propose a different form of entertainment?"

"Different?" Sheikh Zayd had subsided into his seat. His glance slipped to Elyse and away again, causing her to tense against shuddering. "What do you have in mind?"

This time, Arcadius looked in her direction. She lifted her head, but Joseph's was the face he was checking. The servant seemed to understand what was being asked. He gave his master a tiny nod.

"My servant," Arcadius said, waving casually toward him, "is considered a fair storyteller. Perhaps your men would like listening to him, and perhaps you and I might liven the experience with a small wager."

Arcadius spoke as if butter wouldn't melt in his mouth. Zayd leaned back in his fancy chair and laughed.

"You truly do take me for a fool. Even here in the desert we know who Joseph the Eunuch is. We also know his storytelling considerably outdoes 'fair.' Yes—" He pointed an accusing finger at Arcadius, whose jaw had slackened with surprise. "My old friend Samir informed us which Arcadius and Joseph were requesting shelter. The sultan's great commander and his famed magician are quite the guests for humble tent dwellers like ourselves."

Zayd's smile was saturnine. He savored revealing what he knew, including that Samir was his ally and not their own. Since none of them had trusted him to begin with, Elyse didn't think this was important. She glanced at the smoke demon. Samir grinned broadly back at her, white teeth flashing in his smoke head. The display was as unexpected as it was unsettling. Elyse dragged her gaze to her knees again, where her hands had unconsciously curled into fists.

Wait a second, she thought, her overloaded brain catching up by increments. If Arcadius was the sultan's commander and Joseph was a magician, then the bedtime stories Arcadius told her related true events. Joseph must be the apprentice the evil sorcerer had tortured. *Eunuch* wasn't simply a word. Joseph had sacrificed his manhood to save his father's life.

Her understanding turned upside down. The tale telling competition in the tavern had really happened. And the sultan falling in love with the disguised princess. These were actual people Arcadius and Joseph knew, people they were trying to get home to and rescue.

She was lucky her head was down. Her face would have told a story by itself. Poor Joseph! No wonder he seemed sad.

"Forgive my unfortunate omission," Arcadius was saying to the sheikh. "Everyone knows how highly desert people value their freedom from any sultan's rule. I feared the Guardian of the Glorious City might not be welcome here."

"The rules of hospitality don't care who a person serves."

The sheikh's response was terse, as if he'd rather not acknowledge this.

"Of course." Arcadius bowed in response to the reprimand. "I shouldn't have implied you'd act otherwise."

The sheikh snorted. Elyse snuck a glance at him. He didn't appear particularly angry. In truth, he looked like a man secure in his upper hand.

"No matter," he said dismissively. "I hear Sultan Iksander isn't ruling much of anyone these days."

For just an instant, Arcadius's polished facade roughened. Genuine anger cut across his face. When it passed, his features remained stiff.

The insult had been deliberate. Sheikh Zayd's mouth curved the slightest bit. He pressed his fingertips together to hide the smile. "We *would* be curious to hear the eunuch's story," he admitted. "And to consider a wager, if you still wish to propose it."

Joseph spoke up beside her. "I'd be delighted to spin a tale. And I know just the means to determine a bet's winner."

Arcadius blinked and then composed his face. He must not have seen this coming.

"Excellent," Sheikh Zayd said silkily. "What shall we wager for?"

That was the crucial question. Arcadius faced the ifrit squarely. "We want one of your flying carpets, sufficient in size and power to get us safely home."

Sheikh Zayd's smoke gray eyes gleamed with amusement. "That *is* a prize.

I presume you hope to somehow relieve your 'glorious' city's plight."

To this, Arcadius said nothing.

"You know what I want of course," the sheikh continued. He crossed his long legs with a rustle of fine cotton. "Your pet. At my mercy. For all the hours between sunset and sunrise."

Elyse's heart threatened to choke her throat. Had she really almost suggested this herself? Arcadius's gaze held Zayd's so very firmly she knew he must be ordering it not to shift to her. Surely he'd offer the ifrit another prize . . . except what other prize did they have?

"Your 'mercy' poses problems," he said tightly.

"You should have thought of that when you claimed she was only moderately good in bed—and that she was soft. You piqued my interest, 'Cade.' Now I know the human is a tigress, worthy of *all* my attentions."

Despite the day's sunny heat, Elyse's face went icy. How did Zayd know what she'd called Arcadius privately? And why didn't Arcadius seem surprised? He'd made such a fuss about Joseph's sound-cancelling circle. He must have known the sheikh was spying on them some other way.

Her breath burst from her in outrage. Even then, neither man looked at her. Apparently her preferences weren't important to either one.

Arcadius worked his jaw and spoke. "I'd loan her to you on one condition: that you return her unscathed in either mind or body. If one hair on her head is harmed, you concede I may claim your life as forfeit."

"My life!" Zayd exclaimed. "You value this pet highly."

"To an ifrit, no other penalty means a damn—as you'll admit yourself, I think."

Elyse sucked in a breath of shock. Joseph squeezed her shoulder to keep her from speaking. He was going to allow this happen too? After what Arcadius said about Zayd being certain to lose control and kill her? Zayd's life being forfeit wouldn't help her then.

Joseph's fingers dug into her again. "Silence," he said sternly.

Her lips were trembling so she pressed them together. *They have a plan*, she told herself. Please God, let this be a part of it. It didn't take a genius, or a genie, to realize what Zayd meant by all his attentions. Arcadius wouldn't let her be whipped and raped by a sadistic maniac.

"Human minds are so delicate," Zayd observed. "How can I promise not to harm hers?"

"You'll have to err on the side of caution."

Zayd pursed his mouth in distaste. "That would diminish my enjoyment. No, I cannot answer until I know how your man proposes to decide the winner."

Joseph dug his hand into his loose pants pocket. "Here. These are toys from the human plane. This is called a heart-rate monitor. You strap it around your chest and it wirelessly sends information about your pulse to this device, which humans call a cell phone."

The items Joseph pulled out were miniaturized, but he quickly restored them to their original state. True to his djinn love for vivid colors, Joseph's cell phone was bright orange with deep red dots.

"The monitor came free with the phone," Joseph explained to Arcadius.

Bemused, Arcadius shook his head. Zayd seemed intrigued but suspicious. "Those are *human* devices."

"They're easy enough to use," Joseph said. "With your magician's help, I can clone the monitors. I thought you and Arcadius could wager on whether I raise your men's pulses with my tale—say ten percent above their normal resting rate?"

Zayd leaned forward, obviously attracted by the tech. "Which of my men would wear the straps?"

"Whichever you choose. Your sorcerers and I will have to see how many of the clones we can get to work. You could keep them afterwards of course."

Sheikh Zayd rubbed his lips. "I would prefer you raise their heart rates fifty percent above normal."

"Twenty-five," Joseph countered.

"Thirty-five," the sheikh fired back.

"Hm." Joseph made it sound as if he didn't like this idea. "We'd need a referee, someone to track results and announce them at the end. Would you appoint one of your men to submit to an honesty spell?"

"I would," Zayd said. "Are you prepared to have this challenge take place tonight?"

"One moment," Arcadius cut in, his tone as dry as the sand he stood on. "Before my servant enters into this bargain on my behalf, I'd like to speak to him privately."

Zayd appeared to enjoy this sign of dissension within their ranks. He leaned back in his throne and waved for them to go.

Because he held Elyse's leash, Joseph pulled her along for the huddle, which began as soon as they were out of the crowd's earshot. Elyse didn't know if she was expected to share her opinion and was too enraged to care.

"You know," she said to Arcadius icily, "if you'd told me you were making a display of our private moments, I could have acted more vanilla. Then maybe that maniac wouldn't be convinced I'm the only prize worth bargaining for."

"I was concerned you'd give away that you knew we were being watched."

Elyse slapped him in the chest. "That's no excuse. It was a horrible thing to do. That man saw us. You should have given me a choice."

Arcadius rubbed his breastbone where she'd hit it. "You're telling me you'd have agreed?"

"I don't know." She crossed her arms. "I would have worn more clothes at least." Arcadius began to smile. "Don't you *dare* be amused. You owe me the biggest apology in the history of both of our planes."

"I'm sorry," he said. "If you'd allow it, I'd spend eternity making it up to you."

She turned her head away. He'd complied too glibly. "Tell me you're going to win this," she said to Joseph.

"I probably am."

"Probably!"

"Calm down," Arcadius said. "You going ballistic will hardly convince Zayd you're vanilla."

Elyse was so angry she couldn't speak.

"Tell her," Joseph advised. "Zayd has already decided she's worth trading a carpet for."

Arcadius pulled a face but followed his counsel. "We wouldn't hand you over."

"What?"

"If we lose, I'll forswear myself. I'll fight every man he has to keep you safe from him."

Elyse's fury swung so quickly to concern her emotions got whiplash. "He has a lot of men. You couldn't defeat them all."

"I'd try," Arcadius said simply.

"And if he failed, I'd kill *you*." Joseph shrugged when she gaped at him. "Better that than living through what Zayd would do to you, since you'd end up dead either way."

Elyse broke into a ragged laugh. "That's practical, I suppose."

Joseph smiled crookedly back at her.

"Can you win the wager?" she asked, trying to speak calmly.

"I believe I have the measure of this audience. And the human tech gives us an advantage. These desert djinn won't understand the monitor can't be tricked by putting up a stoic front."

"So we're doing this?" Arcadius asked, surprisingly democratically.

"Yes," Joseph voted.

"Yes," Elyse sighed when he turned to her.

~

Together with Zayd's raven-garbed sorcerers, Joseph cloned five working copies of the heart-rate monitor. Arcadius and Elyse kept an eye on their friend. Though too far away to hear what was said, they saw he was comfortable with his ifrit counterparts. Elyse wondered if there was a special geekdom for magicians. Maybe they felt a kinship to each other irrespective of moral differences.

Having had the interval to consider, Zayd quickly named the men who'd wear the monitors. Three of his smoke-haired fighters stepped forward. One of the fighters' ears were pierced with multiple gold rings. A red-eyed albino joined the group, followed by an old man so tall and emaciated he literally seemed to be skin and bone. For all the emotion the group displayed, their faces could have been carved from stone. Elyse hoped Joseph was right about the monitors not caring.

The sixth man Zayd called underwent a charm that compelled him to be honest. Elyse noticed he seemed less than ecstatic over the honor.

After this, everyone took a break to eat.

Darkness had fallen by the time they gathered again at the fighting ground. Joseph stood alone within the large oval. Torches burned to either side of him. Behind him was a leather folding chair he could sit on if he desired. An ifrit servant scurried over with a silver cup and a goatskin that held water. Joseph thanked him, waiting in silence for everyone to sit. He seemed dignified in his tunic and over-robe—big enough to be a fighter but radiating the spirit of a man of intellect.

As before, Elyse and Arcadius sat with Zayd under his canopy. She wasn't terribly religious, but she closed her eyes and thought a silent prayer. She hoped no one noticed. She understood the ifrits didn't approve such things. Arcadius laid his hand on her shoulder and left it there.

"You know who I am," Joseph said in a smooth natural tone. His audience had been stirring on their seats and cushions, but they fell still as he began. Joseph gazed at them and went on. "I am Joseph the Magician. Joseph the Eunuch, some call me. I am different from you, and yet underneath all djinn are made the same. Smoke and fire form our spirits, ash and sparks our bodies. We love God or we do not, but we are one family."

He paused for a sip of water.

"Is this the story?" someone muttered.

Joseph's expression remained pleasant. "This is the truth behind *all* stories, whether we hail from the open desert or a djinn packed city. Every man knows what it means to laugh or cry, to love or hate, to strive for courage or shake with fear." He pointed to his audience. "Do you have the courage to hear my tale? Will you listen or turn away? This story concerns people I care about. *I* will feel it as I tell it. Do you dare to let yourself?"

"Clever boy," Arcadius said very quietly.

"Will there be sex?" a second heckler demanded.

"This is a story of Iksander the Golden, my sultan, the most beautiful ruler the Glorious City has ever known, the most beautiful man the women of the Qaf have ever laid eyes on." Joseph paused once more and grinned.

"There will be sex," he promised.

CHAPTER THIRTEEN

The Sultan and the Sorceress

IT is a fact well established that Sultan Iksander adored his wife, the beautiful Najat, who he rescued from captivity in an ifrit's tavern. She was royal like him and as gracious as she was well favored. Those who knew the couple thought the match excellent. Though it began as infatuation, their feelings soon deepened to devotion. Sultan Iksander took no other *kadin* but her, shamefully neglecting the women of his harem. For her part, Najat did everything in her power to bring her husband joy, whether it be sending a servant across the city for the best figs or rubbing his tired feet at night.

She rubbed more than Iksander's feet of course. The couple's physical affection for one another was infamous. Servants never knew when they'd round a corner in the palace to find the Glorious City's leading couple engaged in coitus with half their clothes torn off. If the sultan traveled outside the city for state business, immediately on his return, he would closet himself and his wife to sate the needs that had gone unmet in the interim. Thumping noises and hungry groans would ring out as they screwed for days, pausing only to eat and rest.

In this manner, they lived blissfully for many years.

One lack alone marred their happiness. Despite much trying, the sultan's beloved wife did not conceive a child.

Iksander assured Najat this could not make him adore her less. They would adopt, he said—some wonderful orphan child who needed parents like themselves. Though Najat pretended to be comforted by his words, she could not accept this idea. She wanted to create a child *with* Iksander, an heir who sprang from both their loins. The failure—for this was how she saw it—wore on her increasingly over time.

It happened that, seven years following her rescue from the tavern, whispers blew to the palace that a powerful sorceress had taken up residence in the lower town. Najat's personal maids were aflutter over the wonders she was rumored to perform: love spells and healings and even messages from the dead.

I must visit her, Najat thought. *Surely she can help me become pregnant.*

Najat knew her husband wouldn't approve of this. His most trusted friend, the commander of his army and all the guards, had in his service a highly skilled magician. If they consulted anyone, Iksander would want it to be him.

Regrettably, Najat had never been easy with this servant, for he was not a whole man. She was accustomed to perfection in all things—not to mention males she could dazzle with her beauty. To make matters worse, the magician was a favorite of the *valide sultana*, the sultan's widowed mother, who presided over everyone in the harem . . . Najat included. As sometimes happens between old mother and young wife, the pair didn't get along. Najat was reluctant to let her mother-in-law discover the seriousness of her condition. Should she find out, the sultana was sure to pressure her son to impregnate a harem girl of her own choosing—likely whichever doe-eyed seductress would annoy Najat the most. Once that happened, no matter how unshakable Iksander declared his love to be, Najat would be pushed to the sidelines.

Any risk seemed worth facing if she could prevent that.

Najat called her deaf mute guard to escort her and dressed in her plainest clothes. She hid her face with a veil borrowed from a maid. Her identity thus concealed, she slipped away to the lower town. The season was high summer and it was afternoon, the hour the wise close their shutters and try to nap. Najat would not sleep today. The streets twisted like a maze through the poor quarter, where the air was hotter than an oven and cooling breezes refused to stir. The shop the sorceress had rented opened onto a cobbled lane. Najat and her escort ducked under the tapestry that hung across the door. Inside, at a table draped with expensive silks and lit by a single lamp, a beautiful, very pale woman sat.

Her hair was long and pure silver, her eyes the milky blue of icebergs. Her flawless skin seemed woven from moonlight. Najat was surprised to see such a young woman, never mind one so finely dressed.

"I am the one you seek," the woman assured her. "And I know who you are. Sit at my table, and I will penetrate the business that brought you here."

Though disconcerted by this welcome, Najat sat in the opposite chair. When she laid a coin on the table, the sorceress made it disappear with a quick murmur.

"Take down your veil," the sorceress said, "and lay your hand in mine. No one will disturb us as long as you silent friend guards the door."

Najat laid her hand, palm up, in the hand of the sorceress. As the woman traced its lines with one fingertip, strangely sensual tingles rippled through

Najat's body. She almost pulled her arm away, but then the sorceress spoke.

"There is a blockage in your womb. This is the reason you cannot bear children."

Najat gasped. The sorceress truly had divined the purpose of her visit. "Can you cure me?" she asked.

The sorceress looked deeply into her eyes, seeming to search for the answer there. Beneath her plain gown, Najat's nipples tightened without warning.

"I can," the sorceress said, "but I shall require two things. I need a golden hair from your husband's head, plus a single ripe strawberry only your lips have kissed. With these ingredients, I can concoct a potion to triple the sultan's sexual potency. After he drinks it, his emissions will be powerful enough to defeat any obstacle. Within a moon—two at the most—I guarantee his son will grow inside you."

Najat was no one's fool. Though her judgment might have been impaired by her anxieties, she knew sorceresses didn't give guarantees—not honest ones anyway.

Seeing her expression, the sorceress nodded in understanding. "You doubt me, yet you believed the tales of what I've wrought for others enough to try your luck. Bring me what I ask and you'll see proof yourself."

"How do I know you won't use your potion to poison my beloved?"

"Would I sign my own death warrant? I am a good magician, who works her wonders in the name of the Creator. But you must do as you think right. Perhaps some other miracle worker can help you."

The sorceress inclined her shining silver head, leaving the decision to Najat.

Iksander's *kadin* stood up from her chair. Her hopes and fears fought within her, making it impossible for her to say "yea" or "nay."

"Return tomorrow," the sorceress said, maintaining her humble posture. "I will prepare the cure you seek."

Her soft words freed Najat to go.

The instant she left, the sorceress sprang up, shutting the shop's wooden door behind the tapestry. If she had seemed beautiful before, as she paced her shop she was glorious. Truth be told, she was no ordinary sorceress. She was the Empress Luna, monarch of the City of Endless Night, where the sun never rises and the moon never sets. No territory in the Qaf was closer to the Glorious City in wealth and might. For years, she had dreamed of annexing Iksander's city and ruling both. When she heard he was the handsomest djinni of their generation, she dreamed of annexing him. She'd come to his capital for the sole purpose of seducing him.

Her present situation wasn't her first attempt. Using her magic arts, she'd convinced his staff she was a member of his harem. His gifted friends protected him from spells, but that did not dim her hope. With the utmost faith in her luminous beauty, she arranged for him to "accidentally" witness her bathing. The ploy earned her a scolding from his mother and not one moment alone with him. Iksander saw beauty only in his wife. He became the first man in Luna's life to resist her.

The mighty can be as foolish as anyone. The sultan's rejection inflamed Luna's lust for him. She vowed she would not rest until she had him groveling in her bed. She spent her remaining time in his harem learning his weak spots. Now she had nearly all the pieces to put her plan in motion.

"*She* will deliver him to me," Luna swore, "she" being his loathed *kadin*.

Luna had no doubt that fish was already on her hook.

~

As the sorceress had anticipated, Najat returned with the requisite articles the following afternoon. Luna made a show of dropping the sultan's golden hair and the strawberry into a brass cauldron.

Alas for Najat's hopes, this was a show only. Every magician, however powerful, can perform sleight of hand. Luna was no exception. As the smoke whirled up and she chanted magic words, she replaced Iksander's hair with that of another man. The substitute belonged to Philip, the sultan's second most trusted friend. Philip was a celebrated artist and the son of the vizier. His temperament was closer to the sultan's than his commander, being passionate and a bit romantic. Luna had bribed a servant to get the strand during her residence in the harem. Now she prayed to her god that it would serve her current plan.

She decanted the finished mixture into a small cut glass bottle with a stopper. Najat took the vessel with trembling hands.

"There is one more instruction I must give you," Luna said. "This is a royal-specific potion. Its powers will not affect your husband's taster or anyone who doesn't have noble blood. Simply slip a few drops into Iksander's food or drink. He will never notice it."

Najat looked at the crystal clear liquid. "How long will it take to work?"

"No time at all. You would be wise to remain available and to prepare yourself to be well ravished. As soon as he ingests the potency elixir, he will experience an uncontrollable need for you. Should you not conceive right away, you may re-administer the treatment."

Najat shivered and then grew hot. Being well ravished by her husband didn't sound unpleasant.

"Thank you," she said to the sorceress. "You have saved my future happiness."

The empress bowed and smiled pleasantly. She knew the *kadin's* future happiness was the last thing she was saving.

~

Whatever her faults, Najat couldn't give her husband an unknown substance without some test of its safety. After returning to the place, she slipped a single drop into her maid's mint tea. Nothing whatsoever happened, which was reassuring and certainly fortunate for the maid. On the other hand, the sorceress had said the potion was designed to affect royals. Having none available except her mother-in-law and herself, she shook the smallest possible droplet into her own wine cup.

When she sniffed it, she smelled nothing but the age-mellowed grapes. When she wet her tongue and swallowed, sensations such as she'd never known exploded through her body.

This was no accident. The potion Luna brewed wasn't intended for the sultan but for Najat. The sorceress had counted on her tasting it. Her stratagem worked as well as she'd hoped. The *kadin* was seized with longing for the man whose hair the sorceress had substituted: Philip the vizier's son, the sultan's trusted and very handsome friend.

The bottle fell from Najat's fingers as the powerful enchantment took hold of her. Her swiftly dampening pussy ached with desire, her button of pleasure swelling to twice its normal size. She knew she must have Philip or she would die.

Frightened by what she felt and desperate to find the man, she ran from her apartment within the harem. She ignored the startled questions of those she passed, her very reason compromised by her lust. Each brush of her thighs against each other maddened her more. She tried pleasuring herself in a small alcove but could not achieve release, no matter how frantically she tried.

Evidently, the attractive artist was the only salve for her suffering.

After demanding his whereabouts from a number of surprised servants, she found him in his studio.

It must be conceded that Philip had a little yen for his friend's *kadin*. The sultan's wife was very beautiful, very charming, and Philip was a healthy unmarried djinni. Certainly, suggestive daydreams featuring Najat and himself had slipped into his mind occasionally. Beyond the teeniest flirtation—which might be accounted as politeness—he'd never acted on these longings. He was a man of honor, and valued his neck besides. Even sultans as principled as Iksander weren't known for tolerating adultery. Not with their wives. Not when they treasured them.

Though no sorcerer, Philip had magical as well as artistic talents. He could spell a chisel to cut through marble as if it were butter. As luck would have it, he was working on a sculpture of Najat that evening. She wasn't bare in the piece but wore flowing robes and a sheer head veil. Seated on a little stool, she leaned forward across her lap to pull on one slipper. Philip was proud of the way he'd captured her graceful figure beneath the draping cloth. He thought his friend would enjoy receiving the finished piece on his next birthday.

Given the subject of his work and his secret affection for the *kadin*, he might be excused for momentarily being too stunned to move when the real Najat rushed in and embraced him.

"Help me," she pleaded, immediately tearing at his clothes. "Take me or I shall die."

Before he could stop her, she ripped his shirt fully off and writhed on his helpless thigh. Her free flowing juices soaked not just her clothes but also his work trousers.

"My lady," he exclaimed as she shoved her hand down his garment's front. "What are you doing?"

Her eager fingers wrapped his cock, which it must be admitted was stiffening. Though the desire she labored under was terrible, she stroked his hard length skillfully.

"You must fuck me," she said, her thumb and finger twisting excitingly beneath his now very swollen crown. "If you do not, I will go mad."

The poor beset artist tried to contain his moans of delight. "I will . . . call your husband," he choked out. "He will assist you."

"You," she said, flinging off her jeweled belt so that her robes fell open. "You are the lover I'm desperate for."

The sight of her naked breasts and belly stunned him anew. Najat was beautiful, like a thunderbolt striking him from above. Here was his forbidden daydream, begging him for the very act he dared not perform. Further inflamed—and no doubt frustrated—by his paralysis, Najat shoved him back onto a crimson chaise he kept for his models and straddled him.

His rebellious cock had escaped his clothes and pointed toward the ceiling. It certainly wished to satisfy his mistress. When she angled the thudding rod toward her hot grotto, the only thing he could think of to prevent her engulfing it was to thrust two fingers deep into her pussy.

Such were the qualities of Najat's enchantment that Philip's fingers were as good to her as his other parts. She groaned with enjoyment, pumping her hips on the penetration until—in almost no time at all—her body seized with pleasure and she wailed out her completion.

Because Fate was not feeling kind that evening, this was the moment her husband burst in on them.

The palace servants had alerted their liege to the *kadin's* strange behavior.

Seeing where that behavior led, white-hot rage blazed through the sultan's veins. His beloved had betrayed him, and—so it seemed—his closest friend had as well. If his other friend, the commander, hadn't followed on his heels, Iksander most assuredly would have slain both lovers.

"Wait!" the commander cried, grabbing his friend's raised sword arm. "This cannot be what we think it is."

"Your Highness!" Philip cried, throwing himself face down on the floor.

"Please listen to Arcadius."

He'd had to squirm out from under Najat in order to make this supplication. Coupled with a form of address that said they were no longer friends, his action pulled a feral growl up in Iksander's throat. The sultan strove to attack again, but the commander held fast to him.

Meanwhile, Najat had collapsed into a weeping ball on the blood red chaise. She pulled her robes around her, wrapping her head between her hands as she rocked back and forth in distress. Now that she had climaxed, her madness seemed to have passed.

"Forgive me," she pleaded. "Beloved, I couldn't control my own actions."

"You see," Arcadius said as Iksander growled again. "It must have been a spell."

Iksander flung out his arm with the scimitar trembling in his grip. He pointed the tip at his sobbing wife, looking rather near tears himself. "No spell does *that*, no matter how powerful its creator. It must have a seed of lust to work on. She was attracted to Philip already!"

Arcadius had sometimes suspected this might be so. Najat liked her little flirtations, and Philip was a glamorous artist type. Because Arcadius knew her devotion to her husband was deep, certainly deeper than any fancy she had for Philip, he'd never thought it would cause trouble.

None of this seemed useful to mention then.

He put his hands on Iksander's shoulders and forced the sultan to look at him. "You must call on your nobler self, my friend, and spare the couple's lives. Poor Najat was charmed, and Philip was trying to, er, help her the best he could without, um, sullying your trust." Arcadius realized this might not be the best way to put it.

"You cannot kill them," he went on more firmly. "You would become ifrit. You would be barred from djinn heaven."

"I don't care!" the sultan cried. "I would brave hell itself if it would burn away the image of her riding him."

In the doorway behind them, a familiar throat was cleared.

"Joseph," the commander said, sounding relieved to see him. "Please establish whether the *kadin* has been charmed."

The eunuch crossed to her carefully, crouching down to examine the merest tips of her right fingers. She didn't like him touching her, but under the circumstances she allowed it. "I sense a foreign magical substance. I believe she ingested it. Shall I check Philip as well?"

Seeing the sultan was a little calmer, Arcadius nodded.

Philip rose from the floor. "Joseph," he said sadly, offering him his hand palm up.

The eunuch studied it. "He is himself," he said reluctantly.

"Himself!" the sultan burst out.

Perhaps Philip feared Iksander would rush forward to attack. The artist stepped closer to the sultan's defenseless wife, his leg grazing her knee as a result. The moment the contact occurred, Najat moaned throatily with desire.

Everyone stared at her in horror. Najat looked horrified herself. She slapped her hand across her mouth.

"My God," said the sultan. "She still wants him!"

He spun away, unable to look at her. "Joseph," he said in a hard tight voice. "I order you to use your magic to banish her. You need not kill her. Simply send her somewhere in the Qaf where I—and *he*—will never, ever see her again."

"Your Highness . . ." Joseph said unsurely.

"Do it!" his superior spat out.

Joseph looked at the commander, who nodded. If Iksander relented in the future, he knew Joseph would have sent Najat somewhere safe. Though she wept and begged for mercy, Joseph performed the spell. A whirlwind sprang to life within the studio, dark gray and thunderous. The power of its raging currents blew back their clothes and hair.

"In the name of God," Joseph ordered the swirling thing, "carry the *kadin* away from here."

Najat wailed out one last plea as the ominous funnel cloud swept her out the window and into the black of night.

The sultan had turned to watch. As the tossed-up items in the studio dropped, Iksander's eyes fell on the sculpture of Najat that Philip had been carving. Though the sultan's expression did not change, the artist tensed. Would the sultan read more betrayal into the work? Iksander's gaze shifted slowly to the face of his former friend. The sultan appeared to have aged a decade in a few minutes.

"Your sentence I shall decide later," he intoned.

* * *

Joseph stopped speaking and bowed his head. For a couple seconds, no one in the crowd reacted. Like Elyse, they expected him to go on.

"That isn't a proper ending," one ifrit cried. "The sultan didn't kill either of the adulterers. Are you trying to raise our pulses with annoyance?"

Joseph's eyes widened as if he were surprised. "The sun is even now creeping over the mountains. I thought it best to find a place to stop."

"You stop at the *end*," the same tribesman protested. "On top of which, you called this story 'The Sultan and the Sorceress.' You hardly put in any bits about her. And she is the best character!"

"Forgive me," Joseph apologized. He looked helplessly at the sheikh. "What do you wish me to do? I can continue another night, or we can measure the results now. I do not wish to interfere with your men's duties . . . or their perfectly natural need for rest."

Lounged comfortably in his throne, Zayd had propped his chin on his hand. He regarded Joseph with raised eyebrows. He seemed aware of the djinni's disingenuousness.

"It is your choice," Joseph insisted, offering him a bow. "Whatever suits your convenience."

Quite a number of Zayd's men looked hopefully at their leader.

"Very well," Zayd relented sourly. "You may continue tomorrow evening, but you had better finish then. I've no intention of letting this contest drag on forever."

"Thank you," Joseph said. "Your munificence is exceeded only by your wisdom."

~

"I assume you did that on purpose," Arcadius said once they were alone in their tent.

"Well, I hoped Zayd would let me break the tale in two. I want to see how I'm doing on the bet."

They'd stepped into his sound-cancelling ring, where Elyse was struggling to turn on the self-heating teakettle. Arcadius didn't know how to advise her. Ifrit implements wouldn't work on prayer power like the ones at home.

"You have to threaten it," Joseph said. "Take a firm grip on the handle and say, 'Heat my water or I'll beat you.'"

Elyse gawked at him. "You're pulling my leg."

Joseph smiled. "Give it a try and see."

She did as he instructed, gasping with surprise when steam quickly began puffing out the nozzle. "I did it! The magic worked."

Arcadius grinned at her delight . . . until he saw the item Joseph had pulled from his pocket for de-shrinking.

"You have a second phone," he accused.

This one was red with shiny orange dots. "Of course," Joseph said. "I force paired it to the first. I can check on my progress without Zayd knowing."

"You have *two* phones," Arcadius repeated.

"It was a two-for-one deal, plus the heart monitor." Joseph saw he was aggrieved. "I offered to shop for you, master. You're the one who wanted to choose your own."

"Mine is still in my overcoat. Which I had to abandon in Elyse's cellar."

"If you like," Joseph said, "when I'm done with this one you can have it."

He was childish enough to want to accept, but that wasn't the point. "You were holding out," he said. "We could have used those phones as our guest gift. You made Elyse give up her wedding ring!"

Joseph gave him a look Arcadius didn't think he'd ever seen on his face before. Though it wasn't precisely rebellious, it also wasn't the expression of a respectful servant.

"First," he said, "these phones are too human for Zayd to have found them sufficiently appealing, especially with no cell network here. Second, I thought we might need them for something more important—which as it turns out, we do. Finally, it's not like *you* mind Elyse's sacrifice!"

The truth of this last point kept Arcadius from arguing the first two. His jaw worked with annoyance for a moment.

"Fine," he conceded reluctantly. "You shouldn't have to give your phone to me. You're the one who had the foresight to purchase a back-up."

A muffled snicker broke out behind him. Elyse was laughing. When he turned to look, she wiped the amusement from her expression.

"What are the results so far?" she asked.

Joseph studied the screen and frowned. "Only three out of five. I pushed two of the fighters and the albino into their 'red zone.' The old man and the champion with the many earrings are resisting."

"Less sex, more violence," Arcadius recommended. Joseph scratched his jaw unsurely.

"More misery?" Elyse proposed. "The tribesmen seemed unimpressed by the sultan's wife getting off so easy. If you have a happy ending, you might want to deep-six it."

"I don't," Joseph said. His sad gaze met Arcadius's.

"One challenge at a time," Arcadius said softly.

CHAPTER
FOURTEEN

ZAYD'S tribe gathered for the rest of Joseph's story with palpable eagerness. Elyse took special note of the old man and the fighter with the earrings. Both looked stone-faced, but so did the other three.

"Get on with it," Zayd said, waving Joseph on from his raised seat.

Joseph heard and obeyed.

* * *

The Sultan and the Sorceress: Continued

As you'll recall, the magician banished the sultan's wife by means of a windstorm. He sent her to a nunnery in the mountains, where she'd be treated kindly but not allowed to leave. Though the eunuch waited every day to be ordered to bring her home, the sultan seemed unable to relent. Perhaps he felt guilty over his hardheartedness. His sentence against the artist was less extreme. Philip was ejected from the palace and obliged to find lodgings. Though he missed his friend, the commander didn't seek Philip out, only kept track of how he fared. According to his spies, the artist was very sad—too sad to paint or sculpt. Other than that, he was enduring.

Back at the palace, Iksander shut himself in his rooms, fulfilling only those duties that were essential to keep the place running. His feelings of betrayal ate at him too much to venture among people. Everyone he saw seemed—to him—to be judging him a cuckold. This withdrawal lasted seven days. On the eighth, he told the master of his harem to prepare a concubine to receive him that evening. He didn't care who it was, simply that she be warned not to expect him more than one night. At precisely midnight, he went to the chosen girl. At precisely three a.m., he left.

The pattern repeated itself for thirty days.

Iksander was a naturally virile man, endowed with needs any male might claim. The commander didn't consider it his business how Iksander satisfied himself. Celibacy wasn't expected of a male in his position. Nonetheless, Arcadius grew curious.

Stories of the sultan's habits began to escape the harem walls.

It was said he made love to the concubines in his smoke form; that he didn't allow them to change but only to lie there and accept him. The women weren't complaining. Though the practice was uncommon, the sultan left them well pleasured. Some even pleaded for more encounters, but Iksander never complied. He seemed to have sworn off taking any woman a second time.

Over the years, the sultan had received many concubines as gifts, but eventually even he ran out. The commander waited to see what his liege would do. Would he start again at the beginning? Or forgive Najat at last? Neither appeared to be happening. The sultan continued to leave his rooms every night, though no one in the harem reported seeing him. When the commander tried to have Iksander followed, the sultan evaded the surveillance.

Now Arcadius heard new reports. These came from the surrounding town. A phantom lover was haunting the female populace. This smoky being —who took the general form of a tall young man—would appear at a woman's window, requesting to be let in. If admitted, he would say, "Good woman, might I have your permission to pleasure you?" If the answer were affirmative, the phantom lover would introduce them to such erotic transports the women claimed to be ruined for other men.

"He is obsessed," the women sighed. "His many orgasms do not exhaust him, and he is *very* interested in bringing women theirs. It is as if he cannot stop himself!"

On one other fact the women agreed. The phantom lover remained three hours and then departed, never to be heard from again by the same female.

Apparently, many women liked the idea of being taken in this manner. A fashion sprang up among the Glorious City's female residents. If a woman was amenable to a visit from the phantom, she displayed a red silk scarf in her bedroom window, thus advertising her availability.

When the reason for this craze reached the ears of the *valide sultana*, she was incensed. She summoned the commander for a private talk in her apartments. As if to compensate for her offspring's indecency, she'd veiled herself more thickly than usual. Of all her countenance, only her flashing eyes were visible.

"You must put a stop to this," she said. "My son is royal. Most of these women are commoners. What if people discover this perverted 'phantom lover' is their sultan? His behavior is completely undignified!"

"I'm not certain what I can do," the commander said. "Your son is my superior, and also a grown man."

"But he listens to you!"

"Only when he wishes. Perhaps we should be grateful he has returned to overseeing affairs of state."

The sultana didn't wish to be grateful. "That girl," she muttered, meaning Najat. "This never would have happened if she'd kept her thighs together."

The commander thought this unfair but was too wise to say so. He also thought the sultana had a point about her son's conduct. As delicately as he was able, he raised the topic during his next consultation with the sultan.

"You didn't use women this way before," he pointed out. "Why are you so bent on it now?"

The sultan glowered at him, his hips resting on the front of his ornate official desk. He was alert and groomed and perfectly outfitted—all of which seemed promising signs. Only his dark mood and manner were altered from before.

"How," the sultan asked haughtily down his nose, "can this be your business?"

"I'm concerned for you, Iksander. You know you risk a scandal. Also, this . . . particular act doesn't seem like you."

Iksander crossed his arms. "What would you know about it? Maybe it *is* me. Maybe I always wanted to, but Najat seemed so sweet and normal I didn't dare. Well, now I don't have to worry about shocking her. She's the one who shocked me!"

"But why a new woman every night? Wouldn't a single female you trust not to gossip be better?"

"Whom can I trust?" the sultan demanded, his voice grating with anger. "The only woman I ever loved betrayed me!"

The commander fought a sigh. He saw he wasn't improving the situation with his questions. "Very well," he said. "Please come to me if there's anything I can do. I promise not to judge but only to serve you loyally."

The words calmed Iksander's ire. Unfortunately, they didn't swerve him from the slippery path he'd chosen.

~

Inevitably, news of the sultan's exploits reached the sorceress. She hadn't given up her plan to seduce him and rule his city. She'd been waiting for the right moment to make her move, and it seemed it had arrived.

The identity of the phantom lover was obvious to her.

Hanging her red scarf out with countless others didn't strike her as efficient. One night when the moon was full, she drew on its influence to work a sly magic. As the lunar orb rose above the city, its rays bleached every scarf but hers. Only hers remained red. Only hers would lure the obsessed sultan. His habit of loving and leaving didn't cause her the least distress. She was the Empress Luna, who drove men mad with her seductive wiles. The only reason Iksander didn't love her already was that he'd never tasted them.

~

On the stroke of midnight, a sharp knock sounded on the empress's windowpane. She'd bathed and perfumed herself earlier. Wearing filmy garments that were more alluring than none at all, she sauntered across her bedroom to meet the arrival.

Her residence was on the second floor above her sorceress shop. A figure cut from a storm cloud bobbed in the air outside. The smoke man was perhaps a foot taller than solid males. Completely naked, he had broad shoulders, narrow hips, and long fit legs. Two eyes lit his nobly shaped smoke head, gleaming the bright green of lime slices. Equally interesting from Luna's point of view was that her visitor had an erection. Its impressive length pulsed with eagerness, the idea of what he'd come here to do arousing him.

The sorceress fully intended to make the sultan's fixation work in her favor. She smiled as she opened both casements.

"Do come in," she said, stepping back to make room for him.

The sultan floated by her, not that she greeted him as such. Anonymity was crucial to his game. That much closer to what he wanted, his upward pointing shaft throbbed impatiently.

"Good woman," he said as he always did. "Might I have your permission to pleasure you?"

The sorceress stroked a slender finger down her neck. "I have needs of my own," she said, pretending not to notice how the sultan's gaze went to her cleavage. "Before I answer, might I convince you to ravish me somewhere other than my bed?"

If it were possible for vapor to look worried, the sultan did.

"You must remain solid," he insisted.

"I shall," Luna promised. Sensing the phantom didn't mind obviousness, she slid both hands around her breasts and cupped them.

The smoke phantom licked his lips. "You must not interfere with my passions. If I wish to—" He hesitated before going on more harshly. "If I wish to fuck your ass or come on your face, you will allow it."

"Whatever you wish," the sorceress purred, "you'll find me eager to receive you."

"Then I accept your condition. Where do you want me to take you?"

"To begin with," the sorceress said, secretly exulting, "over the back of that chaise right there."

The sultan's smoke form pulsed with anticipation. "Take off those garments," he commanded.

This gratified the sorceress too. From the accounts she'd heard, the sultan never asked his partners to disrobe. From the beginning, she was setting herself apart.

She peeled off her filmy clothes—not too fast, not too slow—teasing him by baring her moon pale beauty one transcendent feature at a time. Finally, all the silk pooled around her ankles. The moon silvered the slopes of her breasts, the enticing curves of her waist and hips, the polished sterling curls that wisped between her thighs. The phantom trembled at these sights, his smoke cock jerking with his desire.

Satisfied with his reaction, the sorceress showed off her shapely legs by strolling to the chaise. Aware that her rear was fetching, she bent over.

"Grip the cushions and hold on," the phantom ordered. "My smoke form is very strong."

The sorceress's lips curved as she obeyed. "Shall I brace my legs wide as well?"

"Yes," the phantom lover growled.

Luna moved her feet, first the left and then the right. She liked sex and the teasing that went with it. It was no surprise that she was aroused. When a trickle of excitement ran down her inner thigh, however, that startled her a bit.

The phantom saw the rivulet. He let out a groan so raw she couldn't help shivering.

"Ass *up!*" the sultan snapped like a sexual drill sergeant.

The sorceress barely had a second to comply. The phantom streaked to her, clamped both smoke hands around her hips, and shoved his cock to the very end of her vagina.

Anyone in Luna's position knows a smoke form feels similar to a gale force wind. The edges are almost solid, but they penetrate more deeply than purely physical objects can. Smoke forms hum as if lightning ran through them, providing a delectable vibration. Despite her worldly habits, Luna hadn't done this before. The fetish was too eccentric.

She discovered she liked it.

The sultan had experience refining his technique. He knew how to blur his edges to strum a woman's nerves. Before he'd finished pumping in and out even once, Luna was moaning. By the time he'd enjoyed half a dozen strokes, she'd almost swooned from the strength of her sensations. The sultan's sensual assault couldn't be resisted. He was in her everywhere. He was also bigger than a normal man. Luna felt overwhelmed, a rare state for an empress. Iksander was in control of her, from his driving cock to the fingers that gripped her hipbones like fiery steel.

Sensing she needed anchoring, her phantom lover nipped the bend between her neck and shoulder.

"Do not faint," he warned. "If you do, you'll miss your orgasm."

The implication that he would still take his both outraged and titillated her.

"You'd have to stop as well," she panted, "if I were unconscious."

"I wouldn't be able to," he contradicted. "I am a monster. I need my monstrous release too much."

Well, that was an interesting answer, especially since the mere mention of stopping made him thrust more frenziedly.

"Give yourself up to me," he said. His smoke hands slid down her arms to shackle her at the wrists, which strained from the clutch she had on the chaise cushion. "I need it. I need it. Fucking hell, I need it."

His compulsive chant made her need it too. She arched her bottom higher, inviting him farther in. Her nerves were tightening, her pussy unable to grip him even a little bit. His pelvis made no sound as it hit her buttocks. She cried out hoarsely, still not coming.

"Thirty heartbeats," he rasped, his smoke so dense his next thrust jolted her onto her toes. "Thirty strokes and you'll explode."

She wanted the climax more than she'd ever wanted anything. She whimpered with desire, too agitated to keep count. His cock was bigger, hotter. If he tore her apart, she suspected she'd scream with thanks. She slammed her rear back at him, his nearly solid rod a torturous delight pumping her pussy.

"Now," he roared, shoving in so hard his smoke form and her body overlapped.

Her nerves shot fire from the hum of their spirits occupying the same space. She came and came, from her fingertips to her toes. Liquid gushed. Muscles spasmed. Burning lungs fought for air. The reactions were all hers: her personal earthquake. Her pleasure was unspeakable—a perfect terror of ecstasy.

In the middle of the tumult, the sultan groaned violently with relief. Smoke from his ejaculation overflowed her in a great cloud.

When the cataclysm in her pussy ended, the mighty sorceress could not move one muscle. The sultan, by contrast, was simply warming up.

"Ahh," he sighed, a long mellow sound. "That was excellent. Shall we do it again? Perhaps on your bed this time?"

He had to carry her in his buzzy arms. Her knees wobbled too badly to support her.

The city's phantom showed her many pleasures in the succeeding hours, everything he'd threatened and more besides. Face down, with her hips propped on a bolster and both hands laced behind her neck, the sultan took her anally. This excited him so greatly he had to rub her button with his smoke fingers to speed up her climax. Next he performed oral sex on her— an interesting proposition when the tongue in question was all buzz and no wetness. He made her come many times this way, with no release for himself. Extremely wound up then, he ordered her to pretend she was asleep while he masturbated beside her bed.

Luna would not have guessed the sultan's desires were this unusual. Her city had more of a reputation for depraved sex. Obviously Iksander hadn't exposed these interests to his *kadin*. If he had, they wouldn't have burst out so potently now.

The sorceress hardly minded. She complied with all his requests and savored them. Finally, he ordered her to finger herself to orgasm while his smoke form occupied her body. They came together, two sets of nerves coiling tight and then springing loose in unison.

The sorceress's understandable relaxation caused her to fall asleep without meaning to. Her night with the phantom had been the most extraordinary amatory experience of her life. She understood why his partners never complained. They only had energy for sighs of ecstasy.

Her eyes struggled open as the nearest clock in the quarter gonged three times. Alarmed, she sat up. She didn't think she'd been sleeping long, but her bedchamber was abandoned. Only the disarray of its furnishings suggested she'd had a visitor. The sultan had left without a goodbye. Worse, he hadn't remained to the actual stroke of three.

That wasn't right. Luna was superior to other women. She shouldn't have been given even one minute less. Convinced there must be some mistake, she hung her red scarf out a second time. The sultan did not return. To add insult to injury, she overheard at the market that a rug merchant's plain-faced daughter had been his chosen one. The girl hadn't hung out a scarf. He had simply showed up outside her room and knocked.

Night after night, the same thing happened—no matter what she arranged to befall the other women's scarves. Finally, she changed apartments to make him think she was someone new. He showed up then but took one look at her and gathered his smoke together in preparation for leaving.

"Wait," she cried.

He paused momentarily, green eyes glinting as his cloud shape hung in the air. Luna pressed her hands to her heart. She addressed the sultan sincerely, with a tenderness that surprised her.

"You don't have to go. I am an empress, nobly born like you. You and I can share a real life together. I know our connection was stronger than the others. I see no reason we shouldn't be happy."

The sultan's green eyes blinked. His shadowy mouth opened as if he would speak. He seemed to think better of it. He shook his head twice—unmistakably. Then he streaked away from her.

In an instant, Luna's desperation changed. Fury cut through it like a sword. Iksander had rejected her, probably in favor of some sardine-scented fisherman's daughter.

No one rejected the empress—not without paying handsomely. In a flash, how to make the sultan pay came to her. Whatever he believed about his feelings, he obviously still loved his banished wife. Luna had failed to make him hate her. This was grief he was expressing, not simply erotic obsession.

Luna decided to eliminate the chance that he'd summon Najat home.

~

It is a lesson all mages learn that, no matter how strong they are, someone somewhere will outdo them. Though the eunuch hid Najat's location carefully, before a day had passed, the empress discovered it. Luna had many magical resources and rage had increased her power. She traveled easily to the isolated mountain fortress. Once there, she cast a sleep spell on its inhabitants, leaving only Najat awake.

Najat was unaware of this. She worked in the nunnery's undercroft alone, performing an inventory of their foodstuffs. She had begged the Mother Superior to keep her busy. She loved Iksander dearly. Ever since the whirlwind had dropped her here two months ago, her conscience had tormented her. If only she hadn't flirted with Philip . . . If only she'd fought the potion harder . . . If only she'd done what she knew Iksander would have wished and gone to Joseph the Eunuch with her troubles. *If only* circled in her head like a wagon wheel on cobbles—bump-bump-bump—until she feared she would go insane.

She didn't know insanity would have been preferable to Luna's plan for her.

The empress watched Najat for some time, more curious than she wanted to admit about her rival. Though beautiful, the *kadin* appeared unhappy. Her brown robes were unflattering, borrowed from the nuns, no doubt. Hollows darkened her eyes, each jerky stroke of her quill on the ledger suggesting a temperament turned nervous. Flashes of anger thinned her mouth intermittently—at herself perhaps, or maybe her husband. One thing was certain: she hadn't given up all hope.

That was good. Hope left Luna with more to take away.

She waited among the shadows to be noticed.

After a moment, Najat thought she heard a sound. "Sister Graziela, is that you?"

Sister Graziela was fast asleep. The empress stepped into the open. Because she was veiled, Najat didn't recognize her as the sorceress.

Najat clutched the ledger book to her chest. "Who are you?"

"I come from the Glorious City."

Like the sun breaching the horizon, hope lit the *kadin's* face. Luna couldn't fail to notice she was achingly lovely. "Has my husband forgiven me? Is he asking me to return?"

"He is not," Luna said.

The joy drained from Najat's visage, replaced by anxiety. "Is he well?"

"He is better than you realize," Luna responded.

The *kadin's* brow furrowed with confusion. "Why are you here then? I can tell something is amiss."

"Come. Take a seat for me."

Located among the nunnery's shelves of stores was a small square table with one wood chair. The sorceress held it out for Najat to sit. When the other woman was where she wished—seated and gazing up at her—Luna brought out a golden bowl.

The dish was large, suitable for serving a gallon of soup at a fine table. Many decorations graced it, but around its flattened rim a few simple words were etched.

I will not spill, they read.

Luna placed the bowl on the table in front of the *kadin*. "Do you know what this is?"

Najat's eyes were wide. "A bowl that will not spill?"

She tried to rise. Luna held her down by pressing on her shoulder. The empress was strong. One hand was all it took.

"Do you know what *this* is?" Luna asked as if the little struggle had not occurred. This time she brought out an amphora of shining brass. Whatever was in the vessel sloshed.

Frightened now, Najat shook her head.

Luna stroked her dove-soft cheek with the backs of her fingers. "It is filled with concentrated seawater. As you know, salt is caustic to our kind. The slave who boils down my supply has developed terrible scars."

Luna poured the dangerous fluid into the bowl that would not spill. Again Najat tried to rise, and again the sorceress shoved her down.

"I don't like this game," Najat said. "Stop now, or I shall call the nuns."

Anger made Iksander's favorite as beautiful as hope.

"By the power of the Creator," Luna said, "I command you to stay in the chair."

Najat stayed, even when Luna grabbed the back of the neck and plunged her face into the seawater. The effect was painful. Najat struggled violently. Despite her thrashing, not a single drop splashed on the sorceress. Desperate, Najat attempted to change into her smoke form to escape. Luna's magic kept her from succeeding.

When long lack of air stopped the *kadin's* struggles, the sorceress pulled her up again. Najat wasn't beautiful anymore. Her skin had blistered terribly and turned red, actually peeling away in places. She was, truth be told, a bit of a horror show. Nonetheless, sufficient life remained in her to revive. Djinn are hardy beings, and royals no less so. After a minute, Najat gasped noisily for breath.

"What is your quarrel with me?" she asked, the words distorted by her swollen lips.

"You stood between me and something I wanted."

"Iksander," Najat said, finally understanding. "You're the sorceress who gave me the lust potion. You wanted to destroy his love for me."

Luna didn't like her figuring this out, or the compassion in her tone. Her fingers tightened on the *kadin's* nape.

"If you murder me, you'll turn ifrit," Najat warned. "The gates to heaven will forever be barred to you. For your own sake, do not do this."

Luna had often wondered why she was born a good djinniya. Honoring God didn't suit her character. Honoring anyone but herself didn't. Still, she had never committed the act that would turn her dark—not by her own hand at least. Willful murder of another person was different from deaths sustained in battle or taken for self-defense. It was different from accidents and suicides.

Only murder changed how the Creator regarded them.

Luna wondered if it mattered. Najat would heal her wounds eventually. Also eventually, her husband would forgive her. His nature was over-proud but not pitiless. They would reconcile and likely be happier than ever. Did Luna *want* to share an afterlife with the joyous pair?

"I must be who I am," she said.

With that decision, she shoved Najat's face back into the bowl of seawater. This time, she held her under until she died.

If the sorceress couldn't have Iksander, neither would her rival.

* * *

"Now *that's* how you tell a story!" Joseph's former heckler shouted admiringly.

His words spurred the rest of the audience to roar with approval. Seeming pleased with the response, Joseph bowed modestly.

Good Lord, Elyse thought. She'd guessed Zayd's men would prefer a miserable ending, but she hadn't known Najat's suffering would inspire such delight. She'd cringed at Joseph's description of her death. She couldn't imagine being drowned in a bowl of water, held down while you strove to breathe and your face was burned. She hoped Joseph had exaggerated for effect. The idea was too gruesome otherwise.

Arcadius squeezed her shoulder, not in comfort but warning. The sheikh's gaze had slid to her. He was watching her like a hungry cat outside a mouse's hole. Was he picturing her in Najat's place? Wondering how she'd suffer so he could drink it up?

Elyse fought not to shudder. She shouldn't have let herself become so engrossed in Joseph's tale telling.

"We should check the results," Arcadius said in a deliberately calm tone. "See whether Joseph or you won the bet."

Zayd pulled his attention away from her, a slight hesitation betraying his reluctance. He lifted his hand to summon the ifrit who held the phone with the heart monitor data, the one who'd been spelled to honesty.

The man trotted over, seeming relieved that his duties were almost done. "One moment," he said. "I must 'poke the app' and the answers will come up."

He jabbed the touch screen a few times and scowled.

"Hm," he said and scratched his head.

"Is the device functioning?" the sheikh demanded.

"It is," the ifrit said. "Forgive me. I . . . it seems the eunuch has won the bet. The app tells me all five of your champions went into the 'red zone.' More than once, according to these squiggles."

"You're not mistaken?"

"No, sir. Your sorcerers spelled me to be positive."

This announcement wasn't met with applause. Instead the mood of the crowd around them quieted. Elyse had worried Joseph might lose the wager. Now she saw winning might present challenges.

Sheikh Zayd looked extremely irritated. "Well," he said. "Honor demands I pay up. The bet was for a flying carpet to get you home, wasn't it?"

"*Safely* home," Arcadius emphasized politely.

"All of you, return to your duties," the sheikh ordered his tribe members. "Guards, accompany us to the secure cache."

The sheikh stored his valuables exactly where Joseph thought, beneath an outcrop of rocks not too far from camp. Zayd had brought a torch to light their way. He planted it in the sand, clambering up the tallest boulder to murmur a password that sounded like *hyacinth* to Elyse. The rocks split up the middle, making a grinding noise as they moved apart with Zayd riding them. A cavelike mouth appeared between them.

"Bring out one of the larger carpets," Zayd instructed.

Two guards jogged down the sandy slope. They returned carrying a rolled up ordinary-seeming Persian rug. They laid it on the sand and stepped back from it.

"There," Zayd said. "Never say I don't pay my debts."

Arcadius and Joseph exchanged a glance. Like Elyse, they thought this was too easy.

"Thank you," Arcadius said. "We appreciate—"

Without warning, Zayd blinked into his smoke body. He zipped to Elyse before she could move, yanking her and her leash away from Arcadius. She didn't get a chance to struggle. He pressed a long curved blade to her throat.

"Not another step," he ordered.

Arcadius and Joseph froze. Arcadius addressed the vaporous sheikh carefully.

"You gave you word," he said.

"I promised you a carpet to get you home. The Glorious City is no home to this human."

"Splitting hairs does you no credit."

Zayd's laugh rasped like a match on cement. "Her hairs aren't what I intend to split, trust me."

Elyse trembled. Zayd's cloud form was damp and icy where it held her. Was he drinking her fear already? Was that why her knees felt weak enough to buckle?

More guards materialized from the shadows, all with their scimitars drawn. Arcadius had promised to fight every man Zayd had to protect her. Judging by the way he brought up his fists and readied, he'd meant it. Joseph shifted around until he and his master were back to back, two good djinn against dozens of ifrits. Joseph had magic, but neither man was armed. They were outnumbered more than ten to one.

Then the tribe's sorcerers showed up.

Crap, Elyse thought, her terror spiking uncontrollably. Zayd had so planned this.

"Elyse," said Joseph's voice. He was facing away from her, and no one else reacted. Perhaps he was projecting his words to her magically. However he was communicating, he continued. "I made the rope you wear around your waist. My magic is in it. You can draw on its power to free yourself."

That was fine, but she didn't know how and wasn't sure what good it would do anyway. Even as she wondered, Zayd's smoke arm dragged her another body length away from Arcadius.

"*Don't,*" her protector growled. "I'll kill you if you harm her."

"Why fight?" Zayd asked silkily. "I'm giving you what you want the most. Go save your city. Leave this woman with me. There are plenty more where she came from."

Arcadius answered but Elyse didn't hear. Joseph was speaking to her again.

"You can do it," he said. "Remember how you worked the kettle? All you need is your faith and words of command. You're human, Elyse, the race most beloved by the Almighty. Your words of magic overrule any of our kind's."

What words of magic? Did he expect her to make them up?

Her attention split. Something had happened that caused Arcadius to explode into his smoke form. Apparently, his transformation was a signal for the dark djinn to change as well. Chaotic wind and cloud filled the space around her. Dozens of djinn tornadoes did battle. Strange glows flashed on and off within whirling banks of gray. Zayd's hold on her seemed to keep the hurricane force gusts from tearing her apart, but some fighters were getting hurt. Djinn screamed louder than the cacophony of the wind, smoke forms shredding as lightning-like bolts tore them. Djinn shot these bolts from their fingertips, forming disembodied hands so they could do so. Hitting something that could be injured seemed to be a challenge, but it was happening.

Elyse guessed the seriously wounded couldn't remain vaporous. Solid bodies fell bleeding from the sky. The distinctive blue of Arcadius's eyes told her he was alive. Unfortunately, she kept losing track of him in the confusion.

Her attempts to find him kept her from noticing Joseph was still solid. When she finally did, he was looking straight at her through the tumult. His eyes glowed gold with intensity.

"Grip the rope," he said very firmly without his lips moving. "Arcadius can't hold them all off for long. Speak your command in accordance with your belief."

Speak her command . . . How did she speak in accordance with her belief when she wasn't sure what that was?

She'd have to try. They didn't have time for indecisiveness. She took the rope in both hands. The strands might have been vibrating. It was hard to tell with all that was going on. Zayd didn't notice. The fighting had distracted him.

"In the name of Jehovah," she whispered under her breath, hoping desperately this would work. "God of Jews and Gentiles, God of Djinn, God of all creatures great and small, I command these djinn who want to harm us to lose their strength."

The rope flared within her hands like it had gone nuclear, its matter turning to energy. Brightness flashed out from her in a circle, magically clearing out the smoke.

The smoke hadn't disappeared; it had changed state like the rope. Every djinn except Arcadius and Joseph thudded to the ground unconscious. A heartbeat later, the sheikh collapsed behind her. Elyse staggered forward from gaining her freedom so abruptly.

"Holy sh—" she said, cutting off the curse at the last instant. Under the circumstances, more respect seemed appropriate.

"Whoa," Joseph said, sounding surprised himself. Nice to know he hadn't been convinced she could do it.

Arcadius returned to his solid form. "Hurry," he said. "Help me unroll this carpet. We don't know how long they'll be out."

They also didn't know how far her impromptu spell had reached. Elyse shot a nervous glance over her shoulder at the camp and then ran to help the men. Whether by chance or on purpose, Zayd's guards had pulled out a big carpet. It was large enough to have covered the floor in her living room. Once it was unrolled, it still seemed ordinary. Something that looked like a brass walking stick lay inside. Joseph picked it up as if it was important.

"This rug is old," Elyse said, noting the faded patches.

"Old is good," Joseph told her. "Newer flying carpets aren't as reliable." He gestured her onto it. "We need to get going."

She stepped on suspiciously. Flying carpets sounded romantic until she was about to ride one. Seriously, this was just a rug. Even if it worked, there wasn't anything to keep them from falling off the edge.

Arcadius smiled at her look of doubt. "It's perfectly safe. Just sit down in the middle and—"

"Sirs, wait for me!" someone cried, interrupting his instructions. They all looked up.

"Shit," Joseph said. "It's that two-faced jackal, Samir."

The little smoke demon flew up to them through the litter of unconscious ifrit bodies.

"We're not taking you with us," Joseph said. "You betrayed us to the sheikh."

"Samir introduced you, just as you asked. Now you have defeated Zayd and made me the bearer of bad guests. Zayd will kill me as soon as he wakes up."

"Then go hide somewhere. We're not responsible for you."

"Be merciful," Samir pleaded. "And smart. I am an experienced pilot. I know the way you go. I can help you fly home."

"We can fly ourselves," Joseph retorted.

Samir dropped to his knees and wrung his smoky hands. "Please? None of the tribes will shelter me if they find out what happened here."

"Oh, let him come," Arcadius said. "We haven't traveled this route before. Maybe he'll be useful."

"You try anything," Joseph warned, "and we'll toss you into the Gulf."

"You can trust me, sirs!" Samir scrambled aboard the rug with them. "I know which side my toast is buttered on."

Elyse believed that. She watched with interest as Joseph used the walking stick—if that's what it was—to draw a quick rectangle within the carpet's edge. When he tapped one corner, the border folded up like a box's lid. The top reached slightly higher than the men's waists.

"Safety walls," Samir explained to her with almost convincing friendliness. "So we won't tumble out."

"Uh-huh," she said. She studied their new companion cautiously. His smoke face was hard for her to read.

"Sorry you were almost raped and tortured," he offered.

"No you're not," Elyse said, which caused Arcadius to snort out a laugh.

"I'm a *little* sorry," Samir tried. "Also, I will miss my rocking horse. I had to flee too quickly to carry it."

He shook his head dolefully. Elyse turned away to hide her amusement.

"I'm ready," Joseph said.

"Go ahead and lift off," Arcadius directed.

Elyse sat while she had the chance, doing her best to clutch the carpet to either side of her. Samir sat too, but Arcadius and Joseph remained standing, simply bracing their legs like sailors. Joseph murmured one of his indecipherable incantations.

They rose so smoothly they were five feet above the sand before she realized they were moving. Fortunately for her stomach, the motion was more like an elevator than a boat. Up they went, until the fires of Zayd's encampment dwindled to candle flames. As they did, the men she'd knocked unconscious began to stir. They heard distant shouts below and behind them.

"They're lighting arrows," Arcadius said. He was near enough to the carpet's edge to lean over. "I don't think they can see us, but they'll probably try to shoot us down anyway."

Joseph nodded. Unalarmed, he planted the walking stick on the carpet floor. He pushed the upper half toward one end as if it were a rudder.

"Forward," he commanded.

The flying carpet immediately—and wonderfully—shot out of attack reach.

It soon became apparent, at least to Elyse, that it was good they'd let Samir come. Arcadius and Joseph seemed to have only a vague idea where their Glorious City was in relation to the Great Desert. Samir rolled glowing eyes over their debate, then drifted up to his cloudy feet to help.

"This star," he said, pointing out one of the brighter twinkles. "Steer toward it until you feel the Gulfstream bump under us."

The three djinn navigated together for a while. Elyse guessed Arcadius was satisfied Samir knew his stuff, because he left the others and joined her. To her relief, the men moving about didn't unbalance the carpet. Though it vibrated from the air currents and their speed, it stayed level and steady.

Arcadius's nearness steadied her in a different way.

With a grace that said he was used to traveling this way, he lowered himself beside her. Leaning back on his arms, he stretched his long legs in front of him. The pointed toes of his slippers reminded her how different from normal he and this experience were.

"You must be exhausted," he said. "These last few days have been eventful."

Eventful was one way to put it.

"I don't want to sleep," she confessed. "Now that I'm not fearing for my life, this seems too cool to miss out on."

"You should try to rest. We have hours of flight time left."

She looked at him. Little striations in his eyes were glowing. Despite his casual manner, he was jazzed by their escape too.

"Would you like me to . . . lie down with you?" he asked.

She knew he meant just to rest. The rug wasn't big enough for anything private.

"If you wouldn't mind," she said, glad he'd offered. "You're way warmer than I am."

They wriggled down a bit awkwardly with Arcadius behind her. He let her use his lower arm for a pillow while the other draped her waist.

"Okay?" he asked.

She nodded and hugged his forearm to her. He fit them together better by shifting his legs into the bend of hers. His body heat was like hot chocolate for her psyche. Joseph and Samir were at the opposite end of the carpet, far enough that she couldn't make out their hushed conversation, only that they were having one. The wind rushed steadily above them, proof they actually were flying through the air.

"Are *you* cold?" she thought to ask Arcadius.

"Being near you has a tendency to warm me," he said wryly.

She smiled, belatedly noticing an extra ridge of hardness pressing her bottom. In a way, that was comforting too. "If I were meaner, I'd squirm."

"I appreciate your restraint," he said even more aridly.

Emotion welled in her as she grinned. Maybe it was the result of all they'd been through, but she felt so much for this man: attraction, gratitude, admiration. Her irritation at his highhandedness fell away. So she didn't know all his secrets. In that moment, she thought she knew what mattered. He deserved to be told what he meant to her.

"I love you," she said softly.

Arcadius stopped breathing.

"I know," she said. "You don't feel the same, but we escaped death together. Just this once, you can stand hearing it."

"'Just this once,'" he repeated in an odd tone.

"Sometimes you gotta say it," she informed him.

Losing her dad and David had taught her that. Whatever Arcadius felt, he didn't seem bothered by her words. His strong arms pulled her closer into his warmth. She closed her eyes, strangely satisfied with herself.

Being brave was good, no matter what you were being brave about.

CHAPTER FIFTEEN

WHEN morning broke, they weren't over land anymore. Arcadius recognized the slight turbulence of the Gulfstream bumping under then. Elyse slept on peacefully. Reluctant to disturb her, he took off his outer robe, draping it over her before he got up. The particular sights they were flying over she didn't necessarily want to see.

Joseph wished him good morning from his post at the control stick. Samir had conked out and was curled up in a cloudy ball in one of the rug's corners. The sun was brighter than it got in the human world, the edges of everything he saw razor sharp. Longing futilely for coffee and a bagel, Arcadius peered over the carpet's safety wall.

Far beneath them, the mist that filled the In-Betweens of the Qaf swirled like a restless animal. In some places, the fog was dark. In others, it sparkled as white as snow. Though it resembled a cloud layer, no one could swear it was. Crossing In-Betweens in smoke form was the equivalent of a human swimming the English Channel. Few djinn possessed the strength. Those who fell disappeared forever and couldn't bring back reports. The popular theory was that the mist was the same stuff that surrounded mirror spaces.

Naturally, no one knew exactly what that was either.

"I suppose Elyse wouldn't want to sightsee this," Joseph said, his thoughts on the same track.

"No," Arcadius agreed. "She'd find it unnerving." When he squinted, he thought he spied mountaintops breaking through the mist in serrated teeth. "You made good time. That looks like the next Qaf island."

"This is an excellent carpet. I suspect we're lucky Zayd didn't actually mean for us to take it."

Arcadius hummed in agreement and scratched his cheek. He hadn't shaved in too long.

"She saved our bacon," Joseph said after a little pause. "I wasn't sure she could."

"She's brave," was the only response Arcadius came up with.

Elyse *was* brave, and smart, and totally too pleasurable to be around. Given his previous dearth of romantic attachments, she was also probably the only woman he'd ever love. His memory of her saying she loved him brought waves of heat into his chest. He didn't know what she meant by it. She'd said it lightly. Maybe she'd love anyone she shared an adventure with. Maybe she could have said the same to Joseph. Arcadius didn't know and wasn't prepared to ask.

She *couldn't* love him like he loved her.

Their experience at the portal proved it . . . unless her emotions had grown since then.

He shook his head. If she really were in love with him, it would be both amazing and terrible. He'd have so much more to lose, and likely would lose it after she learned the truth about how he'd schemed to exploit her emotions. Even if a miracle happened and she forgave him, he wouldn't be able to stay with her, not if he and Joseph saved their city the way they were trying to.

I won't exist, he thought. *Not as the person I am right now.*

He pinched the bridge of his nose, contemplating a future without Elyse. Would he mind when he rejoined his original self? Would he appreciate what he'd lost? He'd never heard of djinn accomplishing what he and Joseph had —what Iksander and Philip had accomplished too, God willing. This was uncharted territory. Maybe he'd fall into his old routine like he'd never left. Serving his sultan. Guarding his city. Being the same responsible, half-alive person he'd always been.

The life he was living now would seem like the dream.

Then again, he'd be lucky if he got the chance to feel that way. Saving their people was hardly a done deal. He frowned at that realization, beginning to get a headache from his conflicted thoughts.

"You love her," Joseph said.

"What?" Arcadius's attention jerked back to the other man.

"That's why the portal in the mirror space worked at all, because her not loving you broke your heart. Your energy powered it."

Joseph said this calmly, his gaze on the landmass steadily growing larger ahead of them. Arcadius's heart gave a little skip. That wasn't any island. That was their portion of the Qaf. They were almost home.

"My feelings for Elyse aren't important," he said.

Joseph seemed to think they were. "She cares about you."

Arcadius put his hand on Joseph's shoulder, unable to respond. For no reason he could pinpoint, Joseph seemed taller. When Arcadius was himself again, would he go back to thinking of Joseph as he had before: a servant he admired and was fond of but not an actual friend? Joseph *was* Arcadius's friend, as much as Iksander or Philip. In truth, maybe he was a better one.

"I suppose we can deal with personal matters after we help the city," Joseph said. He gnawed his lip, probably unwittingly.

Arcadius concluded he wasn't the only one worrying about their next challenges.

~

Elyse opened her eyes and said, "Shoot."

She lay in a small but comfortable bed with a light blanket pulled over her. Sunshine poured through the narrow windows that lined the unfamiliar room. The air that drifted in smelled of flowers, the temperature around seventy. None of this was reason to complain. She was just annoyed she'd slept through the rest of the magic carpet ride.

She sat up and pushed off the covers. She was alone in a stone dormitory —or maybe a troop barracks? Everything was spic and span. All the other bunks were made. She wondered if Arcadius has slept in one.

So long, bitches, someone had scrawled in black paint on the whitewashed wall.

"If I knew who'd done that, I'd have him dishonorably discharged."

Arcadius's tone teetered between joking and serious. He leaned casually in the doorway at the room's end, one wide shoulder propped on the wall. He'd changed into tan trousers and a loose white shirt with the tails tucked in. Weathered army boots clad his feet, and he'd strapped various knife harnesses around him. This outfit didn't look borrowed. Everything fit as if it belonged on his body. He reminded her of a mercenary, dressed for some dangerous assignment. Only the gems glinting on his knife hilts were out of place. A human soldier would have worn bullet bandoliers. Maybe djinn didn't do handguns?

He's the sultan's commander, she recalled.

"Where are we?" she asked, disconcerted by seeing him this way.

"Fort Faithful. Just outside the city walls."

"Your city."

"Yes." His handsome face was unreadable.

"We made it then." She hopped off the bed she'd been sitting on.

"Bathroom is that way," he said. "Joseph activated the water."

The bathroom was dormitory style as well: bright, clean, with airy ceilings and smooth stone floors. She used the facilities and washed up at a spotless sink. When she looked in the mirror, her hair was hopeless—curls exploding every which way in corkscrews. A week with her flatiron wouldn't have helped it. She supposed flying carpets were like convertibles that way: fun to ride in but hell on the coiffure. On the bright side, her face was fine. She looked less tired than she had in months, and she'd gotten a little tan. Her formerly pale cheeks were pink.

Okay, she thought. *I can live with this.*

"Where is everyone?" she asked as she came out again. "Doesn't a fort imply soldiers?"

"Theoretically," Arcadius said. "But there's no one to guard right now. Anyone who wasn't caught inside the city walls has left—probably weeks ago. They'll have gone to the provinces, I expect."

"There's no dust."

"The spells to keep it out are still functioning. Fortunately, the food stores are also protected. The local monkeys have been trying to break in."

His lips twisted. This place's abandoned state upset him, but he was trying to disguise how much. She went to him and touched his arm. To her surprise, he gathered up her hand, squeezed her fingers, and brought her knuckles to his mouth to kiss.

She guessed that settled the question of whether her saying *I love you* bothered him. He looked down at her from his greater height, his mesmerizing eyes probing hers. His expression didn't give much away.

"You should probably tell me what we're up against," she said.

His laugh was soft and ironic. "That was my plan. Let's take a walk, and I'll lay it out for you."

He kept her hand in his as they left the barracks. A bright warm day awaited them outside. Lush flowering trees softened the two-story stone buildings. The emerald grass was overgrown but not weedy. Birds sang in random choruses. When Elyse looked up, a cute little monkey perched on a nearby branch widened its eyes at her.

"This way," Arcadius said, pulling her along a tidy path. He was leading her to a lookout point. The fort was on a promontory above a harbor, with its own thick wall around it. The sweet warm air seemed to sparkle, the colors brighter than she was used to.

Everything is so pretty, she marveled.

They climbed steps to a curved platform. A large black cannon stuck out a parapet in the wall.

"There," Arcadius said, indicating the same direction as the gun's muzzle. "Within those walls lies the Glorious City."

Elyse's breath caught in wonder. They were about a mile away, and Arcadius's city was really big. Its mostly white buildings sprawled over three massive hills, between which thick fringes of palm trees grew. Dreamy minarets poked up everywhere, plus church spires and huge gold domes whose curves appeared to be gilded with genuine twenty-four karat leaf. Red clay roofs predominated, giving the place a consistent, Mediterranean look.

"Wow," she said, leaning over the wall to see better. Those big green spaces were probably city parks. Wide avenues suggested main thoroughfares, but mazelike backstreets abounded too. The scene was a travel poster for an exotic vacation spot, one where the sky was always blue, the clouds well mannered, and the temperature perfect. A sparkling turquoise river cut across the metropolis, lovely little bridges arched over it.

"It reminds me of Istanbul," she said, recalling a teenage trip there with her father.

"Yes," Arcadius agreed. "That is the human city easiest to travel to from ours."

She turned to him. He was gazing at the capital and for once his expression hid nothing. Elyse thought she'd never seen anyone so sad. Tears glittered in his gorgeous eyes.

"What happened here?" she asked softly.

"Look at the avenues," he said. "At the parks and the public spaces."

She looked. "Nothing's moving. Well, the palms are swaying in the breeze but I don't see traffic or pedestrians."

He pulled a pair of binoculars from a pouch he wore on his hip. "Look again. Your vision isn't as sharp as mine."

She put the lenses to her eye sockets. Either the focus accidentally suited her or it adjusted magically. She found the biggest park she could. A number of inexplicable white objects sprang into view.

"Why are there so many—" She cut off her own question. She wasn't looking at statues. The poses and the lack of bases weren't right for that.

The white objects were people who had been turned to stone.

"Oh," she said, jerking with the realization. "Who did that to all of them?"

"The sorceress cursed us," Arcadius said.

She lowered the binoculars to gape at him. "The sorceress from Joseph's story?"

"Yes." His mouth tightened, his lips pressed into a thin line. "Luna's thirst for vengeance wasn't satisfied by murdering Najat. She was still obsessed with Iksander. She told him she'd destroy his city if he didn't marry her and make her queen."

"She was that powerful?"

"It was a terrible magic. She gave up her own life to perform it."

"Wow." Elyse leaned sideways on the wall, unable to look away from his troubled face. "If I'm going to help, you'd better tell me everything."

"Elyse, I'm not explaining this to get your help."

"Maybe you should. I've been handy more than once before."

"This isn't your responsibility."

"But you're acting like it's all yours!"

Her anger took him aback. Elyse poked his hard breastbone. "I don't care *what* happened. No way is this all your fault."

"I was the guardian. I *am* the guardian. Saving the city is my job."

"So do your job. Use all the resources at your disposal. I am a resource. Just like Joseph. I'm not a magician but maybe I'll see something you two haven't."

Arcadius looked doubtful.

"I helped us escaped the sheikh," she pointed out. "And found the door that brought us to your world in the first place. Like it or not, I'm part of the team."

The corners of his mouth turned down. "I want you to be safe."

"I want *you* to be safe," she retorted. "And Joseph. And that amazing city full of people. If I have something to offer, let me try. Tell me what happened. *Please*, Arcadius."

The "please" got to him. When he sighed, the sound was a mix of weariness and relief.

"All right," he surrendered. "I'll do my best to tell you what's important."

~

Arcadius knew he ought to sit down for this. He led Elyse back to the overlook's curving steps. She lowered herself next to him, her warm side leaning into his. Helpless not to, he put his arm around her shoulders.

* * *

The nuns weren't long in discovering Najat's death. Naturally, they sent word of it to Iksander. I'm not sure I can describe what her loss did to him. He went a little crazy with guilt and grief, but after that he grew very calm. He called Philip back to the palace—pardoning him, I suppose, though he didn't formally say so. I doubt Philip wanted an apology. He had his own reasons to feel guilty.

In any case, the three of us—myself, Joseph, and Philip—were summoned to meet Iksander in his private office the same night Philip returned. We weren't certain what we'd discuss. A memorial for Najat? An inquiry into her murder? Only I was an official advisor to the throne. The rest were simply Iksander's friends. When we arrived, Philip's father the Vizier was present. Of all Iksander's cabinet, the sultan probably trusted Murat most. Murat had also served Iksander's father and was experienced. He stood slightly behind Iksander, who sat at his fine large desk. Both looked extremely serious.

We saw immediately that the sultan was once again his true self.

In that moment, his true self was angry. Because he was too overwrought to speak, Murat explained that Empress Luna had conveyed certain demands to him. Not only did she want Iksander to forsake all other women and marry her, she wished to rule the Glorious City instead of him. She'd allow him to keep his title, but she'd make all the decisions. If he refused, she'd wreak such destruction on his people that Iksander's name would be remembered for nothing else. His city's terrible defeat would become his legacy.

"That's ridiculous," Philip said in his passionate way. "Her army might be as large as ours but I doubt it's half as good."

My spies told me this was true. The upper ranks of Luna's military were corrupt, more interested in the perquisites of their posts than in training or caring for their troops.

"Unfortunately," Murat said, "she doesn't plan to defeat us by force of arms."

"Then how?" I asked, unaware she had other means.

"Show him," Iksander said tightly.

Iksander's private office was separated from his salon by a curtained arch. Murat strode to it and pulled the drape aside. Behind it a realistic sculpture of a young boy appeared, perhaps five years of age. Dressed in play clothes, he rolled a hoop with a stick and laughed. The various pieces interconnected delicately.

"That's lovely!" Philip exclaimed, his artistic mind distracted by the work's quality.

"It is the grandson of the Minister of Agriculture," Murat said grimly.

Still, we didn't understand.

"It *is* his grandson," Iksander said, rage causing his voice to shake. "Not a likeness. Luna used magic to turn the boy to stone."

This struck even Joseph speechless.

"If you can undo this," Iksander said to him, "I'd be very happy to have you try. The minister has had half a dozen mages attempt it already."

"I will do everything in my power," Joseph said carefully. "I confess, however, that this may be beyond me. Now that you've drawn my attention to what it is, I can sense the boy's spirit within the stone. He's alive, but his consciousness is locked to the . . . being force of the marble, for lack of a better term. I'm not sure I can extricate him without doing more damage."

"There must be some way," Philip said.

I knew Joseph pretty well. He had served me a long time. I suspected he was doing his utmost to avoid saying there was no hope at all.

"What if we kill the person who cast the spell?" Iksander asked. "Would that improve your chances of lifting it?"

"Considerably," Joseph said. Thoughtful now, he crouched down to gently examine the boy's statue. "The problem is, a mage strong enough to do this will also be able to protect himself from attacks."

"Herself," Iksander corrected. "Empress Luna cast the spell. She—" He swallowed. "She informed me she is the person who killed Najat. She has turned ifrit. This magic was powered by a blood sacrifice. She assures me she'd be delighted to spill more."

"She is ifrit?" I said, startled by this news. "Why haven't her people deposed her?"

"Evidently, the City of Endless Night isn't as particular about these things as one would expect God-fearing djinn to be."

We had dark djinn in our city but they were a minority. Ifrits weren't always evil. Some were simply born to ifrit parents. To *turn* dark, however, was a thing most light djinn avoided. Hell is a real place to us. We'd rather not burn for eternity.

"What do you wish of us, sir?" Joseph asked respectfully.

"Too many things," Iksander said, "but I must ask all the same. Joseph, I would like you to oversee the investigation into how we can get around Luna's magic. We need to weaken her defenses so we can kill her, or somehow shield the city from succumbing to this boy's fate. I know it's a tall order. Please enlist whatever help you need—discreetly, if you can, so as not to start a panic."

Next, the sultan turned to me. "Arcadius, I want you to organize an evacuation plan. I know your men will fight but if fighting does no good, our people must have the opportunity to escape."

"And me?" Philip asked.

Iksander looked at his friend, whom he had briefly cast aside but now brought into the fold again. The regret he felt at their recent history was clear in his expression. "From you, dear friend, I need one last cause for hope if all else fails."

"I don't understand," Philip said.

"Do you recall how you imbued the ability to take animal form into Arcadius's raven tattoo?"

"Of course." It was Philip's gift to combine art and magic, in whatever medium.

"I wish you to accomplish something more complicated for the people in this room. We need an escape hatch Luna is ignorant of. Only then can we mount a rescue if worse comes to worse and our city is petrified."

"You have a means in mind," Philip guessed.

"I'm hoping we can exploit the magic that mirror spaces run on to create copies of ourselves, into which we could project our consciousness. Joseph is a better authority than myself, but if we did this near a portal, it seems to me we could send our copies into the human realm. There they could gather strength for a return. Most curses can be undone with time. We'd have another chance to save our people."

"That seems . . . possible," Joseph said. "And certainly creative. Are you thinking Philip could encapsulate a trigger in a tattoo?"

"I am," Iksander said.

"It would require a great deal of power," Philip mused. "And *I* cannot do blood magic. If I attempt this, I don't think we'd be able to test the process beforehand."

"I will forego the honor, if that makes it easier," Murat said.

"Father!" Philip protested.

Murat lifted his hands. "I am an old man. I'd rather wait here in the faith that you'd rescue me than go gallivanting among humans."

We discussed it further—argued, truth be told—but in the end, it was settled. We would perform our tasks as Iksander had assigned them.

Iksander tried to buy us time by requesting a chance to think on Luna's gracious offer. She wasn't interested. She gave him one more day to make up his mind.

She set a deadline of midnight. The sultan called me to his office a single hour before his response was due. To my surprise, he was alone. He stood beside a tall window, holding back the drape to gaze over his city. The fateful letter lay on his desk, lacking only his signature. Though he must have heard me enter, my friend didn't turn around.

"I have refused her," he said, "using every flowery plea for mercy I know. I doubt my pretty manners will help but I thought I ought to try."

He seemed to be soliciting my opinion. "You have to turn her down," I said.

"Do I?" Iksander twisted his head to me. "Should I not throw myself on the pyre to save my people, even if it means pleasuring the woman who killed my wife?"

"No!" I exclaimed, shocked that he'd suggest it. "Luna is a dark ifrit. You know they love suffering. If you set her on our city's throne, she will not stop at tormenting you. I promise you, there will come a day when your people curse you for preserving them. It is better to be turned to stone than to live under a thumb as depraved as hers."

Iksander let the curtain fall across the window again. "Maybe." He turned fully around to me. His face was strange: not simply melancholy but also guilt ridden. "I have pleasured her already."

"What?" I asked, my brow furrowing.

"She was one of the women I visited in my madness. I didn't know she was the sorceress who tricked and killed Najat, but it is likely I am responsible for her obsession."

Perhaps my reaction was influenced by the strain we were under. I laughed at him.

"Forgive me," I said once I'd recovered. "Though I've heard you're a gifted lover, it's clear to me Luna built her own obsession. She lusted after your city before she lusted after you. It was happenstance that you also attracted her. I can see it bothers you to have slept with her, but if you hadn't, I wager she'd have found some other reason for perpetrating these horrors. This is no more your doing than it is Najat's for inspiring you to love only her."

I hoped I'd hit on the words to get through to him.

Iksander rubbed his forehead. "So I should reject her."

"It is my firm opinion that you must," I replied.

I still had hope when he signed that letter and magically sent it off. My troops were disciplined and brave, our people doughty, and I believed Joseph had made headway in finding weaknesses in Luna's magic from which to gain advantage. Philip had given us our tattoos: small overlapped twin suns that we wore inside our right ankles. Considering the unpredictable situation, we were as ready as anyone could be.

Alas, we didn't have the interim we believed. Upon receiving Iksander's refusal, the empress used sorcery to transport herself and her entire army from the City of Endless Night. The following morning, a great host stood massed outside our walls.

When I tried to put my evacuation plan in motion, we discovered Luna's magic had sealed off our escape routes. Unable to flee by land or sky, we prepared for her army to scale the walls. The empress had other plans. Her army, who she'd dressed in black for effect, began to march around us, thousands upon thousands of booted feet all thumping in synchrony. You may imagine the noise spread fear, but it wasn't the worst of what we witnessed. Luna's sorcerers strode in the center of the tramping sea of soldiers. They carried her on a spell-shielded palanquin, where she periodically sacrificed living creatures over a cauldron and chanted. Her sorcerers chanted too, in the old tongue skilled practitioners master.

During the course of that first day, they circled our city once. My men attacked them from the ramparts, but couldn't kill enough of them to disrupt their march. I suppose it's pointless to describe the battles. Suffice to say, many lives were lost on both sides.

The second day unfolded much the same as the first. The main difference was that Luna began sacrificing larger animals. We knew she was tightening a magical noose around us in preparation to cast her curse. No defense we mounted was successful, whether involving our own mages or conventional arms. Our last hope was a stratagem Joseph concocted.

Aware that Luna's third circumnavigation was liable to spell our doom, once she'd made camp the second night, we requested a parley. We led her to believe Iksander was reconsidering his refusal, and that he'd appointed Joseph and myself to discuss possible surrender terms with her. I suppose she did love Iksander, in her way. The chance that we were being honest tempted her too strongly to dismiss us.

We exchanged the usual binding ritual oaths that neither party would harm the other. The empress's magicians dropped their charmed barrier long enough to allow us out the gate. The diplomatic niceties taken care, Joseph dropped down onto one knee.

"Glorious Empress," he addressed her, "my master the sultan wishes me to present you with a humble token of his remorse, that you may be assured of his sincerity."

Luna's sorcerers went into a tizzy at the silk-wrapped object he brought out. Finding no spells hidden in the parcel, they conceded she might open it if she wished.

No matter what their station, djinn love presents. Luna couldn't help peeking at this one. She ordered one of the sorcerers to unwrap the silk.

Revealed within was a cuff bracelet Philip had created, using only the purest gold and the most precious of gemstones. The piece was so lovely everyone who saw it gasped.

"It is not as beautiful as you, mighty empress," Joseph said, "but my master begs you to accept it."

Luna was dazzled. As any woman would, she slid the bracelet onto her arm to better admire it.

Joseph rose to his feet and grinned. He didn't quite say "gotcha," but Luna understood the significance of his reaction.

"What have you done?" she demanded.

"I have bound you to your magic," Joseph said. "What you do to us, you now also inflict on any who have sworn allegiance to you—not excepting your own self."

"That is impossible. My sorcerers searched this gift for spells."

Joseph examined his fingernails. "The spell was very tiny. I enjoy shrinking things."

"You swore not to harm us!" the empress objected.

"I have not harmed you. I only made it possible for you to harm yourself."

The empress tried to remove the cuff, but it was affixed to her as securely as her arm. Joseph warned her severing the limb would also do no good. Still hoping to rid herself of the thing, Luna shifted to her smoke form. Unfortunately for her, the bracelet simply vaporized and re-formed.

Her fury when she realized she could not escape was truly a sight to see.

She swore at us and ordered us from her presence, an invitation we accepted while we could. When we were within the walls again, we sobered. Luna had behaved as if she were lost to sense. We couldn't guess what she would do next, only that admitting defeat and retreating seemed unlikely.

We had our answer when the sun rose the following morning. As if we'd accomplished nothing, her troops formed up and once more began marching. The chanting resumed, along with the sacrifices. The blood Luna's cauldron drank that day belonged to farmers she'd caught outside the walls. Nothing she did horrified her men. They'd become as degenerate as she was.

In our city, people drew together. We have an awareness of the human "9/11." I suspect our feelings were similar. We were facing horrors, and it made us want to reaffirm our closeness to those we loved. Ironically, the curse struck the empress and her army first, turning them all to stone. Though our mages tried, the spell was unstoppable. It swept inward in concentric circles, taking one ring and then the next.

The palace district is our most central. Within it, we have three portals. Iksander assigned us to different ones, to maximize the chance that one of us would escape. We didn't have time to be emotional. Joseph prepared a survival cache for each of us, a sack of miniaturized treasures with which we could make our way in the human world.

We exchanged our last embrace and parted. Together, Joseph and I flew to the portal we'd been assigned. This was at the top of the Arch of Triumph, where the Avenue of Palms begins. From that height, we had a bird's eye view of the sorceress's curse progressing through our city.

"We must concentrate," Joseph reminded me.

He sat and composed himself as I spoke the words to activate the portal. I'd decided on Manhattan, New York as our destination. To improve our chances of reaching it, I gave properly keying the nexus my full attention. Fortunately, this wasn't as complicated as it is in your dimension. The portals' magic is natural to our plane, and no special sacrifice was required, simply a strong mental grasp of the place I was aiming for. When I was satisfied I'd got it as right as possible, I sat on the opposite side of the glowing sphere from Joseph. Though I couldn't see it, I sensed the lattice of the mirror space he'd spun around us.

"Know who you are," he said, guiding me to the same meditative state he'd achieved. "Remember that your spirit is your true essence. It is eternal. It continues when your body dies. More than this, it contains the intelligence to create another shell to house itself."

I knew the new forms we made would be imperfect. We weren't as wise as our Creator. Because of this, it was important to preserve our originals if we could. Consequently, I had one more question.

"How much spirit should we leave behind in our bodies?"

"A tenth part should be enough to keep them from dying when the curse strikes."

The curse was coming closer. We could feel it pushing the air before it like a foaming wave running up a shore. Joseph wouldn't make his leap until I attempted mine. He didn't want to leave me to try alone. Realizing this, I focused on the details of my physical being, hoping to make my copy as accurate as possible. When it was set in my mind, I touched the symbol on my ankle, murmuring the word we'd decided on. Half the mirror space's lattice lines jumped to me, the magic in the tattoo setting my blood aflame. My edges blurred but I didn't turn to smoke. Across from me, I saw a second Joseph pull like taffy from his body. Half a moment later, I did likewise. The new Joseph chanted at the portal, which flared for him.

To our relief, the nexus sucked our consciousness and our copies into it.

We rematerialized in your city on the roof of a large post office, thankfully only scaring a few pigeons. Because being shot through a nexus is a one-way trip, we began searching for a portal to take us back as soon as we were able. The portal in your brownstone was the likeliest candidate we found. You know the rest of the tale from there.

* * *

Elyse had been listening attentively. As Arcadius finished, she shifted on the step to face him more directly. Seen in the sunlight of his world, her clear green eyes were even more beautiful. Though he was aware she'd have preferred straight locks, her hair was a mass of glorious deep black curls with midnight blue highlights. Struck by how very attractive they were to him, he had to force himself to pay attention when she spoke.

"What happened to Philip and Iksander? Did they get out?"

"We don't know. They were headed to different locations. The plan was for everyone to place an ad in the *New York Times* classifieds, to let the others know they'd arrived safely. We've had no response to ours, though we don't assume the worst. Many things could have prevented them from answering."

"And now that you're here?" she asked. "Do you know how to free your people?"

"We believe destroying the sorceress's statue might accomplish it—or at least serve as the first step."

"You *believe* it might."

"We've never seen anyone pull off a curse of this magnitude. It makes the process of undoing it inexact."

"There was that palace whose residents were turned to fish," Joseph said.

Elyse started. She hadn't noticed Joseph's approach. Arcadius recognized the servant's bright blue robes and yellow trousers as a set he kept in their private quarters in the fort. Like Arcadius, Joseph was mentally preparing to become his old self again.

"Fish?" Elyse asked.

Joseph smiled. Arcadius could feel how fond of Elyse he was. "Very beautiful fish but only a few hundred were transformed." He looked at Arcadius. "I estimate we have an hour until noon. We should probably make our attempt on the statue then."

"Because Luna ruled the City of Endless Night?" Elyse asked.

"Yes," Joseph said. "The sun reaching its zenith should mark an ebb in her powers, whatever remain in her current state. Samir has slipped away, by the way. When I awoke, he was gone."

Arcadius's mouth pursed with annoyance.

"Should I have tried to hold him?" Joseph asked.

"We don't really have grounds for that. He's not our prisoner. And he helped get us here, as promised." Arcadius shrugged. "We'll keep an eye out. Hopefully, he'll find somewhere far away to make mischief."

He rose and offered Elyse his hand. She took it and hopped up. She was endearingly eager. "Are we smashing the sorceress now?"

"We're damn well going to try," he said.

CHAPTER SIXTEEN

THEY didn't have far to search for the sorceress. The stone army was at the city's gate, having finished their last lap around the wall before the curse took hold. Elyse found the sight of the soldiers intimidating, even knowing they couldn't move. Their marble expressions were very fierce, their frozen postures determined. Had the sorceress warned them of the fate they faced, or had they walked blindly into it?

"Here's the palanquin," Joseph called.

He'd picked his way through the ranks to find it. Lena's sorcerer-porters must have set it down before they were petrified. The carrier hadn't turned to stone. The black silk awning that shaded it seemed especially animated in the light wind.

"Someone got here before us," Joseph said.

The empress's body was in pieces. Her lower half was separate from her upper, one arm had been struck off, and her head had rolled a short distance from her neck to rest face down in the trampled dirt. A thick steel pipe lay nearby, clearly the implement that had caused the damage.

Along with Elyse, Arcadius gazed down at the stone remains. "One of the soldiers posted at the fort could have done this. I suppose he gave up hacking her when it didn't do any good."

"We could smash her more," Joseph said. "Maybe she needs to be smithereens."

"Hm," Arcadius said, the way men do when they have no idea. Suddenly his attention sharpened. He strode to the severed head. He lifted it, bouncing it on his palm until it was face up. The stone eyes stared, the feminine lips covered by a half veil. Elyse noticed the nose was cracked.

"That's not her," Joseph said.

"No, it's not," Arcadius agreed.

"Well, heck," Elyse said, deflated by this turn of events. "Oh, look: there's no bracelet on either arm."

The men were way ahead of her.

"An imposter?" Joseph asked.

"But why bother?" Arcadius responded. "The bracelet ensured she'd turned to stone, wherever she ran to."

"Maybe she wanted to see Iksander one last time," Elyse suggested.

Both djinn turned glowing eyes to her. Like the fluttering palanquin, the men seemed especially alive amidst the stone soldiers.

"That is an excellent guess," Arcadius said. "We'll search the palace first."

Though she was a full-grown woman, Arcadius's praise warmed Elyse. She understood how he'd risen to commander. Anyone would go the extra mile to earn his approval.

~

Walking through the Glorious City was eerie and fascinating, like visiting Pompeii if the bodies were standing up. The residents had been caught in their last moments. Some wept. Others appeared resigned. Many hugged their children or held the nearest person's hand. Nothing had been harmed but the djinn. Dogs and cats roamed the alleys, and birds in every imaginable hue darted overhead. Small flying carpets had settled to the ground and stopped with their stone passengers. In other cases, the stalled vehicles were wheeled carts, pedaled by more marble folks. They passed some statues that had toppled over and shattered. Joseph assured her the people's spirits would have departed before this happened.

"They'd be extremely hard to break otherwise," he said. "Probably they died of heart attacks from shock."

Though she believed him, she did her best to avoid bumping anyone.

She also noticed, once she was able to see past the pathos surrounding her, that perhaps two thirds of the women wore head veils. Those who didn't seemed to be less affluent, though that was relative in this treasure-laden place. Observing the women's dress made her realize Arcadius had faced quite a bit of adjusting in New York—quite a bit of adjusting to her, for that matter.

With no moving traffic to hinder them, they reached the sultan's palace in about half an hour. The golden domes of the huge white complex dominated the upper portion of one of the city's hills. Inside, the palace was museum big, with long echoing corridors and voluminous arched ceilings. The abundance of embellishments astonished: intricate mosaics and murals and fist-sized gems sparkling from every surface that would take them. The result was overwhelming and beautiful. Elyse would happily have spent a week peeking in every door.

The numerous too-realistic statues reminded her they weren't here for sightseeing.

Despite searching every face, they failed to find the empress in either the grand reception hall or the main corridor.

"Maybe we should go to the treasure room," Joseph said. "That's where the portal Iksander chose for himself is located."

"If Luna's there, that would mean she knew what he planned to do."

Joseph didn't look any happier about this prospect than Arcadius.

"All right," Arcadius said. "That's the next logical place to try."

They proceeded down pretty stairways into silent windowless halls. Elyse fought the urge to tiptoe, but the men walked normally, even when skirting petrified palace staff. The door to the treasure room resembled that of a bank vault—assuming a person would construct one of thick etched gold and then stud it with diamonds. The heavy barrier was ajar, allowing them to simply step around it. Inside, the vault was octagonal. Shelves stuffed with priceless objects lined the walls. A subtle flicker in the air at the center told Elyse where the nexus was.

"Iksander's here," Joseph said, gesturing toward a low folding screen carved of red jasper. The sultan's statue sat behind it in lotus posture on the floor. He was very handsome—tall, she thought, with thick wavy hair that fell frozen to broad shoulders. His eyes were closed and his face was calm. Looking as he did, as if he were carved from the finest Carrara marble, he fit right in with the room's treasures. It must have been strange for his friends to see him like this, but her companions weren't the sort to openly freak out.

"The portal has been used," Arcadius observed. "Iksander must have got away."

Must have seemed like overstating it, but maybe the djinn had a way to tell. Bugged by something she couldn't put her finger on, Elyse wandered back to the hall outside.

A single female servant had fallen to her knees perhaps fifteen feet away. Had she been trying to reach the portal and given up to pray? Not that Elyse relished the idea of thousands of unmonitored djinn running around New York, but why hadn't they attempted to get more citizens out that way? Arcadius claimed the portals here weren't as hard to operate as the ones on her plane. Once they'd found the door thingie in the brownstone, she thought they'd gone through pretty easily.

Guessing this was another topic she had half a picture of, she stepped closer to the statue. The servant's robe and veil covered most of her kneeling form. Her slippered feet stuck out from the pool of her marble hem, giving Elyse a view of their soles. They'd turned to stone as well. What struck Elyse was that they were caked with dirt.

This servant hadn't spent her last day indoors.

"Guys," she called to the others. "I think I might have found Luna!"

Joseph and Arcadius came out to check.

"It *is* her," Joseph said. "You can see the shape of Philip's bracelet beneath her sleeve."

Arcadius had carried the pipe that smashed the imposter inside with him. His hand tightened on it, but he didn't tell them to move back so he could smash her.

"What?" Joseph asked, seeing him hesitate.

Arcadius looked at her. "Elyse and I need a minute."

"Ah," Joseph said, seeming to understand what she didn't. "I'll just . . . check the treasury for more clues."

~

Arcadius felt like his heart was going to explode inside his chest. Walking through his city, seeing what Luna had done to it, hadn't agitated him the way what he had to tell Elyse did. He breathed in and out but couldn't calm himself.

She put both hands on his arms. His sleeves were rolled up. Her thumbs stroked the sensitive skin inside his forearms. "What is it, Arcadius?"

"I have to warn you. If the continuation of Luna's curse depends on her statue, breaking it may awaken the city."

"I thought that was the point."

"It is. I'm not saying this very well. My original will awaken too."

"Oh," she said. "I forgot about that. Will there be two of you? That would be weird." She put one hand to her mouth as something occurred to her. "Gosh, you aren't going to go poof, are you?"

He laughed, despite his rattled nerves. "No. Joseph believes . . . that is, he and Philip designed the spell so that when the doubles are once again together, they'll meld back into one person."

"Okay," she said slowly.

"I . . . won't . . . be the same as I am now. Not precisely. My experiences in your world have changed me. Meeting you has changed me. I can't predict who I'll be after recombining. I can't predict what I'll feel."

She tilted her head slightly. "What are you getting at?"

He tried to calm himself with one more deep breath. "I'm in love with you."

Her eyes went wide.

"I know you don't feel that way," he said before she could interrupt. "I mean, I know you said you love me, but that isn't quite the same. You probably love Joseph too. Actually, you probably still love your duplicitous husband."

"My 'duplicitous' husband." She was fighting a smile. He felt his mouth begin to frown. "Sorry," she said, giving his arms an apologetic squeeze. "I shouldn't joke. Just tell me, exactly how is it that you know I'm not in love with you?"

He didn't want to get into this. He gritted his teeth and explained anyway.

"I know because of what I tried to do at the portal in your brownstone. Traveling back and forth between planes takes a lot of magic. The nexuses we used to leave this city are fed energy over time. Since our sort of djinn don't perform blood sacrifices, it takes months for them to accumulate a sufficient charge for a single trip."

"I wondered about that," she said and then waved her hand. "Sorry. Go ahead."

"When a nexus located on your plane isn't properly pre-keyed—as was the case with the one in your cellar—a sacrifice is required. If a pure heart can be broken, it releases a great deal of energy. When I told you I wasn't in love with you, that's what I was attempting."

Elyse's brows drew together. "You were trying to break my heart."

"Yes."

He waited while she processed this. "And I laughed at you."

"Yes," he said, irritated anew at the memory.

"So you 'knew' I wasn't in love with you."

"Correct."

"But the portal worked anyway."

"Because you broke *my* heart," he said gruffly. "I didn't recognize what I felt until then. I'd never been in love before."

To his amazement, she smiled. "That's the sweetest thing I've ever heard!"

"I assure you, I'm not trying to be sweet. I'm trying to warn you, I might not love you after I'm . . . reunited with the real me. Not that you necessarily mind."

She laughed, which caused him to cross his arms. "Shit. Sorry. I'm not laughing at you. You just look so grumpy." She stroked his shoulders and then his face. "I don't know the difference between *love* and *in love*, but I really do love you." Her voice dropped a bit on the words, as if she were self-conscious. "Love that lasts takes time—at least in my experience, it does. I promise, though, I definitely could come to love you that way."

"You're not angry I tried to manipulate your emotions for my own ends?"

She considered this, which made him regret asking. "I could be angry if I think about it, but you did get your comeuppance so maybe in a while, I'll let you off the hook."

He looked into her wonderful face. Her expression was teasing and worried and tender at the same time. "God, I love you," he said.

Her speaking green eyes welled up. She went onto tiptoe and kissed him.

Her lips molding over his set off a slow fusillade of sparklers along his nerves. He wrapped her in his arms, holding her even tighter than she held him. She clung to his shoulders as his tongue slid into her mouth. When she let out a sigh of pleasure, he wanted to record it. Everything they did felt worth memorizing: her firm little body moving beneath his hands, her breath rushing on his cheek, the fierce rise of his arousal as she pressed back at him.

This had to be the most affecting kiss of his life, breaking him apart and putting him back together so perfectly he felt reborn.

The kiss's only flaw was that it didn't last long enough.

All too soon, she dropped back onto her feet. "Really?" she asked breathlessly. "You might not love me after this?"

"At this moment, that's hard for me to conceive, but I'm afraid it's true."

"Well, that sucks." He watched her struggle, finding every flicker of emotion miraculous. Finally, she hunched her shoulders in surrender. "You have to smash Luna anyway. A whole city worth of people depends on this."

He clasped her face gently between his hands. "You make me think well of who I've become with you. Part of me will always love Elyse Solomon."

She wagged her finger. "Don't you forget it."

She wasn't quite teasing.

~

Arcadius had dropped too many bombshells on Elyse at once. He was in love with her? And thought he might fall out of it when the other him woke up? Was his belief that he loved her more than she loved him reasonable? Did it even matter? Certainly, what she felt for him wasn't casual. She *wanted* him to love her. The idea that his affection would go away made her stomach clench —and she'd only just learned of it! Seriously, where was the "stop" button on the world when she needed one?

Wherever it was, she wouldn't get a chance to use it. Joseph came back into the hall carrying a large shiny candlestick he must have found in the vault. He gave it a Babe Ruth swing to test its balance.

"Titanium," he said, pretending not to notice she and Arcadius had had a moment. "There's another in the stores if you want one."

"I suck at baseball," she said absently, her brain rolling in a new direction. "Is you shattering Luna's statue really okay? It's like killing her, right? Because if that will turn you ifrit, maybe I *should* try to break it instead."

"She went to war with us," Arcadius said. "And committed atrocious acts. By djinn code, this is a justifiable homicide."

"What about Luna's army? Won't they wake up too if you break the curse?"

Arcadius squeezed her tense shoulder. Maybe he sensed part of her was stalling. "They will but I have many trained men within these walls. And I briefed my captains about this possibility. They'll handle any threat the empress's soldiers are able to muster. Without their leader, I expect her forces will cut and run."

"Okay." Elyse tried to calm her nerves by blowing out a breath. "I'll just step back and let you two have at it."

Arcadius kissed her forehead and Joseph smiled at her. She realized she might lose him too. No doubt he'd also changed from who he'd originally been. Crap. She wasn't ready for this to happen.

Ready or not, Joseph and Arcadius went ahead. No more than a dozen swings of their muscular arms bashed Luna's statue to rubble. Both men stepped back. Panting, they contemplated the destruction on the floor.

Elyse shivered. Suddenly, the air in the hall was cold.

"Luna's life force," Joseph murmured. "It's been severed from the stone." He turned his head as if he could see something. "It's dissipating."

The men fell silent so Elyse did as well. The only sound was their breathing and her too loud heartbeat.

"Do you hear that?" Arcadius asked. He cocked his head to listen.

Joseph broke into a beatific smile. "The palace staff is waking up."

Then Elyse heard the noises too. On the floor above them, people were calling to each other.

The same idea turned their heads toward the vault door in unison. No noises came from there. Arcadius marched back first, followed by Joseph and Elyse. The sultan's statue sat unchanged—still marble, still preternaturally serene.

"I was afraid of this," Joseph said.

"Afraid of what?" Arcadius and Elyse asked simultaneously.

"We thought Luna went ahead with her plan because she was too bent on revenge to exercise good sense. But maybe she wasn't crazy. Maybe she had a secret out. Luna's departing life force seemed less than it should be. I suspect no more than half her spirit was inside that statue."

"Are you implying only half our people will wake up?"

Joseph hitched his shoulders and looked unhappy.

"Where's the rest of her spirit?" Elyse asked, fighting an impulse to glance around for it. "Could she have copied herself like you did?"

Joseph rubbed one finger across his lips. "I'm afraid she might have done something simpler."

"Simpler?" Elyse asked.

"She could have sent her spirit through the portal with Iksander—the part she didn't leave here to sustain the curse. We have strict prohibitions against possessing humans, but dark djinn don't obey them. If Luna's consciousness made it through, she could be inside anyone."

"She could be riding Iksander," Arcadius blurted in dismay.

"That might explain why he never contacted us."

"Fuck," Arcadius cursed with heartfelt vehemence. "That would be bad." He squeezed his temples for a moment and shook himself. "We'll look into Iksander's situation when we can. For now, we need to handle what's happening here." He turned his gaze upward, toward the sounds of people stirring overhead. "Let's lock the vault. If Iksander is simply taking longer to wake up, he'll still be able to get out. I don't want to leave the portal or his statue unsecured."

"Right," Joseph said, already moving to the door.

As they left, Arcadius's hand fell to Elyse's shoulder. She had a feeling he was steadying himself with the contact as much as he was steadying her.

Their journey into the upper areas of the palace was punctuated by staff catching sight of Arcadius, exclaiming 'Commander!' and looking as if they very much wanted to fling their arms around him.

Arcadius didn't do hugs while he was working, apparently, but he patted a lot of shoulders and shook a lot of hands. In the process, he also got people organized to restore order. Some he asked to make lists of who in their section had woken up. Others he assigned to finding places to safely store the remaining cursed statues.

She guessed nobody wanted to keep tripping over them.

"Keep records," he emphasized. "People will want to know where their loved ones are."

Joseph set down all the instructions Arcadius issued on a magical scroll he'd nabbed somewhere. Elyse peered curiously at the thick parchment. Words seemed to fly straight from his fingertips onto it.

"These scrolls are similar to computers," he explained. "If we want, we can network sets of them at great distances."

"Cool," she said, which made him grin at her.

Elyse turned out to be a curiosity herself. For one, she still wore the boy's robes Zayd had given her. For two, she was human and unveiled. The djinn who weren't overwhelmed by their immediate concerns didn't fail to notice that. They weren't shocked exactly but they were wary. To anyone who stared, Arcadius introduced her as "Miss Solomon, my valued associate."

That amused her. She really was part of his team now.

A breathless messenger brought word that the portion of Luna's troops who'd recovered were retreating. "Shall we let them go, Commander? Our men are prepared to pursue."

Arcadius thought quickly. "The 5th Battalion should escort them to the port. Make sure they take passage on whatever freighter will carry them. For the time being, we'll store the rest of her men under guard. Before we release them, I want to see who replaces Luna as the ruler of the City of Endless Night. Depending on who does, we might need a bargaining chip."

"Wait," Joseph said before the messenger changed form and flew off again. He tore a strip from his scroll, shot the appropriate instructions onto it, and handed it to the grateful man.

With so many urgent matters to address, they progressed haltingly. Finally, they exited the main palace into a sunny palm-filled courtyard. Arcadius pointed out a colonnaded white structure on the opposite side. "My rooms are in that building. We can catch our breath and hopefully grab a meal before going on with this."

"Arcadius," Joseph said, touching his master's arm.

A tall man in a hooded blue and tan striped djellaba sat on the rim of a round fountain. He rose as they approached, watching all of them with such intense focus that he was impossible to overlook.

Arcadius jolted to a halt. "Oh," he said as the man dropped his hood.

Elyse sucked in a startled breath. The man was Arcadius—his original, she guessed. He had the same stern face she'd looked into from her brownstone steps, the same penetrating blue gray gaze, the same great height and formidable physical presence.

He didn't smile as they stopped a few feet from him. Instead, one of his dark eyebrows arched upward. His gaze swung to Elyse for single heartbeat, after which he seemed to dismiss her.

"It's about time you came back," he said to Arcadius. "The starlings were beginning to roost on me."

"Sir," Joseph burst out. The servant appeared not to know who to stand beside.

"Joseph," the original Arcadius acknowledged. Perceiving Joseph's dilemma, humor curved his mouth slightly. His amusement faded as his attention returned to Arcadius. "We'd best get this over with. The city needs us to be our strongest self."

Her Arcadius nodded. Elyse had clutched his hand without thinking. He turned to her, squeezed her fingers, then let go to cup her face. He didn't say he loved her, but she could tell he was thinking it.

Elyse wanted to say something. She simply didn't know what was appropriate. *I love you too? Everything will be all right?*

"Go ahead," she finally settled on. "I know this is important."

The other Arcadius's brows twitched higher. He must not have thought her Arcadius needed permission.

Her Arcadius went to him. The copies looked at each other, both frowning a little until it seemed they really were reflecting in a mirror, despite their different clothes. Her Arcadius put his hands on the original's shoulders.

Nothing happened.

The original's scowl deepened. "Do we need to say an incantation?" he asked Joseph.

"No, sir. As long as you're touching, you ought to join up automatically."

"But we're not."

"No, sir," Joseph agreed.

"Don't look at me," her Arcadius said when his original glowered. "I'm not doing anything to prevent us from combining."

The original's eyes narrowed. "You'd like to, though, wouldn't you? You let yourself change too much. Damn it, this is unacceptable!"

Arcadius dropped his arms. The original crossed his.

"Joseph," the original said as if struggling hard not to lose his temper. "I realize a lot is going on, but please look into why this is happening at your earliest convenience."

"Yes, sir." Joseph scratched his jaw with the edge of the magic scroll. "Um. Might I ask what happened to the other me?"

Arcadius's irritation drained away. "Forgive me. I should have told you immediately. Your statue didn't waken. I covered it with a cloth and locked it in the portal room."

"I . . . see," Joseph said. His expression was very strange. As if he wanted to hide it, he looked down at his slippers.

"I'm sure we'll straighten this out," the original said. "You won't be separated from yourself much longer."

Kindness made him sound more like the Arcadius she knew. "Maybe we should eat," she found the nerve to suggest. "I don't know about you, but we skipped breakfast. Whatever's wrong, we'll think more clearly after we've had a meal."

"Who *are* you?" the original asked.

His manner was a hair short of rude. Her Arcadius opened his mouth, likely about to spout his *valued associate* line.

"I'm Elyse Solomon," she said, forestalling him. "I met Arcadius on the human plane. The nexus he used to come here was in the basement of my building."

"And you came too?" the original asked disbelievingly.

"I wanted to help," she responded.

She saw what Arcadius meant about his former self maybe not being so impressed with her. He shook his handsome autocratic head, obviously dissatisfied with her brief answer. She suspected her Arcadius knew what the other him was thinking.

"This isn't Elyse's fault," he protested.

"It's someone's," his original said darkly.

~

Arcadius decided they were lucky there was enough work to keep both of them occupied. If there hadn't been, he might have punched his original in the nose. Inevitably, his dining room became an impromptu command center, where they snatched bites of food between interruptions. Every time someone came to the door and said "Commander," his double had to answer first—as if he were the one with the lion's share of their spirit, rather than a mere ten percent.

At least their judgment was in sync. Arcadius would have issued the same instructions as his original, though he hoped he wouldn't have done it so coolly.

"Asshat," he muttered when the other him told a weeping cabinet minister to pull himself together.

"I don't know what that is," his original said after the minister left, "but

I'm sure you'll agree we don't have time for tears right now."

"You didn't have to be an icicle about it. Every member of his family is stone but him."

"All the more reason for him to concentrate! But, by all means, you pat everyone's hands while I do our job."

Elyse didn't quite muffle her snicker. His original shifted his frigid gaze to her. Arcadius was pleased to observe that she met his frost with a pleasant, unruffled smile.

"Perhaps you could see what's holding up the coffee," the other him suggested.

"She's not your servant," Arcadius said.

"*He* is." His original nodded at Joseph. "And there he sits by your side, scribbling notes for you."

"Stop it," Elyse scolded with a firmness that took them both aback. "There's plenty for everyone to do. Maybe you should split up if it's that difficult for you to be in the same room."

"I'm not leaving him to make decisions on his own!"

"Why not?" Elyse said. "Decisions seem to be the one thing you agree on. I'm sure Joseph could find you another assistant. Don't forget lots of folks in this situation would consider having two of them a blessing."

Arcadius's original gaped at her.

"Fine." She pushed back from the dining table, getting up from the floor cushion a little awkwardly. "I'll see about the coffee. You think about what I said."

Joseph probably made things worse by shooting her a grin.

"Why are you with that female?" his original demanded, once she was out of earshot. "You could at least have found her a veil. A face like that doesn't need showing off. She's barely even pretty."

"She's brave," Arcadius said. "And loyal and clever and to my eyes utterly beautiful. I'd say you don't deserve a woman as good as her, but I'd be insulting me."

His original muttered something along the lines of Elyse being good in bed.

"That too," Arcadius said smugly.

His original slitted his eyes at him. "I haven't lost my sense of humor," he retorted, which, eerily enough, was exactly what Arcadius was thinking. "You're simply not funny."

"Oh, boy," Joseph said from the seat next to him. "This is gonna be a long day."

~

The day was long but eventually it ended. Awkwardly, Arcadius and his double headed for the main bedroom at the same time.

"I am not sleeping in the guest room," the other him announced.

Arcadius rolled his eyes.

"Maybe you and Elyse should occupy Iksander's chambers," Joseph said, trying to play peacemaker per usual. "No one's been there all day. I'm sure his staff would appreciate a steadying presence."

"Those are the sultan's rooms!" the other him objected. "I hardly think that's appropriate, especially considering who you're with. You have to be aware that woman doesn't belong here."

Arcadius wanted to wallop him. Elyse was standing two feet away! In the end, he decided against it. She'd watched him lose his temper with himself enough times today. Taking it to blows would be too much.

"I swear, you make me ashamed of myself," he said. "You, or rather *we* of all people know Iksander wouldn't mind. He cared about us, and his staff, and he never was a snob about humans. Humans interested him."

His original frowned with great energy.

"I can stay with you," Joseph offered, "if that would make it easier."

"I'm not two years old," his original snapped. "I don't need company!" He seemed to realize how churlish that sounded. Certainly, Arcadius did. "Forgive me. Of course you are correct about Iksander not minding." He turned to address Elyse stiffly. "I apologize for my insults. I was ungracious. Clearly, you are a friend to our people."

Elyse never let Arcadius down, though sometimes she surprised him. Now she beamed like the sun coming out. "I'm honored to be your friend. And I'm really glad things are starting to turn around for your city."

The other him blinked, knocked back by her sincerity. Arcadius wasn't sure how he felt about that reaction. If it turned out he and his original couldn't be recombined, having the other him fall for her could get trickier than who had the right to sleep in which bedroom.

CHAPTER SEVENTEEN

THE sultan's rooms were ten times the size of Elyse's apartment . . . and that was just counting the footprint. The painted ceilings were so high the huge double doors—all of which bristled with carvings and jewels and gold—only went halfway up the walls. The djinn were lucky Cortés hadn't heard of them. The conquistador would have forgotten all about the Aztecs.

She goggled as Arcadius led her through a reception room, an office, a display room for about a zillion gifts from other rulers, a billiards room, a dining salon, a giant closet with more clothes than she'd worn in her entire life, a jewelry room, a bathroom with a steam pool a person could do laps in, and finally the most eye-popping room of all: a bedchamber as big as a basketball court.

The walls there were covered in miles of pale blue embroidered silk. Giant antique framed mirrors reflected the room at intervals. A balustrade separated the sultan-size bed from the rest of the gleaming space. If the crystal rope chandelier that hung above it ever fell, it would crush the inhabitants. The light its branches emitted came from small hovering sun-like spheres.

"O . . . kay," Elyse breathed. "I'm actually thinking your asshat double was right about me not belonging here."

Arcadius turned and wrinkled his brow at her.

"This is insane," she said, trying to explain her reaction. "All this stuff for one person. I mean, I have a lot of stuff myself, but this is . . ." She trailed off and turned in a slow circle. "This doesn't even seem real to me."

"We can sleep somewhere else," he offered.

"Oh, no," she demurred, gathering her nerve to prowl around and peer at interesting objects. "I'm determined to rise to this occasion."

"Then you like it."

He didn't sound sure, so she stopped snooping to grin at him. "Give me twenty minutes to look around and I'll get back to you."

He restrained himself very well, she thought. "You *are* coming to bed," he said after about fifteen.

"Uh-huh." She stuck her head back into the bathroom. Was the floor honestly paved with *pearls*?

"It's a nice bed. Comfortable. We could open the courtyard windows and let the breeze blow in. Really, we should rest. We don't know what tomorrow will bring."

Something in his voice—a hint of forlornness, she guessed—caught her attention. "Oh," she cried. "I'm sorry! I'm letting myself get distracted from what's important."

"Perfectly understandable," he said, trying to sound like her behavior hadn't bothered him. "These surroundings are new to you."

She ran to him across the long carpet, hugging him and pressing her cheek against his hard chest. His sigh and the way his arms came around her told her this was what he'd been hoping for. She liked it pretty well herself. It was nice to have a hug welcomed.

"I love you," she said. "Today showed me you're even more amazing than I realized."

"Some would say my temper was short."

If the "some" were the other him, maybe so. Arcadius had treated everyone else patiently.

"You were wonderful," Elyse said. "Decisive and caring and graceful under pressure. You being a little grumpy, which you totally had a right to be, just made your good qualities stand out more."

"Did you excuse David's faults this easily?"

The question knocked her off balance. She pushed back to look at him. "There's nothing to excuse, and . . . I don't know, maybe. Are you jealous of him?"

"Maybe," he said. "You still love him."

"I love a memory, which wasn't entirely false. David had his issues, obviously, but he told me the sort of lie every woman wants to be convinced of: that she's lovable and interesting exactly the way she is."

"But you *are* loveable and interesting."

She laughed, her eyes warmed by emotion. "That sort of thing is in the eye of the beholder. David was the first man aside from my father who made me believe that about myself."

Arcadius stroked her hair back from her face. "I want you to believe it. And that you're beautiful."

"I like being beautiful to you."

"My original has crap taste."

"He has 'crap' taste, does he?"

He knew he'd said it right. He smiled down at her, but after a moment his gaze turned sad. "I don't ever want to lose the way I'm feeling now."

She understood. Loving someone could feel as good as being loved. "Maybe you won't."

He didn't contradict her, though she wasn't sure he believed. He slid his hands down her arms, keeping one within his grasp to tug her toward the bed. He swung his long legs over the balustrade, then lifted her over it.

"Going around takes too many steps," he said with a teasing smile.

Happy to repay him in the same currency, she undid the tie to her indigo outer robes. "Too bad my slave rope bit the dust when I did that spell."

She'd hooked his attention. Her breasts were bare beneath her white tunic, their shape and arousal apparent. His breath came more shallowly. "You don't need ropes. I'm your slave now."

Perhaps he was. He undressed just the way she wanted, weapons harness by weapons harness, hanging the straps on a bedpost in easy reach. Watching him tug off his boots was sexy. His trousers followed and his now-creased white shirt. She took the final item from him before he could toss it. He'd had the shirt on all day.

"I'll be wearing this later," she explained when he sent her an inquiring look.

Her answer seemed to perplex him. "I can ask the staff to bring any garment you wish."

"This garment smells like you." She draped the shirt on a chair, grinning at his continued mystification. "Don't you understand the concept of a boyfriend shirt?"

"Evidently not." He considered her. "I'm your boyfriend."

"Is that a question?"

"No-o." He said it slowly, like it might be.

"It's a reasonable place to start."

"I'm not a boy."

"True." He wore the boxer briefs he'd bought in New York. She guessed he liked the style enough to hang onto them. The only sight she liked better than him and his boner in them was him in nothing at all.

"You want me to remove these," he said, noting where her eyes had gone.

"I know *that's* not a question," she laughed.

He shucked the formfitting underwear. The effect that had was as good as magic. They stood naked and excited a foot apart, the atmosphere between them suddenly very personal. Elyse's skin pulsed all over, and Arcadius's big chest went in and out. His erection stretched up his stomach, throbbing and thick and dark. She lifted her gaze to his before wrapping her fingers gently around the shaft. The veins that snaked up it were extra firm. As she slowly stroked him, his face took on a lovely dazed expression.

She couldn't let go of him. Her palm was in love with his heft and heat. His hips rocked into her caresses, making his size even more obvious. He was right. He surely wasn't a boy.

"You are so much man," she murmured.

His daze cleared, mischief glinting in his eyes. He cupped her breasts in his hands, the pads of his thumbs pushing across their pointed tips. "You are so little woman."

She laughed even as wonderful sensations shot from her nipples to down between her legs. "You like me this way."

"I *love* you this way, more than I know how to say."

He kissed her, hugging her slighter body against his. Elyse went liquid at the feel of him: his heat, his hardness, all the parts of him that emphasized his maleness. As his mouth wandered to her neck, he lifted her off the floor.

"You make me dizzy," she said happily.

He laid her gently on the sultan's bed, the covers to which he'd already pulled down.

"My God," she exclaimed, squirming helplessly on the cushioning softness. "This bed is fabulous!"

Arcadius let out a sexy growl. "I hope you like it even better when I'm fucking you on it."

She couldn't doubt she would. When his powerful naked body swung over her, she creamed in reaction. When she pushed her fingertips up the ridges of his abs and into his chest hair, he shivered.

His chalcedony eyes were glowing.

"I want to remember every second of this," he said.

He didn't add *just in case*, but she understood. They could speak of boyfriend shirts and love all they wanted, but with their future hanging in the balance, they needed to make the most of their time together.

Making the most of it didn't involve rushing. Arcadius slid his hands down her arms again, stretching her wrists out from her body. His grip was gentle, but she didn't try to break free of it. The things his mouth was doing were totally worth letting him indulge his fondness for control. He nuzzled her collarbone and her breasts, dragging his handsome face across every dip and rise. He sucked her nipples for long minutes, laving each with his tongue as he pulled firmly. He kissed her breastbone and worked his way down her ribs. His tongue tickled her navel, but somehow she didn't have the urge to laugh.

"You smell good," he purred, using his chin and mouth to forge between her pussy's folds. "Is there a girlfriend shirt?"

She didn't laugh at that either. Her hands curled into fists as he licked her lingeringly. His tongue was pointed, its tip dragging firm and slow up her clitoris. He did this repeatedly: too slow to make her come, too hard to let her arousal do anything but rise.

"Cade," she groaned, her body heaving with desire.

"Yes," he said. "Call me that."

He burrowed in to suck her swollen button, his hold on her wrists tightening as her thrashing intensified. He was panting. Restraining her was a turn on for him. Then again, it was a turn on for her too. His strength and the way he used it got her going as much as the skill of his lips and tongue. Wanting him so much it was crazy, she squeezed his solid torso between her calves. His mouth felt incredible as she rocked her sex toward it. The ache of pleasure rose inside her, the need for the tension to break soon.

"Not yet," he whispered when she hovered on the brink.

He backed off and shifted up her, releasing her wrists in the process. He hung above her on his arms, not moving to take her yet. Him waiting there was an invitation she wasn't going to decline. She trailed her touch down his front, watching his face as she circled his nipples. Their centers were little nubs she couldn't resist pinching. Twisting them made him twitch—but not in a bad way.

"You like playing with my body," he observed.

"Yes, I do." She petted his ribs toward his center, following the enticing line down into his pubic hair. Lightly, with the tips of her fingernails, she scratched the rounds of his testicles.

"That feels good," he whispered.

She cupped the warmth of his sac. "I like having you in the palm of my hand."

He laughed, but he also wriggled, his breath catching with pleasure. A drop of pre-come rolled from his penis to her belly. "I want to be inside you."

She chafed his waist with one knee. "Come and get me."

His eyes flared hot at her challenge. He yanked her second knee upward: one quick, aggressive move, after which he went back to taking his time with her. He kept his elbow crooked beneath her leg as he balanced on his other arm. She had to admire his coordination—and the strength of his erection. His shaft was extremely stiff. He didn't need his hands to search her folds with the rounded tip.

He thrust forward when he found her entry, still not rushing, his ass and thigh muscles clenching to drive slowly him in. Elyse bit her lip as his cock spread her lust-slicked walls, as his weight came down, and his satiny thickness went in and in. When he'd filled her last millimeter, he released her bent leg. She crossed her ankles behind him. One heel dug into his tailbone, trapping him where he was.

"God," he said, his cock quivering inside her.

Her neck arched with enjoyment. "I'll let you move in a minute. You know, once I've memorized every inch of you."

He brushed her curls from her forehead. "I'd like to do the same. You're my first lover in this body. My only. You have no idea how good you feel around me."

"I'm the only person to touch this you?"

"Yes."

"Well." She let that sink in. "I'm not sure I've been anybody's first. I believe I'm honored."

He smiled and executed a tantalizing undulation with his pelvis. The motion pressed the tip of his erection into an especially nice spot.

"Oh," she said.

"Like that?" he asked throatily.

She didn't get a chance to answer. He rolled them onto their sides, gripped her rear in one hand, and repeated his hip wave. "How about that?"

She moaned. In that position, the deep, aching pleasure was even more potent. His fingers loosened, allowing his palm to rove over her bottom's curves. Then they tightened again.

"God, I love your ass," he said.

He drew back to give her an actual thrust. That did delicious things to her.

"Me too," she gasped, clutching his muscled back, which was dampening with sweat. "I mean I love *your* ass too."

He laughed and began to fuck her, making it hard for her to speak. She needed this even more than she'd known. Thankfully, nothing about his lovemaking was halfway. Every stroke was long and deep and just forceful enough to let her know he was claiming her. She gasped and groaned as her excitement swelled. His movements inside her felt amazing.

"Yes," he said, thrusting faster. "Come for me."

She wanted him to come too. Her face was against his shoulder, her upper arm wrapping him. She pushed her hand down his spine, clamping it around one tight butt cheek.

He made another growling noise, jolting into her pussy vigorously. She was so close to coming she wasn't certain she could hold off.

"Is it okay if I order you?" she panted.

He took a second to hear the question. He'd been caught up in her reactions, in his own progress toward orgasm.

"What?" he gasped.

"Can I command you to come?"

His mouth fell open, his grip contracting on her butt as his cock jerked excitedly inside her. "Yes," he said, low and gravelly. "I'd like that."

She didn't wait. "In the name of the god you love, I command you to come with me and not before."

She didn't expect the quick glow that shimmered around them. If Arcadius was surprised, it didn't show. She guessed he liked the idea that he didn't have to worry about holding back. The little spell would guarantee his timing. Taking charge his way, he shoved her onto her back. The way he locked their fingers together felt perfect. She was trapped now, but he was her prisoner too. He dug his knees in to get more leverage. The change did good things for both of them. His hips hammered into her as he snarled with pleasure.

If she'd known how to snarl, she would have. High cries tore from her instead, her excitement so intense she couldn't fathom how one body could contain it. The mattress thumped under them, the chandelier above the bed beginning to *ching* with sympathy. She thrust her hips harder up at him.

"Elyse," Arcadius groaned.

He shifted to a higher angle, his pelvis hitting her rapidly. Each thrust knocked the sharpest possible sensations up the nerves of her clit and deep into her pussy. Her pleasure reached critical mass in a nanosecond. No power on earth could have stopped her climax. It broke into a million glittering diamonds that dazzled her.

"Cade," she choked through the blinding bliss.

Her magical command did its job. He was coming too, lurching deep into her and groaning at his release's strength. His heat poured into her as hers flooded out.

He drew out their pleasure as long as he was able. Then his full weight dropped onto her.

"Need to breathe," she reminded after a few moments. He rolled onto his back, his slightly shaky arms bringing her with him.

Panting, she kissed his pounding chest gratefully. He made a rumbling noise she wasn't sure was supposed to be language. It didn't matter. She understood because the same feelings were inside her. Her emotions ran deeper than happiness. She seemed to have found a person she truly matched, not because they were the same but because their differences clicked.

She knew how special that was.

"Love you," she said.

"Too," he managed to mumble back.

If she'd been a different sort of person, she'd have sunk into oblivion with him. She couldn't do it. Her brain was wired to overthink. She lolled on top of him a few minutes and then sat up.

Arcadius seemed to be on another page.

"Can't move yet," he slurred. "Being compelled to come was—" he paused to stretch and yawn "—like having a mule kick the climax out of me."

He didn't sound like he was complaining. Elyse patted him. "I'm going to open the courtyard doors. Maybe look at the stars a bit."

"Mm," he said and closed his eyes.

She pulled on his shirt, childishly loving how big it was on her as she buttoned it. Wrapped up in his scent, she half expected him to roll out of bed and join her—despite his obvious weariness. She supposed him staying was a commander thing. He slept when he got the chance. She was the stupid one, giving in to her restlessness.

Stupid or not, she kept going. The secluded courtyard she entered was on the roof of a lower floor. The palace's recently awakened residents must be conked out like Arcadius. The complex was quiet, the sky above its domes deep black and strewn with stars. These stars were different from the ones she was accustomed to—not that she saw the constellations much in Manhattan, where the city's lights obscured them. Here, the two brightest stars she spotted twinkled in pink and green.

She wondered what was happening at the brownstone. She'd been gone a bit now, and probably wouldn't be able to travel back until the city's portals were recharged. Were Mario and Cara still camped out, preparing some dastardly welcome for her return? Without her, who'd collect rent? And pay utilities? God, she hoped garbage pickup went off okay. What day was it now anyway?

Had Aunt June reported Uncle Vince missing to the police?

Upset now, Elyse gnawed on her thumbnail. Her questions couldn't have been less calming.

You didn't have enough to worry you right here? she thought. *You had to add things you can't do anything about to the list?*

She glanced over her shoulder at the open door to the room where Arcadius slept. She could go back to bed but doubted she'd drop off. A bushy palm grew beside another door on the courtyard's opposite side. Were more of the sultan's rooms behind it? Maybe further exploring would tire her out.

Giving in to temptation, she padded to the door. The space behind it was pitch-dark. Feeling slightly idiotic, she tried to invent a spell for light. Nothing happened when she said it. She guessed she couldn't do magic unless Arcadius or Joseph were there to support her. As djinn, their faith was unshakable. Hers had to be worked at.

She was about to turn back when she thought she saw a distant luminosity.

Her pulse picked up. Had she done that or was someone here?

"Hello?" she called softly.

The light came nearer. It was Joseph. He was carrying a small lantern. "Elyse?"

She immediately remembered she wasn't wearing much. "Sorry." She pulled Arcadius's shirt closer around her. "I couldn't sleep. I wondered what was over here."

"Iksander's private library. I'm seeing if I can find an answer to the two Arcadiuses' dilemma."

"Could I help?"

He smiled. "Probably not. Though you understand our spoken language, I doubt you can read our books." He hesitated. "I did make tea, if you'd like to keep me company."

She nodded and followed him.

"I'll turn on the rest of the lights," he said. "I didn't want to risk disturbing you."

The rest of the lights were candles, some flickering in candelabra, others protected by glass sconces. Joseph "turned them on" with a whispered word. The library wasn't as huge as some of the other rooms, but it was very tall and floor to ceiling shelves. The kid inside Elyse wanted to climb the rolling ladders and push herself around the room.

"This is great," she said.

Joseph was pouring tea at a small table. He'd been working here a while. The nearby chairs all held fat open books. "This library is one of my favorite rooms in the palace. I'm actually happy for an excuse to do research."

Elyse accepted a glass of hot mint tea. A pretty silver holder with a handle allowed her to sip without being burned. "Did you find anything?"

"Not yet. I'm stumped, to tell the truth. I watched Arcadius's original today. If I hadn't known he only had a fraction of a spirit, I'd swear he was a real person."

"He isn't a real person? Because he acted like my Arcadius is the fake."

"Well, that's the question. While his personality and Arcadius's do seem to overlap, they also give the impression of being separate individuals. I've been looking for precedents in the historical record, but I can't find examples of anyone pulling off precisely what we did."

"I'm not an expert but isn't a spirit a huge thing?"

"I suppose it is." Joseph rubbed his chin. "You're suggesting ten percent of a spirit might be enough to . . . power one small djinni."

"Yes. If we—" She hesitated, not really in her element discussing divine truths. "If that part of us comes from God, a little piece of Him is still a piece of Him. It's not going to be measly. Sorry. I don't know what djinn believe about this stuff."

"We are less certain on this topic than we are on others." He stared into space for a few moments. "Unfortunately, this doesn't help me solve the conundrum."

She was tempted to ask if the conundrum had to be solved. If it didn't, she could keep her Arcadius as he was, maybe even convince him to stay with her in her world. At the least, once this crisis eased, he could make long visits. He said he was in love with her. Was it presumptuous to think he'd consider going back and forth?

This was the downside to jumping into things in the heat of passion, to acting on impulse. When you finally had a chance to think, the flaws in your decisions crashed in on you all at once.

Her face must have revealed her dismay. "I don't think you'll lose him," Joseph said. "The Arcadius with the greater part of his spirit is the one who fell in love with you."

"What about you?" she asked, realizing she was being a bit self-engrossed.

"Me?" Joseph said, startled.

"Aren't you worried that your original didn't wake?"

"Oh, I . . . I'm sure that will sort itself out in time." He turned away to busy himself over the tea things. "Certainly, I feel like a whole person as I am. I'll just continue to make myself useful as best I can."

Elyse squinted at his back. From what she knew of him, Joseph had a highly developed sense of responsibility. If his merged version would have more power to help his sultan and his city, he'd be eager to become it.

The one reason this might not be the case smacked her.

"Holy smokes," she breathed. "You called yourself a whole person. Your copy isn't a eunuch."

He spun back to her, his face blazing with embarrassment and what definitely looked like guilt.

"I'm right," she said, sure of it.

"Shush," he hissed at her.

"But shouldn't you talk about it? Don't you have different options now? Unless . . . when you meld back into your original, will that be the body you live in?"

"Almost certainly," he said. "That's the main point of recombining. That body has more powers. The Almighty made it. This one is inferior."

"Except in one important respect."

"Not that important," he muttered.

"Joseph," she said. "You're a man, not a monk. Of course it's important. Why have you been hiding this anyway?"

"I didn't do it on purpose. I had my concept of myself ready to project into. I *knew* it needed to be as close a copy as possible, so my spirit wouldn't be too changed when the time came to reunite. I guess—" He hitched his shoulders. "I guess I don't truly think of myself as half a man."

His voice had roughened. Elyse couldn't help herself. She pulled him into a hug. Knowing he probably wasn't comfortable with that, she kept it quick. "You're not half of anything, no matter what."

Joseph wouldn't look at her. He was a grown man, but right then he reminded her a miserable teenager.

"You know," she said, "most people in your situation would take this as an opportunity to sow some oats."

"I can't. It's bad enough feeling so . . . relieved that my original remained a statue. I'm afraid I'd never want to go back."

She squeezed his shoulder. She longed to give advice but wasn't sure it would be the right advice for him. At last, he lifted his gaze to hers. When she saw his eyes were swimming, hers welled up too.

"You're the first friend I've had who was a woman," he confided. "I hope my original has enough sense to like you."

She wiped her cheeks and laughed. "Me too. I'm very glad we met."

His gazed dropped again. "Arcadius is fortunate."

"Joseph." She watched him frown. Okay, he didn't want to talk about this. Not with her. Maybe not with anyone. "Arcadius would understand you feeling conflicted."

"He doesn't need any more worries."

She was on uncertain ground. "I don't think he'd see it that way. I'm pretty sure, if you wanted someone to talk to, either of us would listen."

Joseph bowed in thanks, and she saw that wasn't an empty thing. Done sincerely, his bow was a gesture of respect.

"I'm your friend too," she said, wanting that to be clear.

"You honor me," he responded.

~

Elyse left the library with a host of new things to think about—new things to appreciate as well. She didn't just have an awesome lover. She also had a new friend. That was better than treasure, no matter what challenges lay ahead.

Maybe she'd been right to feel proud of herself for being brave. Maybe her impulses had led her somewhere worth a risk or two.

With a lightened heart, she crawled back into the cushy sultan's bed. The room was dim but not dark. Arcadius must have ordered the floating lights in the chandelier to turn down. She assumed he was asleep, but as she settled, he rolled toward her onto his side. His hand covered hers, his thumb rubbing comfort into her knuckles. Part of her longed to blurt out Joseph's secret. Arcadius would want to know. The dilemma was that blabbing would break friend code. She pressed her lips together as Arcadius's eyes opened.

"Did you enjoy the stars?" he asked.

"They were beautiful."

Oh, it was hard to worry with him so close and warm. She nudged his foot playfully with her toe, which made both of them grin like kids.

"Do you miss your own stars?" he asked.

"What stars?" she joked. "We only have streetlights in NYC." She wriggled a little closer, getting comfortable. "I *might* be homesick for a nice crusty bagel with cream cheese."

"It could be a couple months before we can get you home."

"I figured. I am a bit concerned about the brownstone, but there's lots of interesting stuff to do here."

His face grew more serious. "If anything happens to me, with my double, Joseph will look out for you."

"Not that I want anything to happen, but I suspect your double wouldn't let me come to harm."

"I suppose not," he admitted. "If I were him, I'd consider you my obligation too."

She smiled at his choice of words. From what she'd seen, Arcadius didn't regard obligations as bad things. He shifted, one knee sliding between hers until they were closer still. "Maybe it's too soon to discuss this," he said, "since we don't know what will happen . . ."

"But?" she prompted.

He pulled her hand to his chest. "I want us to find a way to be together. I don't know if it will be possible, but I want you to know that's what I'm hoping for."

To hell with not being impulsive. He made her heart go gooey. "Me too."

"Really?"

"Really."

He sighed with relief and smiled. Because he was him and knew a thing or two about being cautious in his own right, a moment later he sobered. "We probably shouldn't make promises we don't know we can keep."

"No," she agreed straight-faced. "That would be irresponsible."

"Are you mocking me?"

"Would I mock my new boyfriend?"

"Absolutely."

She pushed him onto his back and laughed. When she straddled his waist on her knees, gleams of interest lit his eyes. His hips shifted, rustling the sheets and suggesting he might not be that tired.

"Are you going to have your way with me?" he asked.

"I'm going to try," she promised.

~

Halfway to dreamland, Arcadius lay on his back when the sensations hit. A slender woman perched on his waist, drawing her touch down him. He wasn't alarmed. One of the female servants must have slipped into his bedroom. They did this sometimes, though it was frowned upon. Apparently, a big serious man like him attracted some women like catnip. They liked to play with him and giggle, to pretend he might do something dangerous.

Right then he was too lazy. The tensions of the day had knocked him out.

"That's nice," he murmured, his eyes still closed.

The servant bent to kiss his neck where his pulse was speeding up. Her lips were soft, her caresses gentle as they stroked and admired him. He must have moved without thinking, because his hands were on her hips.

"Nuh-uh," she said, firmly removing them.

He almost recognized her voice, but her actions and his rising interest distracted him. She kissed his right nipple and then his left, sucking each quick and hard. Sensation twanged through his nerves, hardening his cock completely.

Did weeks spent trapped in a statue count as abstinence? It felt like they did. His erection ached for release, his fingertips digging into her narrow hips.

"No hands!" The woman laughed, pushing them off again.

She rewarded him for his compliance, kissing a soft path down his torso. Tangled curls whispered teasingly over him. Wanting to obey her, since she was doing what he wished, he grabbed fistfuls of smooth sheets. His thighs clenched, his pelvis offering itself to her.

"Suck me," he said gruffly, unable not to ask.

"That's the plan, Commander."

Her teasing tone said she wasn't afraid of him. She proved it with her delays, dragging her face lingeringly up each of his hipbones. The feel of her lips brushing him was sufficiently enticing to make him curse.

"So impatient," she scolded, giving his throbbing shaft the briefest of kisses.

"I want you enough for two," he said.

She didn't ask what he meant. He wasn't thinking straight anyway. She smoothed both hands up his rigid penis. Incredible sensations burst in it, as if his nerves had regained the responsiveness of a teenager's. He groaned, longing to say "please" but managing to hold back. She pulled the flat of her tongue up him, the trail of wetness useless for cooling his pent-up heat. She flicked the tip against the concentrated patch of nerves under his cock's throat.

"Suck me," he repeated.

"Yes, Commander," her laughing voice agreed.

She tipped him to her mouth, taking just his head into her clinging warmth. He growled with pleasure. Her tongue rubbed excitingly across his crest, her lips ringing him snugly. It was too much and not enough. His fingers threatened to rip the sheets they clutched.

"More," he demanded.

She hummed around him and pushed down.

That was exactly what he needed. He moaned, bliss spreading out from his groin in waves. She sucked him steadily up and down, as if she loved doing it. Her mouth was wet, her tongue moving slow and firm. Her hands steadied him at his base, increasing the pressure she could exert.

"God," he gasped, loving that.

He was spiraling toward climax, urgency building in his balls. Her hands shifted to his thighs, kneading their bunched muscles. The sensuality made him writhe, a ripping sound warning him the sheets were giving way. It didn't matter. He couldn't hold back his request.

"Please," he rasped. "Do that faster."

She pulled in a breath and gave him what he asked for. The noise of her rapid sucking made him crazy all by itself. Though it wasn't his nature to relinquish control, he let her mouth devastate him, let the pleasurable imminence swell and swell until its bounds simply had to burst.

He came with a low rough cry, hot lines of ecstasy rushing out of him. The pleasure didn't end when he anticipated. She milked his climax, her unusual zeal dragging fresh zings of pleasure up his penis. He couldn't remember having a better orgasm. Certainly, it was one of his more selfish. When he was convinced it had ended, she cupped his balls gently. One last delicious shudder rolled through him.

Curious to see who'd given him this delight, he forced his eyes open.

Shock slapped him like cold water. He was alone in his room. His seed soaked the sheets, but no woman sat atop him. No woman was anywhere.

Heart pounding like a drum, he shoved off the covers and sat up. He hadn't just had a wet dream. The details had been too real. He could have sculpted the woman's lips, the slenderness of her hands, the strength of her surprisingly firm thighs.

"*No*," he said at the conclusion that came to him.

The female was his copy's human, and she hadn't been sucking him. She'd been pleasuring his double. Arcadius and his copy must be psychically intertwined. In the twilight state between sleep and waking, he'd experienced everything the other was enjoying.

"Hell," he swore with great energy.

This was going to be awkward.

~

Elyse had finished having her way with Arcadius. He lay in the bed breathing hard—an excellent sign that her work was done. She crawled up and snuggled into him. *Now* she was ready to let her worries go.

"Wow," he said. "I think I came hard enough for two people."

She smiled into his shoulder. He was silent for a while.

"I could—" he began to say.

"No," she refused firmly. "Sleep. You've done enough today."

She guessed he was more awake again. He twisted around onto his side. She touched his cheek, petting the soft bristles on his jaw. The massive space that surrounded them made her feel both small and more intimate with him.

"I'm worried about my friends," he confessed.

She sensed this was hard for him. "Of course you are."

"The portal Iksander chose for Philip was used. We think he succeeded in projecting through, but his original was still beside it, not awakened. We don't actually know how long we can survive as statues—if, after a time, our spirits will slip away and leave empty stone."

Elyse hadn't known that. "That's a troubling idea."

"Yes." Arcadius was silent for a bit. "Do you remember the older man in the sage green robes, the one with the pure white hair?"

"I think so." So many people had been in and out of his dining room Elyse's memory was a blur.

"That was Philip's father, the vizier."

"He revived then."

"Yes. He took Philip's statue home."

"That will be strange for him." Arcadius nodded. She tried to read what else was bothering him. "Are you wondering if you should have brought the stone Iksander here?"

"He's safer where he is," Arcadius said, though he didn't sound a hundred percent certain. "From what the other me reported, he wasn't conscious of anything until he woke up. Iksander's original isn't capable of minding being locked in a treasure room. I just wish I knew he and Philip had made it to your plane, and that they were okay there. I hate that we have to wait months to look for them."

"You wish you could protect them now."

"*Yes.*" He pressed his lips together, seeming embarrassed to have answered so emphatically. He came up on his elbow and looked at her.

Elyse put her hand gently on his chest. "We'll do everything we can as soon as we can do it."

"There's so much to do here as well. This curse has disrupted every part of our city."

She patted his strong heartbeat. "Then maybe you'll admit it's a little lucky there's two of you."

He laughed on a rush of air. When he settled down again, he laid his cheek on her breast. She suspected he didn't let himself seek this sort of comfort often—or possibly ever.

"I think I'm lucky you're here," he said. "I think . . . having someone I can talk to like this, makes the situation more bearable."

She stroked his thick dark hair, wanting so passionately to soothe him she concluded she couldn't be far from whatever *in love* was.

"You have me," she promised the Glorious City's guardian. "And you have the other you and Joseph. Plus, your account of Philip's father makes him seem solid. Together, we'll get through this."

"Together."

His voice rumbled on her breast. She felt him relax slowly against her, his arm across her belly, his leg sidled over hers. The connection between their bodies felt natural and good. She'd experienced similar things with David, but this was . . . Her thought trailed off as she tried to pin down the difference. This felt realer, ironically. Some part of her must have known David was deceiving her. Arcadius wasn't even human, but when he confessed he loved her, her deepest instinct told her to believe it.

I can trust him, she thought. *Not to be perfect but to always try his best.*

If she trusted him, maybe it was time she trusted herself again as well.

Arcadius broke into her thoughts. "Elyse?" he asked, sounding half asleep. "What exactly to 'boyfriends' do?"

She grinned and rubbed his back. "Don't worry. You'll be great at it."

He grunted, seeming to accept this—provisionally, at least—as he subsided against her. The last of her tension left her as his left him. She was aware of being hopeful for his friends and happy for herself. She didn't think that was wrong, no matter how much hardship his city faced.

Happiness and love were the sort of medicines most places could use more of.

EPILOGUE:
THE BROWNSTONE

THE attractive man in the faded jeans and black hoodie stood at the base of the brownstone's steps and looked up. He was tall and fit but no twenty-something. His salt-and-pepper hair receded at the temples, and the lines around his eyes were from more than smiles. The hang of his clothes implied he'd once had more bulk. His intelligent face would catch the eye of many females, from post-pubescent to not-dead-yet. He had a great mouth, a lean jawline, and an expression that seemed perpetually interested in everything around him.

At the moment, he was interested in the building in front of him. The old dame had reached a certain vintage but she had gorgeous bones.

He nodded at the signs she'd been taken care of, narrowing his gaze at the new-looking door to the basement unit. After two years, he supposed changes were inevitable. With a small shrug of resignation, he dug a set of keys from the front pocket of his jeans.

A woman he didn't recognize came out the front entrance. Her trim business suit and the miniature terrier at the end of her leash suggested she was taking her pet for a last-minute before-work walk. The warming weather allowed her to do this without a coat. The man didn't doubt the dog also appreciated the milder temperatures. It opened its mouth and panted but didn't bark at him.

"Going in?" the woman asked, noticing his keys and judging him no danger. The quick flick of her gaze over him said she thought he was good looking.

"Yes." He accepted the door she was holding open. "Thank you very much."

She smiled and he smiled back, in response to which she flushed slightly. The man saved his grin for when he was alone in the vestibule. Whatever else he'd lost during his travails, his charm had survived intact.

Inside the lobby, everything seemed all right. The floor was clean, the old-world wood panels no dustier than usual. On the bulletin board for tenants, beside the wall of mailboxes, he spotted a hot pink flyer. The message on it warned residents they needed to send rent to a new address.

That brought a frown to the man's animated face. The address was familiar, and he didn't disapprove of the choice. It was, however, a reminder that events he *did* disapprove of had occurred here.

He couldn't help that now. He had to put it behind him and move on. Up the stairs he went, even his fit legs beginning to burn by the time he reached the fifth floor. On the sixth and last floor, he stopped.

A little old lady in a pale polyester pantsuit was laboriously shoving boxes out onto the landing. The boxes were small—to enable her to handle them on her own, he supposed—and she had about a million. As she slid them from her apartment into the hall, she muttered beneath her breath about what was the world coming to if you couldn't trust your friends or the god damned movers and this hellhole of a city was too dangerous for anyone with sense.

Every few mutters, she thumped the carpet with her aluminum walker. The man fought his instinctive urge to assist her.

"Moving out?" he asked with a politeness he didn't feel.

"What's it to you?" she snapped peevishly, not bothering to turn around.

"Well," he drawled, resting his rangy shoulder against the wall. "It saves me having to evict you, which I'd be inclined to do, considering you betrayed my daughter and almost got her killed."

That motivated the old lady to look at him. Her double take was comical.

"Mr. Solomon." She goggled at him through thick glasses. "We heard you fell into a volcano!"

"Luckily for me, reports of my death were greatly exaggerated."

He beamed at the shocked woman. Short of a reunion with Elyse, this was more fun than Leo Solomon had hoped for.

#

ABOUT THE
AUTHOR

EMMA Holly is the award winning, *USA Today* bestselling author of more than thirty romantic books, featuring shapeshifters, demons, faeries and just plain extraordinary ordinary folks. She loves the hot stuff, both to read and to write!

If you'd like to discover what else she's written, please visit her website at http://www.emmaholly.com.

Emma runs monthly contests and sends out newsletters that often include coupons for ebooks. To receive them, go to her contest page.

Thanks so much for reading this book! If you enjoyed it, please consider leaving a review.

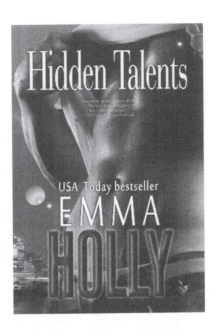

WEREWOLF cop Adam Santini is sworn to protect and serve all the supes in Resurrection, NY—including unsuspecting human Talents who wander in from Outside.

Telekinetic Ari is hot on the trail of a mysterious crime boss who wants to exploit her gift for his own evil ends, a mission that puts her on a collision course with the hottest cop in the RPD.

Adam wants the crime boss too, but mostly he wants Ari. She seems to be the mate he's been yearning for all his life, though getting a former street kid into bed with the Law could be his toughest case to date.

"*Hidden Talents* is the perfect package of supes,
romance, mystery and HEA!"—**Paperback Dolls**

available in ebook and print

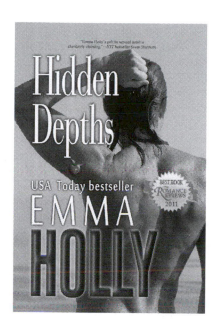

JAMES and Olivia Forster have been happily married for many years. A harmless kink here or there spices up their love life, but they can't imagine the kinks they'll encounter while sneaking off to their beach house for a long hot weekend.

Anso Vitul has ruled the wereseals for one short month. He hardly needs his authority questioned because he's going crazy from mating heat. Anso's best friend and male lover Ty offers to help him find the human mate his genes are seeking.

To Ty's amazement, Anso's quest leads him claim not one partner but a pair. Ty would object, except he too finds the Forsters hopelessly attractive.

"The most captivating and titillating story I have read in some time . . . Flaming hot . . . even under water"—**Tara's Blog**

available in ebook and print

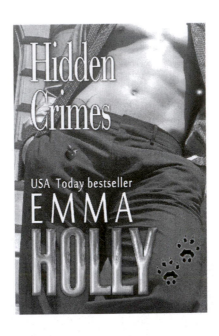

CATS and dogs shouldn't fall in love. Like any wolf, detective Nate Rivera knows this. He can't help it if the tigress he's been trading quips with at the supermarket is the most alluring woman he's ever met—sassy too, which suits him down to his designer boots.

Evina Mohajit is aware their flirtation can't lead to more. Still, she relishes trading banter with the hot werewolf. This hardworking single mom hasn't felt so female since her twins' baby daddy left to start his new family. Plus, as a station chief in Resurrection's Fire Department, she understands the demands of a dangerous job.

Their will-they-or-won't-they tango could go on forever if it weren't for the mortal peril the city's shifter children fall into. To save them, Nate and Evina must team up, a choice that ignites the sparks smoldering between them . . .

"Weaving the police procedural with her inventive love scenes [made] this book one I could not put down."—**The Romance Reviews**

available in ebook and print

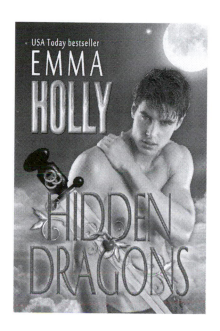

DO you believe in dragons? Werewolf cop Rick Lupone would say no . . . until a dying faerie tells him the fate of his city depends on him. If he can't protect a mysterious woman in peril, everything may be lost. The only discovery more shocking is that the woman he's meant to save is his high school crush, Cass Maycee.

Half fae Cass didn't earn her Snow White nickname by chance. All her life, her refusal to abuse fae glamour kept men like Rick at arm's length. Now something new is waking up inside her, a secret heritage her pureblood father kept her in the dark about. Letting it out might kill her, but keeping it hidden is no longer an option. The dragons' ancient enemies are moving. If they find the prize before Rick and Cass, the supe-friendly city of Resurrection just might go up in flames.

"[*Hidden Dragons*] kept me completely enthralled . . . sexy & erotic"
—**Platinum Reviews**

available in ebook and print

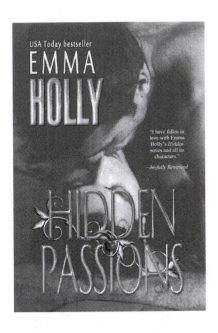

SEXY fireman Chris Savoy has been closeted all his life. He's a weretiger in Resurrection, and no shifters are more macho than that city's. Due to a terrible tragedy in his past, Chris resigned himself to hiding what he is—a resolve that's threatened the night he lays eyes on cute gay werecop Tony Lupone.

Tony might be a wolf, but he wakes longings Chris finds difficult to deny. When a threat to the city throws these heroes together, not giving in seems impossible. Following their hearts, however, means risking everything . . .

"I've visited Emma Holly's magical fantasy city of Resurrection, New York, before and have enjoyed the other *Hidden* stories that take place there. They're all very imaginative and compelling, and absolutely scorching hot. *Hidden Passions* continues in that vein, with characters that are sympathetic and likeable, and storylines that keep me returning for more."
—joysann, **Publisher's Weekly Blog**

available in ebook and print

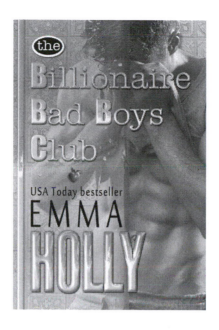

SELF-made billionaires Zane and Trey have been a club of two since they were eighteen. They've done everything together: play football, fall in love, even get smacked around by their dads. The only thing they haven't tried is seducing the same woman. When they set their sights on sexy chef Rebecca, these bad boys just might have met their match!

"This book is a mesmerizing, beautiful and oh-my-gods-hot work of art!"
—**BittenByLove** 5-hearts review

available in ebook and print

65347203R00136

Made in the USA
Lexington, KY
09 July 2017